THE
FIRST
CITY

ALSO BY JOE HART

THE DOMINION TRILOGY
The Last Girl
The Final Trade

THE LIAM DEMPSEY MYSTERIES
The River Is Dark
The Night Is Deep

NOVELS
Lineage
Singularity
EverFall
The Waiting
Widow Town
Cruel World

NOVELLAS
Leave the Living
The Exorcism of Sara May

SHORT STORY COLLECTIONS
Midnight Paths: A Collection of Dark Horror

SHORT STORIES
"The Line Unseen"
"The Edge of Life"
"Outpost"
"And the Sea Called Her Name"

COMICS
"Last Sacrifice"

THE
FIRST
CITY

BOOK THREE
THE DOMINION TRILOGY

JOE HART

 THOMAS & MERCER

Published by Thomas & Mercer, Seattle

www.apub.com

Amazon, the Amazon logo, and Thomas & Mercer are trademarks of Amazon.com, Inc., or its affiliates.

ISBN-13: 9781477818084
ISBN-10: 1477818081

Cover design by M. S. Corley

Printed in the United States of America

To Jade, for all the reasons.

"Once more unto the breach, dear friends, once more."

—William Shakespeare, *Henry V*

BEFORE . . .

"Cleric Asher. Your ward is here."

Simon looked up from where Lee played with two colorful puzzle pieces, trying unsuccessfully to fit them together. For a brief second he thought he'd misheard Assistant Carter, who stood in the doorway looking as if he would rather be anywhere else.

"She is?"

"Arrived this morning. Follow me."

Simon glanced around the large room he and Lee had shared for the last seven months. Lee stopped playing, wide eyes moving from him to the window and the soaring wall of the Advance Research Compound outside.

"I can't leave my son."

Carter wrinkled his nose and adjusted the god-awful green tie he was wearing. "Bring him."

Simon scooped Lee up, clasping him to his chest as he followed the small, shrewish man down the hall. One of the guards, a Redeye, the nickname earned from the convertible infrared goggles they wore, swung into step beside Carter, barely glancing at Simon before ignoring him completely.

When they reached a locked set of doors, Carter keyed them through with his bracelet and they climbed a sprawl of stairs that switchbacked twice before emptying out on a landing and another hall. At the end of the corridor Carter guided them through another set of doors to a long room with a bank of windows lining one side. The top of the ARC's wall was visible from this level, the early summer sun beginning to peek over its edge, coating the floor of the nursery gold along with the row of cribs.

Sixty cribs were crowded together at the far end of the room, their emptiness jarring no matter how many times Simon saw them. Only three, in the center of the nursery, were occupied. Carter moved to the last in line; the goggled guard stopped inside the door.

Simon carried Lee past the first two cribs, the boy leaning out to look inside each one. A girl barely more than two years old lay on her side in the first, deeply asleep, wispy blonde hair splayed across her pillow. Simon glanced at the paperwork hanging from the crib's side, reading the name though he already knew it.

Halie.

The second crib held an infant girl lying on her back. She was asleep as well, tiny fists clenched tight above her head.

Terra.

His heart picked up speed as he stopped beside the last crib, unable to gather the courage at first to look inside. Here it was. The moment he'd been waiting for after volunteering for the program almost a year ago. All of the training, the psych evaluations, waivers, and countless exams had led to him standing here at last.

Carter shot him a look. "What's the matter?"

"Nothing. I'm . . . nothing."

Simon stepped forward and looked down.

The baby girl was wide awake, eyes shifting to him as soon as he moved into view. She was tiny, barely three months old if he had to guess. The beginnings of dark hair curled in delicate strands from the top of her head and a line of drool shone at the corner of her mouth. She kicked her feet, making a quiet cooing sound so familiar from Lee's recent infancy he couldn't help but smile.

"Hello," he said. The girl stared at him and one side of her mouth quirked up. Lee squirmed in his arms, pointing down into the crib.

"Bubby?"

"That's right, baby," Simon said. Lee grunted and he lowered him to the ground, making sure he was balanced before letting him go. Lee tottered around Carter and grasped the bars of the crib, steadying himself.

"Yes, well . . ." Carter said, glancing at the two children before adjusting his tie again. "She's been freshly changed and fed. You'll report to control to have your new bracelet fitted. It will open any door in the facility, save the elevator of course. From this point on she will be your charge, her safety and well-being your responsibility."

"Have there been reports of any more?"

"None at this time."

Simon nodded. "Where was she found?"

"I haven't the faintest."

"Parents?"

"Classified of course. Cleric Asher, you are aware of how the program works, correct?"

"Yes."

"Then you know the questions you're asking me are exactly the things that are restricted for everyone's benefit. Even the infants'."

"Of course."

"You'll look at me when I speak to you, Cleric." Simon tore his eyes away from the girl and focused on Carter. A small seed of hatred for the other man, planted the first time they met, began to sprout and take root. "This is the most dangerous and ambitious venture the United States government has ever undertaken and even now the ledge we stand on grows narrower by the minute. If it is to work everyone must obey protocol, especially those directly responsible for the infants. Is that understood?"

"Yes sir."

Carter surveyed him before giving a clipped nod. "Good. I have other matters to attend to. You can let yourself out I'm sure?"

"Yes."

Without another glance he strode away, stiff and robotic in his movements, which, Simon decided, fit him to a T.

When the door closed behind Carter and the guard, Simon brought his attention back to the girl. Lee had reached through the narrow gap in the crib's bars and was holding her hand in his own. She had turned her head to the side and was gazing out at Lee, who looked back without blinking.

How strange to be here now after so much time. For him it seemed the world had stopped the second he'd entered the ARC, but he knew things were growing worse even as he stood here. Initially he had been curious about the choice of having only men holding cleric's duties and received a clipped reply from Carter about the fact that already women were becoming too sparse to employ, along with being "engaged in other areas of research." Whatever that actually meant. But in the end his questions had come back around to why he'd volunteered in the first place, and he'd told himself it was the honor of being able to serve and protect and not the deeper yearning for a second child he and his wife would never have that had brought him here. But he couldn't deny the sense of completion he felt at knowing the girl in the crib was his responsibility as much as Lee was.

Simon watched them both for a long moment before stepping back to read the paperwork attached to the crib. The urge to simply stay in the nursery and watch Lee and one of the last girls to be born—ever, if the National Obstetric Alliance's scientists failed—was strong, but he would be expected soon in control. The obligations were endless in his position, but he was playing a part in helping humanity continue, even if the world outside the walls was tearing itself to pieces.

"Come on, Lee, we have to go."

"Na."

"We have to let her rest." He gently picked up his son, drawing his arm from inside the crib. "We'll come back to see you soon," he said, smiling down at the girl again. She gurgled and kicked her feet.

Simon carried Lee across the room and stopped at the door, following his son's gaze back to the crib before hugging him close and kissing him on the temple. "Something tells me you and Zoey are going to be good friends someday."

AFTER . . .

1

The thud of the helicopter is in Zoey's head, her body, vibrating the marrow in her bones.

They're coming.

The words reverberate through her, tearing her breath away, paralyzing her. But what the NOA agent said in his last minutes overrides the building panic.

I'm the keystone.

I have a daughter.

Lee and I have a daughter.

I'm a mother.

She turns her head, surveying the scene around her even as everything slows. *I'm in shock.* But the realization isn't enough to get her moving.

Merrill tries to push himself to his hands and knees but fails again, head resting in the dirt.

Chelsea and Tia have Eli sitting up, his face a definition of pain, one hand clutching the bullet wound in his abdomen.

Sherell and Rita are in front of her, mouths moving, but she can't hear them over the helicopter. Over the slamming of her heart.

"Zoey!" Rita yells, and she feels a slight sting of pain as the other woman's hand strikes her. She sucks in a breath as a thousand black moths flutter on the edges of her vision. "Inside!"

"We'll be trapped in there," Zoey says.

"They'll run us down out here."

Zoey moves to Merrill, shaking his shoulder and saying his name. He's completely unconscious now. He'd saved her, once again, blocking the tranquilizer dart meant for her.

She's still trying to figure out how they're going to move him when he's lifted off the ground. Newton hefts the larger man in his arms, eyes asking her a question.

"Inside. Go," she says. Tia and Chelsea have Eli on his feet, supporting him as they move toward the facility's entry. Zoey turns, scanning the black horizon, the cliffs and hills darker shadows below the sky.

There.

To the north two white strobes accompany the growing sound of rotors. As she watches, a spear of light stabs the ground less than a mile away, then a second, both igniting the dead grass of the clearing in phosphorescence.

Zoey runs.

She sprints to the open doorway, where Nell stands waving her inside. A lance of pain shoots through her lower back into her legs but she doesn't slow until she's past and Nell has shut the door. Even then she feels as if she's in free fall, the floor speeding up to meet her.

"Where do we go?" Nell asks, catching up to her.

"Down."

"Shouldn't we try to go out the back? Through the garage?"

"They'll be waiting."

"Then where?"

Zoey blinks. "There's another way."

She hits the stairway leading to the lower level too fast and stumbles on the treads, catching herself on the railing before she plummets headfirst onto the landing. Then she's rushing down the corridor to where the huddled group waits. Lyle stands, wringing his hands, outside the NOA storeroom. Seamus is beside him, his body rigid as he issues a loud bark. Newton leans over Merrill, who's lying on the floor, while Chelsea wraps a large white bandage around Eli's middle. It almost immediately begins turning crimson.

"How did they find us?" Sherell gasps.

"The dead man, he followed us. He was one of them," Zoey says.

"What are we going to do?" Tia asks, her round face flushed and beaded with sweat.

"We have to go out through the tunnel that leads to the storage shed."

"They'll see us when we move from the shed to the fence. There's no way we can go fast enough and hide with Eli and Merrill hurt."

"I'll hold them off," Ian says, unshouldering his rifle, his lined face grim. "It might give you enough time to get outside the fence and away."

"No. We won't let you do that," Chelsea says. Her normally pallid complexion is ghostly white as she struggles to keep Eli on his feet.

Zoey puts a hand against the wall in an effort to keep the entire corridor from rocking beneath her. There's something in her hand: the black cartridge and vial of blood from inside the NOA agent's fake arm. She pockets the items and takes two deep breaths but each inhalation is filled with the scent of blood and fear.

The muffled sound of the helicopters becomes softer, the beat of their blades slower, less powerful.

They've landed.

Only minutes, surely, until they're inside. Minutes before the Redeyes come storming down the stairs and kill everyone she cares about. Minutes before they take her back to the ARC, to the fifth level, and begin their experiments.

No.

Zoey glances around, looking at each face. What she sees wrenches her heart.

Terror.

Despair.

Pleading.

Lyle, hands still fidgeting, jaw trembling below his haggard face, meets her gaze and in that brief contact an idea leaps to the front of her thoughts. She tries sorting through the ramifications but the last audible beat of the choppers shoves her past the barrier of rationality.

"Lyle, how long would it take you to reroute the missile you had ready for the ARC?" she asks.

"I don't know. Five minutes? Maybe more?"

"Do it."

"Where do you want to reroute it to?"

"This building."

The shocked silence is heavy. She turns and looks at the rest of the group.

"Zoey, what are you doing?" Chelsea asks.

"We need to get in the tunnel and out from behind the storage shed by the time the missile launches. If we make it beyond the fence before it comes back down we'll be safe, but they'll think we're still inside. They'll either get out of the way or die."

They glance at one another for a long second before Ian nods. "It's all we've got. Let's go."

Lyle hurries to the computer in the next room and drops into his chair, fingers already on the keys. Zoey follows him, stopping in the doorway as the others continue down the tunnel.

"How long will we have?" she says over the clacking of the keyboard.

"There's a fail-safe in the missile guidance system. Two thousand feet of altitude is required before it will detonate. It's so the missile won't ever explode within the silo. I'd say it will take all of ten seconds to go up and another five to come down."

"Fifteen seconds?"

"You asked."

Zoey flinches as an amplified voice echoes from outside the upper floor. One she recognizes immediately. A chill runs through her.

"Zoey," Reaper says. "You're surrounded. Come out of your own free will and we'll spare the people with you." There is a pause before he adds, "You have bigger things to consider now, Zoey. You hold the key to humanity. And your daughter needs you."

Her heart does a funny double beat and she fears she's going to be sick. Lyle's typing has stopped and he's staring at the ceiling as if it will fall on him at any second.

"Hurry," she says and his fingers fly back into action. "We'll be waiting at the tunnel opening."

Lyle doesn't look up. "I'll put a couple minutes' delay on the launch, give us enough time to climb up and out."

"How far away will we have to get?"

He stops typing and looks at her. "I don't know."

She jogs down the hallway as Reaper's voice booms again. She can't make out what he's saying over her breathing and footfalls. She doesn't need to. More lies and half-truths to get her to surrender.

I'm the keystone.

I have a daughter.

Stop.

She shuts out the thoughts that threaten to make her stumble, slow her movements. There's no time to let them sink in. Maybe there will be later.

And maybe there won't.

She rounds a corner in the main tunnel and sees the last branch to the left leading to the southernmost missile. In the opposite direction is a much smaller hallway, barely wide enough for two people to walk side by side. At the end is a steel ladder that disappears up a vertical shaft. The others are waiting there. As she reaches them she sees Ian has fastened a long belt around Merrill's torso. He and Newton are maneuvering him to the base of the ladder. Eli sits in the corner, Chelsea's hand pressed tightly against his wound. To Zoey's surprise, Sherell leans heavily on Rita's shoulder, blood staining the front of her pant leg over one knee.

"What happened?" Zoey asks.

"I slipped coming around the corner and fell. Bashed my knee."

"Can you walk?"

"With help."

"Where's Lyle?" Tia asks.

"Finishing up. Let's get everyone aboveground. We won't have much time."

Ian and Newton begin hauling Merrill up the ladder. Ian goes first, gripping the belt behind Merrill's back while Newton puts a shoulder beneath Merrill's legs and climbs below. When Ian's voice echoes back down the shaft Tia helps Chelsea get Eli to his feet.

"I got this," Eli says, shuffling to the ladder. He puts his hands on the closest rung and with a grunt begins to climb. Tia follows, then Chelsea. Ian reappears a moment later holding the belt and fastens it in two loops around Seamus's torso. He and Newton carefully draw up the dog, who looks around comically as he disappears out of sight. Before Nell can mount the ladder, Newton's feet reappear and he drops back into the tunnel. He makes a straight line for Sherell and without hesitating guides her arms around his neck, pulling her up onto his back. She clings to him as he mounts the rungs. Before they disappear Sherell twists her head back and mouths *oh my God* to the rest of them.

Rita barks laughter as she and Nell follow. Then it is only Zoey. The empty tunnel is quiet except for the occasional murmur of Reaper's voice filtering ghostlike to her, words unintelligible. She's just about to sprint back to check on Lyle when he appears, huffing noisily toward her.

"Did it work?" she says when he's within earshot.

"I hope so. We have maybe thirty seconds."

She motions to the ladder and he climbs as a loud bang comes from the direction of the stairwell. She whips her handgun up, staring past the sights. Part of her thinks the missile already launched and she's dead, all her sensory input an afterimage of life.

But then the voices float to her. Harsh and choppy yells.

They're inside.

She holsters the gun and climbs after Lyle. Cold darkness embraces her as she's pulled free of the hole and onto rough ground. They are directly behind the storage shed at the northern end of the compound, starlight drifting down and coating the buildings and surrounding hills.

"They're inside," she breathes as Tia hauls her to her feet. A low creaking sound comes from behind her and she makes out Newton working at the lower portion of the fence. He strains against it and with a short shriek one of the wires attached to the steel post snaps and the fence rises a foot.

"Go," Nell says, shoving Rita through first. She follows along with Lyle and Ian who drag Eli and Merrill through after them.

Zoey risks a glance around the side of the shed just as a loud electronic squawk fills the air.

Reaper stands beside the closest helicopter, his attention centered on the facility's gaping entry. Two Redeyes hold positions to either side of the doorway, rifles up and ready. From somewhere between the storage shed and the helicopters the squawk emits again and one of the domes dotting the yard shudders, its farthest end lifting off the ground.

Zoey watches, transfixed as the missile cap opens fully and stops, lights from the silo below shining straight up like an underground sunrise. She sees Reaper glance at the open hole, sees the comprehension hit him like a punch as he spins and makes a gesture to the pilot in the helicopter nearest him.

Two quicker blasts of sound come from the missile silo before the helicopter's rotors begin to turn.

"Zoey! Come on!" Rita whispers.

She shoves away from the building's side and dives under the fencing that Newton still holds up. With an awkward sliding movement he follows her, his shirt catching and tearing on the fence before he's free.

A long, hissing scream from the other side of the shed fills Zoey's ears before the night is lit up in an orange glow.

She climbs to her feet, turning back, unable to look away.

A pillar of fire rises above the shed's roof at least thirty feet into the sky. A moment later a cloud of smoke erupts from the compound, gushing outward through the fence at a shocking speed as something long and sleek shoots upward like a tree growing to its full height all at once.

Then the blaze from the missile's tail end ignites the darkness, washing it away in acrid light.

Hands grasp her shoulder and force her into movement.

The ground is unsteady and she nearly falls before righting herself. Ahead Ian and Newton carry Merrill between them and she sees his feet beginning to push at the ground, his head trying to lift up. Eli limps with one arm over Tia's shoulder while Chelsea holds Sherell's hand.

They run.

Zoey pours on speed, coming even with Eli's free side and pulling his arm over her shoulders.

The missile's light fades, its sound like continuous thunder rising above them. And beneath it, the roar of the helicopters.

The ground dips and rises, a copse of boulders strewn by time to the right, and she angles toward the largest of them, dragging Eli and Tia with.

The missile's howl changes in pitch and becomes a shriek.

The light grows brighter again.

They swing around behind the towering stone, setting Eli down with his back against it. The others stream past, all of them cowering, covering their ears. Zoey steps to the right and peers out past the rock.

One of the helicopters is airborne, angling away so sharply from the facility she's sure the rotors will catch the fence but they don't. The other chopper's blades are still gaining momentum and from her vantage she spots three streaks of black burst from the facility's front, all heading toward the waiting aircraft.

There is nothing but sound.

A flit of movement catches her eye above the compound but it flies down and vanishes too fast to follow. A concussive blast of air rocks her head back and she drops to the ground beside Eli.

The rocks tremble at her back and one of Eli's arms wraps around her head, shielding her.

Dust blasts through the cracks in the boulders, peppering the side of her face, and she turns away, catching sight of something twisting through the air fifty feet above.

It takes half a heartbeat before she recognizes the warped corpse of metal as the second helicopter. Its top rotor is gone, tail blades spin crazily, their tips on fire. Something vaguely human in shape tumbles free, cartwheels, and plummets into the side of the nearest hill.

The chopper corkscrews twice more through the air before smashing to the ground on the edge of a small gorge. It flips end over end once and disappears in a broken rasp of steel.

Dust and debris continue to rain down, an uneven stinging patter that dissipates until the air stills again and Zoey hears only a distant ringing in her ears.

She stands, slowly disentangling herself from Eli. She squeezes his hand and steps to the edge of the rock on unsteady legs.

Inside the sagging fence of Riverbend the night is lit by a hundred sputtering fires. Where the building once was is a ragged hole. Two of the four walls are gone, lost in a wash of rubble that extends almost to the fence line. The storage shed, knocked half off its small foundation, looks drunken in the low light. There is something long and thin swaying in the ground a dozen feet away and it takes her several seconds to recognize it as one of the helicopter blades, at least half of its thirty-foot length buried in the dirt.

A solid beam of light flares and Zoey shrinks back behind the stone.

The airborne chopper approaches the hole that used to be a building, its spotlight stabbing the ruined ground. It's only a moment before the aircraft's sound changes and it lowers into the yard. She watches for another second before turning back to the group, all of them shining eyes and shadowed faces.

"They're landing. Probably going to search the rubble. We should get to higher ground. Is everyone able to move?" she asks.

"Oh yeah, sign me up for a hike," Eli rumbles, his words dissolving into a low wheezing that he quiets with some effort.

"She's right," Merrill says, and her heart lifts to see his eyes open if not entirely clear. "Let's move."

They hoist one another to their feet, supporting the injured, and move in a silent line up a draw in the closest hill like a group of prey on their last legs.

2

The worn pavement hums beneath the ASV's tires, the odd chink in the road throwing a shudder through Zoey as she watches Eli's chest move up and down.

The fatigue that blankets her is nothing short of undeniable. She feels like she's drowning and the rope to haul her free is sleep's embrace. But she can't take it. She's terrified that if she closes her eyes she'll wake to the sound of grieving, to the sound of hearts breaking, and once again it will be her fault. So she won't go to sleep.

They had climbed the side of the hill to a plateau two hundred feet above Riverbend and huddled together for warmth through the long morning hours. The moon made a brief, somber appearance, scuttling behind a bank of clouds near dawn that dropped a dusting of snow on them. It was after the sun had fully risen that she and Tia crept to the edge of the hill and looked down at what was left of the installation.

In the morning light the destruction was even more stunning. The rear and southern wall remained only partially intact. The rest was a landslide of fractured concrete, twisted steel, and sprawling fragments of what was once a building.

She had stared at the devastation with awe for nearly a minute before seeing movement within the wreckage.

Reaper and his men toiled amongst the rubble, moving chunks of concrete and shifting unrecognizable material that used to be floor, walls, and window frames. They worked throughout the morning, digging deeper and deeper into the facility, worming their way down until she could no longer see them.

They had been looking for bodies. For some sign of confirmation that she was dead. Their precious keystone.

She grinds her teeth, wishing Reaper had been in the helicopter that was destroyed. The worst of his atrocities, specifically the one she can't rid herself of no matter how hard she tries, replays once again in her mind: Reaper's blade disappearing beneath Simon's chin, the final dimming of his gaze, the anguish of Lee's scream.

She shifts on her seat so that her back pulses softer with the pain that's been constant since fleeing through the tunnels. She hasn't felt any of the old numbness return to her legs yet, which is a small blessing. And they all made it out alive. But Eli . . . his breathing is faster, his heartbeat more erratic the last time Chelsea checked it.

Zoey glances out through the vehicle's windshield, hoping to see another sign for the small town that was marked on their map. They should've been there by now.

Reaper and his team had taken flight in the late afternoon, the helicopter circling the demolished building one last time before angling away into the reddening horizon. They hadn't dared to move for another hour and when they did it was a slow and agonizing journey back to the facility fences. It took them the better part of two hours to dig the ASV from its grave beside the toppled watchtower. If the vehicle had been any closer to the building there would've been no saving it. After gathering what meager supplies they could, they set off toward the nearest town sixty miles away, for the promise of shelter and medical supplies that Chelsea could administer.

The ASV shudders, slowing as Merrill makes a left turn onto another narrower road, leaving the wider highway behind in the growing evening.

"How far?" Tia asks from beside Eli. She's been holding his hand for the entirety of the ride and won't relinquish her position for anything.

"Five miles," Merrill says. Zoey watches him, studies the side of his face she can see. The tranquilizer hasn't had a lasting effect, but for the past several hours he's been quiet, brooding silently while throwing a look at Eli every so often.

Out the side window, the landscape scrolls by. They've traveled northwest, closer to the Washington border Ian says, but it still looks barren and cold, the last evening light washing dingy shadows past everything it touches. What Zoey wouldn't give to be back in the mountains at Ian's cabin, at their home. She can feel the moisture in the air, the fire warming her fingers, and taste the salty tang of the evening meal while the jug of moonshine is passed around. She can hear the wind's constant murmur through the pines, and Eli is fine, smiling across the fire at her after telling one of his endless jokes.

She blinks away the burning in her eyes and focuses on the buildings that grow steadily outside the windshield.

The town is small, its layout a single line with two neighborhoods flanking the vacant storefronts. They all peer out the windows, searching for movement, signs of life, any threat. The town looks deserted.

"According to the map there's a clinic on the western side. Damn it, I can't tell what street it's on, the number's smudged," Chelsea says. Zoey looks at the older woman's hands. They're trembling. Merrill guides the ASV down the street, taking a left turn at a church the color of a storm cloud, its bell tower leaning hard to the right like a broken neck.

"There," Merrill finally says, coasting into a parking lot before a low building with solid glass lining its front. The sign over an awning reads "Fairfield County Clinic."

They climb from the vehicle, Ian and Newton shoving open the sliding glass doors while Chelsea and Tia get Eli ready to move. He grumbles something under his breath and it takes Zoey a moment to realize he's saying, "Ella. Ella."

Ian and Newton reappear in the gap between the doors. "It's empty," Ian says, hurrying forward. They hover around Eli, everyone helping carry him inside, all of them wanting to bear a little of the burden, share in some of the pain. Zoey holds on to his right arm, her opposite hand locked in his. And even though she knows he's unconscious, she still feels the strength in his fingers as they grip her own.

The air smells stale and bits of dust twirl as they carry him past a vacant reception desk through a set of double doors to a room with a gurney in its center. They lay him down gently, none of them really wanting to let go.

"I need space," Chelsea says, and Zoey hears the vigor returning to her voice, the physician within her taking over. She unbuttons Eli's shirt and removes the stained dressing around his middle exposing dark skin caked with blood. "Merrill, find me an instrument tray that's clean along with a scalpel, shears, and at least six clamps. Someone needs to boil some water."

"On it," Rita says.

"Everyone else, get out and stay out unless I call for you." When no one moves, Chelsea looks up at them and jerks her head toward the door. They file out into the quiet hallway, no one speaking or looking at one another.

"We could try to get some power on. In case she needs it," Lyle says.

"Yes. Even a clinic as small as this one should have a backup generator somewhere," Ian says. "Tia, will you help me find it?"

Tia nods, eyes unfocused, staring at nothing. Ian takes her hand and guides her down the hall with him, leaving the rest of them standing together.

"I'll stay here in case Chelsea needs something or someone," Nell offers. The others mill about for a moment before wandering away from each other. Zoey lingers, unsure of what to do with herself.

"He's going to be okay," Nell says, nodding toward the room. "I know a tough person when I see one, and Eli's tough."

"Yes, he is."

"He reminds me of my friend Robbie. They're different but they have the same resilience and sense of humor. Robbie was one of the only reasons I got up in the morning. Before, I wouldn't let myself think about Rita, couldn't get myself to say her name. I thought she was lost. But Robbie was always moving forward, always kept me focused on tomorrow." She pauses, a hint of sadness crossing her face before she squeezes Zoey's hand. "You just keep thinking about tomorrow too. Okay?"

"Okay. Thank you."

"Anytime."

Zoey slips through the outer double doors, gazing past the parking lot and the ASV to the sun that's fallen behind the row of homes across the street, and despite Nell's comforting words, they look as empty as she feels. The fatigue combined with everything the last twenty-four hours has held compounds into a crushing weight pressing down on her shoulders. Words and images whirl through her mind as if tossed by a storm, none cohesive or useful, only taunting phantoms of pain and confusion.

She walks to the other side of the ASV and nearly collapses against it as a bout of vertigo sweeps through her. What will they do if Eli dies? The idea is too horridly massive to contemplate. And at the base of it all is the sickening knowledge of why he is in the room now, close to death and suffering.

My fault.

Her lungs constrict and she puts a hand on the vehicle to steady herself.

They came looking for me. For the keystone. If I hadn't been there . . .

They might have still killed everyone. She knows this but it doesn't assuage the guilt. It is a physical thing, strangling, draining her strength.

She takes several deep breaths, closing her eyes while trying to concentrate on only what she can feel and hear.

Cool wind coasting through the desolate town.

Cold steel beneath her hand.

A faint call of a crow somewhere to the south.

The smell of winter on its way.

Zoey straightens, no longer sure she's going to pass out. What can she do right now to make things different? Nothing. Chelsea is the only one who can save Eli. The truth infuriates her, but of course it almost always has that effect.

She surveys the surrounding area before setting off at a fast walk. If she can't help Eli directly she can at least make sure they're safe within the clinic.

She circumnavigates the building, looking for access points that a person could enter without their knowledge. There are only three, all steel doors secured from the inside. An office at the north end has a broken window and she makes a mental note to board it up before nightfall. When she returns to the entrance, Newton is there looking stricken but meets her eyes and gives her his small smile. She returns it, squeezing his shoulder as she passes. Inside she smells heated steel and finds Rita standing beside Nell outside Eli's room.

"I boiled two gallons of water," Rita says. "Found a gas burner in one of the closets. We were going to start supper soon. Do you want to help?"

"No. There's a broken window in one of the offices. I'm going to find a way to block it off." She begins to move away but Rita snags her arm.

"He's going to be okay."

"I know."

The other woman's eyes say more, reassurances that Zoey can't stand to absorb. She nods once and strides down the hall.

She's unable to find anything in the office or hallway outside to cover the window with and is about to begin searching for a maintenance room when several lights blink on and a low humming comes from a door near the end of the corridor. A moment later it opens and Ian and Tia appear.

"Got the generator up and running," Ian says. He tries a smile on her that she can't bring herself to return.

"I'm going to check on him," Tia says quietly and leaves them where they stand. The silence invades again and Zoey feels herself on the brink of telling Ian everything. Relaying what the assassin said to her. But the words lodge in her throat, a solid stone that threatens to choke her.

"How are you doing?" he asks.

"Fine. I'm fine," she says, raking a hand back through the stubble of her hair.

"You haven't slept. You should find a room and lie down."

"I don't think I can sleep." It sounds like a lie. There's nothing more she wants than sleep, to sink down away from it all. And when she wakes, maybe it will have been a dream. Something she could laugh about in the moments after consciousness.

"Then at least let's go get something to eat."

They walk down the empty corridor, passing vacant rooms and pictures hanging skewed on the walls. Here is a boy staring out at a tossing sea. There a deer stands by the edge of a wood overlooking a small farm. Another shows the sun rising past an outcropping of rock, the word "WILL" emblazoned over it. Underneath it says, "Without it, courage is only an idea."

She watches the dusty floor, her feet pulling her along as if she is a passenger in her own body.

They find everyone except Chelsea, Eli, Merrill, and Newton in a conference room on the east end of the clinic. Rita and Nell have somehow made a type of dumplings in broth and the smell twists her stomach into knots of hunger.

They eat without comment, all of them staring at different places in the room. When Zoey finishes she cleans out her bowl and sits down against the wall, hands on her thighs. Her back is a dull heartbeat of pain. She readjusts herself and rests her head against the wall. She's about to close her eyes and attempt to drift away for a bit when her fingertips brush a lump in her pocket. She draws it out.

The square cartridge and the ampule rest in her palm. She turns them over, gazing at the red liquid in the vial. It is still cold to the touch. She examines the black square. It is smooth, without markings, one edge of it lined with what looks like brass teeth.

Proof. In the arm.

"Whatcha got there?"

She jumps as Lyle lowers himself to the floor beside her. She considers hiding the objects away but it would be foolish and in the end pointless. She has to tell them eventually.

She drops the square and the vial into his hand. "It was in the man's fake arm. Do you know what they are?"

"Well this is a memory card. But this . . . this I don't know." He holds up the vial to the light. "Looks like blood."

"A memory card. So it goes in a computer?"

He nods. "It's basically storage for whatever you want. Pictures, videos, documents."

"Do you think you could get a computer working here?"

"I sure can try."

They rise together and as they're moving toward the door, Chelsea appears with Merrill close behind. Both of them look exhausted, past their breaking points. Chelsea's eyes are bloodshot and flecks of blood stain the hem of her shirt. Merrill has a hand on her waist, to steady her or himself Zoey's not sure.

Immediately the room erupts in questions. Chelsea motions for them to quiet as she drops into a seat. She licks her lips, glancing at everyone before speaking.

"The bullet nicked an artery leading to his liver. It wasn't terrible and I was able to get the bleeding stopped." A general cry of relief and happiness comes from them, but Zoey stays silent, reading the expression on Chelsea's face.

"The problem is the bullet didn't pass through." The room goes quiet again. "After I got the bleeding stopped his vitals started to drop. I didn't have a choice but to close him up. The bullet's still inside him somewhere." She swallows, looking as if she's about to be sick but merely shakes her head. "If I would've had more time or the right instruments earlier . . ."

"Stop," Merrill says, kneeling beside her. "You did everything you could."

"So what does that mean?" Tia asks.

"It means I have no idea what other damage the bullet caused. If I'd kept going he would've died," Chelsea says, beginning to cry. "And he might anyway."

Tia stands for a long moment, arms crossed as if she's holding herself together before striding quickly out of the room. Zoey watches her go, knowing there's no point in trying to stop her.

"I just need to sit here for a second. Then I'll go find the rest of the equipment for the next operation. If his vitals come back I can go in again and find the bullet."

"You need to rest right now," Merrill says, taking Chelsea's hand and touching her belly. "You and the baby. Besides, you won't do Eli any good if you're too tired to hold your instruments steady." She gives him a wan smile as he rises and ladles a dumpling onto a tray for her.

Zoey watches the two of them, then nods at Lyle. She follows him out through the door and past Eli's room. Inside Tia sits by the bed, the low tones of her voice floating into the hall. Zoey looks away, focusing on the sound of their footfalls. Lyle leads her to a small office off another examination room. Inside a computer sits on a shelf beneath a row of cabinets. The unit is much bulkier than the one in the NOA storage room at Riverbend but Lyle seems to know his way around this model as well. After several minutes the machine hums and the smell of warming electronics fills the room.

When the computer is fully up and running Lyle takes the memory card from her and inserts it into the tower below the shelf. The machine whirs.

A mixture of anticipation and dread fills her. Maybe it was all a ruse. A trick to make her surrender, to confuse and divide her from the rest of the group. Those at the ARC know her, or at least they used to. Perhaps this is their attempt to collect her without ever lifting a finger.

She watches the screen, half hoping the card will be damaged or unreadable, half fearing it will be.

What is worse, knowing or not knowing?

A black box appears on the screen, symbols at its bottom.

"It's a video," Lyle says.

"Play it," she says when she's able to answer.

"Are you sure? I could step outsi—"

"Play it."

He enlarges the box and slides partially out of the way, making room as she approaches the screen. Lyle gives her a last look and she nods before he taps the control on the counter and the video begins to play.

Zoey's stomach lurches.

A woman with dark brown hair and luminous hazel eyes looks into the camera, not moving, simply staring at Zoey as if they're in the same room, without the impedance of technology between them. As unnerving as the other woman's gaze is, the background is worse.

Vivian sits in the room with the opaque tanks behind her, cables and tubes leading to the tower with the swimming lights to her left. It is just as Zoey remembers it from the night of her flight from the ARC, the horrible purpose of the equipment taking on a newer and more personal offense.

"Hello Zoey," Vivian says in a soft voice. "If you're watching this then one of our people was able to find you but unable to bring you home." She pauses as if searching for the right words. "I'm sure you believe everyone here is a monster, that NOA itself is an abomination. I can understand that. But what I ask of you now, Zoey, is to look around you, wherever you are. What do you see?"

Involuntarily she does. She takes in the blank walls of the office, the dust, disuse heavy in the air, the lack of life.

"Hopelessness," Vivian continues. "The world is passing into another age, one without humankind." She pauses, looking down, then back up at the camera. "For a long time I thought it was inevitable, that there was no solving the Dearth. That was before I met you. You've been called the keystone, and that's an apt title, but you're so much more than that, Zoey. You are the single most important person on the planet. You have the ability to transcend, to become something no one else has ever been. A savior."

Vivian rises from her chair and moves it out of the frame, revealing one of the dark tanks mounted directly behind her. She positions herself behind it, places her hands on the top.

"I'd like to introduce you to someone. Your daughter."

3

Vivian presses something on the tank's side and removes her hands.

At first nothing happens but then the darkness of the tank changes. It becomes lighter, smokier, until a shape is revealed within.

"My God," Lyle whispers.

The baby floats in the center of the now-transparent tank. She is curled in on herself, partially turned toward the camera, a synthetic tube extending from the tank's side to her stomach. As Zoey watches the baby shifts, rotating within the fluid, one tiny hand opening and closing.

Vivian touches the tank again and its surface darkens, the girl vanishing in its depths. Zoey catches herself stepping forward, a part of her aching to see the baby again.

Her jaw trembles as warring emotions riptide through her.

Rage.

Fear.

Helplessness.

And something else, a bittersweet tinge each time she replays the image of the baby floating there, unborn, innocent, and defenseless. It is the same sensation she had when the little boy, Isaac, had snuggled against her at the Quiverfull farm.

"I'm sure you doubt what I'm saying, that this really is your daughter. All the proof you need is in the vial that was beside this memory card." Vivian moves closer to the camera, her gaze unnerving again as it was at the beginning of the video. "Please, Zoey, your daughter will be born within the next weeks or sooner. She'll need you just as the rest of the world needs you. Come home."

The video ends, the screen going as black as the tank that holds the baby.

Lyle reaches out and shuts down the window, settling back into his chair without saying anything. Zoey closes her eyes, the whirling mass of thoughts coalescing until she can't define any of them. The scuff of a boot in the hall makes her turn.

Merrill and Ian stand in the doorway, both of them pale and staring.

"Zoey . . ." Merrill says, but she's already moving past him, away from the cloistering room and all she learned there.

She hurries down the hall, turning at the building's double doors and bursting through them, startling Newton where he stands watch.

Her strides double-time until she's running.

The night air whips past her and flecks of moisture sting her face. It is snowing; huge flakes drift carelessly to the street, making everything a white facsimile of itself.

She runs until her lungs burn so much with cold that she has to stop, back beginning to throb again, the threat of paralysis hinted at with a tingling in her legs. She glances around, absorbing for the first time where she's ended up.

The street curves ahead, buildings snowy shapes in the night. To the left the dismal church and its broken tower. She walks to its steps and climbs them, sure that the heavy doors will be locked, but when she pushes at one it swings open as if waiting for her to enter.

The interior is larger than she expected. Thick wooden beams soar thirty feet overhead and her footsteps echo from the darkness of the seating to either side. A curtain of snowflakes fall from the open wound of the bell tower above and she steps through them, their icy touch melting on her scalp.

Zoey moves up the center aisle past overturned benches. At the front, an empty space waits where she feels something should be. A podium or perhaps an altar. On the back wall is an enormous outline of a cross and it takes her several seconds to realize the cross itself is missing. Only the silhouette remains, an afterimage where it once hung.

She lowers herself to the frontmost bench and stares at the outline. She knows the general idea behind most faiths from Ian's books, the prayers, sacraments, and other common practices all similar in one respect or another. The idea of believing in something greater than what can be seen is an attractive one, a type of invisible safety net.

Hope, faith, belief.

Giving away fears instead of giving in to them. She imagines letting go, trusting in fate or a higher power to her life and those around her.

It is a flicker in the darkness that instantly goes out.

Prayers don't stop bullets.

Faith won't bring back the ones she's lost.

She gazes at the outline of the cross, the empty church. Listens to the silence.

All the belief in the world didn't keep the end from coming.

But now she has a choice. An actual way to make a difference.

You have the ability to transcend, to become something no one else has ever been.

A savior.

She breathes out, an exhalation of white in the cold air.

How much is a life worth?

She hasn't asked herself the question in a long time. But now it isn't only *a* life, it is *all* life. The true realization is too large to comprehend, the weight of it crushing.

Come home.

Her throat constricts, panic flaring in her chest as she recalls the feeling of her finger on the button that controlled the missile—a missile intended for the ARC. If she'd pushed it . . .

"I would have killed her," she whispers. "I would've killed my daughter."

She hugs herself, leaning forward, crying silent tears that drop to the cold dusty floor.

Why? Why did this happen? Why was she born when she was? Born into a dying world, having such a burden thrust upon her. The seething hatred returns with the thought of the Director making his speeches. She grits her teeth, remembering the feeling of pulling the trigger and seeing him fall. She'd kill him again if she had the chance, destroy everyone at the ARC: Vivian, Reaper, and every lying face that had kept her and the other women—like Halie and Terra—trapped there and forced this on her.

This responsibility.

This choice.

Keep running or go back?

She slumps to her side and tucks her legs up, tears already cooling on her face.

The thoughts are still churning in her mind as she drops into a fitful sleep, muddied with nightmares of the room of tanks, all of them still dark but seeping blood onto the floor. And the tower of lights becomes a person in black, their back turned to her so she can't see their face. But she knows who it is, she's always known. The figure begins to turn but gravity loses its hold and she floats backward, all sense of direction gone, tumbling over and over, the sensation of falling so strong she jostles awake and barely stops from slamming face-first into the floor of the church.

Zoey props herself up, looking around dazedly.

Night still holds sway. The snow's quit falling through the broken bell tower. All is still.

She rises, stretching taut muscles and blowing on frozen fingers that don't feel like her own. The outside door is still partially open and she pauses on the threshold, gazing back at the lonely outline of the missing cross before moving outside to the snowy town.

Rita is on watch when she approaches the clinic and levels a rifle at her as she nears.

"Just me," Zoey says.

"Where the hell'd you get off to?"

"Went to church."

Rita's lip curls. "What for?"

"Needed to think."

The other woman nods. "Merrill told us. Told everyone about the video." When she doesn't answer Rita says, "They're having a meeting now about what to do. They waited for you but . . ."

"It's fine. Is Eli awake?"

"He was an hour ago. Asked for some water, which Chelsea said is a good sign." Zoey nods and moves past her but Rita snags her arm. "If you want to talk, Sherell and I—"

"I'm fine." She walks away, knowing she shouldn't be angry but is, nonetheless. But when has anger ever been reasonable? She stalks toward Eli's door, ignoring the low voices of conversation in the room they ate in earlier. The door is ajar and she pushes it open slowly.

Eli lies, partially elevated, in the bed, several heavy blankets pulled up to his chest. A small electric heater hums in the corner throwing warmth into the room.

She steps close to the bed, studying his face, how gaunt he appears even though he was only wounded the day before. Zoey finds his hand in the blankets and holds it. After a moment he opens one eye, the corner of his mouth curling up.

"Hey, girl," he says. His voice is a jagged whisper.

"Hi."

He swallows. "How you doin'?"

She struggles with the constriction in her throat. "Good. How do you feel?"

"Great. Tip-top. Gonna go for a quick jog later. You up for it?"

She laughs, swiping at one eye. "I'm in."

He grins. "Good. Better watch it, I'll beat your ass one of these times." He begins to chuckle but it dissolves into a weak cough that flexes his entire body. Zoey puts an arm beneath his neck and holds him until the spasm passes.

"Goddamn. That hurt. Not sure I'll give this hospital a recommendation." He eyes her again when she doesn't laugh. "I'm gonna be fine. Don't you worry about me."

"I know."

"What's everyone else doing?"

"Talking."

"Yeah?"

"Yeah."

"You tired of that?"

"Talking?" She gazes at him and nods.

"Yeah. You and me, same page. Cut from the same cloth. We're doers, not talkers. Ain't too much gets done just by talkin' about it."

She feels like she should tell him then. Tell him what the others are discussing in the next room. She can't even begin to guess what their opinions are, but she's sure Eli would only listen, saving any judgment until she was finished. Her eyes travel down his exposed arm to the dark tattoo. The name he's never spoken until he was semiconscious the day before. He notices her gaze and lifts his arm slightly.

"I never told you about her, my fiancée," he says quietly.

"No."

"Eleanor Dalton. That was her name. But she was always Ella to me."

"You should rest," Zoey says.

"Some things have to be said. Thinking them over and over doesn't always do them justice." Eli shifts, grimacing before laying his head back onto the pillow to stare at the ceiling. "We met in college and we both knew that was it on the first date, wasn't any point in fighting it. Got engaged a year later. The year the Dearth started. She always said she didn't care if we never had children, but I knew the truth. She felt the same as me. We both wanted kids but it was getting dangerous, and what if she gave birth to a girl? At first we just watched it on TV. Watched them ask for women to come in as volunteers. Then we heard the rumors of them being taken by force. Then we saw it happen out the windows of my living room one night. By then it was probably too late."

Zoey puts a hand on his arm, partly to let him know she's still there, still listening, and partly to let him know he can stop if he wants. Eli licks his lips and the dry rasping nearly makes her wince.

"My dad had a boat when I was younger. Had to sell it when he lost his job at the warehouse he worked in. Wasn't much, a little fourteen footer with an outboard that wouldn't have lasted a minute in a storm. But he used to take me and my mom and my brother out for rides on the weekend during summer and those were some of the best days of my life. We would stop at an island that was a wildlife reserve, off the coast maybe a mile, when the water was calm. We'd eat, and Dad and Mom would have a beer together. There was a natural resource building overlooking the rocks and the water. Never saw anyone go in or out of it." He brings his gaze from the ceiling to her face. "That's where I took her when things got bad. Brought her out there in a boat I stole and set her up with water and food. Left a dinghy so she could get back to the mainland if she had to. I thought I'd watch and wait, go visit when I could until everything blew over. Didn't know it wouldn't blow over. Didn't know it would only get worse.

"Figured out they were watching me after she'd been on the island a week. NOA. They had a van on the corner of our street and I'd heard through a couple friends that a few women had disappeared along with their significant others. Started kicking myself for ever leaving her but I didn't know."

Eli coughs and Zoey glances around, grabbing a water glass and straw from the floor beside the bed. She holds it for him and he drinks, face creased with pain when he's finished.

"I'll go get Chelsea," she says, starting to rise.

"No. Gotta finish this. Only told one other person and he's in the next room. She deserves to have people remember her."

"Don't talk like that. Don't—"

"It was my fault. My love killed her. I thought I'd lost them, snuck past and left them behind. But I was wrong. Should have waited, but I couldn't stand not seeing her. They followed me to the island and we were holding each other when they came up from the rocks. There was a team with guns telling us to come with them and I still remember her hand in mine and how she squeezed it, told me what she wanted. So we ran. They chased us away from the building and we were trying to get to the dinghy but she slipped on the rocks." Eli clears his throat and blinks. "Over twenty years ago but time doesn't make some things hurt less."

Zoey feels the prickling in her eyes and takes a deep breath, squeezing his hand again. "She fell."

He nods. "I fell with her. But I hit water and she didn't. She was gone before I could climb back up to her. And they were coming, already shooting at me. I swam away and never got a chance to say good-bye. They even took that from me."

"I'm so sorry," she whispers, knowing if she were to speak louder her voice would crack. "You said you haven't forgiven yourself. You told me that in the ASV, but it wasn't your fault."

He manages a quiet laugh and strokes one thumb gently across her chin. "Look'it who's telling who about guilt."

She squeezes his hand again. "Listen, you're going to be okay."

"Damn straight I will. Too stubborn to die. You better keep runnin' too cause I'm serious about beating you. It's gonna happen."

"You can try."

He nods, his smile gradually fading as he closes his eyes. She's about to stand and leave the room when he speaks again. "Zoey?"

"Yeah?"

"Don't let them go," he says faintly, the effort of talking taking its toll. "The ones you love. They disappear." Then he's asleep, chest rising and falling with steady, shallow breaths.

She sits with him for a time before standing and drawing the blanket up to tuck it beneath his chin.

The hallway is much cooler than the room and she pulls the door almost shut, listening again for a beat to Eli's breathing before moving away toward the muted sound of conversation. She stops in the doorway.

Merrill leans on the table in the center of the room, his posture the same as when planning a movement or contemplating a fight. The rest of the group is split in half to either side of the room. Their voices cease as Merrill straightens, looking directly at her. Zoey pauses, glancing down at the floor before stepping across the threshold.

"I checked on Eli. He's sleeping now." She swallows, bringing her eyes up to them, glancing from face to face, trying to discern how they feel about her now. She recalls one of the first books she ever read, one of two Simon had smuggled into her room without her knowing. Was this how Hester Prynne felt in *The Scarlet Letter*? Gawked at, ashamed, terrified. And none of it truly her fault. She tries to speak but opening her mouth takes a titanic effort, the forming of words something monumental.

I have a daughter.

I am a mother.

I am the keystone.

She wants to run again, her heart calling out to turn from them and flee. She's about to when Ian rises and comes to her, looking once in her eyes before hugging her.

She stiffens, nerves going rigid, then languid. His embrace is like lying down after walking all day.

There is the scrape of chairs then more arms encircle them. Chelsea is there, and Tia. Newton, Sherell, and Nell. Even Lyle at the outermost ring places a hand on her shoulder. She is surrounded, not by words or judgment or the pressing need of decisions, but by the simplicity of comfort. Of love.

Her family.

"We will face this like anything else," Ian says quietly. "Together." She grips him tighter before the circle around her slowly loosens. Ian holds her at arm's length. "But right now you need to rest. We all do."

"I'll stay with Eli," Chelsea says.

"Me too," Tia murmurs, heading for his room.

"Let's get this room set up for the rest of us. I'll stand watch and relieve Rita," Merrill says.

"I'm okay, I'll switch with Rita," Zoey says.

"No." Merrill fixes her with one of his gazes that says she'll be fighting a losing battle. "You of all people need to sleep."

"But—"

"How's your back feel?"

"Fine."

"Liar. Go lie down." He winks at her and is gone out the door.

They carry in some bedding they were able to salvage from Riverbend, and though the tile floor feels hard through the blanket she lies on, it is heaven to stretch out and ease the tension in her back.

She stares at the dusty ceiling; torn spiderwebs drift in the corners. Morning light creeps in around the shaded windows. The soft sounds of the others settling in lulls her. They are safe for now. Eli's hand felt strong in hers; he's going to pull through. She begins to let herself drift but the image of the baby girl floating in the tank rises through her mind, bringing with it all the unanswerable questions. She sighs, closing her eyes, sure that she'll lie awake for hours, the questions churning inside, but it is only seconds until she drops away, falling from a cliff into darkness—and lands in liquid. The water is cloudy, lit only by a vague vacillating light that shimmers from all sides. Zoey struggles upward, in the direction the surface should be but there is only more water.

Her body hitches, screaming for air, and she only has seconds left before she must take a breath.

Her eyelids flutter and close, lips part.

She inhales the water.

And it brings blessed relief.

Oxygen floods her lungs. Her head clears and she opens her eyes.

Movement to her left. Legs and arms froth the water: a group, swimming upward toward the brightest light she sees. She begins to follow them but something else catches her eye.

The baby girl floats in the opposite direction, small legs kicking, tiny fingers opening and closing, and how Zoey would love to place one of her fingers inside that little fist, feel the life there as her daughter held on to her for the first time.

Zoey turns her head back and forth, watching her family and her daughter float in opposite directions, their forms growing more indistinct until she's alone, the cloudy water dimming around her. Closing in. And suddenly she can't breathe anymore.

Her lungs smolder.

Then burn.

The water chokes her, suffocates with serenity the way only water can do. She struggles but the light fades completely and she's falling again.

Zoey snaps awake, legs kicking at the thin blanket wrapped around her. She sits up, completely at a loss as to where she is until she hears the soft snores and rustle of someone turning over across the lunchroom.

It comes back to her at once.

Eli. The clinic. And the dream.

She gags. She can't help it, the sensation of water thick in her mouth. The air tastes used from them all breathing it for hours, but she drinks it in anyway, trying to calm the breakneck speed of her heart. She holds out a hand in the dim light and watches it tremble until it stills. Her mind begins to retrace the vivid outlines of the dream but she shoves it away, unwilling to dissect what it means. Later, when she's had a chance to absorb everything that's happened in the last two days, then maybe—

Movement in the doorway. Merrill stands there, gazing at them, leaning heavily on the jamb. Zoey rises to her knees, then her feet. Something's wrong.

Merrill leaves the door and walks to a chair. He sits, elbows coming to rest on his knees, hands over his face. A sound comes from the hallway, short and muffled, but unmistakable.

Sobbing.

No.

Merrill raises his face.

No.

Solid lines of tears drip off his chin.

No.

"Zoey," he whispers, voice choked.

"No."

"Eli—"

"Stop."

"He's gone."

4

Vivian sits on the concrete bench overlooking the river and watches the helicopter grow out of the center of the setting sun like the expanding pupil of an enormous eye.

The aircraft detaches from the corona and banks high above her, turning into position before settling out of sight below the ARC's walls. A thrill runs through her, laced with anxiety. This could be it. Zoey might be back within the facility at this moment. If she is, one of the nearby guards will receive word via radio. If not . . . well, she'll know soon enough.

She waits, watching the cold autumnal sun glimmer off the water. Listens to the river dropping over the dam's spillway in a symphony of liquid static. She smells the frost in the air and relishes the cold, solid concrete beneath her.

Slowly the pleasure of her surroundings fades.

Soon it's gone completely.

The spike of anticipation gives way to the solemn despair that's stalked her ever since the night Zoey escaped with the rest of the women. She smooths a wrinkle in her slacks, ignoring the sound of someone approaching from behind her.

"What happened? Where's the other helicopter?" she says without looking over her shoulder.

Reaper's gloved hands curl over the back of the bench beside her. They're scuffed and torn, covered with some kind of dust. "We lost it along with one team."

Vivian closes her eyes. "And you didn't get her." It's not a question. "No."

"Why?"

"They launched one of the antiballistic missiles."

"What? No, I don't even want to know. You do realize that was our best chance to get her back. The scout that found her was one of the last men still out looking."

"I know."

"We'll have to send them out again, determine a probable direction she went in and canvass all areas in a radius."

"Maybe—"

"Maybe what?"

Reaper steps around the bench so she can see him fully. He's not wearing his mask; the torn landscape of scars covering his face stands out in stark relief to the rest of his skin. "Maybe we shouldn't send them out again."

"What are you talking about? We have thirty-six men who volunteered to amputate an arm for this mission and you want to, what? Put them to work in the kitchen? They're going to have trouble making the perfect omelet."

"I'm saying it's more dangerous having them out there hunting her. Anything could happen."

"Anything can happen right now, right this instant. She could run into any derelict out there and vanish forever."

"She's got them protecting her."

Something in his voice stops her. She's sure then that this is what's been on his mind over the past months, the subject he's never brought up but carried each time they spoke like some invisible baggage. "Are you saying she's better off with them than here?"

He pauses. "No."

"Then what are you saying? Please clarify because you're really muddying the waters right now."

"I'm saying if she finds the video and the sample, she'll come to us."

She stands, stepping forward so she's only inches from him. "Are you still a soldier?"

"Yes. Of course."

"Then start acting like one. You receive orders and carry them out. That's your job."

His scarred features harden but he says nothing.

Vivian studies him, trying to identify any barriers he's built over the years without her noticing. "You're different lately," she says finally. "You've changed. And not for the better I'm afraid."

Reaper stares at her, and she nearly shivers under a gaze that has gone completely cold. "We've all changed, Vivian."

With that he walks away, leaving her in the cool air by the ever-moving river.

5

The leaden skies hang low, mingling the horizon into a line of gray.

They stand beside the mound of dirt, broken rock ringing its edge and covering its top. Snow crushed with footprints surrounding the cairn.

And ten of them in a half circle. Silent. Staring.

The wind comes in from the west, a dry breath of prairie and the promise of more snow. Zoey stands still as a stone, looking at the grave but not seeing it. She tries to correlate the mounded dirt and Eli, but can't. It's all lost in the last hours.

Merrill's tears.

Tia's sobs, both her hands holding on to Eli's limp arm.

Ian trying to comfort her along with everyone else.

Chelsea repeating what she'd tried to do, tried to save him but the bullet, the bullet must've shifted and cut another artery and how could she not have known that would happen, how could she have lost him, until Merrill envelops her in his arms and she is quiet except for hitching breaths, her whitened fingers digging into his back.

The sound of the pickax still echoes in Zoey's ears. Biting into and through the partially frozen dirt. Digging down with a shovel, and other voices saying that she should take a break, and ignoring them until her back gave out. Numbness crawls in her legs, pain shooting through intermittently like lightning strikes in the desert.

And it is all secondary to the grave and what it holds.

Ian steps forward and lays something on the closest rock. It is a cross, woven from what looks to be paper, string, and stick. She sees the brief image of the missing cross on the church wall. A line of Shakespeare comes to her then—*Hamlet*, her favorite of all his work.

Now cracks a noble heart. Good night, sweet prince.

She tilts her head up, eyelids fluttering at the indifferent sky.

Merrill says something she can't understand, his voice gibberish, meaningless.

Meaningless. That's what all words are in the face of this. No sentiments can withstand the quiet of death.

Tia leans against Ian, and Merrill kneels, placing one hand on the stones before standing and leading Chelsea away. One by one they turn until only she, Rita, Sherell, and Newton are left. Rita says something, telling her to come with, but she shakes her head. Slowly they file away except for Newton who stops beside her and brushes one long-fingered hand down the side of her face. Then he's gone and she's alone on the wind and snow-bitten plain outside the small town that will never shelter life again.

Images swirl in her mind like the snow around her.

The NOA agent saying she is a mother and the keystone.

Her daughter floating in the tank.

Vivian telling her to come home.

Eli grimacing as he tells her the story of the woman he loved, seeing Ella falling over and over again.

The white blanket wrapped around him as he's lowered into the ground.

Zoey's knees buckle and she places a hand out to keep from falling. Her fingers meet the cold, soft earth between rocks.

"I'm sorry," she whispers, letting the hot tears finally fall. "So sorry. I didn't mean for any of this to happen." She cries, the snow accepting each teardrop like a gift. This is exactly what she's feared since the day she felt herself caring about the group—that she would not only lose them but be the cause of it as well.

Should've stayed at the ARC and none of this would've happened.

Not true. Terra would've been sold into the Fae Trade and there's no telling where either of them would be now. She would probably be on the fifth floor, strapped to a table with tubes running out of every orifice.

But Eli would still be alive.

Yes. He would.

There is no rebuttal for the fact. No comfort. He is gone forever.

She cries harder, the sobs wrenching something loose inside her. The memory of Merrill telling her she already has a family comes unbidden. This death, the danger at the silo, is all because she wanted to find her heritage. Because she needed to find who she is.

But now it's abundantly clear. She is chaos. Disaster. Pain.

A murderer.

It doesn't matter anymore who her parents were or where she came from. Nothing can change who she's become. And those she loves have suffered for it.

Don't let them go. The ones you love. They disappear.

She pushes herself upright, hands and face tingling with cold, frozen tear-tracks like burns on her cheeks.

Don't let them go.

Let them go.

Disappear.

Zoey rises slowly and gives the grave a final look. "Thank you," she says, and walks toward the edge of town leaving footprints that start to fill in with snow as soon as she's gone.

♦ ♦ ♦

She finds them in the lunchroom, most settled in their bedding on the floor. Tia, Chelsea, and Merrill sit around the table, the last bottle of moonshine between them. Zoey starts to walk past them but Merrill calls out to her.

"You haven't said a word," he says when she nears.

"I don't have anything to say."

He searches her face but she keeps it emotionless. "You know you can talk to us, any of us, right?"

"I know."

"Can't believe he's gone," Tia says, words slurring. She reaches out and takes another long pull on the bottle. "I keep expecting him to walk through the door or hear him say something smart."

Chelsea puts an arm around the other woman. "I wish I would've—"

"It's no one's fault except the man who shot him," Merrill says, drinking from the bottle himself. "And he's dead so the blame is gone. What we need to do is get some sleep and focus on what our next move is." He looks at Zoey and she drops her eyes before nodding.

Without saying anything else she walks to her bedding and arranges it near the door. The low mumble of conversation gradually lulls her past the visions of Eli in the white blanket and she closes her eyes before the tears can come again.

♦ ♦ ♦

Merrill wakes with a start. He sits up, wincing at the throb in the base of his skull. Too much 'shine. But even then the crashing reality of the day before sinks in. It is a blanket of lead laid over his shoulders. He tries to imagine the coming days without Eli beside him, to rely on, to joke with. He imagines life without his friend and he wants to lie down again and go back to sleep until the hurt is gone. He starts to but stops, propped up on one elbow.

Why did he wake up?

He rolls over and scans the room. Chelsea breathes softly next to him, Tia on the other side of her. There is Lyle against the opposite wall with Seamus dozing near his feet and Nell between Rita and Sherell. Newton lies on his back, one hand holding Sherell's. This almost makes him smile but he doesn't, the persistent inkling that something is wrong like an itch in his mind.

He rises, guessing the time. It's maybe an hour before dawn, the light sterile and cold coming in past the blinds. He tries to remember who was on last shift for watch and recalls Ian saying he would do it, noticing the old man's blankets in a pile, and that's when he freezes.

There is an empty space near the door that shouldn't be there.

Zoey.

He steps quickly over Chelsea and Tia, moving into the hall and through the double doors. Ian stands beside the entry to the clinic. His head snaps around at the sound of Merrill's approach.

"Is Zoey with you?" Merrill asks.

Ian frowns. "No. She was sleeping when I came out around midnight."

"Damn it." He spins away, hurtling through the doors, and calls her name, his voice bouncing down the corridor and back. He steps into each room along the way, hoping against the rising dread that she'll be there, curled up and sleeping, just needing to be alone, but all are empty.

Stopping outside the last office he feels a draft of much colder air coming from beneath the door. He tries to open it but it's jammed. After two thrusts of his shoulder against the thick wood, the chair propped against the handle on the other side snaps and skids across the empty floor.

The broken window Zoey had mentioned to him the day before gapes to the predawn world beyond, a piece of paper with writing on it nailed to the sill. He doesn't need to move any closer to make out the footprints leading away from the clinic through the snow.

6

Zoey hikes up the side of the small ravine to where the wind has blown the ground free of snow.

She gazes back in the direction of the town she never knew the name of, but it is already lost to the distance she's covered. Only a glow in the east tells her she's moving the right way, that she's trekked far enough that the group won't be able to find her easily. She made sure by walking toward the eastern horizon before doubling back at a clear spot in the road and circling well outside the town so her trail will be difficult to track. She doesn't doubt they will find it, but by then she'll be gone.

A hollow ache fills her at the thought of them discovering she's left. Finding the note explaining why. Why she can't risk their lives anymore. Because as long as NOA exists they'll be hunting her, and the ones she loves will be considered disposable or at the very best, leverage to get her to do what they want.

I have to disappear before I lose them all.

The ground levels and she jogs for a bit, the pack on her shoulders sloshing with the two full water bottles she took. Below them is enough dried meat and canned food to last at least a week. But she doesn't know how long it will take her. How many miles she'll have to go before finding a vehicle that runs.

The land is uneven and rough beneath the coating of snow. She trips several times and has to slow as she enters what looks like a field of rock beside a rise that brings her up higher than she's been so far. The expanse stretches on for miles broken only by the occasional hillock or gulley, the curtain of a rolling snowstorm obscuring the northern horizon.

Her stomach turns at the sight of the distance. So far. But there's no choice.

She reaches into her pocket and draws out the vial of blood, turning it over a few times. Something so small with such massive implications. Zoey considers tossing the vial into the snow and turning south. She could walk until it got warmer and the world forgot her. Maybe then she could do the same. Forget the family she's gained, forget the love, forget Lee.

Forget her daughter.

Her hand clenches around the vial. She knows she could never do that. She has to be sure that Vivian's message and the baby aren't all a ruse, something to lure her back. And at the very least Lee deserves to know he is a father. That is if she can find him.

She starts down the opposite side of the hill, walking quickly until she's running, sprinting from all other thoughts except finding a working vehicle.

Because she's not sure she'll be able to walk all the way to Seattle.

7

Lee gazes out over the calm bay, hands chilling through his gloves as he holds on to the support railing of what once was the Space Needle.

He focuses on his breathing, trying to bring it under control after sprinting up eight hundred stairs to the observation deck where he stands now. Closing his eyes, he breathes in slowly through his nose and out through his mouth, willing his heart to slow. Gradually it does.

Lee stretches his right leg, which always tenses up and cramps faster than his left, and watches the boiling fog hanging over the bay. It is as thick as he's ever seen it since arriving here over seven months ago.

A recollection of stumbling into the outskirts of the city sweeps over him. Bloody, beaten, starving, two fingers broken on his right hand. He remembers the failing of his vision, the guard post door opening and the first kind voice he'd heard in nearly a month saying, *God Almighty. What the hell happened to you, son?*

Son.

He grimaces and walks around the circular observation deck, the view unhampered by safety cables that were cut years ago. They hang limp like unearthed worms through support bars, some lank and swaying in the wind, clacking against the sides of the structure in a sad off-beat. Suicides were the reason the cables were strung in the first place.

He'd read it in a swollen and weathered book he'd found in a small shop a stone's throw from the Needle's base. The aversion to even picking up a book had been monumental to overcome; each time he saw one he thought of Zoey, and then of his father.

Lee swallows and bats at one of the loose cables. In the early years of the Dearth there had been dozens of suicides every morning to clean up. Ray had told him this after nursing him back to health in the small, ground-floor apartment in what the old man called "Skid Row"; a tea-kettle almost always hissing quietly on a hot plate. *Garbage men!* Ray had exclaimed, redressing the slow-healing wounds while he lay helpless and weak on a cot. *Garbage men pick up garbage, not bodies, or pieces of them after falling five hundred feet. Damn outrage it was. But our union wouldn't back us. Some bureaucratic bullshit about pulling weight in a time of need.* The old man had batted a hand at the air as if knocking a fly away. *No one else would do it, that's all. We were accustomed to stink and dealing with other people's refuse. But let me tell you, son, no rotting garbage can prepare you for the smell that comes off a human being busted open on the concrete. The mind can't make sense of it even after seeing it over and over. And we cleaned them up every morning for a year. Shoveled them into the backs of the trucks and did our rounds like usual until the shooting got too bad. Then we hung up our keys and hid like anyone had to do who wanted to stay above the soil.*

Lee flexes his hand unconsciously, feeling the last tinges of ache in the mended bones. Ray had told him he'd have arthritis in the fingers when he gets older since they didn't heal exactly straight. The old man had said it in an apologetic way, looking at the floor as if ashamed. But Lee couldn't have appreciated him more. Kindness, he'd found out the hard way, was a limited commodity in the world beyond the ARC's walls. Most dealt in pain and suffering instead.

He stops to gaze out over the opposite side of the Needle, his back to the sea. The air is devoid of cloud and haze, the early morning light graying the mountains beyond the city. Somewhere in that direction she's probably warm in a bed with a fire to sit by when she wakes. There are people to take care of her, Rita and Sherell no longer her enemies. Food and drink and her damn books always nearby.

Lee releases his hold on the steel bar, blood rushing back into his palms, and ignores the memory of her lips and her body pressed against his.

Instead he recalls the howling wind in his ears as he fled down the side of a mountain.

Yells in the dark behind him.

Injuries bleeding beneath his clothes and terror pumping through every vein.

The men had ambushed him at his small camp several weeks after he'd left Ian's cabin, their eyes wild and hungry in a way he didn't understand until they started beating him, tearing at his clothes, saying things in lustful grunts that made their intentions all too clear.

He'd fought, but they'd been stronger. So the choice between hiding away somewhere in his mind while they did what they wanted with him and flinging himself off the nearest mountain edge was an easy one.

It was a miracle he hadn't broken anything more than his fingers.

The fall was quick and shockingly painful since he had no time to prepare himself for impact in the blinding dark. He'd rolled for a dozen yards and come to rest against the base of a huge pine, back throbbing, skin torn, hand mangled.

Then he'd run. Run until his lungs were two burning bags inside him. Run until he'd fallen again in a rockslide above a clearing. And that's where he'd ridden out a day and a half, listening to the calls of the men searching but not finding him, not daring to stand up even to urinate but simply wetting himself like a child until he lay in his own fear and filth. When their cries had trailed off far to the east, he'd walked down to the clearing, which turned out to be a desolate highway that eventually led him to the guard post, and Ray.

The bitter anger at Zoey flares like a fanned ember as he remembers. His injuries and debilitating fear were nothing compared to seeing Reaper's knife edge lick the light before disappearing into the soft skin below his father's chin.

Lee shoves himself from the railing and makes his way to the stairs, jogging down them at a brisk pace, letting his simmering rage fuel him. He hits the street at a run, keeping an easy pace that brings him to the first intersection where he takes a left and heads up the steady incline of hills the city is built on. Most buildings to either side are empty, abandoned, and crumbling into side streets that aren't used regularly. Much life subsists lower, closer to the ocean along the ports and rocky coastline. Above the businesses that still operate daily are the residences; the farther from the water, the less life there is.

Truth be told, he prefers solitude nowadays. Ray and Connor's company is fine, but beyond that he finds the steady rumble of conversation in the pubs grating, the flow of bodies when the workday is done overwhelming. He recalls the order of the ARC, the daily routine, the rigidity of rules. It made sense. It was home.

And it was also there for the sole purpose of keeping some of the last women on earth complete and utter prisoners.

Lee frowns at the inner voice, the one he considers a remnant from before Zoey escaped.

The terror you felt running for your life from the men in the mountains? That was a fraction of what Zoey and the others endured. Still have to endure. Look at where you are. Seattle, the last city in America. Could a woman jog through the streets as you're doing now?

No. The city is civilized compared to what he's witnessed of the outside world, but the answer is still no. A woman would be caught and held against her will, fought over, and possibly killed, just like when the Dearth began.

He pushes himself harder, thighs burning as he reaches a plateaued street and swings right down an alley. The anger recedes as it does when the voice of reason begins to speak and in its place is the haunting ache to see her again. Hold her. Kiss her. He knows it wasn't her fault that his father died. In fact, when looking at it objectively, his father was a major proponent of her escape, smuggling her books the way he did. There is no one truly to blame except perhaps the Director and NOA itself, but the anger is still there no matter how much reason is applied.

Lee trots to a stop before a brick building rising four stories above him. A steel door is positioned beside an exterior zigzag of stairs leading to his living space on the top floor. He takes several cleansing breaths of the cool, moist air and enters the lower apartment.

Inside, the smell of stale tea, soiled clothes, and camphor meets him. The space is largely one room, the kitchen opening off the entry and leading into the dining and living area. To the left is the tiny laundry room where he spent weeks healing, and near the back of the apartment is a single bedroom.

A wet cough issues from that direction and Lee's hope that Ray is getting better evaporates.

"That you, Lee?" The voice is thick, smoky.

"Yeah."

"Bring that bottle of hooch, eh?"

Lee sighs, glancing at the bottle on the cluttered table considerably less full of amber liquid than it was the night before.

"Looks like you had enough last night."

"That's why I need some now."

"Ray—"

"Don't make me get up off my deathbed to come out there. I'll give you a good kick in the ass if I have to."

Lee can't help but smile as he snags the bottle's neck and carries it through the apartment. He considers the state of the place. It's not dirty, just in disarray. Clothes hang from the backs of chairs, empty teacups sit on bookshelves and tables alike, a pedal bike Ray's been talking about fixing for months stands in one corner, wheels up. He'll have to come down later after his shift and tidy up. He stops in the doorway to the bedroom where the camphor smell is the strongest.

The room is ten feet square with a single bed positioned in the center. A desk sits beneath a window looking out onto the street front and a watercolor depicting Mount Rainier in the evening above the city's lights hangs on the farthest wall. Lee's imagined seeing that scene in real life and wondered what it must have been like, all of the life carrying on below the over-watching mountain, people living out their lives in relative peace. Even with Ray's continual relaying of what the world was like before the Dearth it's hard to fathom.

"This hangover's getting more furious by the minute and he stands there gawking," the lone occupant of the bed says.

Ray Ellenbury sits propped up on three pillows, waist and legs hidden beneath a wool blanket. He has a squarish head, white hair framing its top with a matching tangle of beard below. His eyes are bright behind dark-rimmed glasses, and even with the sickness that surrounds him like an aura, there is a sharp sense of wit about him like a knife with a dull edge but a honed tip.

Lee crosses the room and holds the bottle just out of the old man's reaching hand. "Just a swig."

"Give it here, you little shit." Lee pulls the bottle back and raises his eyebrows. "For God's sake," Ray says, "you'd think I'd earned some respect after nursing your broken ass back to health."

"I didn't get drunk every night."

"It's not my fault you can't handle your booze."

Lee laughs and hands the bottle over. Ray uncaps it and takes several long pulls before closing his eyes. "Ah, that's the ticket right there. The only cure for what ails you. My daddy always said you can't drink all day if you don't start in the morning."

"I don't think whiskey is the cure for pneumonia."

"But then again, you don't know that it isn't," Ray says, tilting the bottle once again and winking.

Lee shakes his head and tidies up the rags beside the bed that have overflowed the can he placed there. He tries not to think about the cold wetness in each one, the fluids that continually run from the old man when he coughs and hacks at what's condensed in his lungs. When Lee is finished picking up, he stacks the dirty dishes on a serving tray and carries it to the kitchen sink that's full. Another task that needs doing. He might as well stay here tonight on the cot in the laundry. He won't be done until midnight anyway. When he returns to the bedroom, Ray's settled back into the pillows, chin tilted up, eyes closed, ragged breathing loud in the small space.

"How do you feel?"

"Waterlogged," Ray says without opening his eyes. "But the fever's gone."

Lee places a hand against his brow. "You're right."

"'Course I'm right. I'm in my own body, aren't I?"

"Yeah. Sorry."

"Stow it. I do feel better. Cough comes and goes." He cracks an eye. "How about you?"

"Fine."

"You look wore down. Between your shifts and looking after me it's too much."

"I said I'm fine. And besides, it wasn't too much for you when you took care of me."

"See but I'm a man." Ray grins, light twinkling off a gold tooth in the corner of his mouth.

"Well since you're feeling well enough to give me hell maybe you can walk down to the pub to get your own whiskey," Lee says, snagging the bottle from his hands.

"Come on now, I was only kidding. 'Sides, got something here I'll trade you for that bottle." Ray holds out a folded piece of paper.

"Not falling for that."

"Seriously, it's for you. Take a look."

61

Lee takes the paper and hands him the bottle. Neat handwriting covers half the paper and he reads it three times before glancing up at Ray. "What's this mean?"

"The hell you think it means? He wants to see you this morning before your shift. Can't you read?" Ray releases a chuckle that becomes a wheezing cough.

"But why?"

"You're smart, son. These days that doesn't go unnoticed. Tyee's plugged in to the city, sees most things that go on. That's the only way he turned this place around after the last bastard tried to burn it down. You should've seen the coup he staged. I got to see part of it, but the ones who were close to him said he was like a man possessed. Got shot three times and didn't quit until the dust had settled and his men had the city."

Lee reads the note again and folds it, a quiver of nervousness running through him. "What do you think he wants?"

Ray sips from the whiskey and eyes him. "That's something you'll have to ask him yourself."

8

Lee jogs through the morning air, thick with moisture and the smell of scorched steel from the smelting plant a dozen blocks to his left.

He glances to the south as he comes to an intersection, utterly devoid of activity at this hour, which gives him a clear view of the cityscape below.

Hundreds of blackened skyscrapers rise up out of a faint mist spilling from the impenetrable wall of fog in the harbor. Their towering forms are like charred logs stood on end in a fire, ruins of what they once were. The floors are open cavities, glass fronts shattered and gone. Some have toppled in the years since the fire and crushed lesser buildings into formless humps of debris. The beginning of the new port is the distinct boundary where the flames were halted and eventually extinguished by the coup Ray had told him about.

Lee imagines the scene as he runs: the fleeing men, half burned and screaming as the city erupted into flames. Gunshots and the resounding booms of grenades being lobbed from either side of the fighting. He mentally shivers, deeply glad he wasn't here a decade ago to witness it. Visualizing it is enough.

The street he's on empties out into a network of buildings overlooking another inlet that reaches a dozen or more blocks into the city. The glass facades here are whole and don't climb as high as some of the burnt husks farther south, but they still possess an imposing air. He slows in a cracked concrete pavilion between two of the largest structures. Ray had told him the mayor's headquarters used to be an international company called Amazon that sold nearly everything from bandages to books.

The entrances to both buildings are guarded by teams of six men, all hard eyed and wary of his approach. One of the guards steps forward holding out one free hand, the other clutching a rifle.

"Stop. What's your business?"

"I was sent for by Mayor Tyee," Lee says a little breathlessly. He digs in his pocket, terrified for a moment when he can't find the note. Then his fingers close on it and he hands it to the guard. The man reads it quickly and nods to two other guards who come forward and roughly pat down Lee for weapons before opening the door.

"Up to the second floor. Take a right and go straight ahead."

Lee steps into a silent lobby with granite floors that echo his footsteps to the towering ceiling above. Pendant lights illuminate the staircase to his left, and as he climbs, his heart rate, which was coming down from the run, rockets again at the thought of speaking to the single most powerful man in the city.

At the second floor Lee is stopped by two more armed men who pat him down again before showing him through a door set into the side of a partition that doesn't quite reach the ceiling. Inside is a wide expanse of concrete flooring broken here and there by large rugs. Two of the four walls are floor-to-ceiling glass that look out over the encroaching bay where several fishing vessels bob in the gray light. At the far end of the office is a compact desk, behind which stands a very tall man who faces out in the direction of the ocean, hands clasped behind his back, a long braid of black hair trailing down between his shoulder blades.

Lee walks toward the desk and stops, unsure of what to do. The man hasn't moved or made any indication that he's registered his presence.

Lee's about to clear his throat when the man speaks in a smooth baritone and turns to face him.

"Mr. Asher. Thank you for coming."

Daniel Tyee is perhaps in his early sixties but could pass for a dozen years younger. His skin is like dark leather and without wrinkles save for two small patches of crow's-feet at the corners of his eyes, which are so deep brown they appear black. His prominent features are serene and a stillness surrounds him, as if he is a fixture in the constantly moving world.

Lee fights for the proper thing to say and finally settles for "You're welcome."

"Please sit," Tyee says, motioning to a chair opposite the desk. Lee settles himself, taking in the desktop and the papers it holds as well as a birdlike wood carving balanced on a small pole. He waits for the other man to speak, uncomfortable that the mayor has remained standing. In the back of his mind he tries thinking for the fourth or fifth time since reading the note if he could have done anything against the city's decrees.

As if reading his thoughts Tyee says, "You're not in any trouble, if that's what you're wondering. We deal with people who break our laws in a much more formidable manner than sending them a polite note inviting them here." The mayor gives him a small smile.

"Okay. That's good," Lee says, a knot of anxiety loosening in his chest.

Tyee examines him for a moment. "How long have you been here, Lee?"

"About seven months."

"I've been told you were in very rough shape when you were found."

"Yes. I was."

"Would you like to tell me how that came to be?"

"I was attacked in the mountains and I escaped. Barely."

"I see." Tyee steps around the desk and faces the opposite windows overlooking the small bay. "And before that?"

Lee reviews the story he's relied upon since leaving Ian's cabin. As much resentment as he harbors for Zoey and the others, there is no way he'd ever willingly give up their location or even existence. "I grew up in a small town on the eastern side of the mountains with my father. He got ill and died almost a year ago. I left and decided to come here."

"What was the name of your town?"

"Bristol." Lee shifts in his seat, trying to recall any facts he'd gleaned from the atlas in Ian's library about his cover story before leaving.

Tyee faces him again. "I know of the place but have never visited. Did many people live there?"

"No. A hundred or so."

"Any women?"

"No."

This seems to satisfy him and he moves to his desk again and picks up a sheet of paper. "This is an incident report from a shipping vessel, the *Sara May*, from three weeks ago. It says here the vessel hit an unmarked, submerged object and partially ruptured the hull and damaged the fuel pump on its way into port. The crew had mostly evacuated, and the ship's engineer, along with a small team, was still trying to save it when you appeared and helped them devise a method to seal off the breach as well as repair the pump. Is that correct?"

Lee swallows. Tyee had lied to get him comfortable. He was in trouble. "Yes sir."

"You weren't on shift at the time, were you?"

"No sir."

"Can you tell me why you boarded a sinking ship that most others had abandoned?"

Lee looks down at the floor, wanting to stand and get out of the office, out of the building where he can drink in the sea air and cleanse the panic that's threatening to consume him. "Because I thought I could help."

Tyee sets down the paper and grasps another one. "Here I have a note from Abraham Butler in the transport division saying you stayed late one evening helping redesign a troublesome carriage bolt assembly that would've delayed two major shipments. He said your design was nothing less than 'brilliant.'" Tyee drops the note and holds up another handful. "I have nearly a dozen messages here from various station managers and they all have one thing in common. You."

"Sir—"

"Be quiet." Tyee looks at him for a long moment before pointing at the wooden carving. "Do you know what that is?"

Lee examines it. "A dragonfly?"

"That's right." Tyee sits behind the desk and laces his fingers together. "The dragonfly was an important symbol to my people. Since it lives its life both in the water and air, it is a creature of change and adaptability. The one thing my predecessor lacked was vision for the future. He believed there was nothing to fight for other than power, since almost all the women are gone and those left only bear male children. But he was wrong. Order can be brought out of chaos. Good can still be done, even in a world such as this."

Lee licks his lips. "I apologize, sir, but I'm not sure what that has to do with me."

Tyee smiles. "A city is like a clock. If one of the gears is broken or stripped, the entire system stops. Time stops. We have industry here: loggers bringing in truckloads of trees, ships entering the harbor carrying supplies from distant places, even the Red District serves its purpose. You are familiar with the Red District?"

Lee nods. "I mean, I've never been there, but yes." He's heard the stories of effeminate men dressing so convincingly as women that it's hard to tell they're not until you're close enough to touch them. He's heard how many of the dockhands, Connor included, will spend half their wages on an hour with one of the men in the district. *Just close your eyes and imagine anything you want,* his friend had told him once.

"Tolerance and cooperation. That's the two things that keep the cogs oiled. Seattle was a progressive city before the Dearth. Acceptance of gay and transgender people was very common. In the years since I came to sit in this chair, we've restored some of that tolerance, and the city has thrived. Even the Fae Trade is useful in some respects. When it makes its yearly rounds, the men release the pent-up steam they've been building. Some compete and die for the chance to win one of the women. The ones who have broken laws can join the trade or face exile. Almost always they choose the trade."

Lee can't help the look of disgust that crosses his face. From what he's heard, the Fae Trade is much worse in some respects than NOA.

"You are young," Tyee says, sitting back in his chair. "And I see the righteousness in you. In a perfect world the trade wouldn't exist but in this one we must utilize what is offered to us to keep the wheels turning. And that is why I wanted to see you today."

For a split second Lee is terrified the meeting has something to do with the Fae Trade since he's gathered the traveling auction is only weeks away. "Sir, I—"

"I'm an observant man. I have to be to keep tabs on a city such as this. You have a gift, Lee, it's obvious to anyone who isn't blind, and your quick thinking and innovation haven't gone unnoticed. There's a reason you were assigned to engineering beneath Loring. He's not a young man anymore, and until now there hasn't been anyone who has shown enough promise to someday fill his shoes. I believe you have what it takes."

Lee opens his mouth and it seems like forever before the words come out. "Thank you, sir."

"You're welcome."

"I don't know what to say." His head spins with the implications of what Tyee's hinted at. If he were to someday be promoted to the head of engineering, it would mean more pay, more opportunities to attend to Ray's health. His eyes moisten.

"You don't have to say anything. I simply wanted to meet you and see what kind of person you are. If you continue on your path, I think you'll accomplish great things here in the city." The mayor holds out a folded piece of paper and Lee takes it, finally standing. "If you would, hand this to Mr. Weller down at the pier on your way to your shift."

"Of course."

"It was nice talking with you. I know you won't disappoint me, Lee."

"I won't, sir. Thank you." Tyee nods and Lee understands he's been dismissed. He is at the door, feet moving quicker than he means to when Tyee speaks again.

"Oh and Lee?"

"Yes?"

"I have a scouting team traveling to the other side of the Cascades in two weeks. They're going to be visiting Bristol. If they return with a story that doesn't match your own, you will answer to me."

9

The streets descending toward the port are beginning to course with life as exhilaration and fear propel Lee in equal parts through them.

The knowledge that he's next in line for the head engineer position hasn't set in yet. It's hard to fathom that someday he'll be in charge of the engineering sector, doing what he was meant to do. Born to do.

He swallows the lump that forms as he hears his father telling him he'll create great things someday. The pride that would consume his father's gaze when looking at him used to make Lee so embarrassed he would fidget with anything he could get his hands on to distract himself.

After he watched Reaper murder him, after fleeing from the only life he'd ever known, he'd come to terms with the fact that he'd never design anything again.

But now, with his old life gone, with the first kind and encouraging words about his talent coming from the mayor himself, the yearning to create is overshadowed only by the need to see Zoey again.

Lee pauses at an intersection, narrowly avoiding a logging truck that rumbles past. No. He wasn't thinking about Zoey. He was remembering what it felt like to take apart a problem, the thrill of discovery at finding the solution hiding within its folds. He hadn't been thinking about the feeling of her hand in his. Or how her lips tasted the last time they'd kissed.

He shakes himself back to the present, gulping down the moist air before crossing to the next block. There's no time for contemplating those things. They're part of his old life, and that's gone, burnt and dead as the portion of the blackened city to the south. Besides, he has something more pressing to worry about. Like what he's going to tell Tyee when the scouting party returns and no one in Bristol's ever heard of him or his father. Maybe he should turn around now, go back to Tyee and tell him the truth. Tell him about NOA, the women, how his father really died. The women are all gone. There would be no reason for Tyee or the men of the city to venture to the ARC.

But what if they stumble on Ian's cabin while crossing the Cascades? What if Tyee sees the lies in your face? What then?

He needs to think of a way to defuse the problem before it becomes something he can't handle. He'll go over it tonight at the apartment after his shift. Maybe he'll even tell Ray the truth. He knows Ray won't judge him or say anything to anyone else. All the man has been to him is gentle and kind. Someone who's filled the void left by his father's gaping absence.

Lee feels tears rise around the borders of his eyes and closes his mind to everything except the pattern of his breathing and the steady slap of his falling feet as he begins to run.

Several minutes later the port comes into view, the wide expanses of concrete marred here and there by crumbling edges where massive steel cranes once were mounted to load and unload cargo. In the years since the Dearth they've been sabotaged, dismantled, destroyed, fallen into the sea. Immediately he begins diagramming the broken areas in his mind, adding supports and re-forming the concrete borders as well as envisioning a new row of cranes, compact and versatile in their movements and function.

As he nears the lower platforms closest to the water, Lee gazes out at the thick veil of fog. It's solidified even more in the past hour so that now it resembles a starched bedsheet hung from the roiling clouds above, all the way down to the ocean.

"Look what we have here!" a gruff voice yells. Lee drops his eyes from the blankness of the fog, searching for the man who spoke.

Gibson Weller stands beside a length of coiled rope as thick as Lee's thigh. Weller's bald pate shines with moisture. His close-set eyes are two piercing beads that study him, hands like pieces of rawhide set on his hips, arms knotted with muscles that bulge beneath his long-sleeved shirt. Lee's never seen a gorilla outside a book, but if there is a person he would liken to one, it's Weller.

Lee jogs closer and stops, digging for the note Tyee gave him. "Good morning, sir."

Weller pulls a blunt cigar from behind his ear and lights it, drawing hard until a thin coil of smoke wafts from the end. "What the hell's good about it?"

Lee can't help but smile. Weller's brusque exterior is plating like a machine with a delicate interior. The dock foreman's temper is the stuff of legend, but his ability to forgive and offer a kind word is well known among the workers. Lee manages to draw out the folded note and hands it over just as Connor comes strolling from between a tottering pile of pallets.

"What's this shit?" Weller says, reading. Lee glances at his approaching friend and Connor jerks his chin in his direction.

"Needed your help a minute ago, but you're like a blister. You show up after the work's done," Connor says, slugging him in the arm. The lanky man gives him a lopsided grin revealing crooked teeth.

"I'm sure you could handle it," Lee says.

"That's not the point. As assistant dock foreman I expect service and respect from a lowly engineering lackey."

"Shut it, McKay," Weller growls. He puffs on his cigar and refolds the note before looking at Lee. "Tell Loring when you see him we need a different design for the equipment ramp in the north sector; some of the supports folded under the last shipment."

"Sure thing."

"Note from the mayor's office?" Connor asks. He reaches for the paper and Weller slaps his hand away with surprising quickness.

"Try it again and you'll lose a finger. And how many times do I have to tell you you're not assistant foreman?"

"I might as well be. I've been here the longest besides you."

Weller ignores him and focuses on Lee. "Also, if we could get another cargo ladder built, it would help with unloading; we're two short as it is."

"Absolutely."

"You should come down here and do some real work sometime," Connor says, grinning again. "Get your hands dirty. Strengthen that wobbly back of yours. God knows we could use a few more men on the docks."

"Shut it, McKay," Weller interrupts. "Lee's got his job. You've got yours. And if you had any brains in your skull you wouldn't be rucking supplies up from a hold." To Lee he says, "One other thing, when I saw Loring last night, he said he was going to be undertaking the retrofit of a few machines over at the munitions factory. When you see him, tell him . . ." Weller's words trail off as he glances past Lee toward the encroaching fog. He stands like a statue, squinting into the murk of the harbor.

"What is it?" Lee asks.

"Something out there." Weller takes a couple steps in the direction of the water and stops. Lee follows, searching the impenetrable curtain that swirls and shifts.

"I don't see anything," Connor says.

"It's there. Beyond the mist," Weller says, voice soft. Seagulls wheel overhead, their cries mournful and muted.

Lee stares at the fog, listening. Faintly there is the shush of water against a hull, quiet but steady. "A ship," he says.

"Yeah, I hear it too," Connor says. "Just a ship, sir."

"That's what bothers me," Weller replies. "There's no arrivals scheduled for the next two days."

Weller walks farther out on the pier, slow controlled movements. Lee follows. Something moves through the veil, a darker shadow in the heavy, swirling air. All three men stand side by side at the edge of the broken concrete. Waiting.

The gulls scream.

Water laps below.

The hush of the approaching vessel grows louder.

The shadow Lee's been watching darkens, begins to take on definition and detail. But something isn't right. The top of the ship is . . . strange. Too pointed and long. It doesn't look like anything . . .

His eyes widen.

What at first he'd thought was the very top of a cabin or superstructure breaks free of the fog. It isn't the cabin at all but the bow of an enormous ship, much bigger than he's ever seen in the harbor. Its prow is narrow and curved slightly upward in a predatory fashion that immediately sets off a warning bell in his mind. More of the ship glides free of the mist and several faded numbers appear on the portside. But what's mounted on the top of the deck is what holds his attention.

Turrets supporting enormous barrels point directly at the shoreline, a massive tower rising above them lined with satellite dishes and antennas.

"God Almighty," Weller whispers.

The ship glides fully into view with disturbing silence.

Everything seems to hang on the edge of a second.

Motionless.

Crystalline.

Then there is a blast of fire from one of the enormous barrels followed by a sound so loud it's nearly inconceivable. The boom reverberates in Lee's chest and he feels himself rock backward on his heels.

A drilling whistle fills the air, followed by an explosion almost as loud as the first, and the mortar station three hundred yards to the north detonates in a shower of sandbags and a mist of vaporized cinder block and men.

Lee staggers back, nearly losing his balance. His ears ring and he can feel the heat of the shell but can't get past the vision of men he knew disappearing in a fragmented wash of blood and debris.

Weller is yelling something over and over, swinging one arm around in a pinwheel motion. Lee's mind whirs. What was the protocol for being attacked? What had Ray told him? Assist any clerics with securing the women. Then help distribute arms and ammunition to the guards. After that run extra rounds to the snipers on the walls.

He blinks and shakes his head, the whining from the first shell still blocking out all sound. No. He's not in the ARC anymore. Not behind the walls. He's in the city.

Another flash of fire bursts from the ship's guns. Then two more. The sound is immense, beyond hearing anymore. He feels the shells, their targets destroyed so suddenly and completely it's like they were never there at all.

Then a hand grasps him by the collar and spins him around. Connor. The other man drags him back toward the city and it takes his legs several seconds to remember their job. When he begins to run, Connor lets him go and motions to a reinforced bunker built on a slight rise overlooking the harbor. There are weapons there, rocket-propelled grenades and mortars they can fight back with.

Lee runs as fast as he can but Connor pulls away from him easily, his long legs outdistancing him with each stride. The guns bellow again and something explodes a half block away in a shower of brick. Screams start to filter through the tinny whining in his ears, unearthly yells that aren't sounds human beings should make.

They near the bunker along with several other men, Connor leading the pack as he sprints through the open door and out of sight. Two more dockworkers follow before there is a terrific vibration along the side of Lee's head and he sprawls to the ground but not before he sees the bunker vanish in an eruption of concrete and rebar. It's as if the ground has rejected the structure, shoving it up in the air while pulverizing it at the same time.

Lee's head feels as if it's going to follow the bunker's example. His ribs throb from where he landed on a curb, and he's bleeding from the side of his head. He can feel the blood dripping off his chin like tears. Rubble rains down, pattering like hailstones around him. The bunker is gone; all that's left is a two-foot-high wall at the rear. Something mangled and red slides down a twisted door frame and it takes him nearly five seconds to realize it's the majority of a right arm still encased in its sleeve.

He pushes himself up, a bout of dizziness coming in layers, each worse than the last. He vomits, almost unaware of doing so as the ground jostles below him. Another shell he's sure, though he can't hear it or anything else. His ears pick up only a faint buzzing as he works his jaw, willing his hearing to come back.

Something snags the collar of his jacket and he's hauled to his feet, Weller's bloodied face inches from his own. The older man yells something, but Lee doesn't understand until he's shoved forward and Weller points up the hill.

Run.

Lee moves up the street, pausing numbly and looking back as soon as Weller's hand leaves his coat.

The space between the pier and the first street lining the dockyard is gone.

The land itself is there but it is a muddled, ruined waste without anything truly identifiable. Several men climb and crawl through the ruin. Beyond the pier the massive gunship has come to a stop and there is a flurry of activity on its deck. Things being lowered over the side. Boats.

"Come on!" The words are muted but distinguishable. Lee looks at Weller, whose face is again inches from his own. "Run! Let's go!" Weller slaps him, a stinging pop that sends a jolt of pain down his neck and makes his eyes water. But it does the trick. His feet move again and he realizes that if Weller hadn't hit him he would've stood rooted in place forever, completely captivated by the violence.

The streets are alive with running men. Some take positions behind fences or guardrails, rifles pointed down at the ship and the boats that stream away from its side, while others simply flee up and into the city, disappearing inside buildings and down alleyways.

Lee runs for several blocks before realizing he doesn't know where he's going. He's simply running blind. His heart hammers so hard and fast it feels like one long beat. Faint gunshots ring out behind him and to the left, their pops like the quiet crackle of gravel beneath a boot. Sweat pours off him and he swipes at his face, his hand coming away partially bloody. And all at once he realizes what he's got to do.

The streets leading up to Skid Row are total chaos. Men stream from buildings, wide eyed and stricken. Some race past him in the direction of the harbor where the first sounds of battle trickle through his battered eardrums.

"What is it? What's happening?" someone yells as he passes, and an answer comes from the opposite side of the street.

"Invasion! There's a ship! Get your gun!"

Of course. An invasion. But why? Why now? Why did Connor go into that bunker? Why did the shirtsleeve with the arm in it look so familiar?

Lee slows, lungs full of acid, and bends over, placing his hands on his knees. He sucks in deep breaths of air, trying to force away the darkness encroaching on the corners of his vision. There are more screams coming from the north now and weakly he wonders why that would be. But there's no time. He has to get to Ray, get him up and move him back somewhere safer away from the fighting.

With an effort he gets going again, the many mornings of running the stairs in the Space Needle coming to his aid. He covers the last blocks quickly and rounds the corner, ready to jog into the apartment's alley, when he freezes.

To the south, a horde of men travel through the streets.

From this distance Lee can't tell how many or exactly what weapons they carry; all he knows is that they're armed and organized. They move quickly and efficiently, several peeling off the main group to enter buildings along the street. Near the rear of the cavalcade are two pickup trucks, men in the beds, weapons pointed forward over the cabs. As he watches, a few city residents enter the street only two blocks down, hurrying in the direction of the larger horde.

There are shouts that are cut off in a hail of gunfire from both sides, but those who just entered the street don't have a chance. They're cut down in a matter of seconds and the larger group continues its steady pace. Directly toward Lee.

He forces himself to overpower the fear that grips him. Thoughts whirl through his head. This must be a coordinated attack. First the shock of the ship entering the harbor and now this encroaching army from the south. The screams he heard earlier now make sense. There must be another similar faction moving in from the north, like two waves washing on either side of an island to meet in the middle.

He jumps over a bucket that's fallen into the alleyway and skids to a stop before Ray's door. He bursts inside and finds himself looking down the twin barrels of a shotgun.

"Damn it, boy! Could've killed you!"

"Ray, we have to go." Lee moves past the old man, noting it's the first time he's seen him out of bed in days and that he looks much thinner than before the sickness descended upon him.

"What do you mean, go? What the hell's happening out there?"

"An army, a ship. I don't know. They're coming down the street, shooting people. We have to hurry." He snags a burlap bag from the floor and begins tossing in food from the pantry. "Get some warm clothes on, we have to leave."

"I'm not going anywhere."

Lee turns to face the old man. "What? We have to. They're going to kill us."

"I've lived here for over thirty-five years, son. I'm not leaving now. This is my home."

"We don't have a choice. They're going door to door."

"Then they'll be damned surprised when they come through mine."

"Don't be stupid, they'll kill you."

"Then I'll die." Ray's words are hard as granite, forceful enough for Lee to pause in packing the bag. Ray's face softens some and he glances at the floor. "Wouldn't make it farther than the city limits. Not with what's in my lungs now. But you go. Take that bag and a pistol and go."

"I'm not leaving you. Not again." Lee frowns, the memory of his father lying on the infirmary floor lit in flickers of lightning, there and gone.

"You don't have a choice, son. Get moving. If what you say is true you don't have more'n a minute."

Lee's vision begins to blur. "Please try."

"Don't make me force you out. I'm not young, but I'm still strong." Ray's voice cracks on the last word and Lee goes to him, embraces the man who brought him back from the point of no return, made him laugh and want to live again. Ray claps him on the back once and pushes him away, gently but with enough force Lee has to take several steps toward the door.

"Go," Ray says. "I can hear their boots. Go!"

Lee nods and throws the bag's strap over his shoulder. He doesn't look back as he leaves—if he were to, he'd never step out the door.

The air is laced with soft rain when he enters the alley. Judging by the light it's not even mid-morning yet. Could everything have happened in that short a time? His thoughts are cut off as he hears footsteps echoing from the far end of the alley. He doesn't wait to see if the men will appear there or not. There's one direction he can run.

So he does, not looking back at only the second home he's ever known in his life.

◆　◆　◆

Ray settles himself into his favorite chair and lays the shotgun across his lap. With shaking hands, he uncaps the whiskey and takes two long swallows before setting the bottle on the floor.

So strange to think of things in beginnings and ends. It feels like only the other day he was driving his route, in a hurry to get home and see his wife, who's been gone now for over twenty years. He tries to remember the sound of her voice, how she said his name and ran her fingers through his hair when they fell asleep together. He tries and can't quite summon the memory.

The steady plod of boots brings him back to the little apartment that was once a real home. He'd lied to Lee, saying that it still was. And there's a part of him that had hoped it would become one again since

Lee had appeared at the checkpoint. But people get foolish as they age and he should've known some things never come twice. Not even in a lifetime.

Soft voices discuss something outside his door and he reaches down, drinking the last of the whiskey. He nods at the empty bottle before tossing it away, then brings the shotgun to bear on the door as it bursts open, and pulls both triggers.

10

Lee trips and nearly falls at the sound of the gunfire two streets over.

He braces himself on a nearby wall and looks back in the direction of Ray's apartment, throat closing so tight it won't let the anguished cry out of his chest. He hunches over and wheezes a sob out before slowly straightening, wiping his eyes clear once again. The yells and rumble of trucks are closer now; he can almost smell the army, their scent much like that of the men in the mountains who tried to rape him: briny sweat and body odor that speaks of violence and terrible things done away from the light.

He moves to the mouth of the alley he's in and stops, peering out around the closest corner.

Someone runs by so suddenly and quickly he's afraid his bladder will let go. The man streaks past without a look anywhere but ahead and disappears around a corner into the next street. Lee glances in the direction the man came from and sees nothing but the ghostly silhouette of the Space Needle. Ahead is the northern side of the city. Should he try for the 520 bridge that he first entered the city on or hide in one of the buildings farther north? Maybe he should wait until dark to try to slip past. But from what he's seen of the army, they'll have all routes into and out of the city blockaded by noon.

A short chatter of gunshots comes from the north, their echoes like fading thunder. *So that decides it, only one choice really,* Lee thinks. He'll have to go east and try to cross Lake Washington. Maybe find a working boat along the shoreline.

He watches the street, confirming its emptiness, then runs forward, staying close to the nearest building. More gunfire comes from several streets to the south followed by an earsplitting boom that can only be another shell from the ship. He ducks involuntarily as the explosion cuts the air, making his eardrums flex. His breathing is erratic, untimed with the falling of his feet. He concentrates on matching the two while looking everywhere at once.

The next street's intersection is devoid of life but five blocks to the south a row of vehicles rolls forward at a steady pace, men on foot before them. Lee streaks through their line of sight without stopping, cutting up and through a yard below a three-story home with paint long faded from its siding. He leaps a broken fence and skids into a small alley before bursting onto the next street.

Shouts rise from the direction of the squad to the south.

They've seen him.

His heart feels as if it will come unmoored in his chest. He scans the sides of the street.

More homes, most with tall trees in their front yards and broken glass lining their fronts. The urge to hide inside one of them rises again and he pushes it aside. They will find him if he stops now, he knows it just as surely as he knows Ray is gone.

He runs up a small rise and turns right down another narrow street. Ahead the trees and shrubs are thicker, the homes larger and more lavish in design. He must be nearing the lake. Find a boat and get across, then he can disappear into the wilderness of the nearby mountains.

There is a vibration in the air beside him and a mailbox explodes into a shower of plastic and metal. Lee flinches away, guts clenching in terror as another shot skips off the pavement a dozen yards ahead.

The low rumble of an engine rises to a roar.

He dives to the left behind a car skewed partially across the driveway and lawn of a towering three-story home. There is a plunk and he sees the windshield spiderweb as he rolls away and is up on his feet again, finding himself facing a looming growth of vines littered with thorns.

He's moving too fast to stop.

The thorns tear into his face, past his shielding arms and hands, their bite like a thousand wasp stings. His clothes snag and jerk in different directions as he plunges forward, blind and sure at any second he'll hit a hidden wall behind the biting foliage, knocking himself unconscious.

But then he's free, out in the open again, blood running down his face and off his chin, arms burning with scratches, legs throbbing from exertion. The ground opens into a clearing, large trees spaced a dozen strides apart and several steel benches sprouting from the earth.

And beyond that, the lake.

Lee runs across the park toward the suggestion of a path leading into another heavy section of woods. The rain and wind toss the lake's surface into a tumult, white foam washing onto a littered beach.

The growl of an engine becomes louder behind him and he knows they've entered the clearing. Without looking back, he ducks into the cover of trees and doesn't slow, feet pounding up the trail that winds through the trees, glimpses of the lake speeding by on his right.

The engine's sound lowers with each step. Maybe they didn't see him enter the path. But really there is only one direction he could've gone. They will follow.

His lungs hitch and stutter with each breath, the air on fire every time he inhales. He won't be able to keep running for much longer.

The trail dips and jags at nearly ninety degrees before emptying out into another clearing half the size of the first. Someone has parked two dozen cars and trucks at the opposite end in the direction of the city, their headlights watching him like dead eyes. Ahead a picket fence cordons off a private property but past its end he sees the planks of a dock jutting into the water.

He pours on the last of his speed and vaults over the fence, landing hard on the other side. His ankle tries to turn and he sprawls to all fours, clawing forward onto his feet again.

The home is a massive black and white mansion set on what used to be a manicured three-acre lawn. Everything is overgrown now, weeds and vines invading at all angles. At the lake's edge a boathouse slants to one side as if pushed by a giant hand, but the structure isn't what makes him pause, then hurry down to the water: it's the small aluminum boat overturned beside it.

Lee races to the craft, ears picking up the rumble of an engine along with another gunshot in the distance. The rain falls harder, stinging his eyes as he slides to a stop beside the boat. Hanging from the dock are tattered ropes suggesting a much larger vessel was once harbored here. Praying he will find what he needs beneath it, he flips the boat over onto its hull.

Flattened grass and weeds are all that meets him.

Cursing, he stands listening past the hush of the waves. The motor he heard earlier is quiet now. He scans the ground around the boat before spinning toward the boathouse. The door sticks when he tries to open it and makes an anguished cry when he forces himself inside. It takes less than five seconds for him to locate what he needs and haul them outside.

The oars are made of a black, composite plastic with steel locks bolted to them. He gazes at their hinged pins for a moment, eyes shifting to where they fit in the gunwales. He hesitates only a second before tearing off two pieces of his shirt, wrapping them around the pins before shoving them into the boat's fittings. Anything to help him quietly cross the lake.

He slides the boat down through the grass, wincing as it scratches across the loose rocks and sand, until the stern touches the water. The same fog that hung so thick over the ocean is receding on the lake, its veil being drawn back by the falling rain. He takes a moment to steady himself, knowing this will be his only chance of escape, and the likelihood that someone will see him rowing away is very good. With a deep, calming breath he leans into the bow and begins to shove the craft into the water.

A cold circle of steel presses into the back of his neck and a voice that locks his muscles tight with fear says, "Where do you think you're going?"

11

Hiraku Hashimoto dips the thin-handled brush in the dark ink and traces a curve on the paper that will become the grey heron's neck.

Another blast from the guns above him on deck shakes the table and nearly causes the brush to miss its mark. He breathes in and out slowly, steadying his hand before making the next graceful arc. The bird begins to take shape. He can already see its surroundings: a calm pool in the middle of a lush grove. Perhaps a koi fish in shadow beneath the water. That's what the heron is stalking, his next meal. Hiraku can still recall the feeling of his father's hand over his when he was no more than six years old, guiding, teaching him how to blend the ink to shade the subject realistically. *It is our responsibility to reflect what we see if we have the gift to do so,* he said. *And responsibility should never be shirked.*

In the narrow corridor outside his room he hears the sound of heavy footsteps. Hiraku sighs, lowering the brush. The guns are silent now and he knows what will come next and he dreads it. He would give anything to stay in his cabin and finish the painting, anything not to have to climb up and see what his men have done to the city. What he's done.

The sharp knock on the door inevitably comes. "Give me a minute," he says, and there is silence before the footsteps retreat. Hiraku sets the paper aside, knowing the picture will never be finished, and stands to his full height. He is tall for his heritage— half Japanese, half Chinese—at almost six feet and deep through the chest, the genetic lingerings of his grandfather, who was a champion sumo wrestler. He stretches and rubs the keloid scars on the backs of his arms, their presence like a diary, always forcing him to remember. The folded piece of paper, yellowed with age, sits on his nightstand. He picks it up, tucking it gently in his shirt pocket before donning his heavy jacket. With one last, longing look at the tidy room, he shuts the door and locks it tight.

Shirou waits at the top of the stairs in the open air that's heavy with moisture. The smaller man is ten years his junior but always manages to seem so much older. Hiraku supposes it is his gray eyes, the color or lack thereof speaking of great age. As of late there are more lines on the face of the man who is a younger brother to him not in blood but in bond. The lines disturb Hiraku. They are not only creases that speak of stress but also of cruelty. Grimaces of anger have etched them there over time and he would say something to Shirou now if those lines weren't mostly his doing. Too many years of asking the worst of him, and never once a complaint from the younger man.

"The last barricade was destroyed. The city is yours." Shirou bows and Hiraku waves it away. The mixture of their crew is so diverse, the gesture looks out of place.

"Casualties?"

"Only fourteen."

"And their side?"

Shirou pauses. "I'm not sure."

"Have I not made myself clear that casualties will be counted on both sides?"

"You have. I apologize." Hiraku sees the other man resisting another bow and steps past him to the railing.

The bay is heavy and acrid with smoke that's taken the place of the fog they arrived under. Four small boats buzz back and forth from the ship to land, dropping off loads of men one after the next. The harbor itself is a ruin. The shells flattened half of the buildings lining the docks, tearing massive chunks from the closest streets so that they gape like open mouths. The remnants of the city's defenses lie in rubble and he can see bodies already being stacked beside one another like cordwood.

"It's unreasonable," he says, mostly to himself, "that so much death should have to come before life."

"What?"

"Nothing. What's the status of the munitions factory?"

"Our intelligence was mistaken. There are fewer rounds than we were hoping for."

"How much less?"

"Half."

Hiraku turns to look at his second in command. "That won't be enough. We're already running low."

"I know."

"And the solution?"

"They have one functioning brass machine and plenty of brass as well as enough powder."

"You're saying we'll have to manufacture the ammunition?"

"Yes. But there's a problem." Hiraku waits for Shirou to go on. "A shell clipped the building and a portion of the roof fell on one of the machines. It needs to be repaired."

Hiraku breathes in deeply, trying to keep the sudden anger at bay. He's been able to control his fits of rage for years, but he feels himself nearing the edge once again, the blind fury blistering within him like scorched paint. "In your opinion, are any of our men capable of this?"

"Most are engine mechanics or simple service technicians. I'm told this will require fabrication."

Hiraku stares at the destruction for another long moment, unmoving but for the shifting of the ship's deck beneath him. "Ready a boat for me. I'm going ashore."

12

Lee watches the boat land and the men step from it onto the rocky beach.

He shivers, the remaining adrenaline in his system gone, leaving him weak and cold. He can still hear a slight ringing from the ship's guns and the wound on the side of his head has clotted, the blood on his face crusted and flaking. The shoulder of the man beside him brushes his arm. He doesn't know his name or his face, just another person he never got to meet among the thousands of them standing near the shoreline facing out to sea.

The men who had stopped him before he could cross the lake had hustled him into a vehicle, making him lie flat in the rear storage area while they swerved and jostled their way down through the city back to the port. There had been another man in the back with him, bleeding heavily from a wound in his side, and it was only when Lee had asked him his name that he realized the man wasn't breathing anymore. They'd unloaded him along with the corpse onto the city street closest to the bay and ushered him around the gaping holes left by the ship's guns. When he saw what the remaining pier held, he stopped in his tracks until he was shoved forward by the soldier behind him.

Thousands of the city's men stood in ranks surrounded by just as many of the invaders, guns at the ready as they paced the perimeter. But it was the tangle of bodies being heaped in rows beside the street that Lee couldn't look away from. Blood ran from the mound in a steady stream down the gutter, dropping away into a grated drain.

He had been sick then, he couldn't help it. The smell of blood mingled with the briny air was too much, but the soldier accompanying him wouldn't let him stop so he vomited on his own feet as he walked. Connor was in the pile somewhere, or what was left of him. The thought was enough to force more bile from him and he doubled over, finally stopping only to be kicked into motion again. When they'd reached the pier he'd been guided to the farthest side and told to stand still or he'd be shot.

And so he had, wondering if these were his last minutes on earth. Wondering if he would feel the bullet that tore through him or if it would be so fast there would only be a seeping cold before darkness took him. Wondering if it would be Zoey's face he would see last before everything winked out of existence.

Booted footsteps bring him back to the present and he gazes through the ranks of men to where the latest invaders have stopped. There are three of them, the closest man taller than the other two and standing rigid in a heavy coat. His Asian features are blank as he observes them, eyes cold beneath a short forehead and a shock of dark hair going gray at the temples.

"My name is Hiraku Hashimoto, and I know you hate me. I am aggrieved that so many of you had to die but if we hadn't attacked first, many of my people would've perished." He considers them all for a moment before raising his chin. "Who is your leader?" When no one speaks Lee glances around, searching the ocean of faces for Tyee, but doesn't see him. "It is cowardly not to admit leadership in a time of defeat," Hiraku says. "Step forward and you will come to no harm."

"He's dead!" a voice yells from somewhere to Lee's right. He looks for Weller, knowing the foreman's growl from many hours on the docks. There is a jostle of men and Weller's bald head appears, a thin line of blood running from a wide gash above his left ear. "He was shot a few blocks away along with his contingent."

Hiraku studies Weller. "How do I know you're not lying? How do I know you're not the leader?"

"Because every man here can vouch for me."

"That doesn't tell me anything. Your men would lie for you, leader or not. It really doesn't matter in any case, but things always seem to go smoother when I can speak directly with the person in charge."

"Tyee wouldn't have given you anything, you piece of shit," Weller says, taking a step forward. The two soldiers behind Hiraku raise their weapons but he only points a finger at the tall man. "You might as well get back on your little boat there and sail away, because you'll get nothing from the rest of us, either."

Lee's heart jabs painfully against his breastbone and his legs feel like dropping him to the ground. His eyes flick back and forth from Weller to Hiraku, a terrible tension gathering in the air like a poisonous mist.

"I need someone with fabrication skills," Hiraku says, slowly looking away from Weller. "Someone who can design and machine parts. This person will be given benefits during our stay here and a higher position within my group when we move on."

Lee's stomach twists. Several of the dockworkers who had witnessed him attend to the *Sara May*'s hull turn their gazes in his direction. He sees more eyes darting elsewhere.

"Don't, boys," Weller says. "Don't give him shit."

"Where's Loring?" someone yells from the middle of the crowd. "Loring's head of engineering; he can help you!" There is a chorus of "shut ups," a cry of pain, but the voice rises again a second later. "Loring! Where are you?"

"He's dead too!" someone says from several rows in front of Lee. He thinks the man's name is Ollie. "I saw him in the street outside the munitions plant."

Hiraku motions Ollie toward him through the crowd. "You work in engineering then?"

Ollie shakes his head. "In the munitions factory. But Loring was there enough for me to recognize him."

"Can you repair the damaged munitions equipment?"

"Me? No. I just work the line."

Hiraku nods, his gaze seeming to catch something on the ground. He nudges it with his boot and kneels to pick it up, turning it over enough for Lee to see it's a dried clamshell dropped by one of the thousands of gulls along the port. Hiraku rubs the shell with a thumb before saying, "Someone will step forward to help us or there will be consequences. I don't want to hurt anyone else. In all truth I want you to join us because we aren't what you believe us to be. But I won't be waylaid now, not after I've come so far."

"Stand strong, boys. He's bluffing," Weller says, turning to the crowd. Lee watches as Hiraku frowns and gives the slightest incline of his head.

The soldier beside him draws a pistol and fires a round through the back of Weller's knee.

The entire group staggers back as Weller screams, falling to the ground. He cradles his leg, spitting choked curses through gritted teeth as the man who shot him steps closer, aiming at his skull.

"This man is a natural leader," Hiraku says over Weller's cries of pain. "I can see the respect you have for him and I admire it. If you will not help me, he will die. And then another of you, and another, until there are none left."

Hiraku turns and moves to the edge of the pier, gazing out across the water to where the huge ship is moored. He holds the shell out over the drop and begins to tip his hand sideways.

Lee grits his teeth, looking at the soldier holding the gun to Weller's head.

The shell begins to slide from Hiraku's palm.

The soldier pushes the gun barrel hard into Weller's temple, pinning his skull to the ground.

Tears leak from the corners of Lee's eyes and he remembers how Ray looked as he shoved him toward the door, telling him to run. He sees his father just before Reaper's knife went through his chin and into his brain.

The shell begins to drop from Hiraku's palm.

Lee moves past the men before him, muscles working of their own volition. "I can do it!" he yells, stepping free of the crowd.

Hiraku closes his hand over the shell and turns, motioning to the soldier standing over Weller to desist. The leader approaches him and Lee feels himself wanting to shrink back into the crowd, to become another anonymous face. So what if they're all going to die? Anything is better than having this man's eyes on him, their darkness prodding and piercing while everyone behind him curses his name.

"You can help me?" Hiraku says.

"Don't, Lee!" Weller groans. The dock foreman shakes his head, sweat running freely down his face as he grasps his wounded knee. "Don't, son."

"Look at me," Hiraku says, and Lee does. "If you help me you have my word that no one else will die."

Lee swallows but there is no saliva in his mouth. Several jeers and yells echoing Weller's pleas filter through the crowd. He closes his eyes for a long moment and opens them. "I'll help you. Just don't hurt anyone else."

Lee blinks in surprise as Hiraku bows shortly to him before straightening again. "We have struck an accord. What is your name?"

"Lee Asher."

"Thank you, Lee Asher." Hiraku looks past him, raising his voice so the rest of the masses can hear. "My men have formed a barricade around a dozen blocks of the city. Everyone will be assigned to several apartment buildings within this circle. You will remain there until further notice. Food will be distributed accordingly. Anyone caught in the streets without an assignment will be executed." To the man who shot Weller he says, "Shirou, get him medical treatment, either our own physicians or one of theirs."

Lee watches as the ring of soldiers begins herding the huge group of prisoners away from the pier. Thousands of eyes mark him, disdain and loathing so thick in their gazes he has to look away. But the worst is Weller. As he's helped to his feet by a soldier, he spits on the ground at Lee's boots.

Lee tries to say something to him but he is already gone, lost in the mass of men treading up the closest street, dejection hanging over their number like a storm cloud. Lee begins to follow them but Hiraku grasps his shoulder.

"No. You come with me."

13

The munitions factory looms four stories above them, its full glass front doing almost nothing to break the impression of bleakness it exudes.

The vehicle carrying them slows to a stop and Lee braces his hand on the back of the seat where Hiraku rides. The man named Shirou drives and two other armed men sit in the back with Lee, gun barrels not pointing directly at him but not pointing away either.

They climb out and immediately Lee understands why Hiraku asked for someone with fabrication skills.

The southwestern wall of the factory yawns wide near the roof, part of its overhang gone as well. He can only imagine what the tons of concrete have done to the machines inside.

"Walk," one soldier says and he feels the almost familiar prod of a gun barrel in his back. They move to the factory's side entrance and step out of the misting day and into the shaded and warmer confines. The building smells of oil, hot brass, and scorched air. Half of the overhead lights are off, and the several that are on flicker, blinking the towering machines in and out of darkness. In one of the flashes Lee spots an enormous chunk of cement and steel beside the closest brass conveyor, which is smashed into a *U* shape on the floor. Beyond that, the pneumatic assembly mounted on the side of the machine is a twisted mass of pipes and rods. Air hisses steadily from a severed hose on the wall and somewhere in the rear of the building a generator or air compressor hums.

"Well?"

Lee is so entranced by the damage, his mind already assessing and manipulating the reconstruction on its own accord, he startles at Hiraku's voice. The man stands only a foot to his right, gazing at the broken equipment.

Lee sighs. "It's a mess. The conveyor is destroyed. It'll need all new rollers and pins, bearings, belt, chains. And the pneumatic system has to be rebuilt."

"So?"

"So, so what?"

"Can you fix it?"

Lee glances at the other man and walks forward, stepping around pieces of wreckage, his shoes crunching glass. The thought of fleeing enters and exits his mind. They would surely catch him and maybe they wouldn't be so forgiving this time. Besides, no matter what the other men of the city think, he has to try and please Hiraku if they're all to survive. He sees Connor entering the bunker just before it explodes, hears the gunshots from Ray's apartment and quickly files the memories away for later when he is alone and can break down and mourn for them. Right now he has to do what he intended.

"Yes, but it will take time."

"How much?"

Lee circles the machine slowly, taking in every shattered part, every battered panel that will need replacing. When he circumvents its bulk he sees Hiraku has removed his heavy jacket. He wears a T-shirt that stretches over his heavily muscled torso, but the sight of his crossed arms causes Lee to stare. They are covered in wide swaths of puckered flesh. The scars are upraised and have a pinkish hue in the oscillating light. It looks as if his arms have been held inside a blast furnace.

Lee pries his gaze back to the machine. "At least two weeks."

Hiraku walks forward and touches a curved length of broken pipe. "Ten days."

"I can't do it in ten days."

"You will have all the equipment and manpower you require."

"Even so it will take longer. I'll have to machine half of the pieces from scratch. Then the whole assembly will have to be calibrated, which I don't know how to do."

"But you can fix it?"

"Yes."

"Good."

Lee's eyes stray to the scars again and he weighs his words before uttering them. "You're low on ammo."

Hiraku doesn't look at him. Instead he motions to Shirou and the other soldiers. "Do an inventory of lead and powder." The men obey without question; only Shirou hesitates causing Hiraku to nod before he moves away into the immense space of the building.

When Lee can no longer hear their footfalls Hiraku says, "You're correct. We are low on ammunition, but don't believe that you could rally the men here and try to overcome us. We have plenty of bullets for each of you."

"Then why do you need me to fix this?"

Hiraku pauses, finally turning to face him and holds up an arm. "Keloid scarring. Caused by gamma radiation. Nuclear meltdown to be exact. They itch sometimes, even after twenty-seven years." He drops his arm, touching a particularly fibrous scar. "I worked at a nuclear plant as a young man in China after moving there from my homeland of Japan. There was an accident, an explosion, and one of the reactors melted down. I was tasked with clearing wreckage from a hallway that wasn't supposed to be highly contaminated. While a coworker and I were lifting a shelf that had fallen over, part of the ceiling gave way. My friend was killed instantly and the shelving pinned me to the floor. In the effort to free myself my protective suit tore, exposing my arms. Needless to say there was more radiation in the area than we were told initially."

Hiraku falls silent, lost in thought, and Lee waits nearly a minute before saying, "I apologize, but I don't see the connection to the ammo."

The other man smiles sadly. "The radiation made me sick, of course. But it also had an unanticipated effect, specifically on my Y chromosomes. The doctor explained to me that this mutation had been recorded before in X-ray technicians and others who were exposed to certain levels of radiation. These men had a higher percentage of female children due to the damage the radiation caused to the Y chromosomes. He told me in my case the chance was close to ninety percent."

Lee frowns. "So you think you can father female children?"

"It was explained to me this way before the Dearth."

"I was told the scientists who were working on a solution had experimented on men's chromosomes."

"Yes?"

"Obviously it didn't work. Why do you think—"

"Because this happened for a reason!" Hiraku yells, holding out his arms.

The loudness of his voice startles Lee and he takes an involuntary step back. Anger ripples across the other man's face before gradually receding.

"Okay," Lee says after a moment. "But why are you here? Why come all this way?"

Hiraku seems to compose himself, lowering his arms to his sides. "In my own country the government was very efficient when they realized what was happening. They ordered every woman and female child to be housed in an enormous facility along the East China Sea. From what I understand, the United States attempted something similar but the rebellion was more pronounced here. In China we already had a problem with too few women, but the general public obeyed mostly without question." Hiraku grimaces, bending the pipe before him into a gentle curve. "The tsunami came with little warning. It was the strongest earthquake China had ever seen and the resulting wave was over one hundred fifty feet high when it hit land."

"God," Lee whispers in spite of himself.

"God wasn't there that day. Nor any day since. The facility was destroyed. Every soul inside perished."

The air hose continues to hiss quietly and somewhere deep in the building there is a quiet thumping that lasts a moment before fading away.

"So you came here looking for women," Lee says finally.

"Yes."

"I can tell you that you'll be disappointed. There are very, very few left."

Hiraku smiles and there is genuine warmth behind it. If Lee hadn't watched this man give the order to maim Gibson, he might have felt an inclination to like him. "Unless you know where to look."

Some of the air leaves Lee's lungs and for a long second he's unable to speak. "What do you mean?"

"Nearly a year ago we met a man during our searching, an American who was dying. We took him in, and though the sickness he had was too far along to save him, he was grateful for the comfort we provided. He told me of a place where there were still women left. This is why the men follow me. Hope, Lee Asher. They hope for a future for their sons, of which we have nearly fifty on board who are younger than you. They are aware of my chromosomal defect, which is now a blessing. With my seed, females may be born again, and future generations may thrive. But I know the women will not be won without a fight. Thus the ammunition."

Lee feels as if he's falling. The floor is no longer beneath his feet. His head swims and he has to bite down on the inside of his mouth to bring the room back to focus. Hiraku stares at him in the strange way he has, calculating but not unkind.

"What is it?" Hiraku asks.

"I . . ." Lee's tongue feels swollen, alien against his teeth. The choice before him rises like a mountain he's hurtling toward. "I know where you're talking about. The women are all gone."

Hiraku's face darkens. "What do you mean, gone?"

"They escaped more than eight months ago with the help of some outsiders."

"Impossible. It's too well defended."

"That's what everyone thought, but it's true. They're gone."

"How do you know?"

"I . . . I grew up there. My father was a guard for one of the women."

Hiraku's eyes narrow and his jaw works as if he's chewing on something. "I do not believe you."

"It's the truth."

"Enough."

"I'm telling you—"

"Enough!" The word reverberates throughout the building and comes back to them in a ghostly echo. Hiraku's hands are clenched into fists and the muscles in his scarred arms bulge. The older man closes eyes that are aflame with emotion and draws in a deep breath before releasing it. "I will believe what you say when I see it for myself. We have come too far and killed too many to give up now simply on the word of a stranger. It is my responsibility to see this through, and it is yours to fix this machine."

Footsteps approach and Shirou appears from behind a tall stack of wooden crates, the other soldiers following several seconds later.

"Are you okay?" Shirou asks, and Hiraku nods.

"Finishing up. Franklin, you will stay with Lee. He will give you a list of equipment and supplies he needs. At the end of the day, escort him to the home of his choice within the secured area." Hiraku gives Lee one last look before spinning on his heel and exiting with the other two men. Franklin is a bear of a man wearing a graying beard that reaches down to his navel. He motions to Lee who turns to the ruined machine and begins to evaluate it once again. But his concentration continues to slip away, his thoughts returning to the hint of emotion in Hiraku's eyes just before he left the building.

If Lee hadn't known better, he would have mistaken it for fear.

14

Zoey holds her arm out the window of the rusted car, scooping the air that rushes past and letting it slide through her fingers.

The sun sits directly overhead, changing every shrub, stand of grass, and sage from dead brown to bronze. She gazes out over the prairie to her left, looking past the unending plains to a series of rolling hills so far away they're only low stains against the horizon. On the opposite side of the car a canyon disappears and reemerges again and again as the road winds through the occasional stand of pines. She breathes in their smell whenever they pass. The air is cool enough to numb her fingers but for now she can't get herself to roll up the window. After nearly three days of walking and sleeping on the ground beneath rock overhangs or in animal burrows, the tattered seat she sits in is heavenly, and the air rushing past reminds her of the wind in the trees outside Ian's home.

Her home.

Zoey's brow furrows and she finally brings her arm inside. Her efforts to not think about the group have failed over and over since she left. She's sure that the longest she's gone without one of their faces, especially Eli's, appearing in her mind is no more than several minutes. She wonders if Sherell will be able to help Newton escape the prison of silence he's been locked inside ever since she's known him. She hopes

Rita and Nell will cherish their reunion for many years to come. She imagines what Chelsea and Merrill's child will look like and what wonderful parents they'll be. She recalls every kind word, every sacrifice they made, every laugh they shared.

A deep-seated ache blooms in her chest, as if the tethers to her heart are slowly breaking the farther she travels from them.

She squeezes the steering wheel that's covered in some kind of faded fabric, a design she can't make out bleached by the sun. Maybe that's how her memories will become, pale and discolored by time until they're gone completely.

The road curves again, the drop on the right yawning and traveling away as she steers the vehicle, having to strain against the wheel whenever turning to the left. There's something wrong with the tires, she thinks. She can only guess, but the short grinding and squeal that comes from the driver's side whenever she turns the wheel doesn't sound normal.

"Just hold together a little longer and I'll let you rest," she says under her breath.

She'd found the car at the edge of a town the night before, the house it sat by closest to the main road and therefore the fastest getaway. Peering carefully into the home she'd spied no one in any of the rooms and was about to open the car's door when she realized she wasn't alone.

A man had walked out from the trees near the road and begun passing her by. He was whistling between taking bites out of an apple and she'd frozen, knowing if she moved he would see her. Just when she'd thought he was going to walk past, he stopped, staring at her with wide eyes. There was still enough light to see by and she knew simply by the way he was looking at her that he hadn't mistaken her for another man. Slowly she'd reached back and placed a hand on her weapon, ready to draw it the moment he tried anything. But he'd continued to chew, gazing at her, finally reaching into the pocket of his jacket. She'd pulled her gun then, already aiming at him as his hand reappeared.

With a quick toss he'd underhanded something at her and she'd caught it out of instinct.

It was another apple.

She'd gazed dumbstruck at the fruit, and when she looked up, the man had tipped his hat toward her, continuing on his way down the road without a glance back, the sound of his whistling trailing after him.

She'd stood there for longer than she should have, moving the apple around in her hand as if she'd never seen one in her life, before climbing into the car. She had expected silence when turning the key but the vehicle had roared into life, startling her and for several agonizing seconds she fumbled with the levers, trying to get the car into gear, sure that a bullet would blast through the window at any moment, splattering her stupid brain across the seats. But no gunshots came, and she managed to guide the car up and onto the highway and away from the town without seeing another person. It took her nearly five miles before she was able to find the control for the headlights. After driving for an hour or more she pulled onto a side road, driving the car behind a dilapidated shed that barely hid the vehicle from sight. She'd gazed at the apple for a long time then, feeling a smile beginning to pull at her lips that she couldn't stop before biting into the fruit. It was sweet and juicy, perfectly ripe, and after she'd eaten it her thoughts returned to the whistling stranger, his small kindness warming her more than if she'd been sitting before a roaring fire.

Sleep hadn't come easily and when it did it brought melancholy dreams, as if she'd glimpsed something mysteriously beautiful only to have it slip away upon waking.

Zoey casts off thoughts of the dreams. Even though she couldn't fully remember them they still tinged the entire morning with a longing she doesn't fully understand. But now, with the window down and the cold breeze pouring in on her, they are less substantial, papery things torn through by the harsh light of day.

She reaches to the passenger seat and grasps the water jug there, drinking only two swallows before setting it down. There is barely a gallon left; soon she'll have to find a clean source to refill the dwindling supply. But if the road continues unbroken and without hindrance, she thinks she'll be close to Seattle by evening. It already feels as if she's crossed into Washington State, some internal compass that reads the landscape and scent of the air. But she knows what it really is: the feeling of safety since the mountains can't be too far off. Perhaps she'll even see them by mid-afternoon.

Her eyes flick from the rearview mirror, assuring her she's still the sole occupant of the road, before traveling down to the gauges set in the dashboard. The gas tank is nearing the quarter-full mark. It's emptied quickly from full the night before, and she chews on her lower lip, willing a fuel source to come into view around the next corner. When the next bend only reveals more unbroken landscape she sighs, settling back into the seat. At least the roads are clear of snow and the skies aren't threatening any other type of weather that might slow her down. Though she knows when she reaches the mountains there may be plenty of problems with the passes—at least that's what the others have told her about winter in the elevations.

Her throat tightens at the thought of the group, and she allows herself an image of the last good moment she had with them, everyone gathered around the table eating in Riverbend, Merrill and Chelsea's announcement, Eli saying one of his last jokes.

Her vision blurs and she blinks into the wind, letting it dry her eyes. She supposes the small cuts the past opens are the retribution for what she's caused. Never being able to see them again the punishment for being who she is.

She presses the last of the tears away with her palm and glances into the rearview.

A vehicle straddles the center of the road behind her.

Zoey flinches, arms jerking the wheel dangerously to the right, the drop past the road's shoulder opening up, eager for her to careen into its depths. She yanks the car back into the lane, turning in her seat to stare out the back window.

The car behind her is large, sitting much higher than her own, on wide wheels that extend past the fenders. The grille is missing and the chrome bumper sits at a twisted angle, almost like a smile.

And it is gaining on her.

No.

Zoey presses the accelerator down to the floor, hugging the inside curve of the road as she blasts around and up a slight rise before dropping down into a small valley. In the mirror the trailing car disappears for a long enough span for her to hope they gave up, but then it reappears, steel sparkling in the sunlight.

The motor of her car whines and the entire vehicle shakes, coughing once before picking up speed again. *No, no, no, not now, not now.* She squeezes the steering wheel until her knuckles pop as she barely brakes at the next curve, the back wheels sliding sickeningly sideways before hooking in. She glances into the mirror again and her pulse escalates even higher. The car is close enough now to hear its throaty grumble, like the unabated thunder of an approaching storm.

She has to get off the road. There will be no outrunning the superior vehicle and she doesn't want to be traveling at high speed when it draws even with her. Images of it clipping her bumper and sending her off into the chasm career through her mind and she shuts them out, focusing on keeping control of the car and herself. She scans the road ahead, searching for a turnoff, somewhere to make a stand if it comes to that, but there is nothing but the sweeping plains to her left and the sheer drop opposite.

The car behind her closes the distance as they reach another straight stretch, a dark form in the driver's seat becoming defined. She can make out wide shoulders and two white hands gripping the wheel, their brightness like fish bellies in the sun.

On the left side a paved road appears, shooting straight away toward a gathering of houses in the distance, but she knows the driver will overtake her before she ever reaches any of the structures. Zoey blows past the turnoff at nearly eighty-five, tapping the brake too hard on the next curve so that something shrieks behind her. The smell of scorched rubber fills the interior of the car, so pungent she almost doesn't notice the narrow dirt road coming up on the right.

Without thinking she hammers the brake, noting that the car hasn't yet appeared around the last corner.

She twists the wheel, feeling that stomach-clenching slide of the tires on solid pavement, and aims at the side road.

The rear end of the car skids and clips a road sign, jolting her so hard her teeth rattle. There is a loud bang and the wheel shakes in her hands as gravel kicks up, battering the undercarriage.

The road shoots straight down at a steep angle and as soon as she sees the drooping guard cables lining the hairpin turn at the bottom, she knows she is going to crash.

Her foot goes instinctively to the brake.

The tires skid in the gravel, rumbling over a rough patch that slews her sideways into the cables.

Then she's airborne, drab rock and dust filling up the windshield's view. The car hammers the ground, tips and straightens enough for her to catch a glimpse of the decline she's on. It makes the side road she flew from seem flat. For a terrifying moment she's sure she'll simply blast face-first through the windshield, but her safety belt yanks her back before a towering rock fills up the right side of her vision.

Steel screams and crumples.

The passenger-side window explodes and Zoey squeezes her eyes shut, every person she's ever cared about or killed blazing through her mind.

She rocks back into her seat as the car shudders and rolls in reverse for a few feet before stopping. The motor rattles out a final effort to stay running and falls quiet. A hissing screech fills the air and for several seconds she thinks she's the one making it before noticing the steam blasting from the rumpled right side of the hood. She lets out a long, shaky breath and takes inventory of herself.

Her ears ring and her sprained wrist aches. She touches her face and head, sure her hands will come back sticky with blood, but they're clean and dry. She moves her legs and feet. They work as well. She's unharmed.

A hole punches through the roof and the dashboard shatters. She has a moment to note that the bullet went directly through the gas gauge before she's pulling the door handle, ready to dive out of the vehicle.

The door squeals but doesn't budge.

Another shot thunks into the passenger seat and dust flies into the air.

Zoey lunges hard against the stuck door with her shoulder. It groans but only travels several inches before rebounding.

Two bullets punch into the hood and a third rips through her water jug, spattering her shoulder with moisture. She slams herself against the door again and it gives, spilling her onto the ground. Immediately she hears a voice yelling something, a jumble of words that don't seem to go together. There's a small pop and dust puffs up three feet to her left.

She rolls toward the safety of the cliff, drawing her handgun as she gains her feet. Four more shots strafe the ground beside her, and there is the mad insect-whine of lead close to her ear. Then she's in the shadowed safety of the canyon's side, her back against solid rock, breath smoldering in her chest.

"I know you have some!" the voice yells above her. It is tremulous and high. "You give me the spaghetti and the cheese! He's hurt and he's hungry, damn it! Aren't you a person? Don't you have a heart? He's just a boy!" Two shots punctuate the end of the tirade, snapping harmlessly into the ground six feet in front of her. Zoey turns her head, trying to see where the man is, but he's hidden behind the sheer rise of the rock. It sounds as if he's standing at the hairpin turn where she left the road to see if the car could fly.

She nearly laughs then. She's only learned to drive in the last few months and Merrill had warned her many times to take it slow. *Speed works inversely to control,* he'd said. *The faster you go, the less control you have.* She definitely understands now.

"He needs it! He's starving, you down there! You hear me. You have the ears and functions! Don't lie to me. You probably have more than enough. Too much! Glutton! You eat while he starves!" A shot hits the rear tire of her car, and it deflates in a single whoosh, sinking the bumper almost to the soil. "We had chickens until the fox came and then nothing. Damn him! Damn that fox all to hell and back! The chickens had eggs and they were brown. Brown like the sand in the sandbox at the old house."

Zoey shuffles to one side and glances over a shoulder-high shelf of rock. The wall past it has eroded, leaving a wash of silt at its base. If she were to run that way she'd be exposed. In the other direction the overhang above extends like a jutting chin, but she can't see what's on the other side and might be an easy target if she goes that way as well. She's pinned down.

"The roof leaked but we had buckets. And the rain tasted like blood but we drank it anyway." The voice lowers, becoming acidic. "You don't know. You weren't there in the dark when they came. Took the food and the water. And they knew we'd die but they didn't care. Like you don't care. You eat up the world and you don't care at all. You're just like them."

The man quiets and the silence is even more unsettling. The engine has quit hissing and only a slight breeze winds through the canyon. Zoey listens, trying to make out the sound of movement or the telltale shift of rock, but there is nothing. She tries not to breathe and presses herself harder against the wall, bracing her feet deeper in the dirt. She regrips her handgun with sweat-slicked fingers. Maybe she should run now. The last time he spoke he sounded somewhere off to her right. If she runs around the rock shelf, she should be too hard a target to hit. Plus, judging by the report of his gun, it sounds like a small caliber, maybe .22 or something close to it. She definitely has the advantage with the 9mm. She hopes it doesn't come to that since the man doesn't sound at all coherent. He's most likely disturbed and simply—

White-hot pain lances the side of her right foot and she has time to look down to see the hole in her shoe as the shot meets her ears. Blood spurts from the bullet hole in a dark ribbon, before she cries out and topples over.

The rock scratches her back as she falls but she barely notices. Her foot is on fire, throbbing like a burning coal each time her heart beats. She brings her leg up, grasping her foot with both hands, the part of her mind screaming that she's dropped her gun drowned out by the pain. Blood wells up out of the hole in her shoe and drips between her fingers. She presses hard on it, swallowing another cry that yearns to slip free.

Rocks and sand slide down from above and sprinkle on the ground a dozen feet away.

He's coming.

Zoey lets go of her foot, craning her neck around, searching frantically for the pistol.

"Got you, thief!" the man yells. More dust billows down from where he's gradually descending. "You'll share. You'll share if it kills you. He's starving now and we ate the dog already."

Her gun lies three feet away leaning against a stone, the grip upturned to the sky. Zoey slides to it as the man makes an *oof* sound. He's on the canyon floor. "Gonna get him food and then he'll be better. You'll see. She didn't believe me but that's okay because she's gone now. I promised I'd save him but she went away. Good riddance."

Zoey pushes forward with her feet, gritting her teeth against the pain as she snags the handgun.

"Hey, stop that." A shot comes from so close by she's sure she's dead. Something tugs at her shirtsleeve and then she has the handgun and is rolling over, yanking the trigger three times at the figure standing a few steps away.

The booms of her weapon are so loud she's unaware she's screaming until the reports fade away, bouncing off every rock and stone so that it sounds as if she fired a thousand times.

The man stumbles back, the rifle in his hands tipping up and discharging again as he trips and falls to his side. His legs kick and he coughs wetly. Zoey sits up, her shaking weapon still trained on the fallen man. He groans long and painfully, a sound that turns her stomach and seems to go on forever. Maybe she only wounded him. Maybe she can save him.

She starts to pull herself to her feet as the man's groan trails off and his legs spasm and fall still. She waits, counting to thirty in case it's a trick, before hoisting herself upright, the cold stone biting into her hand. Her foot fills with stunning pain as she puts weight on it, and the world goes gray in the distance. She takes a few steadying breaths before taking a step. This isn't the worst pain. Not even close. She runs through the other injuries she's had, ranking them from the most severe to insubstantial just to get her mind off the burning each time she steps. But with every movement her foot insists that it's suffered the gravest damage in memory.

Zoey nears the man's boots and she notes the rifle is out of reach, several feet away, before examining him closer. He's garbed in filthy clothing, the pants and jacket a matching drab green or brown, she can't be sure. His hands are even whiter than when she first saw them in her rearview mirror and they're balled into loose fists. His face is a tangled nest of shockingly red hair and beard, his mouth open, revealing graying teeth and holes where many have fallen out.

She hobbles around him and kicks the rifle farther away before nudging his shoulder with her wounded foot. He doesn't move but three blossoms of red, much darker than his hair and beard, continue to grow in the center of his chest.

A clatter of rocks comes from above and she snaps the gun up, nearly pulling the trigger again. A small cascade of sand rains down, a stone unsettled by the man's passage dropping to the ground several paces away. She waits in case she was wrong before limping away from the body back to her car.

After gathering the backpack out of the rear seat, she empties the remaining dregs of water from the destroyed jug into the one that's still whole and zips it into the pack. She gazes up at the sky; the sun, now dimmed by a layer of thin clouds, has fallen from its pinnacle to the west. In a few hours it will be dusk and much colder.

Around the opposite corner of the rock shelf is a tumble of large stones that lead up to a washout beside the side road. Wincing at the steady beat of pain in her foot, Zoey climbs. Some rocks shift beneath her careful step and cause her to put more weight on her injury. Blood oozes from the hole in her shoe, but at least it's no longer gushing. She makes the road and trudges up it, the man's big car coming into sight after only a minute of walking. It's parked half on, half off the main road, engine quiet.

She draws her gun again and approaches the vehicle quietly and as low as her wound allows her. There is no one in the torn front seats that she can see and only a bundle of blankets in the back. She lets out a sigh of relief and straightens, but it's only then that she notices the shoes poking from the bottom portion of the blankets in the rear seat. Keeping her gun pointed at the bundle, she speaks.

"Don't move. I have a gun."

The shoes remain still.

Working her way around the back of the car, she stops on the opposite side, checking again to make sure the person hasn't moved. With one motion she yanks the door open and pulls the blanket free.

The boy lies molded into the rear seat, arms crossed lovingly over his chest as if he's hugging himself. She guesses he was perhaps fifteen when he died but that was many, many months ago. His skin is papery and mottled brown and purple. She can see the outlines of his finger bones in his hands and the gaunt shape of his skull where his hair has fallen out. His eyes are mercifully closed and a small stuffed bear is tucked in beside him against the seat.

She looks at the starved boy, and leans against the car's cool steel. For a long time she can only think of the man's words, his final ravings about feeding a son who has been gone for months, taking his father's sanity with him.

The dead grass whispers, urging her to get moving but she can't. A small puddle of blood surrounds her foot, its mirror shine giving her a crimson reflection of her face. She twists her heel, smearing her visage away and straightens. With gentle movements she draws the boy's blanket back over his form.

"I'm so sorry," she whispers, and closes the door. In the front of the car she sees nothing but scraps of the seat's stuffing strewn across the console and floorboards. One larger chunk has half-moon shapes missing from it and it takes her several seconds to realize they are bite marks.

Zoey steps away from the vehicle, the urge to climb back down to the canyon floor and give the man a proper burial nearly turning her in that direction. But she has nothing to dig with except her hands and she's wounded. She has to find shelter somewhere and attend to her foot before it becomes infected. How far back was the grouping of homes? A mile? Two? She can't recall, but even if she were able to walk there, because she'll never be able to get herself to climb behind the wheel of the big car, she has no idea if the houses are inhabited.

She turns in a limping circle, scanning the horizon 360 degrees.

Canyon, highway, plains, plains, hills, highway, canyon.

Wait.

Zoey looks again, to the southwest across the fields cluttered with sage and tufts of limp grass. There. At first it looks like only a part of the landscape but the harder she squints, more details come into focus.

A slanted roof.

Two windows, mere dots at this distance. And maybe some kind of vehicle beside it. In either direction and beyond it there are no other structures.

Hitching her pack higher, she starts walking, leaving tiny smears of blood on the road behind her.

15

The house is a single story, the roof gray steel, dull in the afternoon light.

When she cautiously approached, using the old pickup parked beside the home as cover, the place appeared broken down and unused. But now she sees that the walls are made from mortared stone and the windows she spied from the highway are unbroken.

Zoey watches from the rear bumper of the rusting truck. She listens, the wind louder here far out in the open, its voice howling low in the smokeless chimney protruding from the metal roof. She waits, scudding clouds reflected in the house windows lulling her, the pain in her foot the only thing that keeps her from falling asleep. After what she gauges to be an hour, she crosses behind the pickup, drawing her gun, and moves as quickly as she can to the nearest corner of the building.

The stone is cool against her back as she slides around the side and makes her way to a wooden door set halfway down the home's length beside another window. A tangle of dead vines obscures the view past the other end of the house, their twining so thick it is like a curtain.

The door's handle turns easily and she draws it open an inch, standing well to one side, half expecting a blast of gunfire to come from within, but there's nothing. She steps inside, low, gun held before her, and takes cover behind an island of cabinets in a small kitchen.

When there are no noises or cries of alarm she rises and surveys the space.

The entire area, save for the far end of the house, is one room. She stands in the simple kitchen, wooden countertops reflecting years of use, an empty sink with a window above it, an open pantry with several cans and sacks stacked on the floor. Beyond the kitchen is a living space, a large chair covered in blue fabric, a stone hearth, dark and cold. To the left is a long table cluttered with all manner of things. She spies wooden bowls, a shine of gold and silver, and three tall stacks of books on one corner. Two doors are ajar at the far end of the room and she walks quietly toward them. She swings the left open first, pointing her weapon inside.

The space is nearly bare, only a narrow bed and a desk with a chair tucked beneath it. The opposite room yields nearly the same except there are more books and more clutter, the walls adorned with several paintings. A life-size statue of a young boy holding an umbrella draws her aim in a split second of tension.

Zoey lets out a long breath. There is dust on most everything, and she can't smell lingering odors of food or any other telltale signs that someone's been here recently.

Telltale. *Like "The Tell-Tale Heart,"* she thinks, remembering the tome in Ian's library by a man named Poe. She'd picked it up during her rehabilitation period and read it in the evenings by the firelight while her muscles trembled from the day's physical therapy. She'd barely gotten herself to finish. Not because the stories weren't engaging or well written, but because she could tell the man who'd created them had been in a very dark place. She had almost been able to hear him crying out for help, and to her his voice had sounded much too familiar.

"The Tell-Tale Heart" had been one story that had clung to her mind for days, and now, standing in this lonely, abandoned house in the middle of a prairie with the wind clawing down the chimney in an eerie voice, she can almost hear the faint thumping of the murdered man's heart below the old floorboards.

Thunk.

Thunk.

Thunk.

Zoey sways, grasping the corner of the long table for support. She places a hand against her forehead; a wisp of dizziness comes and goes. Maybe she's lost too much blood.

Thunk.

Thunk.

Thunk.

Her eyes widen. The faint heartbeat wasn't in her imagination. She can hear it.

And it's close.

She turns, limping with the gun held out. Where is the noise coming from? She shoots a look at the floor. *Stop it! It's not a heartbeat!* But as the sound comes again, neither can she pinpoint it.

The floorboards creak beneath her as she moves to the kitchen and looks out the window.

Lonesome land as far as she can see, the highway a dark snaking line in the distance. Clouds gathering in the east.

Thunk.

Thunk.

Thunk.

It's coming from the back of the house. Straining over the sink and wincing at the pressure she puts on her foot, Zoey presses her face against the glass, looking at an angle toward the vines.

An icy hand squeezes her heart as something moves behind the veil of dried vegetation. She sucks in a breath and stumbles back from the window. There's someone outside.

Ignoring the spike of pain in her foot, she hurries to the window set in the living area wall and freezes.

A figure emerges from behind the vines and walks toward the kitchen door.

What should she do? Shoot him as soon as he comes inside? No. She can't do that and live with herself. Not after the man in the canyon, not after seeing his son. She shouldn't have come here.

Her eyes land on the open pantry and she hurries to it, swinging the door almost shut. Her breathing is loud in the enclosed space; he'll hear it for sure and simply shoot her through the door. Maybe she should've hidden in one of the bedrooms and tried to crawl out a window. Maybe—

The kitchen door opens and footsteps come inside. Something thumps softly on the countertop. Zoey puts her eye to the opening and looks out.

At first she can only see the island cabinets and cluttered table beyond, but then someone walks past, a low mutter coming from them, and she jerks back, her fingers aching around the gun's grip.

"Rain, maybe snow. I don't know," the voice says. It is deep but smooth and she leans forward again, peering out through the gap.

A man stands at the island counter, a tin pail in one hand. He is elderly, maybe as old as Ian. He is stoop shouldered and rotund, and his face . . . his face is what holds her gaze. It is pocked with scars and growths beneath the skin so that there is not an inch that is smooth or even. It's as if someone has sewn small rocks into his flesh and not done a good job of it. Above his ravaged cheeks and chin is a large nose and glasses that remind her of Lyle's. A shock of white hair hangs down almost to his ears.

"Nothing for it, huh? Weather's weather. Doesn't change until it does," the man says quietly.

Zoey frowns. He's speaking almost like the man from the canyon, the words not aligning to make sense. Has she stepped into a part of the world where everyone is this way?

Her thoughts abruptly end as the man draws a long knife from a drawer and holds it before his eyes, admiring the gleaming edge.

Then he looks past the blade and stares directly at her. "Are you coming out, or would you like supper served in the pantry?"

For a split second Zoey can't move. Then she shoves the door open and sidles to the left, keeping the island between them while covering him with the gun.

"Don't," she says, throwing a look at the door. "I'll shoot you if I have to."

"Funny times when someone breaks into your house and threatens you. Or maybe nothing's changed, huh?"

"Stay back and I won't hurt you."

"I'm not going anywhere. No one else is going to peel these spuds." The man gestures with the knife at the pail and pulls out a medium potato. With a few deft turns he carves the outer layer off, all in one piece, and holds the spiral up before dropping it to the counter.

"What was that sound?" Zoey asks, glancing toward the door again, the thought of another person outside unnerving. She'd been stupid and careless by not inspecting the surrounding land better and she chides herself for it.

"Sound? Oh. Hoeing the potatoes up. Only got a few more then nothing 'til spring."

Zoey places a hand on the doorknob and opens it a fraction of an inch, looking out to scan the yard. "Are you alone?"

"No one'll hear the shot if that's what you're asking," the man says, head down, hands working at another potato.

"I'm not going to kill you."

"Good. That's good. I like my soup and it's a good day for some. Going to rain later, huh?" Zoey clenches her jaw as she shifts her weight, her foot crying out. The man's eyes flick to her and back to his task. "You should look at that injury before too long."

She glances down and back up. "How did you know I was here?"

"Would you believe that the house told me?" When she squints at him he smiles and it warms his pocked features. "I always leave the pantry door open."

"I'm sorry for intruding. I thought it was abandoned."

"I keep it that way on purpose. No dusting allowed around here. Plus, I hate doing it. Had a couple people come through and been lucky so far. No one's taken more than a few supplies and whatnot. I stay hidden and they normally leave in a day or so. But it's been quiet for years now." The pile of peelings continues to grow on the countertop, his hands seeming to work of their own volition, steady and determined.

Zoey watches him for a time, his movements somehow calming. "I just need to sit down for a minute. Then I'll be on my way." When he doesn't respond she takes her pack off and sets it beside a chair tucked beneath the long table. The throbbing in her foot reduces by half as soon as she sits and she nearly sighs with pleasure. She sets the gun down beside a strange sculpture made of polished steel depicting a person divided in half. But that's not right. They are surging in opposite directions, trying to tear away from the other where they're joined at the waist. One figure has an angelic look while the opposite sports gleaming horns from a broad forehead. And above them both, a prism throws dull showers of light around the base.

She eyes the sculpture like a poisonous snake before unlacing her shoe and drawing it off revealing a red sock with a gray strip around its upper edge. Of course the entire sock used to be gray and is now stained with blood. Gingerly she peels the sticky garment away and eyes her wound.

The first emotion she feels is relief.

The bullet cut a narrow slot in the flesh several inches behind her smallest toe on the very side of her foot. In fact, it doesn't look like a bullet hole at all but instead a nasty gash. If it had been a larger caliber she might've lost the closest toe. Maybe even her entire foot if the bullet had struck bone.

The man moves around the kitchen, clanging a couple of pots together, and she reaches for the gun, but he's oblivious to her presence, his back to her near a small stove. Digging in her pack she draws out the compact medical bag she took from the hospital before leaving and opens it. There is some antiseptic cream in a sealed package and a thick roll of gauze. She takes both items out and examines the wound again, plucking small fibers of leather and wool from it that were pulled in with the bullet's passage. After it's fairly clean she dabs at the wound with the dry portion of her sock and is about to apply the antiseptic when the man approaches from the kitchen.

Zoey picks up the gun but he keeps moving toward her as if she were holding a spoon instead. There is a large bowl in his hands and a towel folded over an arm. He sets the bowl down near her feet and she sees it's filled with water.

"It's warm, not hot. It'll get the blood off, huh?" he says, placing the towel on the table before moving away. She stares after him as he busies himself again in the kitchen. Picking up the bowl, she smells it. No odor, no film on the surface, and nothing on the bottom indicating that he put something in it to soak into her wound and drug her.

She sets it back on the floor and dips her foot into the water. It stings initially but after a moment the pain fades and the warmth seeps in. It's a glorious sensation and she relishes it for several seconds while she watches the old man. He moves slowly but is in constant motion, like a bee pollinating flowers. He mutters to himself every minute or so, but now she's fairly sure it's nothing like the ramblings of the man in the canyon. *Madness sounds different than trying to keep yourself sane,* she thinks, and remembers Meeka's voice in her head all the days she wandered after escaping the ARC.

When she looks down again the water is brownish red. She pulls her foot free. The wound wells a little blood and the rest of her skin is mostly clean. She uses the towel to dry off and smooths some antiseptic cream into the gash, wrapping it tightly with gauze when she's done before covering it with a fresh sock. She knows Chelsea would've insisted on stitching it closed, chiding her the entire time about being more careful.

Her throat begins tightening and she distracts herself by lacing her shoe back up. When she tries putting her weight on the injured foot it hurts much less than before. Now there's only a gentle ache where the shooting pain used to be. Maybe that's true of all things. Maybe someday she'll be able to remember Eli and the rest of the group and not be sliced open on the inside.

Gentle tapping overhead draws her attention upward. It's raining, and it sounds truly beautiful on the steel roof. Several slashes of water run down the window and the sky darkens even as she watches. Despite still being on high alert, a sense of calm begins settling over her and she wonders if the old man did taint the water in the bowl with something. But no, this is simply relaxation, a coming down of sorts from the stress of the car crash and shooting. She recalls the canyon man's voice, the fervency. Even knowing he would have killed her for a scrap of dried meat can't drain the pity she feels for him and the stinging regret of having ended his life.

"I walked two miles in the rain once when I was nineteen," the man says coming to the table with a steaming mug in his hands. He draws out a chair opposite her and finds what seems to be the only empty spot on the table to place his tea. He looks across the clutter, white-haired head bobbing a little. "My car broke down on the way to class. The university, see? It was my first semester and I hadn't made friends yet. Don't know why I remember that fact so clearly. I suppose because it was important then, huh? The rain was warm for fall and by the time I got to class it was mostly over and really I think I learned more walking in the rain than I would've in the classroom."

"What did you learn?"

"That I didn't like walking in the rain." Zoey surprises herself by laughing. The man smiles fully and sips from his tea.

"I don't mind the rain if that's what you're getting at," she says when the laughter's faded.

"Suit yourself, as the saying goes. Don't think it will be too nice walking with an injury like that, though. Person that did it still out there?" She starts to reply and pauses before looking away. "Yeah. Okay. Just didn't know whether to expect more company or not. Only have so many soup bowls, huh?"

Zoey looks out the window at the sheets of rain. It's so thick she imagines stepping outside into a solid wall of water. Maybe it would feel good to do so, to have the rain drown everything out, make it all go away. She places her hand on her pant pocket, feeling the vial there, the vial with her daughter's blood in it, and shivers.

As if reading her thoughts, the man says, "Coming down so hard it could wash it all away, huh?"

"Maybe that would be all right," she says.

"Maybe. Lot of bad things." For the first time he sounds morose. "All the problems that ever were, still there, huh? And new ones to boot. But that's time, I suppose." He turns his mug around and it squeaks quietly on the wood. "Good things too, though. Some of the very best. I think it takes losing a lot to appreciate a little."

She thinks of them all then, not just the group but of Simon and Lily and Lee. She remembers his carefree smile and she would give anything in that moment to have his hand in hers and to be close enough to count his freckles, to kiss him.

Zoey brings herself back to the present with effort and glances at the man. "How long have you been here?"

"Long enough. I taught philosophy for twenty years before I decided I needed to plant a garden. So I came here and that's what I did, huh?"

"Plant a garden?"

"That's right. And you know what? All the answers I needed when I was teaching came easy when I started planting. Sometimes that's the way; you find what you're searching for when you quit looking."

He stands and shuffles to the kitchen, setting his empty mug down before lifting the lid off a large pot. It is only seconds before the smell reaches her, hearty and filled with the strong scent of onions and spices. Her mouth waters. How long has it been since she's had a hot meal? It was back at the hospital before . . .

No, don't think about that.

Zoey turns in her seat, examining the slightly disturbing sculpture to take her mind away from the thoughts trying to overwhelm her. She reaches up to touch the juncture where the demon and angel are joined but stops and lowers her hand to her lap.

"One of my students made that for me after I taught a class about dualism," the man says, coming back to his seat and settling into it. "I think it really struck her, huh? She said it was a comfort to know there were two sides to everything, and that really struck me."

Zoey frowns. "I don't think there is." She glances up. "Two sides. There's always a little bad even in the best things. But sometimes there's only evil and nothing else."

"Warm thoughts for a cold night, huh?" The man grins and shakes his head. "Do you know the Bible?"

"I've read some of it."

"So you understand the basic balance? Good and evil? God and the devil?"

"Yes."

"And old Beelzebub himself, he's about as bad as they come, right?"

"I suppose. In that book anyways."

The man tosses his head back and laughs long and hard. Zoey watches him, half bemused and half annoyed. "What?"

When he recovers he says, "I like that you think of it as a story in a book. Perspective is good sometimes. Anyway, Satan is evil and cast away from the light, out of God's good graces as the saying goes. But God's message is clear. Repent, ask for forgiveness, and redemption shall be given. Life is made up of choices, huh? They get made every day and we have a chance when they come along to do better than the time before."

"You believe that?"

"Every coin has two different sides. I believe that everyone deserves a second chance."

"Even the devil?"

The old man gives her another smile. "If he was sorry, then yes."

The rain pounds harder on the roof and Zoey pulls her gaze from the sculpture to the window once again. After a moment the man rises and goes to the kitchen, returning almost immediately with the pot of soup, two bowls, and spoons. He ladles the soup out evenly, the aroma so thick she wonders if she could survive on the smell alone.

"But even an old optimistic philosopher like me has moments of realism. That's why I know you need to see me dishing out the food yourself. A young woman can't be too cautious nowadays, huh?"

She almost tells him she won't eat, but the scent of the food is intoxicating. And besides, she did watch him ladle it from the same pot. If he was going to drug or poison her he'd be doing the same to himself.

Zoey waits for him to take several bites before picking up her spoon. She looks at the sculpture again, and this time it doesn't disturb her as much. In fact, for some reason when she looks at it, her mind keeps returning to her conversation with Merrill in the watchtower, before the assassin arrived and sent everything spinning off-kilter. But her stomach finally forces aside thoughts that don't involve the meal before her, and she begins to eat.

16

The windows of the little house turn ashen and continue to collect rain until the outside world disappears completely into dusk.

Faint thunder rolls across the plains and Zoey listens, the booms like another language older than time.

They'd eaten in silence together, the odd scrape of a spoon on a bowl the only noise. After she'd consumed two helpings, the old man lit several candles dispelling the encroaching darkness and given her one, leading the way to the uncluttered room in the back.

"There's a lock on the door," he'd said, motioning to it. "I know that's the first thing you'd look for. Extra blankets in the closet." She'd thanked him and he'd studied her then before holding up a finger and moving off into the house. He returned a minute later holding out a tattered paperback.

"*The Diary of Anne Frank,*" she'd read aloud from the cover.

"I gave it to all my philosophy students, huh? Required reading." He looked as if he was going to say more but stopped and simply shuffled away to his own room. She'd looked after him before glancing down at the book. As strange as the encounter had been so far she really felt there was no need to fear the man. And leaving on foot during a storm in unfamiliar territory would have been the pinnacle of foolishness.

So she'd shut the door and locked it, setting the candle on the bedside table, and began to read.

Now she sits on the floor, back against the bed, candle burned down to nearly nothing, and she races, races against its lessening light, because there are only a few pages left. Her jaw trembles as she reads the last sentences and continues on to the epilogue.

Zoey shuts the book, wanting to hurl it away and hug it close to her chest at the same time. She squeezes her eyes shut.

I keep my ideals, because in spite of everything I still believe that people are really good at heart.

A teardrop rolls down her cheek to hang on her chin before dripping to her shirt. All of the beauty and horror coalesce, driving down upon her in that moment like a rockslide on a mountain. Not just young Anne's story, but her own, everything she's witnessed: women locked in rooms and cages, fathers killed before children's eyes, an owl that flew away never to return, a dried husk of a boy in the backseat of a car, and a world gasping for a last breath, a last chance.

And she is it.

She crawls onto the bed, barely getting herself to move, and clasps the pillow that smells of musty cotton and long-forgotten flowers, letting the weight of it all crush her. She smells the clean scent of mountain air mingled with burning hair and skin and feels the button beneath her finger that nearly launched a missile, nearly killed her daughter. She feels her soul waver like the candle flame on the table.

She weeps for everything lost.

And for everything that can be if she's strong enough.

As her crying quiets and exhaustion pulls her into the depths of sleep, the candle sputters its last and winks out.

♦ ♦ ♦

She wakes to the dull glow coming from behind a curtained window. Her internal clock tells her it's well past daybreak, and when she twitches the curtain aside, she sees she's right. The sky is layered in clouds but bright enough to hurt her eyes.

The main area of the house smells of candle wax and the lingering scent of potato soup, sending a grumble of hunger through her stomach. With a cursory glance around, she knows she's alone. She listens for the thunk of the old man's hoe outside but there is only the gentle rush of wind trying to find its way past the windows.

In the kitchen, a piece of paper lies pinned beneath three glass jars of what appears to be stew, as well as a tarnished vehicle key. She moves everything aside and reads the scrawling words written by a hand shaky with age.

Good morning and I suppose good-bye. The canned stew is mostly vegetables with a little venison I traded for sometime ago. The truck outside isn't much to look at but it runs and drives well enough. There is some gasoline in a can in the back. It should burn. Use it to get where you're going. Everyone has somewhere to go except me. I've already arrived and don't intend to travel anymore.

Good luck in wherever you're going. And don't forget that coins are everywhere, and until you pick them up you can only see one side.

She rereads the last sentence and raises her eyes to the window, standing still for a long time before folding the note away into her pack along with the jars of stew. Outside the wind is much cooler than it was the day before and she guesses if something falls from the sky today it will be snow. There is no sign of the man near the front of the house or behind the vines, only a patch of turned earth and the neat rows of his garden void of any greenery. Zoey bends low and writes the words "Thank You" in the soft earth near the edge of the garden before moving around the side of the house.

The truck's cab is cold and dank. The passenger window is damaged, unable to close all the way, the seat on that side wet from last night's rain. But when she turns the key in the ignition, the old engine rumbles to life, an alarming stream of smoke issuing from beneath the hood that eventually dissipates. Placing the vehicle in gear she drives away from the little house, its form growing smaller and smaller in the vibrating rearview mirror. And as she turns onto the highway she pulls to a stop, looking back across the distance.

A second before, she could've sworn she saw the old man standing beside the house, one arm above his head in a gesture of farewell. But now he's gone and there is only the lonely stone house on the prairie.

"Good-bye," she says so quietly she barely hears, and accelerates onto the highway leading west.

17

Hiraku dreams.

He knows he is dreaming, and that is perhaps what is most horrible about it all because he has no power to stop it. And knowing it isn't real makes it hurt no less.

He stands in the entryway to his house. Their house. Can he still call it "theirs" if she is already gone? He tries to back out of the entry, tries to reach behind him and grasp the door to push it open and flee, but the pressure is already there. The pressure is all around him, like he's standing at the bottom of the sea with all the water in the world crushing, trying to fill the place where his body is. And it's this pressure that nudges him forward, making him travel into the short hallway and past the sitting room even though he doesn't feel his legs moving.

Framed pictures glide by on each side, but he doesn't look, doesn't have to. He knows them by heart. Here is he and Jiaying holding hands on their first journey to Japan, the cherry blossoms in full bloom behind them. In the next they are smiling on a dance floor, their wedding day almost behind them. And the last are their outlines looking out over the sea at sunset, faceless in the nearing dark, Jiaying more so than him.

Then he is in their small kitchen. He reaches for one of the knives in the butcher block to slit his wrists or throat; even seppuku would be preferable to what he will see down the next hallway and in the little room painted white with blue trim. Always blue, everything blue. Jiaying had always gotten her way. Toys, paint, even carpet, as though she could control what would happen simply by insistence through design.

Hiraku's arm doesn't reach out to the blades; he can only feel the pressure holding him back, guiding him down the hall, always guiding. He tries to scream as some of his ink paintings pass by. These were his contributions in planning for the new life that would inhabit their home—boy or girl didn't matter, he had simply dreamed of a little voice asking him to help hold the brush and show how to make the curving lines as his father had done for him.

The radiation burns on his arms ignite in agony. It is like the day of the accident, the pain unnameable. It shoves him to the border of madness, to the point of not remembering the name of his ancestors or his own. And still he floats toward the door that opens as he approaches. Floor blue, trim blue, walls so white they hurt his eyes, and the crib . . .

He can see it, see the corner as he's shoved into the room in slow motion.

The spindles are hand carved, snowy and pure like the peak of Fuji in winter.

And their purity only contrasts harder with the red. The blood within the crib that's like a scream.

He tries to cry out but there is nothing, no response from his mind's command. He can't even close his eyes to shut out what he sees. Shut out the white blanket with blue edging and the crimson stain in the center, so small, but shining slick as if there is an endless pool beneath it.

Here it is.

The blanket peels back. Folds away from what's beneath.

From what's left of his daughter after the abortion.

Hiraku wakes to his own yell. It is strangled, his throat hoarse and filled with rusted piano wires. The sight is still there behind his eyes even though he sees his cabin in the ship before him. It is still the small, mangled mass of blood and tissue that has eyes and a face and fingers so small he can barely make them out. As always, the dream feels both familiar and alien. He knows he's had it hundreds of times but each instance is layered with different horrid details that make it seem new. As he forces the dream away, oily nausea squirming through his stomach, he realizes he's not alone.

Shirou sits in the corner of the small room, his outline familiar enough that Hiraku doesn't have to turn on a light to know that it's him.

"You were yelling," Shirou says quietly.

Hiraku lets out a long, shuddering breath tasting of acid. "Why didn't you wake me?"

"My grandmother said it was wrong to wake someone in a nightmare. She told me that if you did, part of the person's soul would be trapped there forever."

The crimson crib swims into shape behind Hiraku's eyes and he squeezes them shut, pressing a fist against one temple. "I hope she was wrong." When he looks across the room again the crib is gone and Shirou's face is illuminated in the glow of his lighter as he sparks a cigarette. "May I have one?"

"You haven't smoked in five years."

"Thank you for keeping track. Now may I?"

Shirou half smiles and tosses him the pack and lighter. Hiraku burns the tip of a cigarette and inhales deeply, the smoke traveling all the way to the bottom of his lungs, and it is like coming home. He sighs, some of the tension easing from him. "What time is it?"

"Early. Three-thirty."

"I won't get any more rest tonight."

They sit quietly, smoking, listening to the creak of the ship around them, its movement like being inside a giant womb.

"The dream. It was her again? Jiaying?"

Hiraku doesn't move, not even to tap the lengthening ash from his cigarette onto the steel floor. Only once before had he spoken of the dream to Shirou. Years and years ago. It seems like a lifetime.

He finally shifts his gaze to the other man. To the only person he truly trusts in the world. "Yes." When Shirou only nods he asks, "How many times?"

"How many times what?"

"Have you woken to my yelling?"

A pause. "Many."

"And you never said anything."

"No. Sometimes I would sit beside you in case you rose in your sleep. You did that once, remember?"

"Yes."

"I believe what happens in a man's mind is his own business. Even his nightmares."

Hiraku draws on the cigarette again, but the smoke is becoming less sweet and more acrid. His mouth tastes foul and his head swims from the nicotine. "It was her father, you know." When Shirou doesn't answer or move, he continues, picking at the wound that's scabbed over but never healed. It seems easier in the dark. "He's the one that caused it. The old ways were ingrained in him. The shame it brought him to have a girl during the two-child policy. And he couldn't try again since Jiaying's mother suffered complications during her birth." Hiraku leans forward, stubbing out the cigarette he no longer wants. Maybe it's the words that have soured his taste for it. "And the shame he passed on to Jiaying."

"It was common back then," Shirou says quietly.

"Yes. But I was a fool. I didn't know how deeply it had grown within her. I remember coming home from the hospital after months of treatment for the burns, the radiation poisoning. She was almost in her second trimester by then, and we knew we were having a girl. I could tell she was not pleased, but I thought it would pass." Hiraku picks up a folded piece of paper from his bedside table. "When the doctor gave me this, told me about my inability to father a boy, she was there. She didn't speak on the ride home and when I went for a checkup two days later, she was gone when I returned."

"She went back to her parents?"

Hiraku nods, staring down at the floor, unable to look anywhere else. "I saw her once after that. I tried to see her at their house and her mother finally allowed me inside while her father was out. The first thing I noticed was how flat her belly was beneath her shirt. When I couldn't speak, she told me I would receive the necessary papers for our divorce in the mail. I traveled home in a fog and when I went to sleep I had the first nightmare."

Shirou was quiet for several minutes. "Your daughter."

"Yes," Hiraku says, the word raw in his strained throat. The boat moves around them, shifting slightly on the waves. There is the bang of a door in the hallway and a muttered curse.

"Perhaps it was fate," Shirou says. "I'm sure you've thought of that."

"Yes."

"The test results on that paper have given many men hope. Hope of rebuilding a future someday. You could do nothing more noble with what's happened to you."

"The lives we've ended. I sometimes wonder if they've been in vain."

"So can be said of any great undertaking."

"But what if we're wrong? What if there is nothing left when we arrive at the location?"

"What are you talking about?"

Hiraku pauses, glancing at Shirou, the words of the young man from the munitions factory like a thorn in his mind. "Nothing. It's early and I'm being foolish."

"Doubt is not foolish as long as it is balanced by hope."

Hiraku manages to smile. "You always were a philosopher."

"Not always."

"Have I asked too much of you, my brother?" he says, recalling how quickly Shirou had wounded the man the day before on the pier, the almost eagerness of his movements.

"Never."

"I worry I have, and that your soul has suffered for it."

"Anything harbored in my soul has always been there. I am yours until you have no need of me anymore."

"I'll always need your friendship. I only hope we have a chance to regain what we've lost of ourselves someday."

Shirou rises and walks toward the door, ignoring his last comment. Hiraku frowns, wondering silently how much is truly left of the friend he met twenty years ago. How much is left of himself. "Has the word been circulated about what we're going to attempt?" he asks as Shirou opens the door.

"Yes. We've had a dozen men from the city volunteer to join us already. By the time we have enough ammunition, there will be a thousand willing to fight and die. We will overwhelm the compound when we reach it."

"If the machines at the munitions factory can be repaired, that is."

Half of Shirou's face is thrown into shadow by the light from the hall. "If the man who came forward cannot repair them, I will kill him myself for lying to you."

With that he is gone, the door shutting solidly behind him, and to Hiraku it sounds like the closing of a sepulcher.

18

"No, no, no. This is all wrong."

Lee presses the creases out of the schematics with the heel of his hand before brushing his hair back from his brow. It is moist from the sweat that beads on his forehead, and though the weather outside is overcast and damp, the air in the factory is humid and clingy like a second skin.

"What's wrong?" Ollie says, coming to lean on the table beside him.

"These pins here that match the housing body, they're supposed to be one point two five centimeters, not point two five."

"How'd that get messed up?"

"The one was folded into the crease on the schematic. If these things wouldn't have been stored like this, I would've caught it." Lee shoves the papers away from him and a piece of steel square stock falls from the table and clangs to the cement, drawing a few looks from the men standing before the dozen machining apparatus against the far wall.

"Look, we're lucky to even have these. Must've been one obsessive-compulsive sonofabitch who held on to these after the digital age." The older man slaps him on the shoulder. "And we're lucky you stepped forward when you did. I know not everyone agrees, and I woulda liked to have told those bastards to pound sand too, but it would have meant a lot of dead men floating in the bay. Martyrs are great and all, but I sure as hell don't wanna be one."

Lee smiles wanly. "I appreciate the encouragement."

"Well I owe you one for picking me to help with this," Ollie says, motioning at the factory. "Sure beats sitting in a house all day staring out at an army surrounding the neighborhood."

Lee glances at the two guards stationed by the factory's main door and lowers his voice. "Has anyone looked for a way to get past them and out of the city?"

"Oh yeah. Couple of ours tried it yesterday in fact. These guys are spread out no more'n fifty yards apart, but once in a while they take a piss break or go to get something to drink and there's a gap. That's when the guys made their move."

"What happened?"

"Got caught and had their asses handed to them on a plate. Broken arms, noses, missing teeth. Lucky to be alive really." Ollie surveys him. "You ain't thinking of making a break for it, are you?"

"No. Not really."

"Good. Because like I said, there's no one else that can fabricate now that Loring's dead, and if you get shot or manage to slip away, we'll all pay the price. At least the ones that haven't gone over."

"Gone over? What are you talking about?"

"You heard the rumors. That this guy, this Hiraku's got goofy sperm. Thinks he can father only girls and that he knows about a secret location where they're keeping some women."

Lee tries to keep his expression steady. "Yeah, I've heard."

"Well they're offering everyone the chance to join and come with them to raid the compound and take control. Basically promising to rebuild the old world. My generation might be shit out of luck, but yours and the younger boys would have a chance if girls started being born again."

"You're not considering joining them, are you?"

"Thought about it. Not sure I trust them, though. But some of the guys have already made friends with a few of their men and say they're decent and this Hiraku's pretty fair."

"He destroyed half the port and killed hundreds of us."

"I ain't defending him, just repeating what I've heard."

"Hey! You two!" They both look at the soldier standing beside the door. "Enough jaw-jacking. Get back to work. Clock's ticking."

"Yes sir!" Ollie calls. "Officer shit bag," he adds quietly, and Lee covers his laughter with a loud cough. He draws the schematics for the brass machine close again, and as Ollie prepares to carry a heavy steel plate across the room, Lee stops him. "Ollie?"

"Yeah?"

"Don't join them. Okay?"

He must have something written in his expression because the other man frowns before nodding. "Okay, chief, anything you say."

Lee watches him walk away, deeply hoping Ollie was being genuine, before staring down at the exploded diagrams before him. He tries to concentrate on the measurements of the next replacement part, but his mind keeps slipping to what will happen if he's not able to finish the work in time and what will happen if he does succeed. Either way people will die because of his actions.

He stares at the numbers and designs. They're the only things that have ever made sense in his life, especially now after having lost his father and Ray. And Zoey. He wishes that everything was as simple as blueprints and measurements. If life was ordered like the schematics before him, he would have no trouble navigating it. But it's not, and now he feels as he did months ago before leaving Zoey on the mountainside: unbalanced and unsure of anything. It's as if he's standing on a barrel floating in the middle of a sea, knowing to a certainty that any decision will push him one way or other and he will fall and drown.

"You gonna stare at that all day or are you gonna get some work done, boy?" the guard who yelled earlier growls from across the table. Lee jerks, unaware that the other man had approached.

"Sorry. Just thinking."

"Less thinking. More doing." The guard places a hand on the rifle slung around his shoulder before walking away.

"Yeah. I suppose that's right," Lee says to himself, and begins writing a string of numbers on the paper beside the schematics.

19

Zoey gazes through the binoculars as a gust of wind rushes in through the open tenth-story window, bringing with it the smell of the ocean and a chill mist that beads on her jacket and exposed skin.

Seattle sprawls before her, the uppermost stories of the highest buildings masked in leaden clouds and a drifting fog that curls down and scrapes the treetops before moving on through the streets. The building she stands in is a half-dozen blocks from the shoreline, its lower levels blackened and gutted from a fire long ago extinguished. Many of the structures are damaged in this section of the city and she wonders absently what could have caused an inferno here when there is no natural fuel to feed such a fire.

People. Of course, that's always the answer when something unnatural or unlikely occurs. Humankind, she's learned, is the factor more times than not when dealing with the inexplicable. People are unpredictable and irrational, to say the least.

"Coming from the woman standing in the last city full of men," she mutters, and sweeps the streets again with the binoculars.

She'd arrived at the city limits near dusk the day before, ditching the old truck as soon as the first skyscrapers came into view. A small contingent of men stood guard at the road she first approached on, and it took her nearly six hours to find a safer route past them by hugging a desolate embankment made entirely out of cement below a road built thirty feet or more above the ground. Even with the men's voices echoing to her off buildings and blacktop, she couldn't help the awe that continued to fill her, forcing her eyes from one place to the next, never able to fully absorb what she was seeing. Such industry and design, it nearly halted her in her tracks every few seconds. The soaring height of the structures so unfathomable to her eyes she barely believed them. Of course, she'd seen pictures of the cities prior to the Dearth in the NOA textbook, but being able to touch the smooth glass and move between the scattered buildings that grew in both size and number until she could no longer comprehend it was something else entirely.

And the ocean. The ocean.

It was more than she was prepared for.

She had gaped at it from the second floor of a house she'd stayed in that night. As the sun fell past the horizon and lit the water in colors of orange and red, she'd simply stared, dumbstruck at the beauty of the way the water moved and how it stretched into the distance forever. Even the massive ship anchored in the harbor couldn't detract from the majesty of the view. She'd eaten a jar of the old man's stew cold, eyes never leaving the water until it had become full dark and then, despite the cool air, she left the window open to listen to the soft shush of waves.

Even now as she scans the city streets, her gaze keeps returning to the expanse of cold gray water, the sight moving her more than anything else she's seen so far outside the ARC's walls. Even the soaring height of the mountains can't compare to the constant motion of the sea. She recalls Merrill smiling when she'd asked how big the ocean was. *Big,* he'd said, and now she realizes that he'd explained it the only way he could, for without witnessing it, there were no words to fully convey its size and presence. But maybe it is more than that. Maybe it's not how immense the sea is but how small it makes her feel.

She comes back to herself even though she'd like to do nothing more than sit and watch the waves until sunset again, because she likes that small feeling, the notion that everything could pass her by unnoticed if she only stays in the water's presence. Reluctantly she checks the sun's height and guesses it will be less than two hours before full dark. That's when she'll have to make her move.

A revving engine brings her magnified gaze down to the street. A large truck rolls into sight and turns a corner, heading away from her position, its back end filled with several barrels of what she can only guess is fuel. She knows there is a refinery set up somewhere within the city's limits; Merrill had told her of the many industries still alive within the city, and she hopes that her intuition is correct about what's drawn her here.

Zoey glances down at the weathered map she found in the house she stayed in the night before. She checks the circled building's location again before looking through the glass again.

There. The top is just visible above another structure several blocks down. At least she thinks it's in the right position, but she's no expert at reading maps. Tia would be able to pinpoint it, or Chelsea.

She pulls the binoculars away from her eyes and gazes down at the drop outside the window, focusing on the vertigo that tugs at her brain until the thoughts of the group fade. She can't afford to lose concentration now, can't become distracted, not here. Her hand strays down to the lump in her pocket and traces the outlines of the vial before she leaves the window and makes her way to the stairs outside in the corridor.

An hour later she crouches beside a pile of rotted furniture near the corner of a massive building made of slab stone. She'd traversed the windswept streets slowly and carefully, ducking behind burnt husks of vehicles whenever she spotted movement. Only two trucks had passed while she moved, their lumbering forms hauling more barrels like the ones she'd seen earlier.

Zoey shifts on the balls of her feet, wincing at the sharp pain as she does so. The wound's healing nicely but it still hurts to put a lot of pressure on it. She rises until she can see over the top of a chair that's black with mold.

An armed man stands a hundred yards away on the next corner below a blank sign, its paint having peeled completely off. Another fifty yards beyond him is another man smoking a cigarette and cradling a short-barreled machine gun. A scuffling sound comes from the opposite end of the alley she's crouched in, and Zoey pivots, hand already drawing out her pistol. She just catches the impression of a figure disappearing behind the building beside her, the movements slow and easy, another sentry patrolling the street below.

Something is wrong.

She feels it as sure as the moisture soaking through her coat and onto her skin. She was prepared for guards within the city but hadn't anticipated how closely positioned their posts would be. And Seattle itself—its stillness is unnerving. She imagined bustling activity, not the solemn atmosphere that grips it now. Maybe it's always been this way, but she can't help notice the familiar sensation. The city has the feeling of the ARC, the air of a prison.

Regardless, she's come this far and isn't turning back now. Not when she can see her destination a few blocks away.

Zoey watches the closest guard before easing back into the protection of the alley, then moves down in the direction of the sea. At the halfway point she turns right, waiting for several minutes to make sure no one is lingering at the mouth of the passage beyond. Dusk continues to fall as she walks through several puddles that seep cold water into her shoes and socks, soaking them instantly. When she emerges from the branching alley, the guard she spotted earlier is turned to the east, gazing up a long line of buildings parallel to his position. Another man appears as she watches, and he greets the first guard before walking onward down the street she just vacated. The next street to her left is occupied by two men in an open-top jeep who talk loudly enough for her to catch every other word, none of them meaning anything to her.

She exhales, her breath steaming the air as she gazes at her surroundings. She's at an impasse. There's no way for her to get to the next street and then up a block to the building she's headed for. To her right a few streetlamps flicker on, their muddy-yellow glow staining the concrete below in ragged circles. The closest guard huddles beneath the corner's overhang, glancing her way before turning to the building's doorstep and relieving himself. She's about to retreat and circle around several blocks to look for another, easier way through when her eyes snag on something above and to the right of the next structure.

Zoey blinks, eyes flicking down to the jeep and its occupants who are busy unfurling a canvas top over the vehicle's frame. She launches herself forward and across the street.

One, two, three, four steps and she's across, a slight twinge of pain in her back that barely slows her. She half expects gunfire to roar from either side and keeps expecting it even as she stops before the building's doors, hoping beyond hope that they're unlocked.

She pulls on one of the steel handles and it gives, emitting a shriek that's loud enough to echo off the walls behind her.

Without looking around she darts inside the darkened lobby, easing the glass door shut behind her. Down the street, the men in the jeep have ducked beneath their shelter as the rain begins to fall in earnest, and the guard on the corner turns, still zipping up his pants, and stares in her direction, turning on a flashlight after a pause.

She shrinks back from the glow, nearly tripping over a steel can that she stops before it can go rolling down a set of nearby stairs. Zoey watches the beam of light catching a thousand streaks of rain. The light doesn't move from the door she entered through.

"Please. You didn't hear anything. The wind," she whispers.

Seconds tick by, her heart beating three times in each one.

The light snaps out.

She peers through the glass and sees the man has retreated back out of the rain. "Thank you," she says, and turns to face the interior of the building.

Its walls are sectioned into dozens of rooms on either side. Some are shuttered by rolls of linked steel extending from top to bottom while others gape open like black mouths.

Zoey crosses the wide space, eyes flicking to every possible place that could hide a person, her handgun drawn once again. Ahead, two stairways ascend in the center of the building to the second level, and beside them two more rise to the third.

With a steadying breath, she glances back the way she came, assuring she's alone, and begins to climb.

20

Lee steps into the rainy evening, bone-tired and hungry.

The men who've worked with him all day file past on either side. After a moment, the two guards exit the factory and slam the door closed with a bang, locking it before moving to the truck nearby.

"You want a ride to your house there, genius?" one of them says, pausing as he opens the vehicle's door.

"No. Thank you," Lee says.

"Suit yourself. Gonna catch your death in the rain." The man laughs and climbs inside as the engine rumbles to life. Ollie appears beside him, pulling his dark hat down tight.

"I would've taken a ride. Why didn't they ask me?"

"Not sure. Hey, good work today," Lee says, starting away down the sidewalk.

"Thanks! You wanna go grab a drink down near the market? Pub's still open."

"No. Too tired. See you in the morning."

"Stay dry, chief!" Ollie cries, and hurries away in the direction of the water. Lee hunches his shoulders to the cold, part of him wishing he'd taken the soldiers up on their offer. The house he's been staying in since Ray . . . since the invasion isn't as high up skid row. He chose it because of the color, blue with white shutters. He tells himself he picked it because it's closer to the munitions factory, but really he knows it's because of what his father told him when he was young. He attempts to shut the memory out, walking faster through puddles that line the sidewalk, but it is like shielding himself from the rain with only his hands. The memory slips through.

He recalls how his father used to sit on his bedside and read to him out of a book. The stories he can't remember now, but they were adventurous: knights in armor, dragons that he'd had nightmares about, and animals that could speak. He'd once asked his father for a story that he knew, not one from a book but something from before, before the Dearth, when his mother was still alive. He had been very quiet for a long time before looking at Lee.

There was a little town on the edge of a bay and it was warm most of the year. It didn't rain like it does here, not as much. There were fishing boats along the shore and men and women who worked at businesses that made things people needed. The sky was almost always clear and the sunsets lasted for hours and hours.

Lee watched him stare at and through the wall in their room and had wanted to see what he was seeing. *That was where you and Mommy lived?*

His father had nodded slowly. *Down by the docks. It was all we could afford, but it was nice. We kept it nice. The house was blue, like the sky in the early spring mornings, and the shutters were white. They were peeling when we moved in, but I scraped and repainted them in our little garage and she was . . . she was so happy.*

A tear had leaked out of his father's eye then, and it had scared Lee so much he sat up and hugged him tight, afraid something would happen to him because he had never seen him cry before that night when speaking of the past.

Lee glances around, his senses returning as if he is waking. He stands in the center of an intersection a block from the Space Needle, its dark shape looming like something out of one of his father's stories. He must've walked here instead of up the hill without thinking. The urge to climb the Needle's stairs and stand in the clean, rain-washed air is strong, and the thought scares him because he doesn't know what he would do once he reached the top of the tower.

Instead he turns east and slogs up through the drenched streets, passing into and out of the sickly light cast by the odd-powered lamp. Hiraku's guards stand on nearly every corner, most not visible until he is within a stone's throw of them, their dark clothes blending in with the night. They watch him warily as he trudges by, knowing if it were an hour later they would be escorting him home at gunpoint since the curfew is strictly enforced.

He ponders the conundrum of the munitions factory as he slogs onward. There is a part of him that doesn't care if Hiraku and his army raid the ARC. After what Reaper and the rest of those in charge have done, they deserve to be gunned down. But another part of him remembers the friendships that were made in his years growing up in the facility. Other clerics' sons, many members of the engineering department—they are decent men and boys, unaware of the people and purpose they serve.

And if Hiraku gets the ammunition he wants, they will all perish. For nothing.

But no matter which angle he approaches the matter from, there is no solution. None without bloodshed.

A sound stops Lee in the middle of the street and he glances around.

The nearest soldier stands nearly a hundred yards away beneath a streetlamp, large hood pulled up obscuring his features. Lee looks the other way, but the road is dark and empty without a soul in sight. The sound had been close and strange. Almost like a scratch and a yelp of pain.

Lee looks up into the rain, sees he's standing under the city's derelict monorail system, its twin beams two darker ribbons against the leaking sky. For some reason he takes a step back, the hairs on his arms rising as if statically charged.

There is something above him on the closest rail.

21

Zoey steps from the last stair onto the third level of the building.

Many of the structure's windows are missing or shattered, the remaining jagged edges like broken teeth. Wind stirs garbage that layers the floor, casting cardboard containers across marble in a hissing whisper.

She turns in a circle. Water drips from a cracked pane of glass overhead. There is a shout somewhere outside on a distant street. Then only the night and the patter of rain.

She moves forward, satisfied she is alone. The east side of the building is open to the weather and she stops at the drop to the street some twenty feet below. A sagging steel grate leading out over open air extends before her.

And beyond that, the rail.

When she first spotted it from the street below, it looked like one of the railroads they'd crossed many times while driving, only hoisted high above the streets and much larger and without any ties between the two beams. Now, standing beside it, she sees that it is even wider than she first estimated.

Glancing up at the surrounding buildings, she searches their roofs for the outlines of men stationed there. She sees none, but it is hard to tell for sure through the weather, though she reminds herself it is to her own advantage as well.

Below, a guard on the next corner paces out into the street, and a second later he is lit by headlights that brighten until a vehicle appears beside him. Another guard climbs out of the passenger seat and the first takes his place. The truck accelerates away, leaving the new man in the prior's position. Zoey studies the nearest rail. It's plenty wide enough to walk on, and if she moves slow she'll be able to stay low and hopefully out of sight from the guards below. She eyes the rail again before looking down at her shoes. Quickly she unlaces them and puts them in her pack, the wet floor chilling her already-cold feet through her socks.

She takes two steadying breaths before moving.

With a leap she crosses the empty air between the building and the rail.

She lands solidly and crouches, the rain resuming its assault on her back. Without waiting she begins to run, bent over and taking little steps.

The guard on the right turns toward her and she halts, sinking down to her knees. He scans the area beneath the rails and continues to pivot, looking back the way she came.

Zoey rises and runs again.

Past the end of a towering skyscraper.

Over another guard who stands directly below her path, a rain hood covering his head.

Trees streak by in the dark, their branches so close she could touch them.

Her socks squish wetly with each step, but the sound is barely audible to her ears with the rain pounding down.

Another man steps out from beneath an awning across the street and for a terrifying moment she thinks he's seen her. He freezes, hands moving to his slung rifle as she halts, drawing her handgun out.

He leans back, head coming up, looking straight at her.

And sneezes twice in quick succession.

She sags with relief as he shakes himself and treads to the street, spitting a wad of phlegm into the gutter.

Then she's up and moving again, noting a man's outline on the roof of the building beside her destination.

She slows, unsure if he is facing her or not, and comes to a stop over the center of a street. Thankfully there are no lit streetlights here, the closest one nearly a block up the hill to her right.

She waits, a cramp beginning to tighten in her hip and upper thigh, the low throb of pain in her back like a chiding voice. The man doesn't move from his post, and she's sure now that he doesn't see her or he would've shot by now, but she still doesn't know which way he's facing.

Ahead, the nearest cover is a large tree with skeletal branches reaching high above the beams. If she can make it there without being seen she can climb down it to street level.

Zoey watches the man's outline. The longer she stays here the more likely she'll be seen.

Move.

But even as she starts to rise, she hears it.

The scratch of boots below.

She freezes, halfway between kneeling and standing, and sees the figure closing in on the street beneath her. Watches the figure draw near as the cramp that was only a mild threat before flexes into a sickening knot of pain.

Her leg trembles and her sock slips off the rail.

Steel bites into her shin and her sprained wrist flares bright with pain as she catches herself. She teeters, unable to keep the quiet cry of pain from escaping her lips.

Zoey hugs the beam, praying the man below didn't hear. But now there is nothing but the rain. No footsteps drawing away.

He's stopped underneath her.

22

Lee studies the shape above him on the monorail.

It is only a slight bulge in the steel, unmoving, unchanging, but he still feels the cold gaze on him, making his stomach turn. If there were only lightning along with the rain he would be able to see that it is some debris or other harmless object on the rail, but here in the dark with the storm pounding down he is sure he is near death.

He tries to make his legs work but they are frozen in place, the seconds stretching out into hours as he stares, trying to discern if the shape just moved or not.

23

Zoey brings the pistol over the side of the beam, centering on the figure below.

If he yells or makes a sudden move she'll have to shoot him, she won't have any other choice. She turns her head enough to see the guard on the building's roof has disappeared. The next closest man is a hundred yards away. She can be gone by the time he hears the shot and comes running.

Rain drips off the gun's barrel and her finger tightens on the trigger.

24

Lee tenses, every sense screaming for him to run.

He's about to sprint forward, away from the rails, when a shout comes from his right.

"Hey! What're you doing?" The guard from down the street stalks toward him, flashlight shining in his face. "It's almost curfew. You're not supposed to be on the streets."

"I'm sorry, I'm just—" Lee glances back up to the beam.

The shape is gone.

He glances left and right, searching the rails but there's nothing there.

"Hey asshole, I'm talking to you." The words are punctuated with a rough shove and he stumbles to the side. "The hell are you looking at?"

"I don't know. Something on the rail," Lee says, pointing upward.

The soldier shines his light across the beam. Only smooth concrete and glistening steel. "You drunk?"

"No, I'm just trying to go home. My house is right up the street."

"Then get there."

The guard's radio crackles. "Everything okay, Vince?"

He looks up at the nearest building top across the street to the figure standing there. "Yeah. You see anything on the monorails?"

A pause. "Clear. No movement."

"Good." The soldier eyes Lee again and makes a shooing gesture. "Get going."

Lee nods, giving the rails a last cursory glance before jogging under them and up the hill toward his house, leaving the guard to study the beams before returning to his post.

25

Zoey drops to the ground beneath the tree, wet bark covering her hands and her pants.

Her lungs burn and her shin aches from where she fell. The man below her doesn't know how close he came to death. When the other guard called out, her finger nearly twitched on the trigger, but instead she used the distraction to move and was climbing down the tree before she could hear any of their conversation.

She scans the area, picking out the shape of another man down the sidewalk, sheltering beneath an eave. He's facing away from her, and she jogs across the street, into an alley without hearing any cries of alarm.

The alley is long with gaps between each of the buildings it threads behind. Zoey slows at each one of them, glancing out to gather her bearings. She's close.

The next gap shows her a slice of the structure across the street, and she stops.

There it is. Seattle Medical Center.

It is at least a dozen stories tall and made of brick. The uppermost windows glow with light while the levels below are dark and streaked with rain. The main entrance is composed of glass, only half of it visible to her. Two men stand before it, rifle barrels pointing at the ground.

Finally, after all of the traveling and risk, she's here. One hand goes unconsciously to her pants pocket, fingertips tracing the outline of the blood vial there. She sidles into the narrow gap, venturing as close to the street as she dares.

The hospital's sides are nestled close to the neighboring buildings, and she sees no stairs or ladders. Someone moves past a window on the top floor, their shadow there and gone. Instinct tells her that is the place she has to get to. Up there she will learn the truth about the child she saw in Vivian's video message.

She will find out if she truly is a mother.

Zoey's about to move to a different vantage point to see if there is another access to the medical center when a figure appears in the street, heading up the hill. Trudging is a more apt word. His head is down and he's soaking wet. It takes her a second to realize he must be the man who was underneath the rails a few minutes before. He doesn't appear armed and the guards at the hospital doors watch him enter the halo of dim light thrown by the nearest working streetlamp.

He's there, framed for half a second before moving out of her line of sight.

And in that moment it's as if someone's struck her.

The solid wall beside her tilts as she presses a hand to it.

Her mouth goes dry.

It can't be. Not in a thousand years. She's dead wrong. Mistaken. A trick of the rain and bad light. A hundred different assurances run through her mind as she wheels back into the main alley and sprints to the next gap nearly bowling over a stack of pallets before ducking into a side lane that's cluttered with large cans and humped shapes beneath torn tarps.

She slows, then stops, hanging back a dozen feet from the sidewalk, nerves tingling because she's too close and being foolish because it can't be, it can't be—

And then he is there, walking faster now, head still down and hands shoved in his pockets.

It is almost too much for her and she shrinks back, stumbling on something under her feet and catching herself on the wall, because she would know his outline anywhere, know his walk and how he holds himself, even after all the months apart.

One hand comes up to cover her mouth, maybe to keep herself from speaking, but it fails miserably.

"Lee," she says, and watches as he continues through the rain.

26

The blue house with the white shutters is cool and quiet when he steps inside, shaking himself of the rain that's soaked him through.

Lee closes the door, dripping and shivering, and leans against it for a moment. His muscles are still trembling and he can't escape the feeling that burrowed inside him beneath the monorail. It was as if a cold hand had closed around his heart, sending frigid knowledge through his veins that he had been on the brink of something terrible.

He pushes from the door and strips off his dripping jacket, as well as the shirt beneath, and moves into the laundry room. Throwing the clothes inside the dryer he sets the machine and turns it on.

Something thumps deeper in the house.

His hand fumbles to shut the dryer off, his jacket buttons clanking a last time before everything is quiet again. What had the sound been? Something falling over? Lee steps into the hallway and peers down its length into the dark kitchen. Only a faint strip of light falls across the floor from the streetlamp outside. Beyond the kitchen is the living room, which he can't see at all, and past that the rear entry.

He moves silently down the hall and into the kitchen, listening intently the whole way. Had he imagined the sound? A residual jangling of his nerves now that he's alone in a home that isn't truly his own?

The floor creaks in the darkness of the living room.

Lee's heart seizes as something moves there, a swirling of shadow.

His hand fumbles in the nearest drawer and he ignores the biting pain of the knife blade as it slides across the pad of one finger before he grasps the handle and draws it out.

"Who's there?" he asks, pointing the tip of the knife at the dark.

A figure takes shape at the border of the two rooms, and suddenly his weapon feels woefully insignificant.

"Who are you?" he says, trying to muster the courage to step forward. Instead he reaches out and flicks the light switch beside him.

27

Zoey stands with her hands at her sides, rain dripping from her finger-tips as the light washes over her.

She absorbs the look on Lee's face as he sees her, this particular moment one she's imagined more than once, more than a hundred times. Slowly she reaches up and pulls the hat from her head.

His eyes narrow and his expression changes.

Confusion.

Shock.

Realization.

The pitiful knife he holds drops to the floor.

"Zoey?" he whispers. She says nothing, only watches him, watches and wonders what he is truly feeling. Lee takes an unsteady step forward. Then another. "Are you . . . are you here?" His eyebrows draw down below the hair that's plastered against his forehead. His hand reaches out to her, reaches for her face.

Zoey winds back a fist and punches him. Hard.

The blow catches him on the side of the jaw and he is completely unready for it. His head rocks back and she feels his teeth bite into her knuckles.

Lee stumbles away from her, feet trying to keep him upright. He bounces off the cupboard behind him and steadies himself, bringing a hand up to the split in his lip that seeps blood.

"Zoey, what—" But that's all he has time to say as she launches a kick at his chest.

"How could you?" she says as her foot connects and sends him reeling back over the countertop. He lets out a short cry and flips to the floor, landing mostly on his feet.

"Zoey!"

"How could you leave?" she says, the unbidden anger overwhelming her. All of the days without him coalesce and fill her up.

The loneliness.

The abandonment.

The love.

She throws another punch that he ducks.

His hands come up, palms out, as he backs into a side hallway. "Zoey, please. Stop. Listen to me."

"I did listen to you. I listened to your voice in my head for the past seven months." She kicks at him again, and he dodges away.

"I'm sorry! I'm sorry I left. I had to."

His words are like a bellows to the fire inside her. She makes an inarticulate sound and swings her fist again, catching him on the temple. Lee's eyes widen and he sags against the wall before shaking his head. He reaches out to her.

"Stop, Zoey. Please."

She's beyond words, only movement now, blind fury driving her forward.

She tries to throw a knee into his stomach, but he catches her leg and pulls her forward, wrapping her in a tight hug.

"Zoey. Please." She struggles, trying to shrug him off, break the hold he has on her, but in the distant regions of her mind she knows she can't, because the hold goes far beyond physical.

She tries to get her arms free but he clamps her tighter to him, and she can smell his skin, wet from the rain, intoxicating even as she lunges to the side, desperate to be free, to keep the anger alive and burning.

Lee loses his balance and they collapse to the floor. He lands on top of her, pinning her to the floor, his breathing harsh in her ear.

"I'm sorry. I'm so sorry for leaving you," he whispers. "I wanted to stay, but every time I looked at you I saw him die. And I couldn't stand it. I couldn't. I was weak and you're strong and I knew you'd survive."

She strains to flip his weight from her but he's too heavy. They lie there, breathing heavily, neither of them moving. Zoey stares at the darkened ceiling over his shoulder, smells the blood she drew from his lip, and suddenly her vision blurs.

"I needed you," she says, voice weakened to less than a whisper. "I was so afraid and then you were gone."

He is still for a long time, and when he raises himself from her, silver tear-tracks streak his face. "I was afraid too. You were all I had left, and I was so scared I'd lose you like I did my father. So I ran. And I've regretted it every day since I left."

A tremor runs through her and a small sob escapes her throat. "I'm sorry. It's my fault he's gone. All my fault." But she can't say any more. Her muscles go languid, frailty beyond anything she's felt before washing over her. Even the unsteadiness of her legs as she relearned to walk doesn't come close to the weakness she feels now.

She is water. She imagines herself flowing outward down the hall and disappearing through the cracks in the floor.

But she doesn't because he takes her into his arms.

Lee slides to the side and rolls her to him, pulling her face into the hollow of his neck. For a brief second she resists, trying to summon the rage that's eaten at her all through the months since she found his good-bye note, but the reservoir is dry.

And beneath it is longing.

How many times has she caught herself thinking of him like this? So close against her, the smell of him, his voice. She knows the anger was only a product of it all, the yearning for him and his comfort, the safety she always felt when he was near.

Zoey leans into him and it is like they are back in her room at the ARC lifetimes ago. Two children huddling together as a war rages outside and the night grows darker, only now it is the fear of letting go that keeps them holding on.

He murmurs to her. She thinks it's something like *don't cry,* his fingers on her chin, bringing her face up to his.

Then he is kissing her.

His lips soft and so gentle, barely grazing her own.

She can taste tears and the salty tang of his blood. He is so real and vivid that the voice in her head saying this isn't actually happening fades completely, leaving only the two of them, arms and legs intertwined, bodies pressed firmly against each other.

She runs her fingers through his hair and feels his hand slide up the length of her thigh, pause on her hip, and continue beneath the hem of her shirt, his palm so warm on the bare skin of her back.

Zoey mashes her lips against his, unable to hold back any longer. The deep, coiled need she felt in her dream at Riverbend returns, except it is tenfold.

Their clothes peel away, sodden and cold, replaced by tender caresses that become feverish.

She realizes neither of them knows what they're doing but it is right since they're together.

Lee hovers over her. He trembles against her, forehead to forehead, eyes staring straight into hers. His breath catches and she grimaces.

Pain. Why pain? She swallows, a quiet cry coming from her. Lee pauses but she kisses him, the need still there through the ache.

The rain beats the roof above them as they move together, and it is forever and only seconds before it is over, the pulsing knot of pain dwindling as he collapses in her arms, heart hammering through his chest against her own. His lips press against the side of her neck and he whispers the same thing over and over as she slides toward the oblivion of sleep.

"I love you, Zoey. I love you."

28

Sometime in the night Lee wakes and guides her to a bedroom off the hall.

The mattress is quite possibly the softest thing she's ever felt, and she melts into it, falling asleep again almost at once, the last sensation of Lee curling in close behind her, his body fitting to hers like it was made for it.

◆　◆　◆

Zoey surfaces from sleep gradually like rising through layers of warm water. Her eyes open to a curtained window on her side of the bed, soft blue light of early morning staining the floor and ceiling. She rolls over, unsure if her memory is telling the truth or not.

Lee lies beside her with one arm bent above his head, eyes shut, breathing slow and even.

True.

She watches him for a time, the knowledge of what she will have to do when he wakes, like the roaring of a distant storm. For the moment she ignores it. She deserves this.

The rain must've stopped shortly before she woke because she can hear it dripping from the eaves in a steady plunking outside. The house is quiet and peaceful. The air outside the covers is cool but beneath she is warm.

Lee stirs, a low sound in the back of his throat, then his eyes blink partially open. He slides his gaze to her and smiles.

"You're really here."

"Just what I was thinking," she says, suddenly very aware of her nudity. She pulls the sheet tighter around her.

He props himself up on his side and, for a long time, simply looks at her. "Can't believe you found me," he finally says.

"Me neither."

"How?"

"How what?"

"How everything. How did you find me? How did you get here? How are you walking?"

She smiles a little. "I got feeling back slowly in my legs after you left. I drove here, and it was completely chance that we crossed paths."

A strange look settles on his face. "It was you, wasn't it? Last night on the monorail. You were sneaking into the city." She nods. He shakes his head and rubs his eyes. "How did you know I was here?"

"I didn't."

He frowns. "Then why did you come?"

Zoey sits up, bracing herself against the headboard, clasping the blankets to her chest as if they can protect her from the words she has to say. Lee pivots to face her. "I have to get to the hospital."

"Why? Are you sick? Hurt?"

"No. I'm okay. I mean I got shot in the foot the other day, but that's a different story."

"What?"

"Never mind." She struggles with the enormity of it. How can words weigh this much? Across the room, her and Lee's clothes hang from the back of a chair. He must have put them there after bringing her to bed. She stands and moves to them, feeling his eyes on her but the embarrassment of earlier is gone now. She dons her shirt, which is mostly dry before digging in her pants pocket. Returning to the bed she wraps the blankets around her bare legs.

"I came here because of this," she says, holding out the blood vial to him.

He takes it, turning it over several times. "What is it?"

She takes a deep breath, stomach clenched sickeningly tight. "It might be our daughter's blood."

Lee freezes. He stares at the vial before bringing his eyes up to her. "What did you say?"

"A man named Jefferson found us at a missile installation in Idaho. Followed us there. He was an NOA agent and he killed . . . killed Eli. I shot him, and before he died he gave me this vial and a video chip with a message on it from Vivian at the ARC." Lee turns so that his legs hang off the bed, his gaze locked once again on the vial. "There was a baby girl in one of the tanks and she said I was the keystone. That I can give birth to girls and that the blood was proof."

"But you said our daughter. How—"

"When the guard Tasered me in the lunchroom after Rita and I were fighting. They took an egg and your sperm. And . . ." She gestures with her hands, a sudden anger returning at the thought of what NOA's done.

Lee shakes his head like he did after she struck him the night before. "So you came here to test the blood?"

"Yes. It's the only way to be sure if she's telling the truth. If it doesn't match then they're lying and just trying to lure me back. But if it does . . ."

Lee stands, crossing to his own clothes, and draws his pants on. He stands silently by the open doorway for a moment, and she has the irrational fear that he will walk out and disappear, leave her again just like before. But he returns to the bed, perching on its edge. "How do you know even if it matches that it's not a trick?"

"I don't. Maybe the doctor will be able to tell me, but I have to try. I have to know for sure." She pauses. "There are doctors here, right?"

He says nothing for so long she begins to wonder if he heard her. She's about to ask again when he says, "Can't be. It's a trick. They're—" His eyes widen and he slowly looks at her, mouth partially open.

"What is it?"

"The army. Oh, God."

"What?"

"The army that's here. They're the ones on the streets."

"I thought they were guards for the city."

"No. They showed up nearly a week ago. Killed hundreds of men and rounded the rest up. The man leading them, he thinks he can father female children. And he knows about the ARC."

"What? How does he know? He's been there?"

"No. He's not from here. They came by ship, the huge one in the bay. He said an American told him where the remaining women were being held so he gathered as many soldiers and guns as he could and came here because he thinks he can bring the population back."

"But why are they holding the city hostage?"

"They're low on ammunition, and the machines at the factory that makes it were damaged." Lee swallows. "I've been tasked with fixing them."

She blinks. "You agreed to it?"

"Only because they were going to start killing people if no one stepped forward." He stands and paces across the room. "I couldn't let them do it."

"How close are you to fixing them?"

"Close. They should be producing rounds in two or three days."

Zoey places a hand against her forehead. "Okay. Then we need to think of a way I can get into the hospital and out before that happens."

"That's suicide. The hospital has guards stationed out front and more inside. No one gets in there without being checked first."

"There has to be a way around the security."

"It's impossible."

"You thought the same thing about escaping the ARC."

Lee stops pacing. "You're right. But this is different. If you'd been caught at the ARC, they'd have thrown you in the box. If they catch you here it will be a riot. You'd be torn apart."

For a second the memory of racing toward the mountain with the men of the trade close behind takes her and she is there again, heart pounding, ears ringing with their cries, her injury along with fear attempting to paralyze her. The smell of burnt hair and skin invades her nose, sending a coil of nausea through her stomach.

"I remember my mother's hair," she says, swallowing bile. "At least I think I do. It's the only memory I have, the feeling of it sliding through my fingers. All my life I wanted to know who my parents were. I dreamed of meeting them and dreaded it because I hated them a little for letting me go, for not protecting me." She gazes up at him. "Now we might have a daughter. What should we do? Ignore the fact that I may be a mother. That you may be a father? Forget about her? Let them experiment on her?"

"I don't know!" Lee yells, startling her. His gaze flares, then softens. He moves to the bed and kneels near her feet. He grasps her hands gently. "I'm sorry. It's just—" He glances away. When he looks at her again his eyes shine with tears. "I made the mistake of leaving you once. I won't lose you again."

The ache in his voice renders her silent. "We'll figure this out together," she finally manages.

He wets his lips. "Let me bring the vial and a sample of your blood in and you can stay here in the house."

"What would you tell the doctor?"

"I don't know. That I want to make sure a boy is mine that the mother claims to be."

"He'd ask where the mother is. And besides, he'd think it was strange that you were already carrying your blood in something. He'd want to draw it fresh."

"Well, that would work too, right? If I'm the father then the blood would match."

"It would, unless Vivian was lying about that part. I'm sure they knew how we felt about each other even though we were careful. It would be more leverage to tell me you were the father even if you weren't." She looks down at their hands clasped in her lap. "I have to go myself, otherwise we won't be sure."

Lee's head drops forward in resignation before he stands, moving to the chair opposite her. "Okay. So how do we do it?"

"I don't know. When do you have to report to the factory?"

Lee glances at a clock ticking on the wall. "In a little over two hours."

"Then we'll have to think fast." Zoey twists the bedsheet in her hands, thoughts blurring into one another. She replays her entry into the city past the barricade and thinks about the hospital's position. "I know how we get out of the city and when we'll have to do it."

"The monorail at night."

"Yes."

"But that's really not the problem."

"No. I noticed the hospital and the building beside it share the same roofline. What if you went to the hospital today and unlocked the access to the roof, then in the evening we could cross from the building beside it and get to the top floor that way?"

Lee shakes his head. "Wouldn't work. That building is a huge apartment complex that a lot of the city's men took residence in. Someone would see us coming or going."

She twists the sheet harder. "How about the alley behind the hospital? Other entrances?"

"There's nothing back there but walls and windows and the other two entrances have a guard at them too."

"There has to be a way."

"I told you, these guys are thorough. They check in everyone at the munitions factory, and no one can even go to the bathroom without their say-so. They have radios they contact each other with. Most of the other men in the city are confined to houses or apartments."

Zoey wrings the sheet once more before releasing it. "Then we need a distraction of some kind. Something to draw the guards away from the doors and occupy them while we get inside."

Lee frowns and leans forward on the chair. As he does, her pants slide from the back making a loud thud on the hardwood floor. He turns, reaching down for the holster and handgun that have fallen free of her clothes. "You have a gun?"

"Of course. Did you think I was throwing rocks at people who were trying to hurt me?"

Lee pulls the pistol from its holster and studies it before glancing up at her as if she's a stranger. "They confiscated all the weapons they could find when they took over the city." He slides the gun back in its case, looking thoughtfully at it. "Say what you said before, about a distraction."

"We need something to draw them away while we get inside."

Lee sits motionless for several minutes before rising and placing her weapon on the chair. His gaze becomes unfocused. "Shower's in the next room, I'm sure you want to clean up. There's a box in the closet with some clothes that might fit you; not sure if they're the prior owner's daughter's. I'm going to make breakfast."

"Are you okay?"

"Fine. Need to think."

He leaves the room and she listens to him tread down the hall; the sound of cabinet doors opening and closing comes a moment later. Zoey sits on the edge of the bed in the blue morning light before moving to the bathroom.

She spends longer than she should beneath the scalding water, but can't get herself to shut it off. She imagines the last weeks washing away like the rest of the filth from her body and swirling down the drain into darkness. If only it were that easy.

When the water finally begins to run cold she steps from the shower and dries off. The large mirror above the sink shows her the first true image of herself she's seen in weeks.

A young woman looks back with the harsh gaze she's come to accept as her own. Her face is a little gaunt and there are hints of dark rings beneath her eyes. She runs a hand through her shorn hair, not liking or disliking its appearance. It's simply what is.

The box of clothes contains a pair of dark pants that are a little large for her. She cinches them tight with her belt before donning a gray button-up shirt that fits better. After some searching in Lee's dresser, she locates a pair of socks she only has to roll down once.

The smell of cooking food wafts from the stove when she enters the kitchen and sits at a short counter. Lee stands before two skillets, his hair tousled forward onto his forehead. She studies him, letting his appearance sink in. His skin is ruddier, as if he has spent much more time outside in the sun and wind, his hair uncut and long. And he's leaner than he was at the ARC, any extra weight he carried stripped down to muscle. The image of him above her in the hallway the night before comes unbidden. The dark shape of his trembling body, how the faint light had thrown shadows across his skin. His whispers in her ear.

I love you, Zoey. I love you.

"How hungry are you?"

She returns to the present. Lee watches her, a slightly bemused look on his face. "Starving," she says.

"It's not much. Potatoes and eggs. The eggs are kind of a specialty, though, since there's a limited amount each week at the store." He hands her a plate heaping with golden brown potatoes and three eggs cooked perfectly. Her stomach is an open hole inside her, and she shovels in two mouthfuls before the taste truly registers.

"This is amazing," she says, though it comes out mumbled through the food.

Lee laughs. "I think that was a compliment." He sets his plate beside hers and sits, eating slowly. They say nothing throughout the meal, though she notices he keeps slipping into a trance between bites, gaze locked on a blank wall across the kitchen. When they're done he stacks the plates and places them in the sink.

"Thank you. That was the best meal I've had in weeks."

"I'm not much of a cook, but I had to learn while Ray was sick." His voice trails off and he begins to wipe the countertop with a towel.

"Did you lose him?" she asks. He nods without looking up. "I'm sorry."

"It's okay. He definitely wouldn't have wanted any pity. He wasn't that kind of man." Lee stops cleaning and arranges the towel on a hanger. "I'm sorry about Eli. He was a good person."

Zoey swallows and bites the inside of her lip. "Thanks. He was very special."

The light outside continues to change, the blue graying until she can make out the next house over through the window. "You have to go soon."

"Yeah."

"What are we going to do?"

"I have an idea," Lee says haltingly. "But it's risky."

"I think anything we come up with will be risky."

"Very true. I don't know if it will work."

"Tell me."

He does and when he's finished she sits back in her chair, toying with the cuff of her shirt. "And you think you can build it?"

"I know I can. I'm just not sure I'll be able to smuggle everything I need back to the house tonight. But that's not even the most concerning part. The doctor is still the weak link. There's no guarantee he won't raise the alarm as soon as we're gone."

"From what I've learned, doctors from before were different than the ones at the ARC. They valued human life above all else." She pauses, sitting forward again. "I recently read something that said deep down people are generally good."

"Something written before the Dearth I'm assuming."

"Yes. But it was also during another terrible time, and the person who wrote it didn't give up hope for humanity."

"So you're saying we just have to trust the doctor won't yell for a soldier the moment we're gone?"

"I'm saying we have to believe not everyone's lost who they were before."

Lee brings a hand up to his forehead, pushing his hair back. He closes his eyes. "I still can't get my mind around it. That it might be true. That we might have . . ." He takes a deep breath and braces himself on the countertop and blinks. Zoey moves to him, grasping him around the waist as his balance falters.

"Here, sit down, it's okay," she says, guiding him to the floor. He's shaking but manages to put an arm around her.

"I'm sorry, it just hit me."

"It's okay."

"I'm not ready to be a father. I don't know anything."

She holds him, his head leaning on her shoulder. "We don't have to be afraid anymore," she says. "We'll face everything together."

Outside, the rumble of a truck nears and recedes, and the light brightens. Lee turns his face to hers, and slowly leans in, kissing her. She feels the need rise again inside her, the warming flow extending outward from her center to her limbs as if she's standing before a crackling fire. She begins to pull him closer but stops and strokes the side of his neck.

"I have to go," he says huskily. "But last night . . ."

"Yes. Later," she says, kissing him once more before standing and pulling him to his feet. He gives her a longing look before moving down the hall to the bedroom, a minute later returning dressed in different clothes. She walks with him to the front entry and he stops, framed there in the growing light of day. For a split second the overwhelming urge to run again steals over her. They could leave the city tonight, together, flee until they are somewhere safe and start their life.

Their life.

It has such a beautiful sound to it. But doubt would always be the third occupant of any room they shared. The unsaid wondering would be easy to ignore at first, she's sure. But time has a way of compacting ideas into dense, terrible things, and she knows eventually it would crush them both.

"Be careful," she says, forcing her voice to stay steady.

"I will. You too."

Then he is gone, the door shut behind him, leaving her in the utter silence of the house, so still and complete it's almost as if he was never there at all.

29

The day doesn't brighten past the early daylight hours.

The cloud-choked sky hangs like a low ceiling above the buildings Zoey can see on the street in front of the house. For the longest time, she sat in the kitchen, gazing out at the world, mind simply taking in the sight, no real thoughts processing. It was relaxing not thinking about anything. She tries to recall the last time she let herself mentally drift and can't. Maybe she's never done it, and the idea saddens her.

She washes her clothes in the downstairs bathroom, filling the tub with hot soapy water. The washer and dryer would have been faster but she doesn't want to risk someone passing by hearing the sound. And besides, she's had enough of washing laundry in machines. Ten lifetimes enough.

When her soiled clothing is relatively clean she drains the filthy water and hangs them on the shower-curtain rod. Upstairs she finds herself looking through the refrigerator. It's only been a few hours since she ate, but already she's hungry again. Ravenous. She finds something that looks like soup and after testing it, dives in and devours every last drop. She drinks several glasses of water before retrieving her handgun from the bedroom. At the kitchen table she sets about disassembling and cleaning it with a rag she found under the sink.

As her hands work, she has no respite from the thoughts that buffet her. What if Lee can't find everything they need at the factory? Or worse yet, he's able to locate all the pieces but gets caught bringing them out. What explanation could he give that would dissolve the guards' suspicions? Beyond that, she runs through the plan if they are able to execute it. What if the doctor doesn't have the equipment necessary to test the blood? What if he's unwilling to help them, even by force? What if . . .

She stops herself, realizing her hands have forgotten their purpose and sit folded in her lap. If there's one thing she's learned since her escape, it is there's no use in worrying about what will come until it does. There is only planning for possible eventualities, and even that can be futile and frustrating work.

When the weapon is clean she reloads it and brings it to the bedroom once again, setting it on the nightstand. Mist beads on the window, and for a time, she watches it form droplets that rush down the glass and out of sight before she lies on the bed. The linens smell like Lee, the scent of him so familiar she curls her hands into the loose blankets and breathes it in. A surety comes upon her then. Everything will be all right. Their plan will work; they'll find a doctor and he'll be able to tell them the truth about the baby.

They'll rescue her, their daughter.

Save her from that terrible place of walls and sterility.

She'll never forsake the girl to years like she spent in hopelessness and despair.

Never leave her behind like her parents had.

Never . . .

The sound of movement in the house brings her up through a collage of dreams so quickly it feels as if she's been physically jerked.

The room is dark, everything around her rounded shadows, and it takes her several dizzying seconds to remember where she is.

A soft scrape comes from the kitchen.

She reaches out, snagging the pistol from the nightstand, and then she's on her feet, padding quietly to the door.

She looks down the hallway and leans out, pointing the gun at the shape that stands at its end.

"Zoey?"

Her breath rushes out and she lowers the weapon at the sound of Lee's voice. "You scared me."

"Sorry," he says, flicking on a light above the kitchen counter. "I figured you were sleeping and didn't want to wake you." It's then that she realizes she's slept all afternoon and evening. Her body's sore from the sleep, but her head feels clear and rested. Lee moves around the kitchen, twitching blinds and curtains shut over the windows as she approaches.

"How did it go?"

"As well as it could. I got everything we need."

"Really?"

"Yeah. But I had to have one of the other workers help smuggle some of it out."

She stiffens. "What did you tell him?"

"Just that I was working on a home project. He was a little leery, but I promised him money from Ray's retirement stash he had in his apartment."

"Can you trust him?"

"Yes. Besides, he doesn't know anything about you. No one here does."

"You never even told Ray?"

He pauses at a window in the dining room. "No."

"Thank you."

He gives her a small smile and comes back to the table, digging in his coat pockets and laying out various pieces of equipment. "I had to disassemble it into as many pieces as I could. Even then I was half sure the soldiers would hear something clanking together when I left."

She gazes at the menagerie of screws, bolts, springs, and levers. In a million years she wouldn't be able to piece it together for what they need. Lee leaves the kitchen, returning a second later from the entry with a small toolkit he spreads out on the table. Immediately he begins assembling the parts, fingers moving deftly among the steel components as the apparatus begins to take shape.

Zoey watches him, the part of her that's always admired how Lee's mind works transfixed by the process. Once again the fact that she's here, standing beside him, stuns her. She smiles and moves to the stove, finding a kettle in one of the cupboards to heat some water.

"Do you have tea?"

"Mmm?" He looks up. "Uh, yeah. There should be some in the drawer left of the sink." She finds the packets and drops the bags into two cups, pouring the steaming water over them. When she sets his mug down beside him she's shocked to see the mechanism is almost fully together. Only one piece remains on the table, which he picks up and bolts into place, tightening it with a small ratchet.

"Done," he says, setting the tool down.

"How will it work on its own?"

"See this part here? That's a spring timer. Four winds and it will trigger the lever four times, which should be about right. Your gun goes here in this clamp." He demonstrates, and she watches the machine work, clicking and clacking before it falls silent.

"It's . . . perfect," she says.

"I don't know about perfect, but it should work."

They stare at the contraption until Zoey says, "What time do you think I should leave?"

"Somewhere between two and three tomorrow morning. It looks like it will be raining for a while, so that should give you some cover too."

She nods before pulling the blood vial from her pocket. "If something happens to me you need to take this."

"Nothing's going to happen."

"It's easy to say that, but things always happen. If something goes wrong, I'll hide it on the top floor of the building across from the hospital in the northwest corner of the ceiling. Find it and go through with the test."

"Zoey—"

"Promise me you will."

He sighs, looking down before meeting her gaze again. "I promise."

She reaches out and takes his hand, and they sit that way for some time, neither moving, taking comfort from each other's presence. Finally, Zoey stands and goes to the refrigerator. "Are you hungry? I have some leftover stew I can heat up."

"That sounds perfect."

"I don't know about perfect, but it should work," she says, smiling.

"I would eat just about anything right now. But first I'm going to shower, if you don't mind?"

She covers her mouth and nose. "Please do."

He narrows his eyes at her before moving down the hallway to the sound of her laughter. She removes the stew from the refrigerator where she stowed it earlier that morning and begins heating it in a pan. A sense of contentment, a rightness, surrounds her, and even with the knowledge that she'll have to leave in a few hours, she savors the moment. *This is what I have to hold on to. These little bits and pieces of warmth between the madness. Maybe that's all life really is.*

The stew bubbles and she sets the pan to the side, turning the stove off. She moves down the hallway and enters the bedroom to let Lee know the food is ready.

He stands at the sink in only a towel, the muscles of his back standing out as he braces himself there. For a second she thinks he's crying, but then he straightens and turns, pausing when he sees her.

"Are you okay?" she asks.

"Just thinking."

"About what?"

"About tomorrow and how I don't want you to go." He comes closer and she can't help that her gaze slides down his torso to where his skin disappears beneath the towel. He stops inches away and she can smell the soap he used as well as an underlying metallic odor she assumes is from the factory. It is familiar, and she realizes he used to smell like this sometimes at the ARC from working in one of the shops.

"I don't want to either, but we don't have a choice."

"No. We only have right now." His hand comes up and his fingers graze her hair. She touches it as well, suddenly self-conscious.

"I know it's ugly."

"There are a few things you'll never be. And ugly is one of them," he says, his breath tickling her cheek. She looks up at him and then his lips are brushing hers, softly at first, then with an urgency that she returns. They stay that way for a moment, embracing, and she can feel the cold speckles of water from his skin soaking into her shirt. Then they're moving toward the bed, the only light in the room coming from down the hall. It dapples his body with shadows of purple and black that shift as he helps her from her clothes.

This time it is slower, less frenetic, and her nerve endings hum in each place he touches her until she feels as if her body is lit from the inside. Lee pauses in his caresses, his fingers tracing the scar on her stomach where the Redeye's bullet entered. And with his touch, even the ugly wound tingles pleasurably. She anticipates the pain like the night before, but it is negligible, only a dulled memory, and in its place is a melting warmth that becomes a heightening desire like she's never felt before.

Again Lee starts to whisper her name, his words airy, breathless. "Zoey, I love you."

"I love you, too," she manages even as the pleasure surrounds her, encapsulates them both in a single span of time that lasts days and only seconds.

Then she's drifting and Lee's beside her, holding on to her as if she'll float away and saying something that comforts and allows her to fall into the soft folds of sleep. Something about never leaving her again.

◆　◆　◆

She opens her eyes sometime in the middle of the night, and by his breathing she knows Lee is awake as well. They rise and dress together before reheating the cold stew for a second time. The house is quiet around them as they eat, only the soft patter of rain and a ticking from the heating registers. When they're finished, she repacks her bag, adding the apparatus Lee assembled. It's bulky so she leaves behind a heavy sweatshirt and a pair of pants.

Zoey moves to the back door that she'd entered by two nights before. It seems like weeks ago now. Time has moved slower in the house with Lee. The rightness hasn't worn off, and when she opens the door a crack to the rainy night, a hollow ache forms inside her. The yearning to stay is strong, and the sensation that she's giving up something she's sought for so long is almost enough to make her shut the door again.

Instead she says, "Tonight."

Lee nods. "Tonight. Before you know it we'll be out of the city." She looks at him for a long time, committing every detail she can to memory before kissing him quickly. He tries to hold on to her but she's already turning and gone into the cold rain.

And as she crosses the little backyard to the break in the fence that will let her out into the surrounding neighborhood, she refuses to look back, even if it might be the last time she ever sees him.

30

The little steel man balances on the pedestal and rocks back and forth for what must be the thousandth time.

She had found the toy beside the desk in the office overlooking the hospital's entrance. It caught her attention after the first true light of day crept into the room, the stainless steel reflecting dimly through the layer of dust covering its surface. When she'd established the best place to wait the day out was the hall since it allowed her opportunity to escape in either direction, she'd carried the steel man and his stand with her, setting it on the floor as she rested against the wall.

Zoey watches him lean to and fro, his sharpened legs on the pedestal, a little curved wire in his hands with two spheres attached to the ends. She understands the mechanics of the toy, how the spheres are a counterbalance to the little man's body. It is mesmerizing to watch, the movement soothing to her nerves, which have calmed from the ordeal in the early morning hours.

After slipping away from Lee's home, she'd crossed two streets without a problem, not seeing so much as a guard in the distance. Then, as she was about to leave the safety of a deep doorway, a man had appeared without warning from around a corner only a dozen feet away. She'd fled without waiting to see if he would pass by her or not and he'd given chase with a startled yell. It took her three blocks of weaving in and out of alleys to find a suitable hiding place in a basement window alcove. He'd run straight past her and she'd doubled back, making her way without incident to the building she was in now. But for several hours she'd seen flashlights passing by on the street, and once the sound of two men talking several floors below her, their voices floating up the stairwell she'd propped open exactly for that reason. They had moved on not long after and she'd seen no more hurried movement in the streets since. Hopefully the soldiers had chalked it up to one of the city's men trying to flee, who, after being pursued, returned to his house or apartment building out of fear.

The steel man slows and she reaches out, setting him in motion again. She understands him. How he balances on the narrowest point without any safe way down.

Outside, the weather looks poisonous even though the rain has stopped. Clouds roil above the buildings, and their reflections paint every glass surface in tones of gray. Zoey draws out the small watch Lee had given her while she packed, and checks it, internally cringing after seeing only an hour has passed. It is barely after one and she'll have to wait until seven o'clock to start their plan in motion. Lee will appear on the street below and that will be her signal to climb down the stairs to the alley and put the machine beneath the tarp concealing a stack of wooden pallets.

After that it will be up to fate.

She shifts on the floor, turning the timepiece over; all at once it is the watch she saw in the mass grave when they passed through the desert in search of the Fae Trade. At first she hadn't recognized all the bones for what they were. Maybe it had been her mind's way of protecting itself but the shock of that much death still resonates within her. Of course it would, since she caused something like it only days later.

Zoey stands, moving out of the hallway, trying to leave the thoughts behind, and into the office. The two guards are still at their positions before the hospital entrance, and the rest of the street is quiet. She returns to the hall and sits again, stifling a yawn behind one hand. She shouldn't sleep, shouldn't take the chance, but exhaustion from the last weeks has taken its toll. Her wounded foot aches and she props it up on her bag. If only Chelsea were here. She would have a remedy for everything.

For the nth time she wonders what the others are doing right now. Have they come to terms with her departure? Maybe they've returned to Ian's house. Maybe they're still looking for her. She hopes for the former, flicking the balancing man into motion. His silent movement draws her heavy eyelids down, and as she succumbs to sleep her fingers open and the watch slides to the floor.

◆ ◆ ◆

Zoey wakes with a start, the vestiges of a nightmare sliding away in shredded images.

The group lying dead on a highway. Lee saying her name through a mouthful of blood. The baby disappearing in the tank as it turns opaque.

She grounds herself in the present. The hallway is much dimmer and her legs remain asleep even as she tries to rise, panic sending a flood of adrenaline through her system.

The steel man is motionless on his pedestal and she swears under her breath, cursing herself for letting rest overtake her so easily. She finds the watch on the floor and holds it at an angle to the wan light filtering in through the office windows.

6:49 p.m.

A sigh of relief rushes from her. She hasn't overslept. With hurried movements she draws the apparatus from her bag and examines it, making sure she remembers how to set it. A few more minutes and she'll stand near the windows and wait for Lee to appear. If anything is wrong he'll signal her by running his hand through his hair twice.

Swallowing the sour taste of sleep, she reaches back into the bag to retrieve her water bottle but stops.

A click echoes up through the far stairwell followed by a quiet cough.

Zoey stiffens, hand drawing her pistol as her vision begins to throb with her pulse.

The hallway is dark, cut only by fans of light coming from the interspersed doorways.

A murmured word floats up the stairwell. The scratch of a boot.

She climbs to her feet, her senses screaming. Only one other direction out, the opposite way down the second set of stairs. She starts to move but stops, trying to gather her bag.

No time.

Instead she grabs Lee's machine and jogs down the hallway.

A flashlight beam slices the darkness at the end, lighting the doorway from below.

She's trapped.

Zoey skids to a stop, frozen with indecision. Fight? No, it would ruin everything. They would be lucky to get a block without being captured or cut down. Hide? But where?

She glances back the way she came and sees light growing outside the corridor. They're seconds away. The room to her left is dark, no visible windows. She steps inside, pushing the door shut without a sound.

The smell hits her like a slap.

Something is rotting in the room, the scent nearly overpowering. Her head swims with it and her stomach clenches, nearly forcing her to double over.

Light seeps from the gap beneath the door.

She moves deeper into the space and her foot brushes something solid, her hand finding a desktop.

As her eyes adjust she sees the room isn't large. In the corner is a narrow closet beside two file cabinets, the desk she leans on taking up most of the space. Two shapes poke out from where someone would sit.

Legs and feet.

She steps over them and sees the man has been dead a long time.

He was large in life and is larger still in death, his stomach bloated to twice its normal size, skin a splotchy purplish green. He is bare from the waist up and a dark stain covers the wall beyond his head. The shape of a pistol lies near his outstretched arm.

"Got a bag here and some supplies. Looks fresh," a voice says in the hallway, and she stiffens.

"I told you I heard someone yell," another man responds. Zoey grimaces. Her nightmare. She must have cried out while sleeping.

"Yeah, yeah. Check the rooms. Gotta be close." A door bangs open in the hall a second later.

Her eyes scan the room. There's nowhere to hide where they won't spot her immediately. Her gaze drops to the dead man.

Without thinking she steps over him, the smell of decay like a physical presence this close. The leg space beneath the desk is small but it's large enough for her to fit. Zoey crouches, sliding past the body, cold skin brushing her hand as she squirms into the alcove.

Another door crashes. Closer. Maybe the next room down.

She sets Lee's machine on the floor and reaches out, finding the dead man's arm, and drags him closer.

The skin on his forearm comes loose and slides free of the muscle beneath. It peels off like a sock in her hands. She gags but doesn't release her grip. The body inches toward her, filling the gap under the desk. Zoey yanks one more time and the corpse gurgles wetly, a soft exhale of gas belching from its open mouth.

Bile coats her tongue but she swallows, tucking herself in close to the body as the door to the room opens.

"Holy fuck. What the hell is that?"

Zoey holds a breath of rotting air in. Footsteps pad closer, light coming with them. Is she hidden enough that he won't see her? She presses herself into the bloated body, ignoring the softness of the skin, the cool dampness of the floor beneath her.

"God Almighty," the voice says, but it is muffled as if the man is covering his mouth and nose.

"What is it?" someone says from the doorway.

"Dead guy. Dead a long time."

How long has it been since she checked the watch? Two minutes? Three? Has she missed Lee already? She can almost feel the seconds ticking by, their opportunity dwindling with each one. Zoey feels the body shake and realizes the man must've kicked it. More gas erupts from it and she hears a deep grunt from the soldier only feet away. "I'm gonna puke, move it."

The light fades and the sound of retching fills the hall.

"*Oooo*, he is ripe," the other man says. "Get your shit in order, Jimmy. Let's go to the next floor. Maybe our guy got ahead of us."

Zoey listens to a muttered reply before the booted feet trail away toward the closest stairwell. When she can hear only silence again she pushes at the corpse, rolling it away. One hand sinks into the doughy flesh and she nearly screams when her middle finger pierces the gelatinous skin.

Gagging again she grasps the machine and climbs free of the recess. The door is open and she steps into the hall, pointing her handgun both ways before crossing to the next office street side.

It is dark enough for several of the working streetlamps to have kicked on, pouring yellowed light onto the sidewalks. Down the block a single figure walks straight toward her building. Lee's hands are in his pockets and he makes no move to touch his hair.

It's time.

Zoey hurries back the way she came, heading away from the stairwell the soldiers took. She leaves the contents of her bag where they are strewn and launches herself down the flights of stairs. The taste of decay is thick in her mouth and she spits, rounding the last turn before stopping at the street-level door.

The fresh air gusts against her face as she checks to make sure no one occupies the alleyway.

It's clear.

Lee will be at the mouth of the alley in less than thirty seconds.

She rushes to the tarped pallets and lifts the tattered cover, dropping to her knees.

The machine feels heavy in her hands as she begins clamping it to the most solid-looking pallet. When it's secure she places her gun in the *V* at the top of the apparatus and twists the knob on its side, locking the grip into place so that the barrel points to the rear of the alley.

The ammunition tester, Lee had explained, was used to safely cycle test batches of new ammo through a weapon. If a round was manufactured incorrectly and caused the handgun it was being fired with to detonate or malfunction, the user wouldn't be harmed. The timer to trigger the gun without a person manning it was Lee's own design.

Zoey twists the timer four times, releases it, and pulls the tarp back into place.

She runs.

The mouth of the alley looms as she draws a small knife from her pocket and slices the blade across her hairline before yanking her hat low.

Warmth trickles down her forehead, gathers in her eyebrows. She hesitates several strides from the street, sure that she hadn't set the ammo tester correctly.

A gunshot explodes behind her and she lurches forward the last two steps, falling to the sidewalk.

There is a brief pause and another shot echoes through the alley.

Yells come from across the street and there is the scratch of shoes beside her.

Hands grasp her shoulders and Lee whispers, "Are you okay?" She barely nods. Another gunshot booms and on cue, Lee starts to yell.

"There's a guy with a gun in the alley! He's got a gun!" Zoey risks a glance at the hospital.

The men guarding the entrance are running toward them, weapons at the ready. As she ducks her head again, blood flows into her eyes and the world becomes a dark red.

The last shot resounds as the soldiers come to a halt nearby. "What the hell's going on?" one asks.

"There's someone in the alley with a gun," Lee says breathlessly, dragging her partially upright. "This guy's wounded."

Zoey places one hand against her face and through the haze of blood sees both soldiers staring down their barrels in the direction she came.

"Bennett, circle down the block and contact Daniels on the roof. See if he's got eyes on whoever it is," the closest man says.

"I'll get him to the hospital," Lee says, pulling Zoey to her feet. He slings one of her arms around his shoulder and guides her across the street. She does her best to hobble, still hiding her face. As they near the doors she glances back, wiping blood from her eyes. Both soldiers have disappeared, and yells come from up the block as more men race into view.

Then they're through the doors and in a spacious lobby.

A man sits at a counter thirty feet away, eyes wide and staring at them. Lee motions to her. "He's been wounded. Where's the doctor?"

"Fourth floor," the man answers. "What's going on out there?"

"No idea," Lee says, ushering her through a doorway that reveals a stairwell. When they're out of the man's sight Lee releases her and they jog side by side up the flights, their footfalls echoing hollowly. At a door marked with a four above it, they slow, Lee opening it and peering out before looking at her.

"You're really bleeding. Are you all right?"

"Fine. Cut a little deeper than I meant to."

"Okay. It looks clear."

The tiled corridor is empty and eerily quiet. Zoey swipes at her eyes and forehead again, the sleeve of her coat coming away bloody. Doors open on both sides of the hallway but light spills from only three of them. Thirty yards away is a curved countertop and across from it the last of the three lit rooms.

A shadow darkens the floor inside the doorway and a moment later a man with steel gray hair steps into view. His head is down and he's studying a clipboard in his hands. He doesn't look up until they're ten feet away.

"Doctor," Lee says. "We need your help."

"What's this about?" the man asks scanning Lee's face before traveling on to Zoey. His eyes widen at the sight of the blood. "What happened?"

"We need to speak with you in private. Which floor do you use for testing?"

The doctor frowns. "Testing what?"

"Blood."

"I don't understand. Now if you're injured," he says, motioning to Zoey, "we should get you in a room and . . ." His words trail off as she takes her hat off and steps closer. "My God," he whispers.

"Doctor, we need your help and there's no time to explain," she says. "Please."

He gazes at her for several more seconds before blinking. "This way." He moves past the lit doorway, which houses a single bed, the occupant lying propped up on pillows, his arm bandaged from the shoulder down to his fingers. He doesn't look at them as they file by.

The doctor stops at an elevator and touches the up button, glancing at Zoey again before looking away.

"Are there any guards on the top floor?" she asks as the doors slide open and they step inside.

"One man does rounds every hour. He came through twenty minutes ago," the doctor says.

"If you're lying it won't end well for you," Lee says.

"I'm not lying, young man."

The elevator chimes and the doors open to an almost identical hallway. The doctor doesn't hesitate, moving quickly out and to the left. Zoey and Lee follow, her attention focused on the doctor, but unease at the surroundings keeps making her glance over her shoulder and into each darkened room they pass.

The lab at the end of the hall gives her a jolt when the doctor flips an extra set of lights on. It is strangely similar to the fifth level of the ARC. Along one wall behind a bank of floor-to-ceiling glass are several partitions, each containing counters full of machines and equipment. The doctor stops beside the first one, turning to face them.

He looks them over, dismay creasing his aged features, and it's then that she realizes he's much older than she first thought. "What's this all about?" he asks.

"We need to test this against my blood," Zoey says, holding out the vial.

The doctor takes it. "Direct relative?"

"Maybe. Can you do it?"

He sighs. "Yes. But it will take a little time."

"How long?"

"Twenty minutes, a half hour? I'm not sure. It's been a long time since I did this." He sets the vial down and moves to a compact machine sitting beneath a cabinet, drawing it out into the light. The top opens, revealing a small wheel with clear oblong tubes attached to it. He draws one of these out and twists it open at its center.

"What is that?" Zoey asks.

"The machine is a bioanalyzer. In the early days of the Dearth, NOA made it a requirement for every major hospital to carry at least one. They were developed as a rapid DNA-testing device for determining blood relation in patients." As he speaks his hands work at the vial. There is a quiet click and the vial opens, a cap at one end snapping free. He pours the blood into the tube and shuts it once more. After replacing it in the wheel he opens a drawer, drawing out a plastic sealed syringe. "I'll need a sample."

Zoey takes her coat off and draws up the sleeve of her shirt, exposing her pale forearm. The old man is gentle, hands steady and sure as he slides the needle into a barely visible vein. She doesn't even feel it.

"So tell me," he says, not looking up, "why would a person such as yourself ever risk coming to this place?"

She takes a long time answering. "The truth."

He nods, pressing a cotton ball over the point of the syringe as he withdraws it. "Good a reason as any, I suppose."

"We'd like his blood tested as well," she says, motioning to Lee. The doctor studies him briefly before depositing her blood into another tube. When he's drawn Lee's blood and labeled each of the tubes, he pushes a button and the wheel recedes into the machine. He fold ups a digital screen from one side and presses two buttons.

The machine whirs quietly.

"I can only guess at what this all means," the old man says, busying himself with several plastic-wrapped items before turning to Zoey. "But I'm not going to ask. My mother used to say wishing for things out loud broke the spell and your wishes wouldn't ever come true." He opens some packages and spins the cap off a bottle. "I'm going to clean that head wound if it's all right with you."

"Okay."

Again his hands are gentle and sure. He dabs at the cut she made in the alley, some of the disinfectant stinging, but the pain keeps her alert, listening for the ding of the elevator arriving above the bioanalyzer's humming.

The doctor finishes cleaning the cut and places two small bandages over it.

Zoey touches his work lightly. "Thank you."

"You're welcome."

"Why are you helping us?" She asks the question before she's truly registered thinking it.

He pauses at a trash bin before tossing the plastic wrappers inside. "Because you need it."

The machine on the counter beeps softly. The doctor moves to the screen and touches it three times. Its whirring begins again.

"What's it doing?" Lee asks.

"Phase one is complete. It separated the white blood cells from the red. There's no DNA in red blood cells so it needs to divide the two before it can analyze and compare the samples."

"How accurate is it?"

"Very. Ninety-nine point nine percent. The machine scans specific portions of the DNA and superimposes them. There's an extremely low error rate. The program will match any DNA that it's given. Fifty percent match between two means blood relation. Less than five percent is no relation."

"You know a lot about this," Zoey says.

The doctor smiles sadly. "I've lived in the city all my life. There were a lot of people here when the Dearth hit. I ran that machine many times during those years. That was when I still believed NOA was trying to help."

"What made you change your mind?"

"When they started bringing women and children here in handcuffs to be tested."

A low roar comes from outside and Lee hurries to the window, glancing down. "Four trucks just went by."

"They're not stopping?" Zoey asks.

"No. They headed toward the pier."

"Those gunshots were yours then?" the doctor asks. Zoey looks at Lee and neither of them say anything. "I hope you didn't hurt anyone."

"We didn't," she says, glancing down the deserted hallway. An itching sense has begun to build on the back of her neck, extending into her hair. She reaches up, swiping fingers across her scalp, but the feeling doesn't recede. If anything it strengthens.

They're running out of time.

"How much longer?" Lee says, coming away from the windows.

"Not sure." The doctor moves to the machine and shrugs. "There's no countdown or anything. I can't tell."

"We have to go soon," Zoey says, putting words to the sensation prickling her scalp.

"I know," Lee says.

"Will you tell anyone?" she asks, looking at the doctor.

He meets her gaze and holds it, unflinching. "I just bandaged a wound for you. You're my patient, and that means I'm bound by oath in confidentiality."

Zoey's lips tighten in a smile. "Thank you."

"It's my job."

There is a louder hum, like a fan speeding up, followed by a short chiming.

They all look at the machine. The doctor walks toward it and touches the screen.

"It's finished." He glances at her, an unreadable expression on his face. She crosses the room, Lee to her right, not moving any closer.

Her heart pummels the inside of her chest.

She's never been this afraid. Not in the box. Not when she'd been shot. Not even when she thought she'd never walk again.

The fear is in her lungs, filling them up so she can't breathe.

The doctor tilts the screen toward her and she reads it.

Sample—Subject 1, DNA Segment Span 1–15

Sample—Mother, Segment Percentage Match: 50%

Sample—Father, Segment Percentage Match: .04%

Zoey's mouth opens.

She tries to breathe. Can't.

Tries to say something, anything. Can't.

She's frozen, unable to comprehend what the screen is telling her. She tears her gaze from the digital numbers and looks at the doctor. His mouth is a thin line and there's an apologetic look in his eyes.

"What's it say?" Lee asks. His voice is weak, as if he doesn't have enough air.

Zoey swallows, shimmers of light trying to invade the edges of her vision. She looks at Lee, blinking the spangles away.

"We're her parents," she says.

Lee's face is bone white, the look of shock there something she can handle, but the relief that floods his features a moment later rends her heart in half, and the pieces are two different times: before she lied to him, and after.

She realizes then that he was terrified of being the father, but even more afraid that he wasn't.

He starts across the room, arms reaching out to embrace her, but a sound stops him, a sound that sends a lance of dread straight to her core.

The ding of the elevator fades as the doors open to the hallway.

31

Zoey watches, skin prickling with fear, as two soldiers step off the elevator and turn their way.

Her hand goes to her back out of reflex, brushes the empty holster. Nothing. No way to defend themselves.

The men's posture straightens. They've spotted the three of them.

She glances around the room. There is a single way out, through the doorway they entered. She turns, looking for a weapon. There are only chairs and partitions and medical equipment. Maybe there's a scalpel somewhere in one of the drawers but what would a blade do against the rifles the guards carry?

Her gaze locks onto Lee's and he shakes his head.

The men enter the room, weapons up, eyes hard behind them.

"Don't do anything stupid," one of them says. The doctor steps forward, hands out before him.

"Please, they were just trying to get medical help." The guard snaps his rifle around, its stock connecting with the old man's face.

He falls to the floor and doesn't move.

"You bastards," Lee says.

"Hands on your head."

Zoey glances at Lee again and they both thread their fingers together atop their heads. The men approach and pat them down.

"God she's young," one of them says, and shoves her from behind. She stumbles forward, and she would run in any other scenario, make a break for it now and take her chances if it weren't for Lee. If something were to happen to him she wouldn't be able to bear it.

The men usher them into the elevator and Zoey has a split-second view of the lab before they're shoved inside the car, the bioanalyzer's screen still glowing with the words and numbers.

They ride to the ground floor in silence but when the doors open there is a chatter of voices. A dozen soldiers stand in the lobby talking over one another; a thin, unarmed man, perhaps five years older than Lee, waits outside their circle. The man's eyes register Lee, then Zoey, and his eyes widen slightly.

All of the soldiers stop talking at once, and it's then that Lee swears and lunges forward before being yanked back by one of the soldiers.

"Ollie! You piece of shit!" Lee screams. "How could you?"

The thin man shakes his head as their captors lead them past and to the outside door. "Knew you were up to something, Lee, but didn't know it was this big."

"Why?" Lee asks, voice weak and hoarse.

"I'm tired of this place. Going with these guys when they leave so thought I'd start off my employment with an act of goodwill." The doors open and the night air streams in, cooling the lobby. "I'll help myself to the money in Ray's apartment you owe me. Don't think you'll be needing it anymore," Ollie shouts after them as they're shoved outside.

A truck waits at the curb, idling roughly. Two new men come forward and boost them into its rear, and the soldiers who discovered them in the hospital follow.

Zoey waits and watches them as the vehicle pulls away. Could she signal Lee somehow? Get him to move at the same time as she does? Maybe they could jump out the back of the truck and lose the men, hide somewhere until they were able to sneak out of the city like they planned.

But she knows it won't work; Lee's head hangs and his hands lie loose and open on his thighs, a look of wondrous despair on his face. Zoey reaches out, drawing the barrels of each guard toward her, but she doesn't stop. She grips Lee's hand.

He looks at her, but only for a second before staring back at the truck's bed. "I'm so sorry," he whispers.

"It's okay."

"It's not. I shouldn't have trusted him. He must've followed me and saw us go into the hospital."

"It's not important."

"How can you say that?"

"Because it's done. Nothing we can do about it."

"But I—"

"Shut up, both of you," one of the guards says. Zoey stares at him and he holds her gaze for a beat before looking out at the dark street sliding away behind them. Lee gives her hand a squeeze and she returns it, the memory of the test results slamming back into her all at once.

Lee isn't the father.

She lied to him. One of the few people she trusts and loves. But she couldn't get herself to utter the words, to crush him like that.

Even though the conception was completely medical, it still sends a shudder through her to imagine anyone but Lee as the father. But the real question now is if it's not Lee, then who is it?

She makes an effort to coax her thoughts out of the tangle they've become, but everything is a jumbled mess. And it doesn't help that their escape is lost, the chance destroyed as quickly as it presented itself. But there has to be another way, some kind of option she hasn't recognized yet. There is always weakness even within the greatest strength.

The truck slows and lurches to a stop. The smell of the ocean is stronger, and when the soldiers motion them to the pavement, she sees why.

They stand at the edge of a pier, dark waves crashing against the rocky shoreline.

"Move," one of the men says, pointing with his weapon to a set of stairs descending out of sight.

"Why are we going down to the water?" Zoey asks as they walk to the edge of the pier. *To shoot you both and drop you in the ocean,* she answers herself.

"Because it's the only way to get out there," the other soldier says, nodding toward the shadow of the ship in the harbor.

◆ ◆ ◆

The room they leave her in is made entirely of steel, one bulkhead curved slightly near the floor. There are no windows.

Zoey rubs the place on her arm where the guard grabbed her, forced her into the room as she tried to keep Lee in sight, but he was already being dragged in the opposite direction down the narrow hallway on the ship's second level. He'd yelled something to her, but his words had been cut off as the man escorting him jammed his fist into Lee's stomach, doubling him over.

Then she'd been pushed into the room, the door locking tight behind her.

Zoey grasps the door's handle and strains against it. It barely moves. She turns, inspecting the space.

A low bed is bolted to one wall, a bare mattress, no pillow. There is a bathroom so small she barely fits inside, the door missing, nothing else except dust and a few floating cobwebs in one corner. She searches the floors, corners, ceiling. There is nothing loose or moveable anywhere, the only break in the uniformity of the gray metal, a wall grate much too small to crawl through, even if she were able to pry it open.

Zoey sits on the bed. The tension of her muscles makes her body ache and she tries to relax them but fails. The ship moves ever so slightly, causing her to sway. And even as she tries to focus on the threat before her, the impossible task of escaping not only the ship manned with armed men everywhere, but then the sea and city itself afterwards, the memory of the digital screen arrives once again. She had been so stricken with shock at Lee's test results she hadn't truly absorbed the ramifications of her own.

I have a daughter.

I am a mother.

No question now, no doubt. It's true, just as I felt it always was from the moment I saw Vivian's message.

She finally sags with the knowledge, muscles giving up their rigidity. Her helplessness is only compounded by the thought of a tiny life locked away in an artificial womb, at the complete mercy of those surrounding her, those who would have no qualms testing her uniqueness, the miracle of her existence. They may have already begun their examinations, begun to poke and prod before her daughter has even taken her first breath of air or felt the sun on her face.

Zoey comes back to herself, gripping the door handle, twisting it with all her strength.

It turns in her hand. She steps back, surprised and elated as she pulls it open.

A dark-haired Asian man stands in the doorway, surprise locking him in place.

A second passes, their gazes fused, before Zoey swings a fist at him.

He blocks it, not without effort, managing to pin her arm to his body. With a shift of weight, he sends her reeling back. She's already resetting herself, planning a strike at his groin with a kick, when he holds out his hands and speaks.

"Stop. I'm not going to hurt you."

She pauses, seeing two men behind him in the hall holding guns. She straightens and takes a step back. The man nods once and flicks a hand. The men split, disappearing to either side of the door, which he shuts quietly behind him.

"My name is Hiraku." When she doesn't say anything he asks, "May I have yours?"

She debates before answering. "Zoey."

"Zoey." He inclines his head. "I'm glad to meet you."

"What do you want with us?"

"To talk."

"Talk? That's it?"

"That depends."

"On what?"

"On what you have to say."

Zoey swallows. "Let us go. Please."

"What were you doing in the hospital?"

"I injured my head." She points to the cut near her hairline. "Lee was helping me."

"How do you know one another?" She remains silent, looking past his shoulder. "Is it from the place where Lee says he grew up?" Still she says nothing. "I will assume that is correct. Lee told me that all the women are gone, that they were taken."

She returns his gaze, calculating if she could overcome him. He outweighs her by at least a hundred pounds, maybe more. And though he must be nearing sixty years old, he is solidly built across the chest and shoulders.

"I see you judging me, and I can assure you if you attack me again, you will lose. All I want is information, Zoey. Please. Are the women gone like Lee said?"

"Why do you want to know?"

"Because I can help. I'm able to father female children. This"—he gestures around at the ship—"this is all because of an accident that made me who I am. I have an obligation to make a difference if I can. And the men who have followed me believe in what will come if we can change things."

"If you want to change things, let us go."

Hiraku sighs, looking at the floor. "I cannot do that until you tell me what I want to know. If you won't tell me, I have no choice."

"There's always a choice."

"That is what people say who have not seen the darkness of the world."

Hiraku turns and exits the room without looking back. The door locks with a solid click, leaving Zoey alone with the blank walls that seem so much closer than before.

32

Hiraku finds Shirou in his quarters, the other man standing shirtless near his bed.

He can't help looking at the network of scars crossing Shirou's torso. They are like a map chronicling the years since they first met, each one containing a story, a fight, and he remembers every one; he knows his own body carries much of the same timeline. But there are other, much older scars that Shirou has never spoken about, not in all the years they've known one another, and Hiraku has never asked. Some memories are better unshared, left to weaken and rot in the past.

He closes the door as Shirou dons his shirt. "Something wrong?" the younger man asks.

Hiraku moves to the nearest seat and lowers himself into it, feeling every minute of his age. *It must end soon,* he thinks. *Under pressure something always breaks, and before much longer it will be me.*

"Yes, my friend, I'm afraid there is."

"What is it?"

"The man who was repairing the munitions factory was just found in the hospital with a woman. A young woman."

"What? How did she get here?"

"She won't say, but I must apologize, I haven't been entirely truth-ful as of late. When I first brought the man to the factory to see if he could repair the machines, I told him of my accident, of our journey. He said that he had grown up in the very place I spoke of and that all the women were gone, had escaped, and that there were none left."

Shirou's face darkens and he slowly sits on the edge of his nar-row bed. "How can that be? What type of force could overcome their defenses?"

"I don't know."

"He must be lying."

"I would agree, except for the presence of this woman. She is young, too young to have come from anyplace but the one we seek." Hiraku reaches into his shirt pocket and draws out the folded paper. He holds it delicately, beginning to unfold it, but stops. "Neither of them will talk. But if this is true, if the women are gone, we are finished. Every man who has followed us, all of their sons, each life we took to get where we are, it is all for nothing." Without really meaning to, he drops the folded paper on the floor. It lands without a sound, inconsequential, as if what is held there is already useless. They are quiet for a time, neither of them moving, until Shirou breaks the stillness and picks up the paper. He stands and comes to Hiraku's side before dropping to one knee.

"You are my oldest friend. I consider you a brother and would even if my own hadn't been taken from me when I was a child. You have led us admirably and made hard decisions that kept us alive." Shirou grasps Hiraku's hand in his own, placing the paper in his palm. "Do not despair before it is necessary."

Hiraku closes his fingers over the paper, feeling its coarseness, the rough tangibility bringing him back to the present. "I'm not sure I can do what is necessary."

Shirou's gaze doesn't waver. "Then you must let me."

◆　◆　◆

Zoey's eyes open, and she realizes she's no longer alone.

She had feigned sleep shortly after Hiraku left her, wanting to lull their captors into thinking she would be defenseless if they were to come for her.

And now they have.

She shifts her gaze to the wall, her senses humming.

Two distorted shadows shrink and become the shapes of men coming closer and closer to the bed.

Wait.

Wait.

Wait.

Zoey flips herself over and swings a wild kick. She aimed a little low and it catches the man reaching for her feet in the throat. He chokes, staggering back, and nearly falls into the bathroom.

The other man tries to snag her wrists but she rolls free of the bed, slinging an elbow at his crotch. The blow only partially lands but he lets out a muffled woof of air, bending over.

Then she's on her feet, lunging for the door.

Get out, get a weapon, get Lee.

She's through the entry and slamming the door shut to lock the men in when she sees him. A compact Asian man who looks as if his parentage was mixed. That's all she discerns before he grasps her by the neck.

He is strong, fingers biting deep into the side of her throat. Her pulse slams in her ears, louder with each second as his grip tightens. She tries to break free but he holds fast and gray mist forms at the corners of her vision.

Her legs weaken and she starts to fall.

He catches her, holds her upright, and begins marching her down the narrow corridor as if she weighs nothing. Consciousness returns almost at once, but the weakness won't leave her legs and arms. She coughs, blinking, looking for anything she can use as a weapon as they move.

"Don't," the man says. "It will only be harder for you. Just walk."

Though she continues to search for something that can help her, she does what he says. They move to a set of steel-grated steps that lead down to a lower level. Pipes, wiring, and bulky panels marked with large dark text surround them. They pass through a claustrophobic tunnel in which she has to duck her head before she's stopped by the man's hand on her shoulder. The wall beside them is smooth with only half a dozen pipes threading through it overhead. Two doors are set five paces apart, and it is toward the right one she's guided. The man opens the door, keeping a firm hold on her shoulder.

The room is perhaps four feet deep by eight feet long, the ceiling a mass of cables and conduits, several with red handles attached to their sides. The left wall is made of a clear plastic, thick enough that it warps her vision at its corners from this angle. In the middle of the little room is a tall steel chair.

The man pushes her inside even as she tries to recoil.

Zoey stumbles over the doorway lip and catches herself on the chair. It is unnaturally warm in the space, the air cloying and hard to breathe. Spinning, she tries to bring the chair up in a whirling blow, but it is bolted to the floor and only utters a stilted squawk.

The man laughs and enters the room as she steps around the chair, keeping it between them. "You are a warrior, like me. I admire that, an unwillingness to be broken."

Zoey watches him, glancing to the handgun on his hip. "What do you want?"

The man smiles, and it is cold. "To break you."

He moves faster than anyone she's ever seen. Faster than Eli, faster than Meeka. In a single stride he is around the chair and has an arm encircling her neck.

He pivots in a tight circle, taking her with him, and his strength is uncanny again; there is no way she could overpower him.

Steel digs into her spine before she's lifted up onto the chair's seat. Zoey flings a fist back in a weak attempt at a strike and it is caught, bent around the back of the chair and secured there. A moment later her other wrist is tied as well. She struggles and manages to slide to her feet, but the pressure on her shoulder joints is too much, and she climbs back to the seat, panting.

The man steps in front of her, tipping his head to one side. "Thank you for complying." When she doesn't say anything he continues. "My name is Shirou, and I am here for one purpose: to listen to what you're going to tell me. I'm not going to repeat what we want from you; you already know. Remember, the faster you speak, the faster this will all be over."

He leaves the room, locking the heavy door behind him. Zoey takes several deep breaths, heart still booming like gunfire in her chest. She looks around the room, reassessing it again. The ceiling is low, only two feet over her head. The pipes above her sweat and drip and the heat she felt earlier is stronger, radiating from above. Steam or hot water must be running through them. She twists her wrists against the restraints but they hold fast, some kind of plastic straps. Her feet reach to the transparent barrier and she pushes as hard as she can. The bolts in the floor groan and the chair shifts back an inch. She rocks forward and back, throwing all her strength and weight behind the movement each time.

After what seems like an hour, she lets her feet fall and rest on the chair's lower rung. Sweat runs down the sides of her face and drips from her chin. She is wrung out, adrenaline fading, leaving her muscles weak and spent. As her breathing comes back to normal, she takes a second to look through the partition at the room beyond.

It is twice the size of her own with a steel track attached to the ceiling running through the middle. On the floor is a large bin full of water, a cable attached to one side that snakes to a control panel in one wall. Otherwise the space is empty.

As she's readying herself for another assault on the chair the door in the other room opens.

Lee is shoved through, hands bound before him with iron manacles.

He nearly stumbles on the bin of water but rights himself, his eyes finally finding her through the barrier as Shirou enters the room.

"Zoey!" His voice echoes loud and clear through a vent between the two rooms and he tries to move toward her but is struck by Shirou on the jaw. The blow sends him off balance but he remains on his feet. Another man appears, and as she watches, helpless to stop them, he assists Shirou in hauling Lee to the bin and hoisting him above it. They quickly latch the manacles around Lee's wrist to the track in the ceiling. He begins to struggle again, kicking at the men and swearing, but they move out of his reach. Lee quiets, his body growing slack. Shirou's assistant walks to the control panel in the wall and puts his hand on a dial there, watching with disinterest as Lee twists again, trying to keep his eyes on both of them. As his body slowly relaxes his bare feet dip into the water in the bin.

Zoey's eyes widen as she sees Shirou glance at her before nodding to the other man. The assistant twists the dial.

Lee screams, his body going rigid before he yanks his feet up from the water. The muscles in his arms bulge, straining to hold him up as he draws his knees to his chest.

"What are you doing to him!" Zoey yells.

"There is a small charge of electricity being fed into the water. If either of you tell me what I need to hear it will be turned off," Shirou says over Lee's strangled curses.

"Stop it!" Zoey says, yanking at her restraints until she feels her wrists begin to bleed.

Shirou approaches the clear divider. "Save him. Tell me."

An acidic burning fills her. The words are there at the back of her throat, yearning to come forward. She can save him from more pain and all she has to do is speak.

"No, Zoey! Don't tell them! Don't!" Lee yells, knees still pulled to his chest.

"You are strong," Shirou says. "Both of you are. But eventually your muscles will give out and your feet will touch the water."

"Please," she says, shifting her gaze from Lee to Shirou. "Please stop." But he doesn't look at her, merely contemplates the blank wall near the door.

A minute passes.

Two.

Lee begins to shake, arms quivering, face wrenched with pain.

Gradually his legs begin to drop.

An agonized moan comes from him as his feet extend toward the waiting water.

Zoey feels hot tears streaking down her face, mixing with the sweat. Her teeth hurt from clenching her jaw and she thinks she might be sick. The room tilts around her.

Lee lets out another grunt of pain and tries to hoist his legs up but his toes slip into the water.

He convulses, body flexing back and forth, before he manages to swing his feet free and pull his knees up only to drop them back again, exhausted. His head tilts back and he makes a guttural sound unlike anything she's ever heard before. The hairs on the back of her neck stand up, and all at once she hears herself speaking.

"The women are all gone, okay? They're gone, he was telling the truth. Now stop!"

Shirou makes a quick jerking movement with one hand and the man turns the dial.

Lee falls quiet, body going completely slack. Drool hangs from his mouth and drips into the pool at his feet.

Shirou approaches the thick plastic. "This is the truth?"

"Yes, yes, they're all gone. There's no reason for you to go there, just please, don't hurt him anymore."

"Who did this?"

Zoey pauses, swallowing the acrid taste of fear. "I did. Me and a few others."

Shirou's face draws down. "Impossible. It would take thousands."

"I grew up there, I knew their weaknesses."

He stares at her for several long seconds. "You're lying."

"I'm not. Please believe me."

"Where is this place you speak of?"

"Don't tell him, Zoey," Lee says, his words slurred as he looks at her through slitted eyes. "Don't."

"Where?" Shirou asks again.

Zoey wavers, impaled on the choice. Give him the location of her daughter, or watch Lee suffer. She meets Lee's gaze and there is a solid resolution there that rends her heart in two. He is willing to die for the child that isn't his.

Something must have changed in her expression, for in the next instant Shirou flicks his hand at the man across the room and he turns the dial once again.

Lee shudders, lips peeling back from his teeth, as he yanks his feet free, crying out again.

She looks away, unable to watch anymore. If she does, she's sure she will break. She'll tell Shirou whatever he wants to know.

So she hides, hides within herself, goes back to Edmond Dantès's cell in Château d'If and curls into a corner where the screams she hears are someone else's, another prisoner she doesn't know, even if it's her name that's being called over and over.

33

A drop of water hits the back of her neck and slides down her spine.

Zoey sits up, body aching, vision fuzzy as she blinks at her surroundings.

She is still bound to the chair. She must have fallen asleep or passed out some time ago. What's the last thing she can recall?

Lee, yelling her name.

She sits up straighter, violently awake now, terrified at what she might see through the plastic and unable to stop herself from looking.

Lee hangs limply from the ceiling in the next room, feet submerged in water, chin resting on his chest.

No.

"Lee? Lee!" He doesn't move and there is a plummeting sensation in her chest. He's gone. They pushed him too far and now—

Lee stirs, his feet treading the water as if he's trying to walk away from the torture.

"Lee, can you hear me?"

His head raises enough for her to see his eyes through the sweat-dampened hair hanging over his forehead. "Hey."

She sags with relief. "Are you okay?"

"Yeah, doing great."

A choked laugh comes from her and she clamps the insane sound off. "When did they leave?"

"Don't know. Maybe an hour ago? Hard to keep track of time." He licks his lips, which she can see are bloody from him biting them. "I didn't tell. I didn't say anything."

"It's okay, we're going to be okay."

He shakes his head slowly. "I don't think so. Can't take much more of this. But I won't break. I promise, I won't."

"We're getting out of here." She places her feet against the plastic barrier and begins pushing again.

The bolts in the floor squeal. Something pops in her knee but there is no pain.

She releases the pressure and kicks out again.

The chair rocks.

A ping comes from below her and she stops pushing, leaning to one side.

One of the bolts in the chair's feet sticks up a half inch. The other a quarter.

It's working.

She begins to set her feet against the plastic again when the revelation of what she's doing hits her. If she manages to break or strip the bolts she'll tip backward . . . onto her hands that are still attached to the chair. She'll be on her back without any way to break free.

Zoey lowers her feet. Another droplet of water hits her forehead and she looks up. One of the pipes above her has a threaded nozzle sprouting from it with a long handle set into its side. A ringlet of water hangs from the nozzle's edge, another drop ready to break free.

"It's okay," Lee says, bringing her focus back down. "They won't hurt you. You can wait until their guard is down, then get away."

"Don't talk like that."

"W-what should we name her?" Lee brings his head all the way up, his jaw working soundlessly. And now she can see the tears spilling from the corners of his eyes. "What should her name be?"

"Lee—"

"Something pretty. She deserves something pretty. You'll tell her about me, won't you?"

"Stop, stop it. We're going to get out." She looks away, unable to weather his hopeless gaze any longer. She shifts in the chair, trying to get a clear view of the straps holding her to the chair. They are plastic like she suspected by their feel. The part of the chair they're attached to is angled iron, not a rounded bar like the rungs her feet sit on.

Zoey sits up as straight as she can and shrugs her shoulders, pulling hard at her wrists.

They both slide a fraction of an inch.

She shoves down. Up again, gathering a rhythm even as she feels the lacerations on her wrists open once more. The sound of plastic rasping on steel fills the little room, almost like a promising whisper. Lee seems to have passed out again, the crown of his head facing her. The guilt from her lie stings like the wounds on her wrists. She should have been honest with him.

But it gave him hope.

It doesn't matter, it was wrong.

Kept him from telling Shirou where the ARC is.

He wouldn't have told anyway.

Even if he knew he wasn't the father?

Yes, she tells the nagging internal voice, but it is without conviction. She doesn't know how he would have reacted to the truth. No one ever does until they're confronted with it.

Her wrists burn from the friction and the biting straps that hold her, but she continues to saw through them. How long will it take? Minutes? Hours? Do they have either? Another drip of water strikes the top of her head maddeningly. She rubs faster, simply wanting to escape the leaky pipe.

As soon as I'm free I'm going to smash that nozzle, break the pipe in half. But of course that wouldn't solve the problem. It would only release all the water and flood the room. Then what—

Her eyes widen as she registers a sound outside the door.

Footsteps, heavy and sure.

She works at the straps furiously until there's a click of the lock disengaging and the door's handle turns.

Zoey falls still, controlling her breathing.

Shirou enters the room, cold gray eyes finding hers. "Hello, Zoey. Glad to see you're awake." He holds a small canvas bag in one hand. "I was afraid this was all too much for you."

She watches him for a moment before glancing into Lee's chamber. "Where's your helper?"

"Asleep. I told him to rest. It is what I should be doing now, but I'm afraid I couldn't drift off. Not with you alone down here." Shirou steps in closer and pats the bag against his thigh. A tingling of fear threads through her as he leans in. "I was forbidden to hurt you in any way, but my leader underestimated the both of you. I had guessed Lee would crack first, and if he didn't, watching him go through such pain would persuade you to see reason." He moves around to her other side, still bumping the bag against his leg. "But I was mistaken about that as well. While I was lying in my bed I realized my error. Since you can see through the divide either way, I knew I had started with the wrong person."

Shirou unzips the bag and pulls a short length of black hose out, a copper fitting on one end. He reaches above her, threading the hose to the leaking nozzle. When it's secure he retrieves something else from the bag she can't make out. It looks like some kind of dark fabric.

"What are you doing?" she asks, putting tension on the straps, praying for one of them to snap.

"What I should have done in the first place," Shirou says, and leaps forward.

The fabric opens into some kind of mask or bag. He tries to shove it over her head but she jerks away and his fist catches her in the temple.

The bag slides halfway over her skull and she yells, straining to the side.

Shirou grunts and the fabric continues down to her neck and cinches tight.

Zoey shakes her head but the bag stays put. She's blind, only the vaguest hint of light filtering through the dark material.

"What are you doing?" she says again. But the only response is the squeak of metal and the patter of water on the floor.

"Zoey?" Lee says weakly.

A hand grabs the hood and yanks, pulling her head back.

She has a split second of terrified anticipation before the water sprays onto the hood.

The fabric soaks through instantly, hugging tight against her face.

Water runs into her eyes, nose, mouth.

Suffocating.

Choking.

"Zoey!" Lee screams.

"Tell me," Shirou says from somewhere above her, and it sounds like he's miles away.

She convulses as water courses into her nasal passages, burning and blocking the air she so desperately needs.

She coughs, but the water keeps coming. She's drowning.

Her legs kick, striking the wall.

"Stop! I'll tell you! I'll tell you!"

But the water doesn't stop.

She inhales.

Liquid fills her windpipe and she gags, feeling her stomach heave in rebellion.

Her feet walk up the barrier and the water eases for a moment as Shirou knocks them back down.

"Please! I'll tell you!" Lee yells.

"I think you're just trying to get me to stop," Shirou says, as Zoey sucks in two watery lungfuls of air. "You need more motivation."

Shirou's hand yanks her head back farther and the water splashes against her face again.

She's going to die.

Drown in this steel room while Lee watches.

Never see her daughter.

Never hold her.

No.

Zoey walks her feet up the partition again.

Shoves with all her strength.

There is the sharp bark of steel coming loose. Then she's falling, tipping backward away from the pouring water.

Shirou gives a yell of surprise, something in another language, and she feels some resistance as if he's trying to hold her and the chair upright.

Then there's a screech of rubber slipping and she's dropping again.

The chair crashes into the floor, her arms screaming as they're crushed between the two.

She turns her head and vomits into the bag, screaming and coughing all at once.

Her mind tries to fade into nothing, but she tethers herself to the pain. This is the only chance she'll get.

More of her weight rests on her left side and she shifts that way, yanking hard on her right wrist.

It comes free, the plastic snapping audibly.

She pivots to her left, rolling onto her hands and knees, ripping the bag from her head at the same time.

There is a quarter inch of water on the floor, more spraying from the hose above.

Shirou is sitting partially up across from her, one hand grasping a plate in the wall as he tries to hoist himself to his feet. Blood drips from one elbow where he slipped and fell, and his eyes are wide, teeth gritted into a line of white between his lips.

Zoey rises to her knees, twisting her bound arm against the plastic strap.

It breaks at the frayed point where she'd been working at it.

Shirou pulls himself into a crouch as she leaps toward him with both feet forward. She catches him full in the face, slamming the back of his head into the wall as she falls to the wet floor.

What air she had is gone, knocked free from the impact.

Somewhere Lee is yelling her name.

Zoey pushes up onto her hands and knees, crawling away as Shirou grasps her ankle feebly. She kicks free and rises, swaying like a tree in a high wind, sucking in great heaving breaths that have never tasted so sweet.

Shirou lies on his side, blood leaking from his nose and mixing with the accumulating water around him. He presses a hand to the floor, pushing himself up.

Zoey reaches over her head and grasps the nozzle's valve, opening the flow fully.

She twists the handle sideways.

It bends, then breaks free of the pipe.

Water sprays in a powerful stream from the hose.

"Stop," Shirou mumbles, blood running from the corner of his mouth as she backs toward the door. He fumbles with the pistol at his side as she opens the door and spills into the hallway.

She slams the door shut, locking it as Shirou aims his pistol.

Leaning against the steel hatch, shoulders shaking, saliva drooling from her open mouth, she doubles over with another coughing fit, hacking out more water as she stumbles to the left, sliding against the wall. Distantly she can hear Shirou shouting as the water rises.

Lee's door opens by spinning a wheel set in its center. She crosses the room as he struggles to watch her.

"Are you okay?" he asks as she stops beside him, studying how his manacles are attached to the rail.

"Yeah," she croaks, her vocal cords like open wounds. The restraints around Lee's wrists are thicker than she first thought, their size spreading out the weight of his body through his forearms.

Please don't be bolted in, she thinks, casting a look around the room. A lone chair, much like the one she was bound to but shorter, sits in the corner. She drags it close to the water bin at Lee's feet and stands on it.

A cry of rage pulls her attention to the partition between the rooms.

Shirou stares at them, teeth bared, handgun aimed in their direction. In the instant before it happens, Zoey grasps Lee around the waist and pulls him close to her.

Shirou fires.

She waits for the bullet's sting, the memory from the other times she's been shot magnifying until she's sure it's already happened.

No pain comes. She looks at the other room.

There is a mushroomed crater on Shirou's side, the plastic otherwise unharmed around it. The man himself looks stunned and it takes him a full second to fire another round.

The bullet hammers the plastic but it doesn't break.

He shoots again and again, a look of panic beginning to take over.

The water level rises into view, nearly three feet deep now in the little room, as the hose continues to hemorrhage.

Shirou faces the door, firing several muted blasts at the door handle.

"We have to go," Zoey says, returning her gaze to Lee's shackles. Now that she's closer she can see they're hooked over the rail and latched out of reach of his fingers. She turns the catch and steps down from the chair before moving it into the water bin for Lee to stand on.

His legs barely hold him, but he manages to unhook himself and drop to the floor.

Zoey catches him and they nearly fall over together. His skin is slick with cold sweat.

"Thought I was going to lose you," he breathes, leaning heavily against her.

"I'm here. Can you walk?"

"I think so."

She slings one arm around his waist and they move toward the door.

The water in the next room covers the bullet marks in the partition but none leaks onto their side. Shirou stands navel deep watching them leave. He raises the gun and fires twice more at Zoey's face as she passes, the plastic splintering his visage into something inhuman.

They step into the hallway and close the door behind them. The ship hums. Somewhere above them a ringing begins but quiets almost immediately.

How much time do they have before someone notices Shirou isn't in his room?

They move past the door to her cell, which weeps water from its lower half, a hollow banging coming from within.

To their right the hallway extends in a murky red light along a section of doors. Ahead are the stairs she was brought down earlier.

"We have to get up to the top deck and off the ship," she whispers. "Can you climb the stairs?"

"I think so." She lets him go and he wobbles but stays upright.

"Okay, hold my hand."

"You couldn't get me to let go."

She can't help but smile at this even as her throat burns and the cuts on her wrists flare with pain.

They climb the stairs carefully, Zoey first, their footsteps masked by the thrumming noise of the ship itself.

One flight.

Two.

At the third a flash of movement above makes her pause. A guard strolls past on the next level. If he looks down, there's no way he can't see them.

He walks out of sight.

Below them a door slams, and a conversation begins to grow in volume.

Two men coming toward the stairs.

She squeezes Lee's hand and he returns it.

They move together, climbing fast and steady even though her legs feel as if she's just run several miles. The next level is an open corridor three times the width of the ones she's seen so far. Straight across from the head of the stairs is a doorway.

And beyond it the early morning sky.

Almost there.

Zoey checks both ways, seeing the back of the man who had passed moments ago farther down the ship.

The men's conversation continues. They are perhaps twenty seconds from being spotted if they don't move.

The guard on their level turns a corner.

She tugs Lee with her, and they cross the open space, vulnerable and easily caught if they're seen. She fumbles with the door for a stomach-shriveling second before it opens.

The fresh sea air welcomes them, and she's suddenly aware of how suffused the inside of the ship is with competing odors. The sky is overcast with only a thin swath of lighter clouds on the horizon.

Zoey closes the door behind them and they stand with their backs against the wall, listening to the men talk, voices louder, louder, then softer until they're gone completely.

She exhales, moving away from the door toward the rear of the ship. The deck is wide and slick with moisture. In the half-light the shape of the rear gun turret is like giant fingers reaching out from the ship's surface. A towering structure rises high above the rest of the vessel, lights shining down from its top. A man walks the perimeter of the tower, glancing down near their position before continuing on.

Zoey eyes the harbor, its distance much more intimidating than it was on the ride out to the battleship.

"I don't know if I can swim that far," Lee says, bringing his manacled hands up. "Not like this." She inspects the steel but there are no catches or releases she can see that would set him free. They'll have to cut them off somehow, but it will have to wait for later. Any second Shirou will either break loose or someone will discover their absence, and daylight is not their friend.

They have to leave now.

"There," Lee says, pointing to a round ring almost the size of a tire hanging from the railing across from them. "It's a life preserver. We can use that."

She nods. "Okay. We grab it and go over the side. Head for that spot over there," she says, pointing at a length of shoreline slightly north of the ship's position.

Lee swallows and jerks his head, not looking at her.

Zoey watches the tower guard pass by again, making his circle, and holds out her hand, folding her fingers in one at a time.

Three.

Two.

One.

They run.

In seconds they're at the railing. Lee yanks the life preserver free as she glances over the side.

The distance to the sea makes her take a step back. Hitting the water is going to hurt.

Lee is already climbing up the railing. He tosses the preserver over. "Land with your feet," he says, reaching out to hold her hand.

Zoey steps up beside him and has a fractured second to orient herself.

Then they leap together.

Air rushes past, an animal howl in her ears.

The water speeds toward her and she holds her breath.

It's like jumping into a pit of needles.

The water bites with fangs of ice, and she opens her mouth in shock, shutting down the impulse to suck in a breath. She's breathed enough water for one day. Lee's hand is gone and the ocean drones eerily around her as she kicks and paws at the inky water. A sickening bout of vertigo comes and goes, the unmooring loss of direction so strong that down and up are interchangeable in the near dark.

Then her head breaks the surface and she sees Lee clasping the preserver to his chest a dozen feet away. She swims to him and they begin propelling themselves as quietly as they can toward shore.

Every few strokes Zoey glances back at the ship that looms less and less over them. The deck is still empty at the early hour, and so far the lookout on the tower hasn't spotted them.

"So cold," Lee says, gripping the preserver with white knuckles.

"We'll make it. Keep going."

The sea continues to brighten around them, their wakes no longer hidden in shadow.

The shore is closer with each passing minute but she knows they're not going fast enough. Lee's teeth chatter briefly before he clamps his jaws together in a grimace, breathing hard through his nose. The water was unbearably cold at first and has gotten colder, but now it has the effect of an anesthetizing agent. Her body is less her own and more an idea highlighted by the fact that if she quits swimming she will drown.

A cramp forms in her right leg, quickly tightening to a solid knot of pain. She gasps and water laps at her chin and nose as she slows. Without saying anything, Lee shifts almost completely off the preserver and shoves it toward her. She grabs it and tries to stretch her leg but the cramp only strengthens.

"Come on, Zoey, we're almost there," Lee says in her ear.

"Can't . . ." she says breathlessly, trying to kick with the opposite leg.

"Yes you can. You saved me, you can make it." He shifts so that he's swimming backward, and begins to tow her, kicking hard with his legs. "Look at me, keep looking at me."

She blinks, her vision a smeared mess of monochrome, and focuses on him.

And in that moment, with his hair plastered to his head, lips blue, and a look of gritted determination on his face, she has never loved him more.

After several seconds she realizes there is something wrong with her feet. It's not numbness or pain.

They're touching something.

Shore. They've made it.

She looks up, seeing a long patch of dirty beach set before a layer of brush and trees. Beyond the barricade is the suggestion of a fairly tall building.

Lee stands, shoulders emerging from the water. He drags her in closer to the sand as she manages to get her feet working. They slog up onto dry land, clothes weighing a thousand pounds, breath pluming white in the morning air.

"We made it," Lee says, "We reall—"

A startling siren shreds the silence, shearing his words off, as a red beacon begins flashing aboard the ship. Spotlights erupt out of the last murk of night and slice across the water.

She reaches out, not taking her eyes off the vessel that's coming alive with motion, and Lee's hand is there, cold but strong.

Together they run.

34

Brush slaps at her face, claws at her soaking clothes, trying desperately to hold her back.

The cramp in her leg loosens before cinching tight again, causing her strides to become a rushing hobble.

Lee pushes through the bare foliage ahead of her, hand still gripping hers. Behind them the ship's alarm howls and distantly engines rumble to life.

After struggling through the brush for another ten seconds they burst into full view of the building she spotted earlier. They are in its parking lot, its slanted architecture rising several stories above them. Beyond the structure is a road and a row of homes.

"Hide here or run?" Lee asks between heaving breaths.

"Keep moving."

They rush side by side to the road, crossing it with a brief glance.

Empty.

The neighborhood they enter seems to be laid out in a rough crescent, the drive in front of the homes curving away back toward the center of the city. Zoey adjusts their course, running north through several side yards before coming to a stop at another cross street. It's vacant, so they continue to the next neighborhood. Each house becomes the same, every alley and yard identical. At a low one-story she comes to a stop, slumping against its siding before sliding down. Her legs are on fire and the warning throb of pain in her lower back has returned.

"Have to rest," she says, stretching out her leg to banish the persistent cramp. Lee nods, bent over, elbows bracing against his knees. The sound of engines hasn't gotten any closer but neither are they farther away.

"Maybe they didn't see us at all," Lee says, straightening. "Maybe they just realized we weren't on the ship anymore."

"Could be." She leans into the stretch, the coiled ball of muscle straining to the point she thinks it will snap before it grudgingly begins to release. Her heart rate gradually lowers, and the frenetic anxiety running through her drops several degrees as the vehicle's growls fade slightly.

When she's sure the cramp has relinquished its grip, she stands, surveying the surrounding homes and yards. Nothing moves. The tepid light continues to spread, brushing back the shadows. "You know the city. Is there a way out that isn't watched?"

"I haven't been outside the city limits since they showed up, but I'm sure every road and bridge is covered."

"Can we slip around them? Off the roads or through the trees?"

"I don't know."

"I think that's our only chance."

Lee looks at the shackles on his wrists. "Wish these were gone."

"We'll get them off somehow when we're safe. Are you okay otherwise? Are you injured anywhere?" she asks, looking him up and down.

"Are you trying to get me to take my clothes off?" His grin is back, the one she knew so well from the ARC.

She shakes her head. "You're terrible."

"Maybe. No, I'm okay except for aching all over. It feels like I was beaten everywhere." He winces, stretching his back. "Thank you.

I wouldn't have lasted much longer. Especially seeing him do that to you, I would've told."

"It's okay. We made it."

"Yeah, we're totally free," he says, gesturing around them.

"If we do it right, we will be." She frowns. "One thing I don't understand, though, is why Shirou kept asking us where the ARC is. You said that's where they were headed from here, right?"

Lee squints at her. "Right. Their leader told me they had the location."

"That doesn't make any sense. Why would they need us to tell them?"

"I don't know."

They sit quietly for a time listening to the distant rev of engines until finally Zoey says, "We should get somewhere safer before it's full day."

"We can try for the north bridge. It's not too far, and there might be a way around the roadblock, but you won't like it."

"Why?"

"It involves swimming again."

She groans. "Ready?"

"Whenever you are."

She walks to the corner of the house and peers around it.

Beyond is an intersection. Several old cars are parked on a corner and a few seconds tick by before she dismisses them. The chances that they would start are near zero, and driving away will draw too much attention. They'll have to go on foot.

She glances in all directions before motioning to Lee.

They jog into the street and head for the next yard that's fenced in, a low door halfway down the barricade promising access. Three steps from the edge of the road she falters.

Something is wrong.

"Stop!" A man steps out from behind a large, knurled oak near the corner, his rifle trained on them.

Her muscles tense, eyes flitting up the street, searching for an escape, but the soldier is closing on them fast.

"Don't move! Get down on your knees."

Her mind whirs with thoughts. Rush him? Run opposite directions?

The man stops several steps from them, rifle barrel centering first on her, then Lee. He's young, perhaps only five years older than either of them. His eyes are wide and a bright blue that contrasts with his dark jacket. A layer of whiskers covers his cheeks in sparse patches, and he's trembling, the gun shaking in hands that are very white.

"I said get on your knees!" he yells, raising the rifle to his shoulder.

"Let us go," Zoey says, surprising herself by how even her voice is. It still hurts to speak but the tattered sound is gone from her words. "Please. Pretend you didn't see us."

"On your knees." A plea.

"Okay." She holds out her hands and slowly kneels.

"Zoey . . ." Lee says.

"Do what he says."

The man swallows and reaches into a pocket, drawing out a small black radio that he holds to his mouth.

"Please," Zoey says again. "Don't. They tortured us on the ship. Please don't send us back."

The guard studies her, blinking as his lips work silently. She puts as much feeling into her gaze as she can, beseeching him.

He hesitates a moment longer before pushing the button on the radio. "I've got them. We're at the corner of"—he looks at the sign leaning heavily into the street nearby—"Thirteenth and West Dravus." There is a snap of static before an answer comes from the speaker.

"Good work. Hold them there. We're inbound."

Zoey feels her head cock to the side. That voice.

The soldier swallows loudly again and takes a step away from them, glancing up and down the nearest street. Several motors rumble, their acceleration audible from the direction of the city.

"You can still let us go," Zoey says quietly. "Bloody your lip and say we overpowered you."

He brings his gaze back to her and she sees that he is nearly crying. "I'm sorry. They'll kill me."

"They're going to kill us," Lee says, standing.

"Get down!"

"Lee," she says, reaching for him. But he's moving toward the soldier with steady steps.

"You have no right to hold us. We're leaving."

"Get down!" the man screams, and now there is desperation in his voice. Zoey stares at his trigger finger.

Tightening.

Tightening.

"Lee, stop!" she yells, and he does.

A teardrop rolls down the soldier's face and he motions at the ground. "On your knees." Lee hesitates before taking a step back and lowering himself beside her.

The sound of engines is louder.

Closer.

"You're never going to forget this," she says. "This moment."

"Shut up."

"You'll always wonder if you did the right thing."

"Shut up!"

"I know because I've been wrong before. And it never goes away."

The soldier bares his teeth even as another teardrop courses down his face. He stares into her eyes and she holds his gaze.

With a quick movement, almost like tearing a bandage away from a drying wound, he holds out his rifle to Lee. "Knock me out. It's the only way they'll believe me."

Lee glances at Zoey as they rise. He takes the rifle from the guard who turns partially away from them. Zoey steps close to him, grasping his hand. It's so cold.

"Thank you," she says, and he jerks a nod but doesn't look at either of them. She steps back as Lee hefts the rifle, and without warning snaps the stock across the soldier's temple.

He folds like an empty suit of clothes.

"Come on," Lee says, grasping her hand. She has time to spare the soldier one last look before they're running again.

The steady rasp of tires comes from the south even as headlights appear from the opposite direction. Zoey jerks Lee into the nearest yard and they streak to the rear of the property, fighting through a tangle of bare hedges.

An alleyway runs the length of several houses and they race down it, catching a glimpse of two vehicles blasting by on the main road to their left.

They cross two more intersecting streets before the smell of open water pervades the air. Ahead, the alley ends and they jog onto a path looping away into a thick stand of trees. The path leads them through narrow and wide openings in the forest, all the while the first impressions of water can be seen ahead in the gaps between trees. When they finally stop to catch their breath they are at an opening leading up to a street attached to a massive bridge spanning a width of water perhaps two hundred yards wide.

Zoey searches the bridge's length but sees no movement. No trucks. No men.

From several blocks behind them comes a yell. They must've found their unconscious savior.

"Do we swim or chance the bridge?" she asks, still straining for air.

"Don't know. They might've abandoned the post to come for us. How long do you think it will take to swim the channel?"

"Too long. They'll be back by then. Go."

They break cover and jog up the incline to the bridge's entrance. The road to their left curves away around the bend of trees. The bridge is empty.

They barely hesitate, their strides matching again, each second a breath, each second putting more distance between them and the city. She can make out a hill peppered with homes and buildings across the bridge, a thousand places to hide, a million directions to go. If they can only get across the bridge, they'll be safe.

A large vehicle appears ahead just as the rumble of engines sounds behind them.

Zoey falters and Lee slows as well.

They are halfway across the bridge, equal distance in either direction to cover.

"Zoey?" Lee says.

She looks over the side of the bridge, but the drop is too great; there's no way they would land uninjured or unnoticed.

"Zoey? What do we do?" Lee holds the rifle the best he can with the limitations of the shackles, centering it on the nearing truck. Because it has to be a truck, it's too large—

She blinks.

For some reason the shape of the vehicle reminds her of the voice on the soldier's radio.

Familiar.

Three vehicles come into view around the bend behind them.

A guttural purr grows as the closer vehicle looms, its form becoming distinct.

Zoey grabs Lee's arm and runs forward, eyes traveling over her shoulder at the convoy that is only blocks behind them. The other vehicle swings sideways and shrieks to a stop in the middle of the bridge.

The ASV idles as the side door opens revealing Tia, who steps onto the street, a rifle tucked to her shoulder. "Get in."

Zoey grasps Lee's arm and drags him forward as Tia opens fire.

Disbelief washes over her as she climbs onto the rear bench, Ian holding her arm as Newton and Nell drag Lee away from the door. Merrill turns partially in the driver's seat and they lock eyes.

There is everything in his gaze.

Anger.

Terror.

Panic.

Relief.

And love. Mostly love.

"You just had to see the ocean, didn't you?" he says before facing the windshield again.

Tia yanks the door shut as a hail of bullets ping off the reinforced steel.

Then they're moving, backing up before turning in the direction they arrived. Zoey catches a glimpse of one truck barreling down on them while another rolls toward the steep drop beside the bridge and plunges over. The last is nowhere to be seen.

Bullets chatter against the ASV as Merrill begins to accelerate.

"They're going to catch us," Tia says.

"Counting on it," Merrill says. "Everyone grab on to something!"

Zoey has a split second to grip the bench she's sitting on before the ASV shudders almost to a halt.

An eerily still heartbeat passes.

The sound of rending metal fills the cab and they're all shoved backward.

She loses her hold on the bench and tumbles into Ian who falls against Lee. The rear end of the vehicle is suddenly elevated. Merrill guns the engine and everything levels out with a bone-jarring bang.

Then they're cruising forward, accelerating away through quiet streets. Merrill glances into one of the large side mirrors. "They're done. Front end's smashed to shit."

"They shouldn't have tailgated us," Tia says, checking the load on her rifle.

Zoey rearranges herself on the bench and looks around, absorbing what just happened. "How?" she manages as Ian wraps her hand in his callused palms.

"Your false trail in the snow only threw us off for about a day," Merrill says, glancing over his shoulder. "I knew where you were headed. You're so damned stubborn there's only one place you could've gone."

"When did you get here?"

"Two days ago," Tia says. "It was clear right away that something was off, so after a little reconnaissance we decided to hang back and observe."

"We were also able to monitor their radio channels," Merrill says, tapping the dash of the ASV. "Your capture was all over the airwaves yesterday. We took a position up the shore to watch the ship since we knew that's where they took the two of you. We were still formulating a plan when Tia spotted your escape this morning through the binoculars. After that we moved in closer in the hopes of finding you."

"It was you on the radio," she says, a smile tugging at her lips. "You answered the soldier that captured us."

"Did I sound official?"

She laughs. "Yes."

"Good."

"Where are the others?"

"We left them at a house about an hour away. They're safe," Merrill says.

"I can't believe you came for us. I can't believe you're here."

"And I can't believe you're stupid enough to have gone to the last major city in the continental United States," Tia says. "I'd ask what the hell were you thinking but I know you weren't."

"I had to know. For sure. And"—she gazes around at them, her throat tightening—"I didn't want anything to happen to you because of me. Like Eli," she says, her voice failing her at the mention of his name.

Ian squeezes her hand. "You know that we wouldn't forsake you. Everyone knew the risks when we accepted you and the other women into our group. I told you before, once we get an idea in our heads it doesn't go away."

Her vision blurs but she blinks away the tears. "Thank you. Thank you for coming for us."

"Yes, thank you," Lee echoes and glances at Nell. "I'm sorry, I don't know you. I'm Lee." He holds out his hand, which Nell takes.

"Nell Carroll. I'm Rita's mother," she adds, and Zoey can't help but smile as Lee does a double take.

"Rita's m-mother? But how . . ." He looks to Zoey, eyes wide.

She leans back into the bench, its embrace more comfortable than anything she can recall. "Later," she says, and the steady rumble of the engine carrying them away from the city draws her eyes closed.

35

Hiraku hurries down the ship's hall, two of his men trailing closely behind.

He rubs gritted sleep from one eye and tries to calm the growing unease in the back of his mind. Zoey and Lee escaped. That much was clear from the jumbled message one of the men behind him had given. Shortly before dawn. Not much else was known yet.

When he'd asked for Shirou the men had said his quarters were empty.

That's when the worry started to gnaw at him.

They take a shortcut through the galley before emptying out into another hall that leads to a set of stairs.

Down.

Down.

Down.

At the bottom of the last flight his feet splash in water. The entire floor is covered in a thin layer of liquid. Ahead, a group of men stand outside the rooms they've used for interrogation before. He hates this part of the ship.

As he strides forward, the men standing in a circle begin to part. There is something on the floor in their center, outside the smaller of the two rooms. The dark shock of hair belonging to one of their physicians is visible, but what he bends over is only partially clear.

"What happened?" he says, as he nears the group, and the ones who hadn't seen him approaching flinch. The physician, whose name he can't remember at the moment, turns his head and slowly rises, moving enough for Hiraku to see.

Shirou's pale face turned to the ceiling. Eyes open and staring at nothing. His clothes sodden, and the water all around him.

Hiraku's breath catches. It's like he's walked into a wall. He falters, stopping as the sight of his oldest friend's body sets in.

This is my fault.

The men look at him, and the quiet is as thick and tangible as a soaking wool blanket. Soaking with water. His feet are wet with cool water.

And he can't break his gaze from Shirou's dead eyes.

"What happened to him?" he hears someone say, and it is only when the physician begins talking that he realizes he asked the question.

"He drowned. When the men found him the smaller room was full of water and locked. There was nothing to be done."

Hiraku tries to get himself to look away from Shirou, to examine the situation, determine how Zoey and Lee escaped the rooms, but the gears within the leadership part of his mind strip and spin, freewheeling, as he realizes he will never be able to speak to Shirou again.

"Leave us," he manages after a moment. The men look to one another but none of them move. "Leave us!" he screams, and before the sound of his voice has faded they disappear, hurrying away down the corridor and up the stairs.

Steel creaks around him. Water sloshes against the walls. One of the pipes overhead gurgles faintly.

Hiraku kneels, cold water saturating the knees of his pants. He reaches down and lifts Shirou's head and shoulders off the floor, letting him rest against his thigh. His skin is freezing and he feels heavy. Not for the first time Hiraku wonders if the dead weigh more, but he already knows the answer.

A tremor runs through his chest and shoulders, seeping up into his throat until it bleeds from him in a long moan.

"I'm sorry. I failed you. I—" But there is nothing more. Nothing beyond the truth of what he spoke. If he had never been exposed to the radiation, if Jiaying had never left him, never had the abortion, if the Dearth . . . But there is no end to the regret. He could go further and further back, blaming himself and everything that happened.

It is all wrong. This should never have happened.

None of it.

Even as he registers the tears that drip continuously from his chin onto Shirou's pale face, heat begins to flow across his skin.

White-hot, prickling heat.

He swallows the knot in his throat and gently lays his friend down. He places his fingers against Shirou's eyelids, drawing them shut, but they come partially open, forever staring at whatever arrives when life slips away.

Hiraku rises, bypassing the room where Lee was being held. There is only the rage now, the burning across his skin that he hasn't felt this strong since—

—*he followed him to the store while it was raining. He had taken to drinking in his car outside their new house after he'd seen the announcement on every social media site Jiaying used. The declarations of "It's a boy!" along with the ultrasound pictures had split him in half, one part brimming with jealousy and envy of the man he watched strolling with his ex-wife through the parks, as he used to do. The other part was blackened by the rage that left him sweating and breathless at times. And the night that it was raining the half that was purely rage was in complete control. He had followed him to the store and—*

Hiraku finds himself passing two men waiting at the head of the stairs one level up. They straighten as he moves by, not pausing as he says, "Take care of him." Then he is moving to the next stairway and climbs—

—*out of his car as the man exited the store, a paper sack clutched close to his chest, trying to shield it from the pounding rain. Perhaps a late-night snack for Jiaying, some craving she demanded due to the pregnancy. Hiraku moved forward, blocking the man's way to his own car, and saw a flicker of alarm on his features before recognition and surprise took its place in the dim—*

Morning light streaming through several windows to his right as he turns away from them, away from several sets of watching eyes, into the hall leading to his quarters. Then he is inside, the door shut behind him, but he can still feel the water on Shirou's skin, can still feel it soaking through his—

—*clothes as the rain pounded down on them. There were flecks of moisture on the man's glasses and a soft look about his mouth, as if he were used to keeping it shut while others told him what they wanted. They stood absolutely still for a moment, eyes locked on one another until a flicker of lightning lit the empty parking lot, and Hiraku launched himself—*

Forward and puts his fist through the cabinet beside his bed.

Wood splinters and—

—*teeth broke against his knuckles.*

He throws a chair and its legs snap, pieces flying as—

—*his ex-wife's new husband crumpled to the wet cement, blood streaming from his face. And Hiraku wound back a foot and kicked him, again and again and again, all of the rage boiling out through him.*

The bedside table snaps beneath his foot and he kicks it against the wall, battering it into—

—*a pulp that he couldn't recognize anymore. And the rain fell around them, mixing with the river of blood that flowed steadily away toward the—*

Drained, he crumples to the floor amidst the destruction. Ink runs in dark rivulets outward from the shattered bottle. He watches it transfixed as his heaving breaths slow and his heart quiets from its thundering in his ears.

The ink looks like old blood as it pools against the base of the doorway.

Like a man in a dream he reaches to his pocket and draws out the folded piece of paper. He grips it in both hands, meaning to tear it to pieces, because that is what he's become, pieces of what he once was, and now another is missing.

The paper begins to tear, its fibers splitting with glacial slowness.

He stops, heart thudding in his temples, hands shaking.

With a blast of held breath, he lets the paper fall into his lap. It sits there accusatorially.

Time passes. Minutes or hours, he doesn't know, but then there is a sound from the hall, a shuffling of feet as if the person isn't sure about what they're going to do.

A knock at the door.

Hiraku doesn't move. "Come."

The door opens, and a man with skin so white it looks bleached steps inside the door. His eyes take in the ruin and Hiraku at its epicenter, but to his credit he doesn't blanch.

"Sir?"

"What is it, Draiman?"

"They've escaped the city."

"What did you say?"

Draiman swallows loudly. "They escaped the city."

Hiraku lets the news set in, waiting for another bout of rage to flood him, but there is only a dull throb of anger. "How?"

"They managed to get to the northern neighborhoods outside the secure zone before they were picked up."

"Picked up?"

"By a military vehicle of some kind. Several of our men were killed, but the ones who survived said they think it was another woman who helped them escape."

Hiraku sits motionless for nearly a minute before reaching out with a single finger, dragging it through the ink. He brings it close to his face and smears the ink with his thumb, looking at the way it coats his skin.

"Which way were they last seen heading?"

"North, sir."

Hiraku nods. "Send up the drone."

36

Elation.

She can't help it. The sight of everyone standing outside the single-story brick house at the end of the lane they've been following for nearly a half hour lifts her spirits and dulls the pain in her throat, discards the weariness like an old shell.

Zoey opens the door to the ASV and scrambles out. She's met immediately by Seamus who nearly bowls her over before Chelsea is there, hugging her and cursing her at the same time. Then it is Rita and Sherell and Lyle, all of them welcoming her back and saying how worried they were. She cries, and she can't help that either. Through a bluster of tears, she says she's sorry, sorry for everything, and Lee is there, her arm locked through his as her family forgives her.

The inside of the house is warm, a small fire burning in a hearth. There is food at a long table and she and Lee eat voraciously, his hands now free of his shackles after Tia had worked a half hour on them in the attached garage.

The food begins filling up what feels like a bottomless pit in her stomach. When they've finished the group sits expectantly around the table as they relay the story of their capture and escape. When they're done a deep quiet invades the house except for the faint crackle of flames.

"So it's not a trick. What the woman said on the video," Merrill says quietly, stretching out his artificial leg, which clicks loudly. For the first time she sees it is a new prosthetic, not something cobbled together by Tia. They must have found it for him somewhere along the way while looking for her.

Zoey takes a deep breath. "It's true. She's my daughter."

"Our daughter," Lee says, glancing at her as she cringes internally. "Our daughter."

There is a stunned silence. "You're sure?" Ian asks.

"Yes."

"It doesn't make sense," Chelsea says, shaking her head. "Like I've said before, the male determines the sex of the baby, not the female. So it's back to the old question: why was NOA so determined on keeping women to test on? And how were they able to succeed with you?"

"I don't know. But they're not lying this time. I saw the test results with my own eyes."

"What are we going to do?" Rita asks. "We aren't going to leave her there, right?"

"No. I could never do that," Zoey says.

"Then what?" Sherell asks. "We go back to the ARC and ask nicely if they'll give you guys your baby?"

"No. But doing what we did to get the both of you out won't work either. They'll be ready and waiting for us."

"So what are you thinking?" Chelsea asks.

"We need to talk to them. They'll speak with me. The entire reason for them even being there is my existence."

"Wow. You're so humble too," Rita says rolling her eyes. The group chuckles but it's strained.

"Think about it," Zoey says. "If I'm able to speak to Vivian one on one, I could convince her. I'm the keystone, so they've finally found what they're looking for, right? If that's true, then there's a possibility that we could turn the Dearth around. There would be no reason to keep any of us locked up if girls were able to be born again."

"Your sentiments toward humanity are uplifting," Ian says. "But ultimately I believe they are unrealistic. NOA hasn't shown the slightest hint of compassion when it comes to the treatment of women. They have ruled with an iron fist because they fear exactly what you three have become." He looks at each of them individually. "Smart, strong, beautiful, and resilient young women. They fear what they cannot control, as do most people."

"You don't think there's hope for people to change?"

"There's always hope, but change is the most difficult thing in the world for human beings to do. There is safety in static. Change is the great disrupter, even when it is for the good."

"But what other choice is there?" she asks, glancing around the table. "They know we'll try to get her out of the ARC, it's exactly what they're expecting. The reason we were able to return the first time was because they never dreamed I would come back. But now . . ." She lets her voice trail off. "The risk is too much for everyone to try, including for the baby. It's the reason I wanted to go after the Fae Trade alone. It's the reason I left after . . . after Eli. If we try to do this by force, we could lose everything."

"You can't go in there without a fail-safe," Lee says. "We need to find a way to get us out if something goes wrong."

She looks at him. "Us?"

"I'm going with you."

"Lee, no. You can't. We have no idea what they'd do to you."

"And I won't stand by and watch you go in alone. She's mine too."

Zoey falters. She should tell him, tell them all the truth. Right now before it's too late. Her jaw begins to work, trying to disgorge the words that don't want to come.

"What is it?" Lee asks. "What's wrong?"

She glances around, all eyes on her, wondering, waiting. The moment passes. "Okay. We'll go in together."

He nods. "Good. Now, the fail-safe, in case we can't sway Vivian—any ideas?"

"We won't be able to use the power failure again as cover, they'll be expecting that," Merrill says.

"How about we come in from the opposite side?" Tia asks.

"The dam is on that side," Zoey says.

"Exactly. We can use scuba gear to get to the spillway and lower ourselves down with cables."

"And then do what?" Merrill says. "There's still no way to get in."

"Grappling hooks."

"Tia. That's crazy, even for you."

"Okay, how about the elevator attached to the side where they had boats docked. We saw it the night we went in, remember?"

"It'll be locked and guarded for sure."

Tia makes an exasperated sound. "Well then you start throwing out ideas, genius."

"All I'm saying is the obvious ways in won't work. We need to come up with something different."

"The most obvious way to get in would be helicopter," Ian says. "But of course we're short one of those."

"Along with a pilot to fly it," Tia says. "Unless one of you is holding out on us."

"I say we sleep on it. Everyone is exhausted, especially these two," Merrill says, motioning to Zoey and Lee. "Tomorrow things might be clearer."

There is a general mutter of approval from the group, but Zoey says, "We don't have much time."

"Why do you say that?" Chelsea asks. "NOA doesn't have anything to draw you in besides your daughter. They have to wait for you."

"It's not NOA that I'm worried about. It's Hiraku and his men."

"It would take a miracle for them to stumble onto us," Merrill says. "We're over seventy miles from Seattle. No one followed us and this place isn't exactly on the main road."

"Hiraku knew about the ARC," Lee says, and silence returns to the room.

"What?" Tia asks. "How? You told him?"

"No. He said he met a man who was from there and gave him the location. This army he has is following him because they believe he's the answer to ending the Dearth. He's promising them a new life, and the ARC was his destination. When I told him the women were all gone he got furious. He didn't believe me."

"I thought you said when they were interrogating you they asked where the ARC was," Ian says.

"They did," Zoey says. "It struck us as odd too. All we can figure is they wanted a confirmation of the location to prove we were telling the truth."

Merrill lets out a long sigh. "So you think he's going to go there?"

Zoey nods. "Yes. That's why we don't have much time."

"This is really bad," Sherell says. "What are we going to do?"

Merrill slowly stands. "We're going to leave in the morning and devise a plan on the road. But what I said about resting stands. Everyone should get some sleep. We won't be good to anyone if we're dead on our feet. Tia, take first watch."

Everyone disperses from the table reluctantly, several of them squeezing Zoey's shoulder as they move off to separate parts of the house. The air inside is close and the heat that felt so inviting earlier is now too warm. She spots a sliding glass door leading to the backyard and steps through it into the coolness of the late afternoon.

She finds herself on a deck overlooking a sprawl of overgrown lawn, brush encroaching on the clearing. The outline of something catches her eye in the corner of the yard and it takes her a moment to realize it is a child's swing set nearly consumed by the woods. One of the swings sways, uttering a mournful sound.

Where is the child who once played here? Did they survive or perish in the terrible years since the world fell into chaos? For a beat she's lost in the thought of all the homes and yards that are empty now, the families gone as if they never were. What had it been like then? No more simple choices, only harsh reality and the crushing fallout of decisions and paths taken. But really it is no different this moment.

How much is a life worth?

She closes her eyes. *That's always been the question, hasn't it? And now it's time for me to decide.*

The door slides open and closed behind her, and a second later Merrill leans on the railing to her right. They say nothing for a while, simply readjusting to the other's company.

"Do you remember what I told you after we found out about Riverbend?" Merrill asks after a time. "About how your actions and decisions affect everyone else?"

"Yes."

"Then why do you insist on choices that put others in danger?"

She turns to him, feeling as if she's been struck inside. "I left to keep you all safe."

"I know that's what you thought you were doing, but you forgot what I told you after we talked about repercussions." He pauses, straightening to his full height and crossing his arms over his chest. "You have a family now, Zoey. Do you know what that means?"

"Yes."

"But you don't, not really, because if you did you wouldn't go running away every time there's trouble."

"But—"

"Stop and listen to me," he says, voice stern as iron. A father's tone. "This group, what we've become, each of us would die for one another. That's family. The bad with the good, okay? When you think you're protecting us by putting yourself in harm's way, you're not, you're endangering everyone and to be perfectly honest it's beginning to piss me off."

She shrinks slightly from him, her brow creasing. "I'm sorry—"

"See, you say that, but how do I know you won't leave tonight? Or tomorrow? And once again we'll have to go find you."

"No one had to come. I didn't want anyone to get hurt like Eli." She's tearing up now, her abraded throat stinging again.

"You're right, no one had to come, but they chose to. That's what family is, Zoey. That's what I want you to understand. You didn't grow up having one, and I'm very sorry for that, and I've tried to help make up for it, but you have to realize the consequences of what you do."

She feels as if she's being pulled apart. "I don't know what to do." A tear runs down her cheek and Merrill's stance softens.

"Come here," he says, holding out an arm. She leans into him and he holds her close. "Listen, I loved Eli too. He was the closest thing I had to a brother, but he died doing what he chose, and that's the truest form of love."

Zoey sobs once into his chest. "I'm sorry."

"I know you are. It's okay."

They stand there together until her tears are gone. She slowly draws away from him and he gives her a smile. "Family?"

"Family."

The sliding door opens and Lee steps out, glancing between the two of them. "Sorry . . ."

"You're fine," Merrill says, letting her go. "I'll leave you guys alone."

"Feels good to be back with them, doesn't it?" Lee asks as Merrill disappears inside the house.

"Yes, it does. I don't deserve it."

"Why would you say that?"

"Because of all I've put them through." She's wrung out, barely able to stay on her feet.

"Sherell and Rita are free now because of what you did. Rita has her mother. By the looks of things Sherell has Newton."

"What about Meeka and Crispin and Lily? What about Terra and Eli? What about . . ." Her voice catches. "What about your father?"

Lee's jaw hardens and he looks away, staring into the quiet forest. "My father loved you and he believed in you. He isn't gone because of what you did; he's gone because of Reaper." He turns and intertwines his fingers with hers. "None of us asked for any of this to happen, but you've always done what you thought was right."

She looks away from his gaze, sure that he'll see the guilt swimming in her eyes. "You don't know what I've done."

"I don't care. I know who you are." He comes closer and places her hand against his chest so she can feel his heart beating through the layers of clothing. "We're going to get through this together. I promise."

She tilts her face up to his and he kisses her. A second later the sliding door opens and they both glance toward it where Rita stands with a stricken look.

"Uh, sorry," she says, backing into the house.

"You should be," Zoey says, unable to keep her face straight as incredulity washes over Rita's features.

"Get a room!"

"Is there one open?" Lee asks.

"You two are gross. Both of you," Rita says, slamming the door shut to their laughter.

They hold each other, still giggling. It feels good, this frame in time. She could live here, settle into it like a new home and thrive. She could not think about tomorrow or the next day or the day after that. It could simply be here and now.

Her laughter dies away as she comes back to reality. Maybe some-day, but not today.

She draws back from Lee, studying his face, how it lights up when he smiles, and some strength goes out of her, knowing the fight that will come when she tells him.

"I need to talk to you about something," she says.

"Oh no. This can't be good."

"It's not good or bad, it's necessary."

"Necessary is almost always bad, but go ahead."

She starts speaking haltingly and at one point the way he looks at her is almost enough to stop the flow of words. But she continues until she's done, feeling empty and used up, mostly because she is. There is nothing else past this. Once things are set in motion it will be a one-way track with no return.

"Zoey, you can't—"

"I can't not do it. There isn't another way."

"There has to be."

"Not without endangering everyone else, and I won't do that. Not again."

"I'm going with you."

"You know you can't. She's going to need you."

"Someone else—"

"Someone else isn't her father." She spits the lie out as fast as she can, the taste of it lingering in her mouth sourly. But is it so terrible, telling him this? Is it worse than what's become of the world? If he believes the girl is his, it is a good thing, even if the good grew from something bad.

Unable to hold his gaze, she glances away to the swing set again. "It's the best option we have."

"It's terrible."

She sighs. "Yes. It is."

They are quiet for a long time before he finally says, "When do we tell the others?" There is defeat in his voice. Acceptance. And it both gladdens and breaks her heart at the same time.

"Not until the last minute. Otherwise they'll fight me on it, and that could ruin our chance."

He places his hand in hers again. "*Us*. Otherwise they'll fight *us* on it."

"Yes," she says quietly. "Us."

37

They drive into the cold morning sun.

The interior of the ASV is cramped with everyone riding together. Shoulders and knees touch, and after a time the air begins tasting used and stale.

They stop once to fill the large gas tank with fuel they've brought in cans attached to the roof. Everyone takes advantage of the break to stretch their legs. Zoey walks with Sherell and Rita across a little clearing beside the road, listening to them talk about what's happened since she left them in the clinic, which, according to Rita was the stupidest thing she's ever seen, and she's glad Zoey got shot in the foot since maybe that will keep her from running away again. Zoey takes the admonishments and smiles as Sherell rolls her eyes behind Rita's back.

As they start to return to the ASV, Sherell frowns, walking slightly slower so that they have to match her pace.

"What's the matter?" Zoey asks.

"Something's going on with Newton."

"What do you mean?"

"He's acting strange."

"He always acts strange," Rita says, flicking a piece of dead grass she's been rolling between her fingers in Sherell's direction. The other woman shoots her a look.

"He's been jittery since last night. When he didn't come to bed, I went outside and found him in the yard. He was looking around at the trees and the sky like he was lost."

"Wait, wait, wait," Rita says, stopping. "Come to bed?"

Sherell raises her eyebrows and a smile surfaces on her face. "What?"

"You know what! I can't believe you didn't tell me!"

"I don't tell you everything, you know."

Rita stands with her mouth open. "When did you . . ."

"A few nights ago. We were sitting in my room near dark and I was telling him about one of my new drawings. And . . . well, it just happened." Zoey smiles, both at Sherell's apparent happiness as well as Rita's disbelief. "Anyway, he's been really distant today and jumpy. I touched his shoulder before we left the road and it was like I'd hit him."

"Maybe being away from home for so long is affecting him," Zoey says as they continue walking.

"Maybe he's traumatized by you two . . . you know . . ." Rita says.

"It's definitely not that. He can't talk, but he speaks very well with his body," Sherell says with an evil grin.

Rita stops dead again. "You're unbelievable."

"I think he'd say the same thing if he could."

Rita's mouth drops open once more, and Zoey and Sherell both laugh as they step back onto the road.

Merrill stands beside the ASV, head tilted up toward the clouded sky. Zoey moves toward him, and he glances at her before returning his attention overhead.

"What are you looking at?"

"I don't know. Thought I saw something."

She brings her gaze upward and scans the intermingling clouds. "Like what?"

"Not sure. Like a bird, but . . ." he says almost to himself before looking around. "Is everyone back?"

"I think so."

"Good. Let's move out."

Zoey waits for the others to climb inside and notices Newton standing a few yards behind the vehicle looking at a large, gnarled tree beside the road. Its branches extend out over the highway like dead, reaching fingers tipped with razor points.

"Newton?" she says, and he flinches, turning toward her. His eyes are wide, large portions of white surrounding his irises. "Are you okay?"

It's almost as if he doesn't see or hear her. He moves past without acknowledgment, climbing inside to sit near the door without looking back. She touches his arm as she takes her seat across from him, but he doesn't react, his complete attention on the floor.

Zoey and Sherell share a look as the door slams closed and the ASV begins to accelerate.

"Six or seven hours and we'll be close to the ARC," Merrill says from the driver's seat. "We're taking a roundabout way since the last few storms probably dropped snow on the passes we usually use. We'll go south, then northeast."

"Gee, I'd love to spend more time in here breathing everyone else's air," Tia says. "Can you take an even longer route?"

"Unless you want to chance sliding off the side of a mountain, I'd stow that shit," Merrill replies.

"If we all can't keep our bodily functions to ourselves for the next seven hours, I'd prefer plummeting to my death. I'm looking at you too, dog," she says, pointing to Seamus, who stares up at her from where he lies on the floor. His tail thumps. "Rotten mutt."

"Tia . . ."

"Just saying."

Zoey leans into Lee, who sits beside her, and almost automatically he puts an arm around her. The vehicle sways and rumbles. There is low, comfortable conversation. Some of it is trivial, only to pass the time, but some is serious: ideas about how to retrieve her daughter from inside the ARC's walls. But of course there is only one way.

There has always only been one way.

The symmetry isn't lost on her. She's returning to the only place she never hoped to see again. She feels like the sculpture of the angel and demon in the old man's house—half of her screams to run away while the other half is steadfast, an anchor of resolution.

She doesn't know how long she's been lost within herself, only that something is wrong as she sits up. Sherell is repeating Newton's name, but he is standing, face and hands pressed to the window in the side of the vehicle. Ian begins to rise, reaching for him, and Merrill is asking what's wrong, when Newton puts his hand on the door and opens it.

They are all jerked forward as Merrill steps on the brake. They lurch into one another, the ASV shuddering as it struggles to slow, and all the while Newton stands by the open door, staring out at the decelerating landscape.

Before anyone can say or do anything else, he jumps out.

He hits the ground running and doesn't stumble. Then the ASV stops and everyone is piling out.

They're in an intersection in a town. Small buildings line the street for the next quarter mile before the road curves away out of sight. Broken overhead cables lay by the sidewalk and dead leaves clog a nearby drain. Newton hurries away, arms swinging at his sides, his head jutted forward, strides stiff and quick.

"Newton!" Sherell yells, and starts after him, jogging to keep up. "Stop!"

They're all moving, Zoey realizes. All going after him, but for some reason none of them are running like Sherell is.

She glances around the street they're on. It's unremarkable except for a huge yellow house on the corner that looks like it's over a hundred years old. It leans hard to the left and she's sure a strong wind would blow it over. Newton continues down the center of the street, head turning first one way and then the other as if he's looking for something.

"Newton!" Sherell says again, finally catching up to him and grasping his arm, but he pulls away from her gently, as if she's part of the landscape he's hooked himself on.

"Sherell," Merrill says from beside Zoey. "Let him go." Sherell gives him a long piercing look before starting after Newton again, but she keeps her distance this time, trailing him by a dozen steps.

They follow him down the street to another block that turns to the left, the opposite way ending in an empty lot filled with torn plastic bags that flap like waving hands. Newton doesn't pause at the junction. He goes left, up onto the narrow sidewalk, stepping over several tree branches that are dry and clean of their bark.

There are residues of life everywhere Zoey looks.

A car with a door half open in a driveway.

A child's bike on its side.

Two lawn chairs on a deck; a coffee cup on the railing beside them.

Newton runs past a two-story house with blue siding, bleached almost white with time, before pausing in front of a low home with an attached garage whose doors are open and gaping. The house itself is unremarkable, brown trim peeling around dark, hazy windows. The lawn is long grass folded over and brown beside a walkway leading to the small front porch. Newton stands statue-like, staring up at the house as they gather behind him.

"Newton, what—" Chelsea begins to say.

But he's no longer there. He's moving up the walk, traveling faster and faster until he's running as they call out his name, and Zoey hears herself say it as well even as something registers to her.

A tall piano sits at the back wall of the garage, a sheet draped partially over its top.

Her attention is brought back as Tia nudges her shoulder. "Zoey. Come on."

They go up the walk and into the house in a line, entering through a small foyer that holds only dusty furniture and a row of shoes of different sizes. Next is a kitchen, yellow flooring and beige walls. Some used dishes sitting beside a sink, dust motes hanging in the light from a window above it.

She stops with the rest of the group in the archway of a larger room, a slight smell of decay drifting past her. A picture hangs on the wall to her left, and she swipes a hand across it, clearing the glass of dust.

Four people smile out at her, forever locked in the single second. A good-looking man with graying hair at his temples and a wide smile, his arm around a petite woman with sparkling eyes, her head tilted to the side. Before them are two boys, one nearly as tall as his father, a crooked grin creasing his features, the other no more than three years old holding a tiny guitar, but anyone could easily see Newton's handsome features hidden in the young boy's face.

"Oh no," Zoey breathes. "This is his house."

"What?" Rita asks from beside her, but she's already stepping past Ian and Chelsea into the larger room.

A long rug with dark blotchy stains in its center is thrown back revealing a trapdoor set in the floor that reminds her of the attic access she hid in after escaping the ARC. Beside the rug are two bundles of white cloth laid side by side near the wall. It takes a second for her mind to recognize the shrunken shapes beneath the sheets as people.

"Newton. Can you hear me?" Merrill says, kneeling beside the trapdoor. Sherell stands next to him, looking down into the space below, and it's only when Zoey moves closer that she can see what they're looking at.

Cobwebs dance around the hole in the floor and Newton sits beneath them in the dirt under the house. He rocks in place, staring off into the darkness surrounding him. His hands flick as if he's playing an instrument.

"Newton, come back up," Sherell says. "Please. It's okay." She stoops forward and reaches down to him but he scoots away from her hand, still not looking up.

Merrill touches her arm. "Give him a minute." Sherell shoots Zoey a look that's both afraid and sad at the same time, but steps back.

Newton continues to rock, his boots pressing little ridges of dirt up each time he leans forward. The house is silent around them, the sweet smell of old decay more pungent.

"Can you hear me, Newton?" Merrill says in a low tone. "I know you're scared, but we're right here." He pauses. "This was your home, wasn't it?"

Newton's rocking increases. He turns his head to the side.

"We found you fifty miles north of here. Remember? You fell out of the tree. And that's how you got your name. But it's not your real name, is it?" Zoey sees Merrill turn something in his hand. A small photograph in a frame, Newton's young, smiling face filling up the picture.

Newton's hands move faster.

"Merrill," Zoey whispers.

"You already had a name, didn't you?"

Newton's head cranes around and his eyes are wide like they were on the road, bright against the darkness he sits in.

"Merrill, stop."

"Your name is Alex. Isn't it?"

Newton freezes, blinking long and slowly as if he's on the border of sleep. "This is you when you were very young," Merrill continues, turning the frame so Newton can see. "You're Alex."

Newton stares at the picture and the left corner of his mouth begins to pull down until his teeth are exposed on that side. His jaw lowers and his eyes close and open in another drawn-out blink. A breathy grating sound like fabric drawing across concrete comes from his throat.

Zoey feels a collective hush fall over all of them, much thicker than the silence of before. They're all huddled around the hole now, looking down at the man in the dirt who resembles the little boy in the photo so much they could be the same age.

"Ahhh . . . I," Newton whispers, and Zoey feels her lungs hitch. "I w-was pl-playing a-and they c-came." He looks away from the photo and finds Merrill with his gaze. "They h-heard m-m-me playing. Dad s-said hide. D-d-d-d . . ." Newton struggles, his face growing red. "D-d-don't m-make a s-s-sound. Don't ma-make a sound. Don't make a sound."

His voice breaks into jagged pieces with the last word and tears slip from his eyes as he starts to sway in place again. Zoey feels the air around her head become thinner as if they're suddenly at a higher elevation. She puts a hand out and Lee is there, clasping her fingers in his palm.

Merrill sets the picture aside and moves to the hole, lowering himself down easily. He settles into the dirt beside Newton and gradually draws the younger man to his chest. Newton tries to keep rocking for a moment before leaning hard into Merrill's shoulder, burying his face against the side of his neck.

And the sobs that quake through him are the only sounds in the quiet house.

38

They bury Newton's father and brother in the backyard beneath the boughs of a pine tree.

Ian says that his mother must have been taken after his father had him hide beneath the floorboards. Or perhaps she was already gone by that point, and it was only the three of them. But Zoey can't get past the notion that Newton was forced to listen helplessly while the rest of his family was murdered above him. What had he endured afterwards? How long had he sat in that house with the bodies of his father and brother? For it must have been him that wrapped them in their shrouds. She can't fathom the trauma it must have inflicted, but the fallout is something all of them are familiar with. Newton followed his father's final instruction long after the man himself was gone.

The conundrum of his name is also something they discuss as they place the last few shovelfuls of dirt over the graves. Should they continue to call him Newton or use the one given to him by his parents? For now they agree to continue calling him what they always have.

"Give him time," Merrill says, collecting the few shovels to return to the garage where they found them. "The dam is broken now. He'll tell us eventually what he wants."

Zoey gazes at the two mounds of dirt in what was never meant to be a graveyard. Burying the dead is fast becoming commonplace, another task to be completed, but she knows she'll never get used to it. She's sure it would feel unnatural even under ordinary circumstances, almost as if something is being stolen without ever knowing what it is.

Inside she walks through the rooms. It looks to have been raided at least once over the years since Newton departed. Several crushed cans lie in a room that might've been where his parents slept. There is a bird's nest in the bathroom, no sign it was ever inhabited except for two frayed feathers stuck to its top nodding in a draft. The last room she looks into keeps her locked in the doorway.

The wood of the many instruments is glossy beneath layers of grime. She recognizes another, more elegant piano than the one she spied in the garage. There are several guitars on stands as well as a set of drums that she knows by sight only because of one of Ian's record covers. A band called the Beatles.

This is where Newton learned to play the music that spills from him at times. She guesses it was the only solace his parents could provide after the events of the Dearth came calling, and ironically the very thing that brought death upon them in the end.

She closes the door tightly.

Outside it is barely past midday, the sun a bright disc behind the clouds. Everyone is gathered by the ASV that Tia and Lyle went and retrieved from where they left it on the main road. Newton sits inside on the bench with Sherell inches from his side. She hasn't left him since Merrill helped bring him up from beneath the house, turning him over to her care. Newton appears tattered and thin, like a work shirt ready to be retired. He sips on some of Ian's tea, the porcelain mug wrapped in both his hands.

"How is he?" Zoey asks Chelsea as she stops beside the vehicle.

"Okay. I think he was in shock when we came into town. The area must've kick-started his memory the closer we got. When he saw his street and house it must've been almost like reliving what he'd gone through."

"So terrible," Nell says. "No wonder he was quiet all that time."

They stand in the drive looking back at the house before Merrill finally says they should go. And Zoey agrees. This is a bad place, but more so, a necessary one. Lee had said most necessary things were bad, and she can't disagree with him. What comes next will be necessary. Bad but necessary. She hopes everyone else will see it that way too.

♦ ♦ ♦

"We'll be there in half an hour," Merrill says from the driver's seat. There are thankful groans and several colorful comments from Tia as they coast down a lonely stretch of road beside a length of water, upthrusts of dark rock in its center.

Zoey knows this place.

They passed through it while looking for NOA's agents, the southern approach to the ARC still forty miles distant, but close enough to raise the hairs on her arms.

She is going back.

Across from her, Lyle coughs and takes off his glasses to rub his eyes before replacing them. The older man has been particularly quiet since leaving the safe house that morning.

Zoey stands, moving to the other side of the narrow aisle, and gestures to the small opening in the seat beside him and he nods, scooting closer to Nell.

"How are you doing?" she asks as she sits down.

"Fine. I guess I'm nervous as much as everyone else about this place we're going to. Maybe more so."

"You're right to be."

He gives her a sidelong glance. "Is it true? Did they really put you and Rita in a sensory-deprivation chamber?"

"A sensory . . . oh, the box. Yes. They did."

"But I understand it wasn't only dark and soundless inside."

"No. It was worse."

"And pairing you with one another, keeping you tethered like that . . ." He shakes his head in a disgusted manner.

"It was their way of control. Without it I think they realized we would've finally done something about how we were living."

"And you did."

"Yes."

He seems to struggle with something. "I'm sorry you have to go back. I'm sorry about your daughter."

"Thank you. We appreciate all you've done for us. I'm thankful we found you."

"It was nothing, nothing compared to what you all saved me from."

"You've definitely repaid us. I'm guessing you were the one who suggested tapping into Hiraku's radio frequency."

Lyle blushes. "That was fairly simple, a matter of finding the right shortwave band."

"So you could do it again?"

"Of course."

"Good. Thank you," she says, squeezing his arm.

She stands and returns to her seat, trying to ignore the concerned look he continues to give her until they pull off the highway onto a side road that leads them over a rise and into the deserted parking lot of a long building with dozens of windows set in its front. The lot is surrounded by several smaller units of the same design. The sign above the main building's door reads "Everlasting View Inn." They pull to a stop behind one of the smaller structures, a concrete bowl carved into the ground before it. There is a foot of brown water choked with leaves at its bottom along with what might've once been a dog floating in its center.

When she steps out into the early evening air she sees why the cluster of buildings carries their name. There is a precipitous drop ringed by a sagging chain-link fence thirty yards past the unused pool. Beyond it, a narrow valley cups a stream at its base, the walls rising up in striped suggestions of other times the flow might've been a roaring river, carving away corners and sediment for millennia, yearning to be a straight line, constantly searching for an end. But now it looks weakened and pitiful and she can imagine it drying up completely, leaving only a shadow of what it once was. It's like she's looking in a mirror, the stream running not only through the canyon but through her as well.

Just a little longer and it will be over, one way or another. I'll find where the river ends. We all will.

Lee steps up beside her. "Did Lyle say he could do it?"

"Yes."

"Then it's for sure. It's what you want?"

"Yes. And it's what has to be." She turns to him. "You know it is."

He dips his head, not looking her in the eye. "Doesn't make it any easier." He grimaces and she sees he's trying to hold back tears. "Come on. Let's do it."

They return to the ASV, where most of the others are milling around, unloading some supplies while Merrill and Tia check the resort's buildings. When they return, Merrill gestures toward the main inn.

"Rooms are in good shape. There's multiple exits and the roof gives a clear view of the road. We'll be able to see anything moving toward us. Let's get the gear inside and eat. Then we can talk more about what's going to happen."

Zoey clears her throat and all eyes move to her. "Lee and I have something to tell you." She draws in a breath, readying herself. "Merrill, you said that we're family, that we'd die for one another, right?"

He sets down the gear he's holding. "Yes."

"And that when you're family you do whatever it takes to keep everyone safe. You all trusted me and went after me when I ran. You saved me." She pauses, nearing the cliff before leaping off it. "The baby inside those walls is my family, and that's why Lee and I decided I'm going to trade myself for her."

There is a stunned silence from the group before they all begin talking at once. Lee draws closer to her side as they listen to the squall of arguments everyone is making. Finally, Lee holds up a hand and they slowly quiet. "We decided this together. It's what Zoey and I want."

"How can you do this?" Rita asks, and Nell grips her arm but she shrugs it away. "How can you go back? They're going to lock you up again."

"Maybe. And maybe they won't," Zoey says. "We spoke about a plan before and I have one. Hiraku's army is coming here, I can feel it. Vivian and the rest of NOA value me. I'm what they've been searching for, and now I have the upper hand. I'll tell them about Hiraku and try to persuade them to evacuate the ARC before he attacks. Against his forces we'll have to be allies. They can't see it any other way."

"Wait, you're saying we're going to join them?" Sherell asks. "We're going to join NOA?"

"Until we're out of harm's way there isn't any other choice. Vivian and whoever's in charge now will have to listen to me."

"And if they don't?" Merrill asks. His voice is tired, threadbare and cracking.

She swallows. "Then none of you will be caught in the middle of the fight." She looks at Lee. "And our daughter will be safe."

"That's a shitty plan and you know it," Tia says. "Tell her, Merrill."

Merrill meets her gaze and she feels her throat trying to close but she forces the words out. "There's something else that you've all done for me without even knowing: you've taught me. You've taught me about strength and sacrifice, honor and right from wrong. You've taught me patience and persistence. You've taught me about love." She looks around at them all. "So after everything I've learned, you can't expect me to abandon our daughter. She's my family, just like all of you are."

Merrill frowns, glancing away as he massages one hand with the other. Everyone watches him. When he brings his eyes back up to her they are shining wetly. "If this is what you want, then it's what we'll do."

Zoey has to repress the urge to leap at Merrill and hug him.

"Are you serious?" Tia says, mouth partially open. "Did I just hear you agree with her?"

"They're two adults, Tia. Two parents," he corrects himself. "The world we grew up in is gone, but I'm not willing to go against someone's wishes for their child. That's what happened to me."

Tia flicks her fiery gaze from Merrill to Zoey to Lee. "I'm not listening to this bullshit anymore," she says finally, shoving past those in her way and disappearing into the deepening dusk. Zoey watches her go, wishing she could rush after her, plead with her to understand, but she knows Tia will only accept what she's said in her own time.

"So how do you intend to orchestrate this plan?" Ian asks quietly.

"I'll need to speak with Vivian over the radio and make sure our daughter's been born. Jefferson said she was close, so did Vivian in the video, but we need to be sure before anything happens."

"How do you know they'll tell you the truth?" Rita asks.

"I don't, but I have a way of testing them."

"What way?"

"If Lyle will find the ARC's radio frequency I'll show you."

She gauges Merrill's reaction. His jaw hardens, but then he looks to Chelsea, his gaze dropping to the slight swell of her belly.

"Okay. But we'll need to keep it short. I'm not sure if they have any way of pinpointing a transmission source, but they'll definitely know we're close."

She nods, her heart picking up speed as Lyle climbs into the ASV. She follows him and sits directly behind the front passenger seat as he works the knobs of the radio, pausing here and there listening to a blast of static. She's aware of the others crowding into the space behind her.

She would rather do this without an audience but now there isn't a choice. Like any family, she supposes, one person's business is everyone's.

There is a loud crackle and screech from the radio's speaker before a man's voice floods the cab.

"—on down to level two. You should punch out and get some rest."

Another voice a moment later. "Sounds good. The team get back okay?"

"Yeah. Nothing though. Harley can fill you in better than I can."

Lyle glances at her, handing over a corded microphone attached to the radio. "Hit the button and start talking whenever you're ready."

Zoey takes a breath, her thumb over the button.

Here it is. What everything's come to. This second. This decision.

She isn't ready. She'll never be ready.

She presses the button.

"This is Zoey. I want to speak with Vivian."

The airwaves are silent for a beat before one of the men comes back on, and when he does there's a tremor in his voice. "Repeat that. Did you say Zoey?"

"Yes. Put Vivian on within the next thirty seconds or I'll be gone."

"Okay, okay. Hold."

The radio goes silent and she counts in her head, hitting a hundred and three before there's a click and Vivian's voice streams from the speaker.

"Zoey. Is that you?"

"Yes."

"I'd like confirmation. What books did you have hidden in your room and where?"

"*The Count of Monte Cristo* and *The Scarlet Letter*. They weren't hidden in my room. They were in an alcove outside a loosened windowpane."

A long pause. "Hello Zoey. How are you?"

"I'm fine."

"Are you alone? Of course not. What a stupid question. You're with your companions, aren't you? The ones who helped you and the others escape. The ones who killed ten soldiers at the missile installation."

"I did that," Zoey says with vehemence. "I'm responsible, not them."

"I don't doubt it. Not after what you were able to accomplish here. Where are you now?"

"A safe distance from the ARC."

"I don't believe that since you're calling on a radio frequency, but in any case I'm very thankful to hear your voice. You received my message then?"

Zoey grits her teeth. "Yes."

"So you believe me?"

"Yes."

"Good. Since we're on the same page we might as well discuss what will happen next."

"Has she been born yet?"

Dead air. "Yes."

"Prove it."

"Zoey, isn't—"

"Prove. It. Or we're done."

Vivian lets out an exasperated sigh. "Okay. It will take a second."

Zoey glances around the vehicle and Merrill taps his wrist where a watch would rest. She's running out of time. But that's nothing new. The calendars were always there to remind her before, and now the seconds, minutes, and hours flee with a mind of their own.

The radio crackles and a sound issues from it that causes her heart to stutter.

The cry of an infant.

Loud and clear there is no mistaking the tremulous wails, the sound awakening something in her.

This is her child. Crying, afraid, and alone but for strangers that care only for her existence to serve another purpose.

But within Zoey there is the singular need to comfort, to quiet and assure the baby girl that everything will be all right. The power of the emotion shocks and robs her of her voice for a moment.

Her hand shakes as she brings the microphone up to her mouth. "What did you do to her?"

The baby's cries diminish slightly and Vivian voice returns. "I woke her up from a nap. You have a lot to learn about being a mother, Zoey. Children can be very trying."

She wants to throw the microphone down. Bash it to pieces on the steel floor. At the center of her rage is helplessness, and it's this that fuels the anger itself. "You . . . you . . ."

"Enough of this. We don't have the time and I lack the patience. When will you be here?"

She steadies herself, trying to keep her voice strong. "Soon."

"Then you've realized your responsibility? How much you mean to the world?"

"I've realized what I have to do."

"Good."

"On one condition." She turns to gaze at the people gathered near. Her family.

"And what is that?" Vivian asks.

"I'll give myself up if you let her go. I'll trade myself for my daughter."

A tangible shocked silence comes from the speaker. Zoey can feel it as an increasing pressure in her ears similar to the kind that accompanies leaving the mountains.

"Trade?" Vivian says.

"That's right. We'll meet tomorrow. You give her to us and I'll go with you."

"There is so much we can learn from her, from both of you," Vivian says. "Do you understand what's at stake here, Zoey? This isn't a game. This is the fate of humankind."

"I understand exactly. I understand you violated me and did this without my consent. I understand you killed my friends and sentenced some of them to a life worse than death. Believe me, I've had time to think about this. Either you make the trade or I disappear."

She releases the button and waits.

"Okay," Vivian says. "Okay. You win. We'll hand her over. Where do you want to meet?"

"There's a grouping of houses in the hills above the river where I went after the helicopter crash. We'll meet on the road running past the homes at noon tomorrow. If I hear a helicopter it's off."

"Very well. I'll see you then, Zoey."

She reaches out and turns the power control off. It snaps with a finality that seems much louder than it should. When she turns back to the rest of the group there are mixed emotions in all their expressions, but Lee is who she focuses on because there she sees only admiration and love.

"This place we're meeting at," Ian says. "I'm assuming you picked it to cut down on the possibility of an ambush?"

"Yes. It's wide open before you get to the houses," Zoey says, thankful that the conversation has steered back in the direction of planning. "We'll be able to hear a helicopter from a long ways off."

"How many should go?" Chelsea asks.

"Lee and me of course. Merrill, Newton, Tia if she'll come with us."

"She will," Merrill says.

"Ian can cover us from higher ground. We'll go a couple hours early and if anything looks wrong we get out of there."

The feeling within the vehicle becomes morose, as if a cloud has slid across the sun. Zoey knows what caused it. It is the finality, the sense of end that's snuffed out any more conversation. *That's it,* she thinks. *As simple as that, and everything is decided. Everything has changed.*

Rita leaves first, giving her a sidelong look that is part hostility and part resignation. Sherell and Newton exit next, both of them allowing a strained smile before they're gone. The rest file out until only Zoey, Lee, Merrill, and Chelsea remain.

"Thank you," she says to Merrill.

He nods. "It's not that I wanted to agree with you. If I had my way, we'd figure something else out. But I couldn't go back on everything I've told you. I just wish we didn't have an army riding up behind us."

"When do you think they'll get here?" Chelsea asks.

Merrill shrugs. "No way of knowing. But a force that size, I'd guess it would take at least a day or two to mobilize on land, and they'd move slower than a smaller convoy." He sits back, gazing past them. "Maybe a day from now, possibly sooner if they left right after you escaped."

The thought deflates her. What if Hiraku attacks the ARC before they can make the trade? What would she do? Before the anxiety can set in, Merrill stands and motions toward the main inn. "We should get some sleep; it's been a long day."

They step out of the ASV, and Lee walks halfway to the inn before he notices Zoey's not with him. He cocks his head at her when she remains beside Merrill and Chelsea.

"I'll be there in a minute," she says. He watches her for a long second before finally nodding and heading away.

"He's a good man," Merrill says. "He'll be a good father."

Zoey nods as Lee steps through the front entrance of the building. "He's not the baby's father."

Chelsea shakes her head as if to clear it. "What did you say?"

"Lee's not the father," she sighs, feeling as if some of the lie's weight has been removed from her. But only a small portion. "When we tested the blood my DNA matched and Lee's didn't."

"And you never told him," Merrill says, rubbing a hand up the side of his head. "My God, Zoey."

"I couldn't. I don't know what it would've done to him. No, that's not true. I do know. It would've crushed him. Besides that, I don't care who the father is if it's not him. He's the only one I want raising her. But he's going to need help." She moves her gaze from Merrill to Chelsea. "Will you help him? He's so afraid, I can see it whenever he mentions her. So will you help him take care of her? And . . . and . . ." Her throat closes off and Chelsea embraces her.

"Of course we'll help him."

"I know you'll have your hands full with your own baby, but . . ."

"Don't worry about it," Merrill says. "And besides, you're going to be there anyway. Don't think for a second that we're just going to let you sit in that facility for the rest of your life. Army or not, we'll get you out if they won't listen to you."

She smiles as he takes her hand and she squeezes it. Even with their comforting contact, the thoughts of tomorrow and what will come induce a squirming fear inside her, filling the space a child might have occupied.

"One last thing," she says, still clinging to Chelsea. They wait expectantly as an errant breeze rushes past in a frigid caress. "If it doesn't look like I'll ever get out of the ARC, please don't tell Lee the truth. As far as I'm concerned, he is her father."

39

She finds Lee in a room on the second floor overlooking the magnificent drop of the canyon behind the inn. He's drawn back the covers of the bed, and though the room smells stale, and there are blotchy stains on the carpet that might be ancient blood, there is a permeation of safety in the room as he looks at her. Tomorrow will be terrible. Nearly unbearable. But they can have tonight. Tonight is safe.

She crosses the room, pulling him to her and laying her head against his chest. She listens to his breathing, trying to memorize the sound.

They sway there together for a long time, the final light of day draining from outside the window until they are only shapes in the dark.

We're dancing, she thinks absently, remembering how Merrill and Chelsea moved with one another at Ian's home one night not long after she took her first steps unassisted. Music had been playing from Ian's old speaker, something slow and soft with a man's crooning voice saying words brimming with love and sadness. And they had danced, holding each other like she and Lee do now.

"What if you can't get out? What if you can't come back to us?" he whispers after what could've been hours. She blinks, wondering if she might've been dreaming. Maybe she still is.

"I will."

"But what if you don't?"

She draws a little away from him and lets a small smile emerge. "Then I guess it'll be your turn to rescue me."

He dips his head and kisses her, deeply, long and sweet.

They move to the bed and lie down together, and in the darkness with his skin against hers, the coiling fear unwinds and drifts away like a nightmare unraveling in a sunlit morning.

◆　◆　◆

She is awake before the horizon is even a hairline crack of gray.

She dresses, sitting on the bed beside Lee as he sleeps, one hand on his chest, feeling the rise and fall. He looks peaceful, dreaming something pleasant she hopes. He is strong, much stronger than she ever gave him credit for. He will be a terrific father, just like his own was.

Zoey leaves the room, pulling the heavy door shut behind her before moving down the dark hallway of the inn. It's easy to tell which rooms the others are staying in: almost all of them are open. Tia lies on top of her covers in one, facing away from the door, her rifle standing up at the foot of the bed; Ian snores in another on his back, hands folded neatly on his chest. At the end of the hall, the stairs branch in two directions and she climbs up, pushing through a door that's ajar at the top, onto the roof. A knee-high wall surrounds the roof's edge and a layer of rock covers some kind of springy material beneath it. The air has a snap to it that stings all the way to the bottom of her lungs. Nell stands at the southwest corner of the building, looking out over the shadow-stained landscape beyond. She glances over one shoulder as Zoey approaches before returning her gaze to the dark slithering line of road past the inn's drive.

"How was the night?" Zoey asks, tugging her jacket tighter around her shoulders.

"Quiet and cold. How was yours?"

"Good."

They stand without speaking for several minutes before Zoey turns her attention to the east. "I always liked this time of day, right before the sun comes up. There's something about the way the light washes over everything. It's like a cleansing. A new start."

"Anything can happen," Nell says. "That's what Robbie used to tell me. Each day is an opportunity, you never know what's in store." The older woman smiles sadly. "It's been a long time since I really believed that."

Zoey studies her, this remarkable woman. "How did you get through it? Losing Rita?"

Nell's brow furrows, and a hardness settles on her features. "I didn't. I died over and over after they took her. I replayed every single second of it in my mind, so much so that life became less real. I lived in my own head, drowning in misery. I'm sure I was insane." She frowns, chewing on the inside of her lip as if trying to remember something crucial. "But there was always something that kept me going: the vague notion that Rita was still out there somewhere, still needing me, scared and alone. I would try to forget and drop into depression so deep it was like I was at the bottom of a well, looking up at the world I'd lost like it was a dream, not caring, not daring to hope, but it would always come back. The tiniest notion that if I kept going there was a chance that I'd see her again, if only for a minute. I tried not to think it because it hurt so much, but it was always there." Nell seems to recede somewhere inside herself before returning. "Now it's like I'm dreaming again. A sweet dream that will come apart as soon as I open my eyes."

Zoey takes her hand. "You're awake."

Nell looks down at their hands and finally nods. "I'm sorry you never found them, your parents."

Zoey feels the back of her eyes burn, but she lets out a small laugh. "I did, though. I was lucky enough to have two fathers and a grandfather. I have two mothers, one of which wants to slap sense into me most of the time. I have brothers and sisters and someone who is the other half of me I never knew was missing." She pauses, struggling to go on. "And now I have a daughter who's going to have a family right from the start, and if that's all I accomplish in my life, it will be enough."

Nell studies her. "You're an incredible woman, Zoey. I'm thankful Rita had you while I wasn't there."

"To be honest, Rita and I—"

"Oh I know how she treated you, she told me. But it doesn't change the fact that you were there for her."

She can't think of anything to say to that and resigns to simply hold Nell's hand and watch the sun bleach the darkness away.

40

Good-bye again. Always good-bye.

She gazes at them lined up beside the ASV in the newborn light. They are ashen, downcast, and taciturn, but they are hers.

Zoey hugs Lyle, telling him thank-you again, and when she pulls back from him his eyes are wet behind his glasses, but he manages to smile for her. Next is Chelsea, who embraces her so tightly she can feel the roundness of her growing belly through their jackets.

"You're coming back to us," Chelsea whispers. "Don't get comfortable in that place."

Zoey laughs, but it is a strangled sound. "I won't." Chelsea kisses her on the cheek and steps from her, turning and walking away without looking back.

Seamus sits next to the ASV's running board as if he is planning on a ride, and she kneels before him, rubbing both hands on the sides of his wide head. "You keep them safe. All of them. I'm counting on you." The dog examines her with his quizzical gaze just as he did when she'd first awoken at Ian's cabin. He licks her chin once and issues a whine deep in his chest.

Beside him, Rita and Sherell wait. Sherell is already crying and without hesitation the three of them latch onto one another as if a high wind is trying to tear them apart.

"You're so stupid," Rita says in a tear-strained voice. "When are you going to stop being so stupid?" But Zoey feels the other woman's hold tighten on her.

"In my nature, I guess."

"We love you," Sherell says as they finally pull apart. "Even if she can't say it, we do." Rita gives the barest of nods, her face so red it nearly matches her hair.

"I love you too. This isn't the end," Zoey says, even as her intuition tells her otherwise. "We'll see each other again." They both nod and it takes a monumental effort to let go of them, all instinct telling her that if she does, it will be for the last time.

As they part she gives them the bravest smile she can summon, sure it doesn't appear brave at all with tears in the corners of her eyes.

Then she's forcing herself up and into the ASV, unable to look at them all for another instant, because one more second and she knows she won't be able to leave.

Those accompanying her pile in. Merrill first, climbing into the driver's seat. Ian next with his rifle. Then Tia, glowering and silent, and last Newton and Lee. As Lee begins to shut the door, Seamus steps up on the running board and tries to lunge inside with them but is halted by a hand signal from Ian.

"Not this time, boy. You stay." With a chuff the dog reluctantly backs out, throwing Zoey a dejected look that tugs painfully at her heartstring. She focuses on the floor as the door slams shut and the vehicle begins to move. Lee's hand finds its way to the inside of her arm, giving her a modicum of comfort, but it is like being covered by a thin blanket in a bitter wind.

She doesn't look out the windows as they drive because she knows she will recognize their surroundings, the memories of fleeing through them returning as tangible and vivid as if she had left the ARC only yesterday. No, she'll need her strength when the time comes, when she'll have to say good-bye and step away from all she loves.

And she doesn't know if she'll have the courage.

Merrill guides the vehicle around a long turn before slowing it to a stop.

Here already. So soon.

Lee squeezes her arm again and they emerge from the ASV into a strong breeze tasting of winter. Here in the high hills above the river the soil is already hardening with frost.

The road is only a suggestion before them, its lane barely discernable amidst the washed sediment and detritus littering its width. It runs straight for nearly a mile before dropping and curving away. She recalls the pain and fear, running for her life up that incline, away from the downed helicopter with its counterpart landing near the broken wreckage of the crash.

Her stomach had been a gash of pain.

Head ringing, nerves shredded with terror.

Each breath possibly her last.

"Zoey."

Lee stands directly before her, blocking her view of the road. She'd been looking straight through him, lost in the before.

She shakes herself free of memory. "I'm okay."

"Are you sure?"

"Yes." She looks to the rest of the group, their expressions dour and worried. "I'm okay," she repeats to them.

Merrill drags his gaze from her and points north. "That house across the field is the closest shelter. Ian, you can set up there. The rest of us will cover Zoey from here when . . . when it's time. I'm going to scout a little bit, make sure we don't have company." He looks as if he's going to say something else but instead moves away, climbing a nearby swell in the ground to walk its ridge.

Ian approaches her, his eyes two glistening pools. "I suppose this is good-bye," he says quietly as Lee takes a few steps away to give them privacy. "I have to say, I'm quite tired of seeing you go." His voice breaks on the last word and he reaches out a hand that she holds. "I don't know if I've ever told you, but you remind me so much of my daughter, Lynn. She was as one-minded as you are, you know. I hated that about her after she was killed, her persistence. I thought it was the reason why she died. But now I can see it was her life, it was who she was." He smiles through the tears. "You're strong like her, and I am so proud of you, Zoey."

She hugs him, feeling his chin rest on the crown of her head. She tries to find something to say to this man who brought her back from the brink of death, who always had a kind word for her, never ceased believing in her. Instead she absorbs his comfort like a balm, letting the future fall away outside his embrace.

A sound begins to build somewhere to the east. A low chuckle that slowly becomes more defined. At first she thinks it is only the wind careening up through some of the large cuts in the hills, but soon it changes and takes on a huskier growl.

Engines.

Ian stiffens and releases her, his gaze locked on the highway before them. With a final look they part, his last smile as warm as a summer afternoon as he runs across the field toward the nearest house.

Then Tia is by her side, pulling her back toward the vehicle. "Bastards are early. Why are they so early?" she growls, raising her rifle.

Zoey feels Lee's hand searching and finding her own as she stares down the length of road.

"Merrill!" Tia yells, and a second later he appears at the top of the nearest hill, sprinting toward them, his gait partially hindered by his prosthetic. Newton stands to her other side and centers his rifle on the horizon.

A dark blob appears in the road as if rising directly from the cracked asphalt. Seconds later another follows. The shapes solidify, their edges sharpening until she sees they are two armored vehicles, much smaller than the ASV but still heavily built. A guard stands near the rear of each one, manning a turreted gun.

The wind carries the stink of diesel fumes to them. Above, a roil of clouds she hadn't noticed before suffocates the sun. The vehicles decelerate and come to a stop fifty yards away. Inversely, Zoey's heart picks up speed until it feels like there are no spaces between beats.

This is it. The circle is complete. I'm going back.

Home.

That's what Vivian had called the ARC. But it was never her home. NOA and all of its agents have never known the meaning of the word.

The front passenger door on the closest vehicle opens and Vivian herself steps out. She is much as Zoey remembers: slim and tidy, wearing beige slacks and a dark coat, her narrow features mirroring her dress. Her brown hair is pulled back tightly, leaving her hazel eyes unhindered to find Zoey and pin her where she stands.

The wind drops and an uneasy quiet falls between the two parties.

"Hello Zoey," Vivian says.

"Hello," she replies, trying to keep the warble from her voice.

"I'm not surprised to see you here early. I assumed you would be more than punctual." Vivian takes a step forward and Tia matches it, partially blocking Zoey from her line of sight.

"Why don't you just stay right there, bitch," Tia says. "Or we'll see how well I can do a lobotomy with a hollow point."

The gunmen on the trucks swivel their weapons up but Vivian makes a batting gesture with one hand and their barrels sink.

"My, my, Zoey, you've found some colorful individuals to take up with."

"I think you—" Tia begins, but Vivian cuts her off.

"You know what I think? I think you should lower your weapons and quit this charade of force. You're outgunned and we all know no one is going to start shooting with Zoey and her child in the crossfire, so let's cut the posturing, shall we?"

"Lower your weapons," Merrill says. Newton does as he's told, but Tia holds steady and Zoey can see a bead of sweat roll down from her temple. For an instant she imagines Tia firing a bullet straight through Vivian's head and the return strafing the gunners in the vehicles would retaliate with. Despite the importance of the exchange, she doesn't doubt it could still end in absolute ruin. When had reason ever kept people from violence?

"Tia," Merrill says.

The tension of the moment holds for another agonizing second before dissolving as Tia lowers her rifle.

"There. Now we can speak to one another like human beings."

"If you were a human being, you'd give us our daughter," Lee says, his voice carrying across the distance.

"If you had any sense of duty, Lee Asher, you wouldn't be standing on that side. You'd be next to me, trying to get Zoey to see reason. But of course I'm not surprised. Your father was a liability just as you are."

Lee's hand leaves Zoey's even as she tries to grip it harder. He takes two steps before she lunges from behind Tia and snags his arm, pulling him back.

"Stop," Zoey says. He stares with pure hatred at Vivian for another beat before letting her guide him back.

"You're all the same," Vivian says, and Zoey can see the snarl carved into her lips. "Weak. You fight and loathe me, but I've dedicated my life to ending the Dearth. And now that I have, how do you thank me?" She shakes her head. "With threats."

"Where is she?" Zoey says quietly. "Where is our daughter?" Vivian hesitates, eyeing her with the cold consideration of a scientist watching an experiment. Zoey clears her throat. "Just so you know, you have crosshairs on your forehead right now. I've never seen the man holding the gun miss, so despite all your talk, if you don't give us our daughter right now, none of this will matter if you're dead."

An almost satisfied smile crosses Vivian's face and she motions toward the lead vehicle.

The rear passenger door opens and a guard emerges. It takes Zoey a second to realize the man is Steven, Lily's cleric. Within the shock of seeing him in this setting she registers that he's holding something: a bundle of blankets, pink and fluttering. Steven walks to Vivian, transferring the bundle to her arms carefully.

Comprehension slams into her as if she's just dropped to the ground from the top of a building.

That is my daughter. Right there in that woman's arms. She's a part of me, wrapped up in blankets, able to think, and breathe, and see the world around her.

The knowledge might as well be the bullet that stole her ability to walk. All the strength leaves her legs and she has to reach back and grasp Lee's arm to keep standing. Dimly she registers he is trembling as they start moving forward.

At the same time Vivian walks toward them, gazing down at the blankets in her arms.

The gap closes several yards before Zoey falters and turns, looking from Tia to Newton to Merrill. She's on the brink of running back to them, all the things she wanted to say trying to spill free, but Merrill lifts his chin toward Vivian, heartbreak plain on his face.

"Go," he says, and silently mouths the words, *We love you.*

I love you too, she returns, finding each of their faces for a brief time.

And it's in that moment she knows she'll never see them again. She feels it as sure as she's felt anything. This will be the last glimpse of them she'll take with her. The idea that nothing can be done to her at the ARC that will strip her of this moment, or of any of the time she's spent with them, gives her enough courage to continue walking.

Lee's grip tightens on her hand and she squeezes back.

They meet Vivian halfway between the two groups. She stops several feet away, gazing intently at Zoey.

The nerve that brought her the last dozen steps flees as Vivian unfolds the blanket's edge and turns slightly.

Every sense sharpens to a needlepoint.

She can see each fiber of the blanket, smells what could be a flowery soap paired with the field loam. She feels sweat running down her spine despite the cold, tastes the dried briny parch of her mouth, and hears grit skating across the road over the vigorous slam of her heart.

A hand so small it defies reason pokes from the blankets.

A hand that tiny can't exist. The little fingers and joints are impossible and the pinkness of the skin nearly matches the blankets surrounding it. Then Vivian shifts the bundle a little more and a face appears within its folds.

Zoey drags in a breath and finds she can't release it.

Her daughter looks out at her.

Sapphire eyes find her and hold above a minute button of a nose. Hair, dark and already beginning to curl, grows from the top of her head and she holds the hand not reaching into the air below her chin so that her lips purse out slightly.

She is the most beautiful thing Zoey's ever seen.

Lee makes a gasping sound beside her.

"These are your parents," Vivian says in a low voice to the baby. Zoey finds herself taking a lurching stride forward but Vivian backs away. "Now Zoey, you can't think I'd hand her over to you, do you? What would stop you from simply running away? You'd have no fear of getting shot. No, Lee will have to take her, not you."

"But—"

"Do you want to make the exchange or not?"

Breathless. Dazed. "Yes."

"Then do exactly what I tell you. Move past me and I'll give Lee the child."

She finds herself balancing on a narrow ledge over an incredible drop. It has all come to this. And yes, the fear is there, but something more prevalent casts it aside like an insubstantial barrier. She would die for the girl in the blanket, easily give her life through some atavistic instinct more powerful than anything she's experienced before.

She's being pulled around, away from the beautiful little face peering at her, and she almost begins to fight before Lee says her name.

She looks at him, knowing the time has come. So much to say. How can she put into words days and years of love's potential lost? How can she pour forth the sentiment that she's finally found what she's been looking for, and it is so much more than she could have hoped for? Love is too small a word. How can she tell him?

"Take care of her," she whispers.

"I will." He blinks and a tear escapes, glittering down his face. "I'll find you. I promise."

"Okay."

"Like you said, it's my turn to rescue you."

A sob wracks her but she holds it at bay, kissing him before drawing away. Vivian watches without reaction. She might as well be seeing the disassembly of two machines for all the emotion she exudes.

Zoey looks in through the blankets as Vivian walks by her. The little girl yawns, eyes scrunching shut before blinking at the solemn sky.

Then she has passed, and all she can see is Vivian depositing the baby into Lee's arms, who looks as if he might faint. He cannot tear his eyes away from the bundle and the greater part of her wants to fight, to stay with them both no matter the cost.

"Good. That's done," Vivian says, coming even with Zoey. She roughly grabs her by the upper arm and guides her toward the two vehicles. They're fading away, her family. Growing smaller and smaller by the second, and she wonders if the memories of them will follow suit over time. Will she forget their faces, their names? Will she forget who she's become, who she finally is?

All her thoughts fray as she nears the first vehicle, Steven holding the rear passenger door open.

"Hello, Zoey," he says, guiding her into the dark interior. But something stops her. Lee is yelling, yelling something she can't understand. She begins to step back out onto the road but Vivian flicks a hand at Steven and he shoves her onto the hard seat.

The door slams shut and Vivian climbs in the front beside the driver, another guard wearing reflective sunglasses. Zoey looks out through the side window at Lee holding the swaddled child. What had he been yelling? Something about a name?

Eli's last words come back to her then. *Don't let them go. The ones you love. They disappear.*

The vehicle's engine rumbles to life and they begin to reverse.

Wait. I'm not ready.

Wait.

Wait.

"Wait," she says aloud, sitting up to the steel grating separating the front and rear seats. She hooks her fingers through it. "There's an army coming."

"Really Zoey, I'd expect a better story from you."

"I'm telling the truth. They're—"

"They're going to storm the ARC and break you out, right? That's kind of a weak intimidation tale, don't you think?"

"You don't understand. There are thousands of them." She scrambles for something to make Vivian believe her, because if she can convince the other woman now before her family is out of sight, maybe the insistent premonition of losing them can be refuted and dissolved.

"Relax, Zoey, everything will be okay," Vivian says, reaching for something beneath her seat as the vehicle bucks into gear and begins to pull away.

"His name is Hiraku and he's coming here. He knows the location and he's got an army of men."

Vivian turns, holding a small canister with a short steel tube attached to it. "Just relax," she says, and presses a button on its top.

A mist sprays out of the tube's end and Zoey reels back coughing as a pungent chemical odor clogs her nasal passages, forces its way into her lungs as she takes an involuntary breath.

Can't inhale. Don't breathe.

But already her muscles are weakening and she's slumping back, melting into the hard seat as if it's a plush and enveloping bed. Vivian's voice follows her down the tunnel she's fallen through. Because darkness is eating the corners of her vision and her tongue is too heavy to move.

In the last seconds before she loses the slipping hold she has on consciousness, she realizes what Lee was yelling on the road.

He was asking what he should name her. What he should name their daughter.

41

The man watches the two Humvees roll away down the road before they disappear from sight.

He trains the binoculars on the remaining group of people beside the larger transport. The man holding the bundle of blankets walks toward them like a zombie, feet shuffling and head down. He's crying, that much is apparent. The others gather round him and the old man from their group, who had taken a position in a house nearby, emerges, rifle slung over one shoulder.

He's seen enough.

Quickly he tucks the binoculars away in their case and slings it into his small pack along with the last of his energy mix he hasn't finished yet. He stands, hoisting his rifle from where it rests on its tripod in the open window, the water-warped desk he drug to the opening supporting its stock. Even at the half-mile distance between him and the two groups he's sure he could have picked each of them off without a problem. But that wasn't his mission, and from what he's heard through rumor and conversation before he was sent on reconnaissance, the girl that just got into the Humvee and disappeared toward the river is Hiraku's property. As he descends the rotting stairs of the abandoned house he wonders, not for the first time, how she was able to get the better of Shirou. The man had been one of their best: smart, fast, tough, and brutal. The idea that that waif of a woman could outthink and outmaneuver him is as unbelievable as it is unsettling.

He leaves the house through the rear entry, checking the remaining group's position once more before departing. They are all inside the vehicle now and he watches it trundle away. But they aren't his concern. Hiraku made it abundantly clear that those with her didn't matter. If he was honest with himself, he would concede that their leader has lost his grip since Shirou's death. Preservation of the species and a new life are no longer driving the mission. Instead it is vengeance.

Not that he truly cares as long as his son gets a fair shake at a better life someday. The boy is almost nine and he deserves to have children of his own. The end, for him at least, justifies the means.

He crosses the gap between the house and the low hill nearby. With the camouflage he wears he would be nearly impossible to see even while moving. When he's behind cover his nerves relax slightly from the tension that's built inside him during the surveillance, and he begins to jog.

It is early afternoon when the encampment comes into view. He exits a dense patch of woods into a clearing that might've once been a hay field, now grown over and encroached by bramble. The convoy takes up the better part of the forty acres before him. There are masses of small tents and nearly two hundred vehicles of all sizes. Some of the men even rode motorcycles when they'd moved out of Seattle two days before, which turned out to be a terrible mistake when they reached the first mountain pass covered with snow. Even going slow there were several accidents and one bike's rider slid from the highway and fell a dozen feet before coming to rest on a bed of rocks that broke his fall, as well as his left femur.

He heads across the field, noting several of the other scouts are already back and enjoying a hot meal. They nod his way as he passes, eyeing his route directly toward the largest tent at the center of the field. Six soldiers guard the entrance and relieve him of his rifle and sidearm before he enters.

The inside of the tent carries a harsh smoky aroma of burnt wood and cooked onions. The latter of the two sends a spike of hunger through his stomach. A long folding table takes up the majority of the space and several men sit around it, a map splayed out across its middle. Hiraku is at the far end, elbows propped on the table's edge, eyes cast down at the map, hands folded beneath his chin. When he enters, the commander glances up at him.

"Sir, I located her."

"Where?" Hiraku says, leaning forward.

"About twenty miles to the east, near the river. I was moving south when their transport came into view, so I set up position and observed when they stopped in the highway."

"What happened?"

"There was an exchange."

"An exchange?"

"Yes. Her group handed her over to a woman who must be from the facility we located with the drone. In return they gave the group a bundle of blankets."

"Bundle of blankets?"

"Yes sir." He pauses. "I'm sure it was a baby."

Hiraku sits back from the table as the other men stare at him. He passes a hand across his lips. "You're certain they took her to the facility in the river?"

"They were heading in that general direction, so I'd say yes."

Hiraku shuffles through several papers along with some hand-drawn sketches. "Draiman, you're sure these estimates are correct about the wall thickness?"

The pale man to Hiraku's left nods. "As close as we can tell from the drone footage. Give or take a couple inches."

Silence falls over the room. The fire crackles in the little stove situated in one corner. All eyes hold on Hiraku who continues to stare at the map.

Finally, he glances up as if realizing he isn't alone. "Make the men ready. We move out at 3:00 a.m. tomorrow. Attack is at first light."

42

Lee stares down at the tiny girl in his arms, tracing the lines of her face over and over as the ASV rumbles along the road.

He knows he's in shock, but the awareness of the fact does nothing to pull him free of it.

Zoey is gone, and now he's holding what's left of her.

The baby makes a cooing sound and her eyelids flutter before she yawns. She's done this at least four times now since he took her from Vivian and it's yet to fail to enthrall him. This little life is his complete responsibility now, the gravity of it almost overpowering. He manages to drag his attention from her for a moment as he realizes someone's saying his name.

He looks up at Tia. "I'm sorry, what?"

"I said, are you okay?"

"Oh. Yeah, yeah I'm fine." But his voice sounds like someone else's speaking in another room. The detachment isn't alarming. In fact, he welcomes it because otherwise he'll start thinking about Zoey and how they shoved her into the back of the vehicle and out of sight like she was being eaten and—

"Would you like me to hold her?" Ian asks, dragging him away from the thoughts that are trying to close over his mind like cold water.

"Um. No. No, I'm okay." Lee glances out the window past Tia's head, thinking that they've been driving almost as long as they did coming to the meeting point. When they return to the inn he'll have to find something for the baby to eat. Milk. He'll need milk. But where are they going to get milk? He hasn't seen a cow since stumbling across one after fleeing the mountains before his arrival in Seattle. He's about to open his mouth and ask out loud what the others think about food for her when Merrill begins to slow the vehicle.

They've driven up a slight incline and turned a corner onto a dirt road that empties out onto a plateau. A squat brick building stands at one end of a long parking lot and a series of heavy electrical cables run in sagging lengths between several towers in the distance. Below the flat lookout they've stopped on, the river valley drops away. Far to the east he spots something that catches his gaze and holds it as Tia crosses the aisle and reaches for the door.

The southern lip of the ARC is barely visible beyond the rim of the rise they've parked on. Its concrete shelf rounds outward like a blossoming flower petal. Slightly to the right he can see the impassive wall of the dam. They're maybe four miles from the structures but seem so much closer, the open air between the positions as deceiving as it is breathtaking.

"What are we doing here?" he asks as the others begin to file out of the vehicle.

Merrill pauses on the steps leading outside. "Come on. You'll see."

The wind tugs at his jacket as he steps from the ASV, snapping the blankets around the baby like an animal trying to tear her from him. He hugs her closer, tucking the loose folds of material in around her face. She gazes up at him with a long look before scrunching up her nose and letting out a brief cry that turns into another yawn.

"It's okay. We're going to be okay," he says, following the others around the side of the ASV. When he looks up, he's stunned to see another vehicle there, a small car the color of turned soil, with rims of rust adorning its wheel wells. The rest of the group are climbing free of it, looking at him expectantly. All except Lyle, who is opening up a black folding case on the hood of the car, a strange crosshatched piece of aluminum in one hand attached to it with a length of cord.

Chelsea hurries to Lee, giving him a brief hug before brushing back the blanket to look at the baby.

She inhales quickly, and when she speaks her voice creaks with emotion. "Oh Lee, she's beautiful. She's absolutely gorgeous."

"Yeah. Yeah, she is," is all he can manage.

"Can I?" Chelsea asks, reaching out.

Lee frowns but slowly transfers the bundle over, an unfamiliar reluctance coming over him at the request. He doesn't want to let her go.

"Hello," Chelsea whispers, beginning to sway in place, her face only inches from the baby's. "I'm Chelsea. I—" She abruptly looks up at Lee and he shakes his head.

"We didn't name her. There was no time. We ah . . ." He feels heat prickle at the back of his eyes and bites his lower lip.

"Oh Lee." She leans into him, holding the girl with one arm and wrapping the other around him. "Don't worry. We're going to get her back."

When she draws away, he reabsorbs his surroundings. "What's going on anyway? Why are we here?"

"Merrill hasn't told you?"

"No."

"Come on. We'll explain."

They move to the car where Merrill, Tia, and Ian huddle around Lyle and the case that rests on the hood. Lee inches in beside them close enough to see the case is filled with electronics. Several open circuit boards glow with dots of red and green, a number of places patched with soldered lines and jumper wires. A corded headset sits over Lyle's ears, and the older man squints at a dial as he turns a knob attached to one side of the conglomeration.

"Tia, hold this, will you?" Lyle says, passing the antennae to her.

"Where?"

"Take a couple steps in the direction of the ARC."

"What's going on? What is this?" Lee asks, moving his gaze from the apparatus Tia holds to Merrill as he turns to face him.

"It's a rudimentary tracking device."

"For what?" Merrill says nothing and waits for the understanding to finally wash over Lee. "For Zoey?"

"Yes. When she started talking about returning to the ARC, I had Lyle and Tia begin scrounging for parts." He motions to the open case on the hood. "They cobbled together all this from a store they found in Newton's hometown along with some electronics that were in the basement of the inn last night. Lyle can read the signal's strength and gauge distance by its intensity. More or less we can narrow down her location by a hundred yards or so."

Lee frowns. "How? You said a signal, but where is it coming from?"

"A small, battery-powered transmitter," Ian says. "I attached it to her jacket beneath her hood when I hugged her good-bye." Lee stares at the old man and sees a flicker of guilt on his features.

"We couldn't let her go in there without having a way to find her," Merrill says.

"Why didn't you say something to me?"

"Honestly because we couldn't trust you not to tell her."

"But what if they find the transmitter?"

"We have to hope they don't."

"But—"

"There was no other way," Merrill says, teeth gritted. "Zoey is willing to give herself up, but I'm not."

"Okay, signal is about three and a half miles away," Lyle says, motioning Tia to the right. "Growing stronger."

"They're coming back toward us?" Chelsea asks.

Merrill nods. "It's what I was hoping for."

"What do you mean?" Lee asks.

"I always wondered if there was another way into the ARC besides over the wall. We searched for a long time before our first attack but never found anything. If they bring her in any way other than by the elevator or a chopper, we'll know it."

"Signal's staying steady," Lyle says, turning to stare out over the drop. "They've stopped somewhere this side of the river."

"Can you tell where?" Merrill asks.

Lyle shakes his head but holds out both his arms, sectioning off an area of the river valley. "Somewhere in this range give or take a quarter mile."

"The town," Ian says, meeting eyes with Merrill. "They've stopped in the town somewhere."

"Wait." Lyle's eyes go wide and he turns back to the case, adjusting a dial for nearly thirty seconds before straightening up and drawing the headphones away from his ears. "It's gone."

"What, the signal? How can it be gone?" Lee asks.

The baby begins to cry. Quietly at first but then with more volume until the plateau rings with her shrill voice.

"It's like we thought," Merrill says. "There's another way in. The signal's working off radio waves that can be interrupted by any number of things, but if they were just going behind a building or through a stand of trees, it would return as soon as they were clear. Still nothing, Lyle?"

"Nothing. It's gone."

"It's got to be underground. Some way into the ARC from below."

"You mean the entrance is under the river?" Lee asks, moving to where Chelsea rocks the baby, her cries slowly beginning to quiet.

"I don't know," Merrill says. "But we're going to find it. Lyle, Tia, get points of reference we can search within based on the last signal. As soon as it's dark, we go."

"Zoey wanted a chance to talk to them, remember? She wanted to see if she could convince them about Hiraku and the army."

"She'll have until we find the entrance. Then we're going in and getting her out."

"Merrill—"

Merrill holds up a hand to silence him, eyes blazing with emotion. "Lee, I lost one daughter in that place, and I refuse to lose another."

43

She's in a boat of some kind.

Bobbing, swaying. The movement of water beneath her unmistakable. Zoey groans, pain invading her consciousness in buffeting waves. Her head aches at the base of her skull. With one hand she reaches back and rubs the spot, half expecting it to be swollen and sticky with blood, but there is only smooth, undamaged skin. Someone must have hit her though, what else could cause—

Her eyes come open as she remembers.

Steven shoving her into the vehicle.

Lee yelling in the distance.

Her pleading with Vivian about Hiraku.

The blast of mist in her face.

Sinking darkness.

She blinks. She's in a room, not a boat, and she can't move except to lick her dry lips.

The room is unlike any place she's been before. The walls are a comfortable beige lined with richly stained bookshelves laden with texts. Exposed beams matching the shelves arch up and meet in the center of the room, which appears to be circular in shape, and in the middle a chandelier hangs, dripping with crystal and light. An enormous desk sits across from her on a woven rug the color of wine, a leather chair empty behind it. Two more overstuffed chairs rest to either side of a small table several feet away.

Zoey attempts to sit up and makes it on the second try. She looks down and notices she's wearing a comfortable pair of cotton pants and a buttoned shirt made of the softest material she's ever felt. Her feet are shod in a pair of slippers, and a light blanket is draped over her middle.

She tosses it aside, perching on the edge of the leather couch she's been placed on. How long has she been sleeping? There's no way to tell but it feels like more than a few hours. A tall glass of water rests on a table to her right and she only resists the compulsion of her thirst for a second before downing the entire thing. There would be no reason for them to drug her again, now that she's here. But where exactly is she?

Zoey rises slowly, tries her balance and finds it intact, though she feels slightly sluggish, her senses lowered a notch. The hardwood floor beneath her creaks, and she turns in a circle, examining the office. She's in the ARC, but where? She never encountered a place like this in all her years in the facility. Even as she tries to recall the blackened stretch of memory that is the last few hours, a sound comes from behind her and she turns.

A door set between two bookcases opens, and a figure steps into the room, his face lost in shadow for a split second before it is revealed.

But even before her mind registers the impossibility of his features, it is already computing how he moves, the set of his shoulders, the suit he wears.

The Director stops a dozen yards from her and smiles. "Hello Zoey."

She stumbles back, knees catching on the couch, forcing her to sit. "No," she hears herself say even as she's rising again, her brain trying to uncouple what she's seeing from what she knows. "You're dead."

The Director smiles, glancing over one shoulder, and it's then she sees he isn't alone. Vivian steps into the room behind him and closes the door, but not before Zoey glimpses what's outside.

A sterile hallway, the corner of a stairway visible to the left. And it's all she needs to know where she is.

The Director's room.

"Not the welcome I was hoping for, but the one I expected," he says.

Zoey scrambles to her feet again, beginning to circle away from them. She glances at the desktop, searching for a weapon, but there's nothing but a neat stack of papers, a small lamp, several books. Maybe in one of the drawers—

"There's nothing in this room to fight us with," the Director says, moving closer. He stops near the low table in the center of the room. "Though I'm guessing you could become pretty creative with one of the heavier books. It wouldn't be the first time someone was injured with knowledge."

"How did you . . . ?"

"Survive? With quick treatment and through many hours of pain." His handsome features twist slightly with anger and become an ugly facsimile, as if there is another face hiding beneath them. His true self surfacing. Then it is gone, replaced by the easy smile he wore during all his speeches. "But that's neither here nor there. You were under duress at the time. Your actions were perfectly reasonable."

"You killed Terra," she says, her anger trumping the disbelief at seeing him alive.

"Yes. It was most regrettable and probably somewhat hasty on my part. Needless to say, it didn't have the intended effect." He waves a hand through the air, a dismissive gesture. "But let's not focus on the past. What's done is done, my mother always said. Please, sit." He motions to one of the chairs and lowers himself into the opposite one. Vivian remains silent, watching her closely as she stands several feet to the Director's left.

Zoey makes no move to sit, looking past both of them at the door. Could she get by them and out into the corridor? But where then? She's on the fifth floor, surrounded by guards and concrete walls.

"I know you're trying to gauge your escape," the Director says, folding his hands in his lap. "But you and I both know the first time was a fluke. A brilliant fluke, but a fluke nonetheless."

"What about the second time when we broke in under your nose and took the rest of the women with us?" She sees a flicker of what could be amusement on Vivian's face.

"I would call that reckless, since you caused the deaths of several people. Simon, Terra, Penny, Lily. Not to mention all the men your friends killed in cold blood. Need I go on?"

"You're a bastard."

"Let's be civil, shall we? I mean, you're here under your own volition."

"You had my daughter."

"Regardless, you're back and here we are. You understand as well as anyone how important you are, Zoey. As I said before, any choice besides the greater good—"

Vivian raises one hand, holding a small pistol to the side of the Director's head, and pulls the trigger.

The gunshot is like a slice of thunder in the enclosed space, deafening and gone in an instant.

Zoey jumps as the Director's head snaps to the side, a fan of blood and brain matter spattering the chair and floor.

For a full second he sits exactly where he is, still looking directly at her, his mouth open and struggling to finish the rest of the sentence. A teardrop of blood slips from the corner of his right eye and his shoulders jerk, spine stiffening.

Then he tips forward and slumps to his face, blood jetting out in two feeble pumps before drooling down the side of his ruined head to soak into the rug.

Zoey feels her jaw working, mimicking the Director, as she tries to give birth to the scream that must come. The unreality of what happened continues to loop in her mind's eye.

Vivian stares down at the corpse before examining the pistol's barrel, and frowning, wipes it on her pants leg before tucking it into a pocket.

"Wh . . . why?" Zoey finally manages.

"Have a seat," Vivian says, nodding toward the couch. "Before you fall down."

Zoey shuffles over to the couch and sits. The smell of burnt skin and hair mixed with cordite is almost overpowering and sends a sickening wave through her stomach. When one of the Director's feet death-twitches, she forces herself to look away.

Vivian grasps the arm of the chair the dead man hadn't been sitting in and drags it toward the couch before lowering herself into it. Her expression is unchanged from when she first entered the room.

She's insane, Zoey thinks, fear suddenly returning amidst the aftershocks of violence. *She's insane and now she's going to kill me too.*

"Why did you do that?" she asks, reasoning the only way to stay alive is to keep the other woman talking.

"Because the time had finally come and he was no longer needed. Besides, I was absolutely sick of his voice."

"What do you mean?"

Vivian turns her gaze to the corpse. "His real name was Dennis Anderson. It's very strange to be telling you this now after so many years of him being 'the Director.' He came up with that, you know? Everyone thought it was fine to use his real name but he wanted a title."

"Who was he?"

"A political wannabe. Before assuming his position, he was an aide to the Secretary of State under President Andrews. He was young, impressionable, and truly believed in our purpose." She becomes quiet, almost introspective, and Zoey feels as if she's seeing for the first time who Vivian truly is.

"You," Zoey says, drawing Vivian's inward gaze back to the present. "You're in charge, aren't you? It was never the Director. It was you."

The barest of smiles. "You always were very smart. Yes, I became lead scientist late in the Dearth, after my predecessor decided our pursuit was hopeless. I answered only to the president himself along with his idiotic team of advisors, none of whom would've known a chromosome if it bit them. They were arrogant, even in the end. All of them old, gray-haired white men who had made a career out of their titles, just like Dennis over there did. All of them riding on the backs of the taxpayers and completely derisive of anyone who was better educated or happened to be a woman. Needless to say, none of them were pleased whatsoever when I became the head of the National Obstetric Alliance."

Vivian sighs and runs her tongue across her teeth before standing and striding to the desk. She rummages in the drawers for several seconds before straightening, a small metal bottle in her hands. "Talking about the past always causes me to drink. I know for most people it's reversed, but . . ." She shrugs and unscrews the cap before waving the bottle at the Director's body. "To you, Dennis. Good riddance." Vivian takes a long drink from the bottle, and Zoey uses the moment to study the door. She can see no locking mechanism and wonders if the Director would have required one. But again she's faced with the decision of what she would do if she were able to make it out of the room. There is nowhere to go.

Vivian finishes her drink, wincing. "God, I miss good Scotch. This is nothing like it." She crosses the room and sits again, offering the bottle to Zoey.

"No thank you."

"Probably smart." Vivian sets it down on the floor beside her chair.

They look at one another for a long moment. This woman is the reason for her suffering, for all of what's happened. Not the Director, not Reaper, not any of the clerics—Vivian. A boiling rage begins to well up within Zoey from an unknowable depth. It sends a tremor through her, a reflex of movement she has to fight down because it carries the urge to rocket forward and tear this woman to pieces. She could do it. In this second it is within her to destroy, to kill. What restrains her is the image of the baby in Lee's arms.

She shuts her eyes so she doesn't have to look at the monster before her. "Why did you do this?"

The other woman doesn't respond for so long Zoey begins to think she didn't hear her, but when she opens her eyes Vivian is staring at her, gaze as cold as stone.

"Why? Why did I do this? You need to ask?"

"There were other ways."

Vivian launches to her feet. "There was no other way! You weren't there! You didn't see the things I saw. It was hell on earth. People running rampant, destroying, pillaging. Men raping every woman they saw, and not because they were trying to keep the species alive, as if there would ever be a conscionable reason for it, no, just because they could. People ran when it was their duty to stay and try to fight what was happening. They went to war with each other when the fate of humankind rested on us working together." Vivian's gaze is alight with a fevered intensity. "Our only hope was the research we were doing, and even that was taken away. Shut down by a bunch of men who were afraid for their own lives when we were on the brink of discovery. You ask me why? I had to because people are too stupid to save themselves. The president was going to end NOA and shelve all our work." Her voice lowers and her chin sinks to her chest. She seems unsteady, drunk not only from the alcohol but from her fury. "I couldn't let him."

The words slowly sink in, taking on a new meaning, and Zoey can't help but shrink away from the woman, comprehension like a shower of ice water. "Shepherd," she whispers, and at the name Vivian's head snaps up. "You sent the emails to the rebels. You helped them kill the president. All those people . . ." She lacks the power to go on, seeing the truth in the other woman's eyes.

"How . . . ?"

"We found them. All the messages. It was you."

"They were supposed to take out the president and his staff only," Vivian says, in a weak voice, her fervor gone. "I had no idea what they were planning. They were insane using a bomb like that. I was nearly killed."

Zoey can't respond. What can she say to a person who could make a decision like that? Who could put her profession above others' lives? It is like she's looking at a species utterly alien to her.

"I know what you're thinking. How could someone do that? How could they decide to end another's life? Well I'll tell you: if I hadn't done it, I would've been dooming the entire human race. The president was going to call for a cease-fire with the rebels and the end of the National Obstetric Alliance was his peace offering. All of my work, the sacrifice and dedication—for nothing. He and his advisors were willing to throw it all away." Vivian pauses, looking down at her hands. "So I did what I needed to and when everything fell apart we retreated here. The ARC was built in secret, made to withstand centuries, a last-ditch effort to combat the Dearth. So that's what it became, our final hope.

"And now I know I made the right choice because you're sitting here with me, living proof that it wasn't all for nothing." Vivian brightens, as if casting off the events of the past. "You're special, Zoey. I always believed I'd witness the fruition of all the toiling hours and endless theories, and now here we are at last."

"I'm not special." It's all she can think to say.

"But you are, Zoey. To say anything different would be a lie."

"Why?"

Vivian lowers herself into the chair again and leans forward. "You'll have to forgive me; I wasn't honest with you the night you returned here. I told you that the Dearth caused female embryos to become male no matter what we tried. That wasn't a lie. But I also said we didn't know why. In truth we've known for many years."

Zoey sits back in her seat, despite everything a tingle of anticipation flowing through her. "What caused it?"

"The SRY gene. I'm sure that doesn't really mean anything to you, but in short, it's located on the Y chromosome and causes an embryo to become male during the early developmental stages. Twenty-five years ago, for reasons still unknown to us, there was a widespread duplication of the gene onto the X chromosome as well, so in essence, no matter which sperm reached a female's egg first to fertilize it, the child would always be male due to the presence of the SRY gene."

"So you're saying it affected men?"

"Yes."

"Then why were women taken and held against their will?" She tries to keep her voice even but fails. "Why were we kept here?"

"For several reasons." Vivian stands again, as if filled with manic energy, and begins to pace, walking around the pool of blood still spreading from the Director's body. "At first it was to eliminate the possibility of a female defect such as the SRY duplication. When we found nothing, we realized there would be an unprecedented fallout, that women were going to be considered a limited commodity by some. We knew there would be groups that would abduct them, sell them on the black market. During my tenure the NSA worked closely with the CIA to foil over a dozen attempts at mass kidnappings by foreign perpetrators. Long story short, we continued gathering women and young girls to protect them."

Zoey laughs. She can't help it. She doubles over on the couch and lets the maniacal laughter out like black vomitus. When she sits back up, wiping away tears, Vivian stands motionless without a smile, her hands laced together before her. "I'm sorry," Zoey says, coughing out the last bit of mirth. "You stole them away from their homes so someone else wouldn't?"

"It was necessary."

"That word, 'necessary,' I've come to truly despise it."

"Regardless, it was what had to be done."

"Coming from someone who helped murder thousands of women and children, I find that deeply ironic."

Vivian's lip curls, but she turns away, pacing to the farthest book-shelf before returning. "We tested hundreds of thousands of men over the course of years, searching for someone who didn't carry the duplicated gene, but to no avail. It was much later, after I assumed control of NOA, that we began work on my theory. And that's where you come in."

She tries to still herself and simply listen, but the question she asks comes out of its own volition. "Who are my parents?"

Vivian's face hardens, a flicker of some unknowable emotion there and gone. "That is maybe best left for another day."

"Tell me. You know who they are. You took me from them, the least you can do is give me their names."

"I knew them," Vivian says quietly. "A lifetime ago. And they would have wanted you to know the truth, and that is you are special, Zoey. You were meant to bring the human race back from the brink of extinction."

"So they're gone? Is that what you're saying?"

Vivian gives the barest of nods. "Yes."

Zoey stands, stepping away from the couch, unable to keep looking at the woman before her. She paces unsteadily, the drug still lingering in her system, to the wall where an oil painting depicts a dirt road winding away through trees on fire with fall's colors. She can't see the end of the path in the picture, and she assumes that was the artist's intent: to evoke a sense of longing in the observer, to wonder where that road might take them if they traveled it. But for her the road is at its end. She's found what she came looking for and really she feels no surprise at hearing her parents are gone. They were always absent and now the only difference is she can finally let go of the hope that surrounded thoughts of them.

Vivian clears her throat. "After the president's death we gathered as many test subjects as we could. As I said, my theory differed from that of my colleagues, not to mention the president's advisors, in that the solution wasn't going to be found in a male subject, but a female." Zoey tears her gaze from the painting and faces Vivian. "I believed that genetic weakness was a factor in why the SRY duplication occurred initially, so I built my theory on the hope that we would eventually find a subject that was the opposite: a woman strong enough to withstand what was required to turn back the Dearth."

"The keystone," Zoey says.

Vivian smiles. "The keystone. Yes. You see, it's not to say you aren't remarkable, Zoey, you are. You're a specimen of health: great immune system, blood counts, everything about you screams strength and vigor. But we witnessed dozens of women like you give birth to males over and over again. If women were to be born again, they needed help."

Zoey feels herself being drawn toward the couch again, but doesn't sit. "What do you mean, 'needed help'?"

"Did you ever wonder why the women's food plates in the cafeteria were color coded differently than the clerics' or their sons'?" Zoey's eyes narrow at the memories of all the meals eaten in the large, mostly empty, cafeteria. Never once had she seen a cleric or guard eat off the same color plate as a woman, and never once had she thought to question it. "There is a specific protein called Beta-catenin encoded by a gene in humans that serves several purposes, but one of particular interest to me is its importance in embryotic sex development. It was theorized that it could help promote female sexual development and repress the SRY gene."

"You put it in our food?"

"Actually we put an enzyme that promoted Beta-catenin overexpression in your food and gave you injections of the protein itself on your visits to the infirmary."

The way Vivian says it, the cold, scientific statement sends chills through Zoey, and she shakes her head. "We thought you were taking care of us."

"Don't you see? We were," Vivian says, coming closer. "It was what had to be done, and keeping the truth from you was part of the program."

"It was all part of the program, wasn't it? The control, our segregation, the propaganda, the box, the lies. All for our own good, right?"

"It was for the greater good! The only good that mattered!" Vivian yells. "If we had let you choose you would have been like all the others when the Dearth began: too stupid to save yourselves."

"You took away our freedom."

"Freedom is more times than not a death sentence."

They stare at one another, less than a foot separating them, and Zoey realizes her hands are balled into fists, muscles taut, ready to uncoil into violence. She looks away, willing herself to relax. Fighting this woman won't get her out of the ARC.

Vivian seems to deflate as well, taking a step back and rubbing her arms as if she's cold. "What was done was done for the benefit of humanity, even if lines were crossed. It's how any great disaster is averted, with sacrifice. If you would've known . . ." Her voice trails off.

"If we would've known what?"

The other woman wrestles with something before saying, "There were noted complications to the overexpression of Beta-catenin."

"What kind of complications?"

"None that concern you. You're perfectly fine."

"What kind of complications?"

Vivian hesitates. "Possible heart disease, multiple forms of cancer: lung, colorectal, ovarian, breast, endometrial."

Zoey stares, a lump of sickening dread forming in her stomach. "You did this to us, knowing it could cause these things?" Vivian's mouth becomes a white line. "You said it was no concern to me. Who was it a concern to?" She waits, willing the answer to come, and fearing it at the same time.

"Terra was diagnosed with ovarian cancer before she was inducted, and Lily's heart was enlarged." Vivian blinks rapidly. "She wouldn't have made it to induction."

Zoey launches herself forward. There is no stopping the reaction this time.

It is animalistic: raw reflex and rage combined.

She slams into Vivian, her weight carrying both of them into the chair and over it.

The floor meets them and Zoey rolls, coming up on her hands and knees, scrambling back to lock her hands around Vivian's throat.

Because now all other thoughts are gone.

Returning to the group, to Lee, to her daughter is an ebbing concept overshadowed by the fury bursting from within.

She lands on Vivian as she's trying to lift herself from the floor. The older woman's air discharges in a long gasp as Zoey grabs her neck and begins to squeeze.

Thumbs pressing into soft skin.

Adrenaline-fueled strength locks her grip in place even as Vivian convulses beneath her.

Vivian twists to the side, and Zoey moves with her, tightening her hold. The other woman's eyes bulge. Then her arm is coming up faster than it should be, and Zoey has a split second to remember the gun.

The pistol connects with her temple and flashes of light glitter in the room like the sun glancing off ice on a bright day.

Her hands come loose to the ragged sound of indrawn breath.

She tumbles backward, trying to put out a hand to break her fall, but her arm is suddenly weak and she drops to her back.

The office's ceiling spins then stills, the glinting ice melting away.

She forces herself up into a sitting position, rallying the will for another assault, but Vivian is already on her feet, the pistol in one hand, her other loosely clutching her rapidly bruising throat.

"Stop," Vivian croaks, choking on the word. She coughs, the gun barrel wavering. "Don't move."

"I'm going to kill you," Zoey says, crawling to her feet and rocking there as an internal gust of wind nearly bowls her down again.

"You don't want to do that," Vivian says, voice returning to something vaguely human.

"Why?"

"Because. Then you'll never meet your daughter."

"You won't let me go so what does it matter?" She stares at the gun's muzzle, readying a strike that will send it flying.

"No," Vivian says, reaching out to touch a button on the Director's desk phone. "I mean your other daughter."

44

Lee watches the dark masses of crumbling homes on the slope far below for the signal.

He sits in what Ian called a rocking chair, the places where the feet should be, only rounded lengths of wood allowing him to tip back and forth with the baby in his arms. At first the notion behind the chair was strange, almost silly, but once he settled into it, the squalling infant in his arms, red faced and breathless with hungry cries, he'd silently sent up a prayer of thanks to the chair's inventor.

She had begun to cry again in the early evening as they were stopping before the home on the bluffs above the river. Tia, Newton, and Merrill were already gone, vanished down the valley's side and into the dilapidated town standing along the river's edge. Ian had volunteered to go with them or set up a sniper's position directly above the town within sight of the ARC, but Merrill had refused, saying that if they were able to locate the hidden entrance there would be no helping them in or out once they were inside. He'd sent the older man with them after a brief embrace and a long look shared between them saying more in silence than could be put in words.

The house above the river was large and singularly alone. "Forgotten" would've been the word Lee used to describe it after pulling to a stop in its turnaround drive. It was two levels with a rounding expanse of windows, all miraculously intact, looking out over the impressive views made even more so by the setting sun. Far below, at least two miles, was the small town above the riverbank, and slightly past that, the hulking shape of the ARC set before the dam, its top crenelated by an intermittent line of lights on its walls and the occasional strobe from what he assumed was the helipad.

He brings his gaze down to the child in his arms, a warm ball of blankets fit tight to his chest. She's asleep, tiny lips parted, the smallest of squeaks coming with each inhale. Hunger was what had caused the screaming and fitful movements of her small body, for her diaper had been dry when he'd checked and she had only just woken from a nap. They had no milk of any kind and she refused the water he offered, though he wasn't sure if it had been the liquid itself or the system of delivery it was in; they'd found a clean plastic bag and poked several tiny holes in one corner. It had been Chelsea's idea, in her indelible wisdom, to mix warm water with a bit of flour and sugar together to make a milky substance. At first the baby had refused the makeshift meal, but in the end hunger had won out and she'd drunk nearly half of the mixture, falling asleep with the plastic still between her lips.

Lee shifts her weight into a more comfortable position, a sense of marvel washing over him. She is so small, vulnerable in a way that nearly brings tears to his eyes. This tiny life in his arms is part of him, a notion he'd only given fleeting thought to over the years, but now is overwhelming in its immensity. It's like he's stepped from one life into another.

He breaks his gaze from the girl and looks out over the blackened landscape. The clouds that were high and thin earlier have clotted and hover over the river valley, the water itself flowing in a deeper shadow below. He scans the area the others were going to be searching in, Merrill's last instructions being to watch for several flashes from his light in case the radios failed.

Someone approaches from behind him, and a second later Chelsea appears in the gloom.

"How is she?"

Lee smiles, not sure she can see his expression, but unable to repress it. "Sleeping hard."

"That's good. I was worried we might not be able to get her to eat."

"Glad you didn't show it; I was worried enough for both of us."

Chelsea laughs. "You're doing fine."

"This isn't how it's supposed to be."

She is quiet for a time. "I know. But we'll get her back. One way or another."

Lee finds himself looking at the baby again. Studying the lines of her face. Will she have Zoey's nose? His eyes? How will her tiny hands ever get bigger? "It's funny, I gave up hoping for a future after my dad died. Everything was so convoluted, so strange. It was like I didn't know who I was anymore without him, without the structure of the ARC, my job. I didn't understand any of it. I didn't . . . didn't know how important she was to me until I left."

Chelsea lowers herself onto the edge of a small table, her face toward the window and the town below. "Before the Dearth, I used to drink this tea that had sayings and quotes on little pieces of paper attached to the strings. They were meant to be inspirational and deep. 'A task unfinished is an opportunity missed.' Or 'It's always darkest just before the dawn.' I read them and always kind of thought they were silly. I lost my father fairly young, and when my mother passed away, I was basically in charge of raising my sister. Life seemed meaningless at times, even cruel, like there was a force out there with a sole purpose of causing pain, and if it got a glimpse of you, it never let you go." Her head droops a little. "I quit reading the quotes on the tea bags. I'd tear them off and throw them away. They felt like a mockery of my life, especially after the Dearth started." She straightens, putting one hand on her belly, which is beginning to round beneath her shirt. "Now I regret not reading them because they weren't a mockery: they were another perspective I didn't understand."

"I'm not sure I'm following you."

"My sister made a sacrifice to save me. Your father died for you and Zoey, and now you and Zoey are doing what you have to for her," she says, motioning to the sleeping infant. "We don't always understand the bad parts of our lives until they've passed, most times we're blinded by the pain. But there's things to be learned even when we're hurting. Especially then."

They share a comfortable silence that's broken when the baby wriggles in her blankets and yawns, issuing an unmistakably satisfied sound.

Chelsea laughs quietly. "At least one of us is enjoying herself."

"You should get some sleep. I'll stay here with her, I'm not tired."

"Are you sure? Because—"

"What is that?" Lee rises from the chair, vision hooked on something in the distance. Chelsea moves to the window, pressing her hands against the glass.

"I don't know. They look like lights."

Over a mile away a glittering line bobs and blinks like a glowing snake slithering from a draw in the land. It grows from only a few tiny dots to a dozen, two dozen, a hundred. As the string of lights comes closer and closer to the edge of the river gorge, they begin to wink out, one after another.

"Oh God," Chelsea says, pushing away from the glass. "They're here."

45

Merrill exits the remains of the small house and glances up the street to where Tia appears a moment later.

She jogs toward him as he steps off the rotted porch. "Nothing."

"You're sure?"

"Yes. Checked each level. No new footprints or any other sign they passed through here."

"Where's Newton?"

"At the last one in the block. Here he comes now." When he stops before them Tia says, "Find anything?"

"N-no," Newton says, and it still sends a small shock through Merrill every time he hears the younger man utter words.

Merrill glances around, gaining his bearings. "Okay, so we've covered these four streets. There's one more along with the rest of the town on the other side of the river."

"You're sure they would've hidden the entrance in a building, not in the ground somewhere or the side of the riverbank?" Tia asks.

"No, I'm not sure, but it's where I would put it. Besides, if it's not in a building it could be anywhere and I'm not ready to start considering that just yet."

A ripple of static comes from the radio attached to his belt, quiet enough to pass for the rustling of leaves, but Merrill hears it. A breathed word issues from the speaker as he brings it up to his ear but he misses the rest of the sentence.

"Didn't catch that, say again," he whispers into the radio.

Silence, another crackle of static. Then Lee's voice, hurried and strained. ". . . ight above you."

"Above us?" Tia says, turning to look up the steep grade beyond the houses.

"Say again, Lee."

"They're coming down the . . . ope. Right . . . ove you."

Merrill snaps the radio off, the thumb of his right hand flicking the safety of his rifle as he stares up past the nearest houses toward the shadow-laden hills. "Listen," he whispers.

And below the other night sounds comes the tread of many feet trying to be silent.

46

"What did you say?" Zoey asks.

She balances on the balls of her feet, the explosion of motion held back only by the other woman's words.

Instead of answering her, Vivian speaks to the phone. "Bring her in."

Zoey settles onto her heels and shakes her head, looking first to the door then at Vivian. "No. You're lying. You're calling for help."

"Why would I need help? I have this," she says, waving the gun slightly. "And I'm not lying."

There is a sound at the door, a faint electronic beeping before it swings open. Standing there is a man she recognizes as Doctor Calvin, his bald pate and goatee bringing back the aftermath of Rita's and her fight in the cafeteria. He wears the same smile as he did then, the crooked canine peeking out from beneath his pale upper lip. In his arms he holds a swaddled bundle of pink blankets almost identical to the one that was passed to Lee on the highway.

"No," she hears herself saying as she backs away.

Calvin continues to smile and moves across the room, unperturbed by the Director's corpse on the floor. He transfers the blankets and the weight within them to Vivian.

"Anything else, Doctor?" he asks.

"That will be all, thank you, Calvin. We'll be fine from here out."

He turns away, giving Zoey a barely noticeable wink, and she wonders absently if he assisted in her violation while she was unconscious.

The door thunks closed with finality, and the room is quiet again.

"Come here. I'd like you to meet your daughter." When she doesn't move any closer Vivian tucks the gun away in her pocket once again and cradles the bundle with both arms. "One of the first rules we learned in school was to always duplicate our experiments. Comparative data within the same trials is very useful and necessary to draw conclusions from. We fertilized two of your eggs and I can't begin to express our elation when they both developed as female."

She smiles down at what she holds and Zoey feels an inexorable force pulling her forward.

She crosses the distance separating them in a gliding motion, as if her feet aren't really touching the floor.

As Zoey nears, Vivian turns her gaze up and extends her arms, offering the blankets.

Zoey reaches, heart skipping every other beat like a flat stone across water.

The weight is transferred to her and she looks into the folds of the fabric.

The baby girl is sleeping, fists tucked beneath the shape of her chin. She is so very much like the child Lee accepted on the road, but also different. She has lighter hair, and it's wispier, *like Lee's,* she thinks, immediately casting the thought aside. Also the baby looks slightly larger, fuller in the face and the pink chub of her tiny arms.

Zoey's jaw trembles, all the fight leaving her.

She retreats to the couch and sits, unable to break her gaze from the baby even though she feels like she's looking at her through someone else's eyes.

Disbelief wars with anger, all the while overshadowed by an unnameable elation.

Her child. She's holding her daughter.

One of her daughters.

A teardrop slips down her nose and falls to the baby's blankets, soaking into a dark circle.

"She's eight pounds, four ounces, twenty inches long. Her sister was a little smaller: seven pounds, one ounce, nineteen inches long," Vivian says, coming closer. "They're both very strong and healthy baby girls. You should be proud."

Zoey finally manages to break her gaze from the infant and looks up. "You knew I'd try to trade myself, didn't you?"

"It occurred to me after you escaped, yes. I postulated that if I could get you proof you might try to do something noble."

Zoey returns her gaze to the baby who extends one arm lazily before tucking it close again, a soft snore coming from her. She begins to ask the question but stops, her throat and mouth filled with sand. Does she even want to know? But it's not a question of that. She has to.

"Who is the father?" she manages to ask.

Vivian tilts her head to the side, wearing a puzzled smile. "Didn't Jefferson tell you? It's Lee."

Zoey shakes her head. "That's not true."

"It is. Lee Asher is the father. We always paired the clerics' sons with the women. As I told you they were specifically chosen for their virility and overall healthy genetics."

"I went to Seattle and found a doctor there who helped test the blood you sent me in a bioanalyzer. We compared a sample of my blood and Lee's against it. Only mine matched."

The color visibly drains from Vivian's face. She blinks rapidly, her throat bobbing as she attempts to swallow. "A bioanalyzer?"

"Yes. And now that I know the truth you need to tell me who the father is. I deserve that much. Was it one of the guards? Was it him?"

She nods toward the Director's body, hoping with all her being that it isn't.

Vivian puts a steadying hand on the nearby chair back. She seems to wrestle with something before raising her chin. "I didn't anticipate you testing Lee's blood."

"Obviously not."

"I wanted to give you time to adjust to all this before you had to deal with anything else."

"Now you're concerned about my well-being? You did this to me, to everyone around me, and now that you've finally got what you want you're being compassionate?" Zoey stares the other woman in the eyes. "Fuck you."

"I know you're upset, but you don't understand."

"I think I understand perfectly."

"The blood sample I sent you didn't come from one of your children."

She begins to reply but the venom on the tip of her tongue dissolves. "What did you say?"

"The blood sample didn't come from either of your daughters: that's why Lee's didn't match, but I can assure you, he is the father."

A lazy spinning sensation fills her head, trying to scatter her thoughts. "If it wasn't their blood, then whose was it?"

Vivian looks down to the floor as if the answer lies there before bringing her gaze back up. "Mine. It came from me." She lets out a shuddering breath. "The reason only your sample matched is because I'm your mother, Zoey."

47

Hiraku steps to the edge of the drop and looks across the river toward the paling horizon.

Dawn will come within the hour, and they're nearly ready.

Beside him Lawrence Cree settles into a folding chair before a portable desk. On its top is a computer console hooked to a small battery array on the ground. Another long cable snakes out from the compact processor leading to a complicated joystick. The screen flickers as the technician begins typing in commands.

"How long until it's airborne?" Hiraku asks.

"Ten minutes. Maybe less," Cree answers through his thick beard without looking up. "You're sure you want to go ahead with this?"

"If you ask me that again, I'll assume you're questioning my authority," Hiraku says. The man's typing pauses before continuing. Hiraku turns his attention to the town to the right and below their vantage point. The houses and decrepit businesses are smudges in the early light, nothing moving but the river between the banks. The facility itself is much higher in person than he expected, and he supposes at another time it would inspire some type of awe, but this morning it is only an obstacle, another barrier between him and what he seeks.

He glances up at the hills to his left, seeing nothing marring the landscape besides the long, sagging lines of power cables between their towers and a single house past them, its shape a rounded lump against the lightening sky. He pulls the radio attached to his collar close and depresses the button.

"Are we in position?"

A short silence then, "Three minutes, sir."

He turns to the men who accompanied him to the vantage point. "You two watch our flank. If you see anything, don't engage. Notify me and we move."

"Yes sir," they reply in unison before melting into the shadows.

Cree exhales slowly. "Bringing the drone online now."

Hiraku imagines the aircraft coming to life on the highway a quarter mile behind them, its deadly cargo ready and waiting.

All at once a hyperawareness blankets him. Not simply a sharpened cognizance of his surroundings as is customary before a battle, but an internal one as well.

What the hell am I doing? Is this really happening? How did it come to this?

But just as quickly as the observation arrived, it evaporates with the memory of Shirou's lifeless gaze, the blue tinge of his lips.

Hiraku closes his eyes, letting the rage return to his limbs, soaking his veins with its flow.

"Beginning takeoff," Cree says.

"Good." Hiraku steps back to the edge of the slope, staring at the rounded wall of the ARC as if he's able to see through the concrete to its very center. "I want you to split that thing in half."

48

"Get inside," Merrill whispers, grabbing Newton by the collar.

"What the hell is that?" Tia says, sweeping her rifle toward the sounds of approach.

"Inside. Come on."

They move as one, retreating up the steps as the cracking of brush and the crunch of footsteps become louder. They step inside the house Merrill just searched, closing the door behind them and backing into the center of the first small room, each covering a different direction.

"They're early," Tia says.

"Damn it," Merrill breathes. A bead of sweat rolls off his temple and down to his jaw despite the cold.

"Wh-where do w-we go?" Newton says.

"In the next room. It's got fewer windows. Move."

They creep through the low archway, Merrill going last. Why? Why does it have to be happening now? They need more time. In a few minutes all hell will break loose. He curses under his breath, mind like skipping frames of film. How to get Zoey out and not engage Hiraku's or the ARC's forces?

All of his thoughts halt as a squeak comes from the next room that can only be the outside door opening.

49

Zoey is on the boat again, the world rocking around her, unstable and unmoored.

"You," is all she can manage at first, and it's more of a coarse, scratching sound than a word. Everything is untethered, as if the room, Vivian, the baby in her arms, even the very fabric of herself, is coming apart.

Vivian nods, trying to keep her face tilted up, but Zoey can see it's an effort. "I know. I know what you're thinking. How? How could this be?" She surprises Zoey by laughing, but it is harsh and without humor. "I used to ask myself that every day. When I first found out I was pregnant, later when I learned you were a girl, and last when I gave you up." Vivian looks away and there is a sheen to her eyes.

"I don't believe you. You said my parents were gone," Zoey says, trying to gather the pieces of her wits that feel as if they've shattered like a glass pane. "It's just another ploy, another wall."

"I told you that because I wanted more time. I needed a better way to tell you, but it's true. Believe me, things would be a lot easier for me if it weren't. I was irresponsible, I admit that. I got caught up in the moment and the power of being in charge and I thought I was invincible. Love can do that to you. My work was my life, but when I found out about you, things changed. I nearly left NOA, nearly walked away from years of research, but I couldn't do it. I was too important. And so were you."

Zoey feels an internal tumbling sensation, as if something stable has broken loose inside. She looks down at her daughter. None of it seems real. A layer of numbness covers her; a full-body paralysis that reaches deeper than her muscles and nerves.

"I gave birth to you right before the rebels made their move. We barely got out of the compound alive. You were so small, just like she is now. And I would have died to protect you."

The full weight of what Vivian's saying settles onto her. She shakes her head, trying to hold it back.

"When we came here I had no choice but to place you in the program with the rest of the girls we'd collected. You were one of the last females born on record, and I couldn't ignore that fact. There was something greater at stake than either of us." Her voice trails off and it looks as if she will cry for a moment before smiling sadly. "Sometimes when you were little I would come to your crib in the middle of the night and hold you while you slept. Once in a while you'd wake up and just look at me and let my hair slide through your fingers."

The ghost of the memory washes over her in that instant, stronger than ever before, and any will holding back the reality of what Vivian's telling her crumbles.

At last she's found her mother.

Her jaw works for a time before she can form the words. "I always wondered where you were, what you looked like, and the whole time you were right here." Vivian bites her lower lip as a tear escapes one eye. Zoey swallows and it feels as if a piece of jagged rock is lodged in her throat. "You said I was important. I was important to the research," she finally says. "But not to you."

"That isn't true."

"You would have never given me over, never put me in the box, never let me suffer if you loved me."

"I had to, Zoey. You were too crucial for me to keep you to myself. I needed to test you like all the other girls, make you follow the same rules, and it killed me inside. But don't think for a second I wasn't looking out for you. Why do you think you were allowed to keep that owl or the books or the chewing gum?" The look of astonishment must be apparent because Vivian continues. "Oh yes, we knew about your hiding place, knew Simon was the one giving you the contraband. I allowed it both because you were my daughter and I never thought it would cause a problem. I was wrong, of course, I never should have underestimated the power of a great book. But I loved you then and I love you now. What was done had to be done."

Disgust wells up inside her at the sight of the woman, Vivian's self-pity and righteousness overwhelming.

"You said you were in love," Zoey says. "Who was he?"

Vivian pauses, becoming very still. "He was my personal bodyguard while I was lead scientist. He saved me more than once and was injured very badly." Her posture stiffens. "He's gone now."

So there it is. Her heritage laid bare.

Zoey's gaze drifts down to the child. She's starting to move in the blankets, struggling up from sleep. *What were you dreaming? Something beautiful, I hope. Something that might come true someday. Because that's what dreams are for.*

If only all this could be as insubstantial as a nightmare. If she could wake up and leave it behind in tatters of fading memory.

But she won't.

"It doesn't matter," she says, still looking at the baby.

"What? What do you mean, it doesn't matter?"

"The past. None of it. I was obsessed with finding who I was and didn't realize I already knew." She brings her eyes up to her mother. "And I'm nothing like you."

Vivian's mouth wobbles before hardening. "That's fine. I didn't ask for any of this. All I could do—"

"We need to leave."

"What? Why?"

"I told you in the vehicle. There's a man on his way here with an army." Vivian sighs. "Zoey, please. There's—"

"He took over Seattle in one day. He has a thousand men with him; vehicles, weapons, everything he needs to destroy this place."

"Even if I believed you, the ARC is impenetrable. We revamped our backup generators after your last visits and shielded all of them from the possibility of an electromagnetic pulse. As long as we have power, we have defense. The autoguns will tear apart anything that comes within five hundred feet of the walls."

"You don't know this man, he's different. He'll find a way."

"Enough of this nonsense. You're here now, and that's all that matters. Now we have a chance."

"We have a chance no matter what. You're in control. You can decide what happens. Evacuate the ARC and we'll go somewhere else, somewhere safe. If I'm the keystone you can still do everything you set out to do. You can save the human race. Rita and Sherell are with me. You can use what you've learned to help them have baby girls. There are other women out there, hiding and afraid, but you can change that. Once the world knows what you've accomplished there won't be a need to hide anymore. In my time outside the walls do you know what I've seen?" She stares at Vivian, locking her gaze with her own. "Fear. Every terrible thing I've witnessed stems from it. You can take away the fear and replace it with hope."

Vivian watches her for a long span, the quiet in the room delicate and precarious like a precious artifact balanced on the edge of a table.

Finally, the older woman raises her eyebrows. "That was quite the inspiring speech, Zoey. But why would I risk everything I've worked for by stepping outside these walls?"

"Because it's the right thing to do."

Vivian barks a laugh and Zoey recoils at how cold it sounds. Her daughter squirms again, making an irritated cooing. "The right thing to do? You have no idea what the right thing is. You didn't see the world before, you know nothing of it. It wasn't a good place, especially for women. People's actions after the Dearth only further proved that. Your head is full of fairness and truth and honor, but those things are daydreams. They're not real, they never were. There's only advantage and who has it."

Her voice has risen to a crescendo, and she seems to come back to herself before continuing in a quieter tone. "You had your turn to paint a picture, now it's mine. There once was a young woman who had everything she ever wanted. Good parents, a nice home, a great college she attended, and a bright future. She was in love with a young man who was her mirror image: smart, handsome, successful, athletic. She thought her life was perfect; blessed you might even say. She had just started working under a supervisor who headed one of the most cutting-edge genetics research programs in the country when she went to a campus party. Lo and behold her new supervisor was there. He talked to her all evening and was charming, eloquent, and extremely intelligent. She wasn't afraid of him at all until he forced her into an empty room and locked the door. Then he raped her."

Zoey blinks, the moisture in her mouth evaporating as she watches her mother relive the moment.

"When it was over he told her it would be a shame if someone were to find out. She would lose her student funding, respect from her peers, a future in the field, even her boyfriend. She would become a statistic, maybe an accuser at best. Then he left her lying there, shaking and horrified because what he'd said was true."

Vivian bares her teeth as if tasting something terrible. "It nearly broke her. She lost her identity and became something else- a shell of what she once was. She had to spend her days working alongside the man that had done this to her, but she couldn't get past the fear of what he'd said would happen if she told someone. So she didn't. She kept it inside. She eventually broke up with her boyfriend and her grades slipped. She tried killing herself once before she was finally able to transfer out of the program to a different college. But what happened never went away. She carried the fear and the weakness with her from that night forward."

Zoey can see her mother's hands shaking as she clenches them together.

"So please don't talk to me about 'the right thing to do.' We have a chance to remake the world, Zoey, and we don't need to leave these walls to do it. There are thousands of eggs preserved here along with hundreds of artificial wombs. The beginning of women's dominion can start here with you and me and her. Mother, daughter, and grand-daughter, united."

Nausea squirms in Zoey's stomach, her mouth arid and sour. She feels a shimmer of sympathy shining through the darkness Vivian's sur-rounded herself with.

I keep my ideals, because in spite of everything I still believe that people are really good at heart.

"I'm sorry for what happened to you," she says quietly. "But you can't control everyone's life, even though I understand why you tried."

"That's enough."

"You tried to control everything because you never wanted to feel that way again. Helpless and afraid."

"I said that's enough."

"And your fear made you do things you never would have done otherwise."

"Shut up!" Vivian draws the gun and points it at her, the pistol wobbling in her hand.

"You saw the women who couldn't have girls as weak, weak like you felt when you couldn't tell anyone what happened. And you couldn't stand to look at them, so you sent them away even though they ended up enduring horrible things. Just like you did."

Vivian's face is tear streaked, heart-crushingly vulnerable, and Zoey can see the young woman she'd spoken about still inside her.

"Please," Zoey says. "Come with me."

Vivian sniffles as she lowers the pistol. She stands still, gazing down through swollen eyes at the floor before shaking her head. "No." She looks at Zoey and now the scared young woman is gone. "I won't leave everything I've worked for. Not now that we're this close. You have a decision to make, Zoey. Either cooperate and help me finish what I started, or you'll never see either of your daughters again."

Zoey opens her mouth to say something, not truly sure of what it will be, as a deep, throbbing alarm begins to sound from everywhere around them.

50

Lee crawls the last few feet to where Ian lies, overlooking the vast open canyon.

The old man has folded his coat several times to provide a rest for his rifle, which he holds tight to his shoulder, staring through the large scope atop its bulk.

"What do you see?" Lee whispers.

"Barely enough light but it looks like they're amassing along the western edge of buildings. They're holding there out of range of the ARC's guns."

Lee looks to the area Ian mentioned and the drop combined with the overall distance creates an unpleasant swirl in his vision. He clamps his eyes shut and reopens them.

The eastern horizon is growing brighter by the minute, slowly shedding more and more light across the vista below like a shade being drawn up from a window. Without the amplification of a scope or binoculars, along with the fact that they've shut off all their lights, he can't see Hiraku's army anymore.

"Can you see Merrill and the others?"

Ian is quiet for nearly a minute, panning the rifle with mechanical fluidity before saying, "No."

"Should I radio him again?"

"I don't think so. We don't want to draw any unneeded attention to them."

"Then what do we do?" When the old man doesn't answer, Lee puts a hand on his shoulder. "Ian?"

"I don't know. We'll . . ." He stops, and Lee can see the line of one eyebrow draw down.

"What is it?"

"There's men on the plateau below us."

"How many?" Lee's chest tightens at the thought of his daughter still sleeping soundly inside the house behind them.

"Four that I can see. One is standing, looking out at the ARC, another sitting at a table with some kind of computer. Two more guarding their position."

"What are they doing?"

"I can't tell."

A vague humming begins rising in Lee's ears and he wonders briefly if it's the rush of blood in his veins driven by the hammering of his heart, but a second later Ian's head comes up from the scope and he glances around as well, looking for the sound's source.

"What is that?" Lee manages before something catches the corner of his eye.

From behind the farthest slope to the south, a strange shape appears, bringing with it a slight increase in the humming sound. At first he thinks it might be a bird, possibly a hawk or vulture of some kind gliding calmly on a draft of air, but then he catches a strobe of light, first from one wingtip, then the other. The plane increases in size, shape defining in the breaking light. It is dark in color with a half-rounded nose and several sharp and jutting tail fins behind its long, straight wings. As it glides closer, the sound of its approach seems to diminish instead of increasing, and the sight of it stabs a lance of unease through Lee, pinning him to the ground.

"What the hell?" Ian breathes as the plane banks hard, a sudden alarm issuing from the confines of the ARC, its bass emission carrying eerily across the valley.

Gunshots begin popping from the top of the ARC. First one, then a steady rattle as the snipers on the walls fire at the aircraft.

The harsh chatter of the autoguns overshadows the other gunfire, and streaking lines of light he realizes are bullets zip toward the plane.

A plume of white smoke comes from under the aircraft and for a beat Lee thinks it's been hit, but then something leaps from beneath one wing, moving faster than his eye can follow.

A split second, then a shrieking hits his ears, reminding him of the battleship's shells before they connected with the mainland.

There is a blinding flash of light in the center of the ARC's southwestern wall and a ball of fire erupts from its middle, spewing tendrils of flame, concrete, and black smoke in all directions.

"My God," Ian says as he hears his own voice make an inarticulate sound of horror, which is drowned out by a concussive blast that thunders toward them through the canyon and flutters his eardrums, shaking the organs inside his body.

The aircraft angles up, cruising through the cloud of debris before skimming over the ARC into clear air.

An enormous chunk of cement tips from the wall, falling like a gargantuan tree into the river. At its top, Lee spots a tiny, flailing dot he realizes is a man, now plummeting with the tons of cement into the water. The splash cascades up onto land, washing fifty yards or more onshore.

Through the smoking ruin, Lee sees a *V*-shaped darkness his mind doesn't compute for a moment until he realizes he's looking into the promenade that circles the main building within the walls.

The aircraft flies up, closer and closer, banking until it is coming straight for them.

It's going to kill them. Any second another missile will detach and race toward their position and there will be nothing left of either him or Ian.

Instead the plane turns, hissing by them and tipping once more to angle back the way it came, the first rays of sun flashing off its wings.

It levels out and descends into the valley, dropping lower and lower until it is in line with the ARC again.

51

Merrill eases back farther into the small room, his shoulder brushing Tia's.

He shoots her a look before holding up one finger and pointing toward the sounds coming from the next room. She nods, leveling her rifle.

There is the snap of dirt beneath a boot.

A breathed question.

Another step. Closer.

Merrill touches the safety, making sure it's off, and steps forward into the doorway.

Two men stand half turned away from him, their focus on the window facing out toward the river. As Merrill clears the doorway one of them issues a surprised grunt and raises a pistol.

Merrill's finger twitches on the trigger, the report a thunderclap in the room.

The man jerks, legs folding, his hand finding the bullet hole in his chest as Merrill feels a concussion beside him as Tia fires, and the second man stumbles backward, connecting with the wall. He tries to raise the rifle in his hands but it becomes too heavy and he drops forward, crumpling to his face.

Merrill sweeps the outer doorway with his rifle, ready to open fire on the next person who comes through it, but already he's turning to the window, toward the sound of muffled gunshots. The deep strafing boom of the autoguns starts a second later, and before he can move, an explosion shakes the entire house, rattling the windows that are still whole in their frames.

52

"Direct hit," Cree says in an almost bored voice.

Hiraku watches the operator tip the joystick before glancing to the drone, which mirrors the movement. "Again."

"There's already a substantial breach. If the men go now in the boats they'll be inside in a matter of minutes."

"Again."

Cree licks his lips. "Yes sir."

The drone banks and coasts overhead, nearly soundless after the deafening explosion of its missile. It swoops lower, falling in line with the facility again.

"Targeting now. Ready to fire."

Hiraku doesn't hesitate. "Fire."

53

"Ian?"

Lee feels a noose cinch his throat closed. Within the panic and fear his senses sharpen to needlepoints.

The drone hums.

His jaw aches from clenching it.

He can smell the scorched scent of the explosion on the air.

And worst of all he sees the other missiles beneath the plane's wings.

Which one? Which one will kill Zoey?

"Ian," he manages again, but the older man isn't focused on the aircraft anymore. He's sighting through his scope down at the plateau below them. "What?" Lee starts to say, but it's cut off with the deep blast of Ian's rifle.

54

An enormous insect buzzes by Hiraku's ear and he instinctively shrinks away.

But of course it's not an insect—he would know the sound of a high-powered rifle's bullet anywhere. He turns in time to see nearly three quarters of Cree's head shear away in a fan of brain matter and bone so shockingly white in the morning sun it almost transfixes him before he drops to a crouch.

Cree rocks to the side in his chair, taking the joystick control with him.

The drone yaws hard to the right.

Cree's finger death-twitches on the trigger.

One of the remaining five unfired missiles ignites, launching from its attachment as Hiraku watches, mind still trying to comprehend what's happened in the last two seconds.

The missile rips past the ARC, going wide by a dozen yards, and slams into the dam beyond.

The explosion fills the valley with its roar even as the drone follows the missile's path through the smoke and massive pieces of shrapnel.

There is no pause to the detonation, only a multiplying of it.

The sound staggers Hiraku to the ground. It is mind splitting. His blood vibrates in his veins. He tries to brace himself but falls to his back and a single thought surfaces in his mind.

Sniper.

The word doesn't need summons; it is there even as he starts scanning the hills around him. The shot came from high and to the left, nearly behind them.

There.

A flash of movement, already gone.

He flips to his stomach and crawls to a nearby boulder. From behind it he scans for the two men who had accompanied them to the lookout. Gone. Fled. So be it.

Voices are screaming from the radio on his collar.

"This is Hiraku. Status report."

A man comes back, he thinks it's Draiman. "What the hell happened?"

"Cree is down. We have a sniper somewhere in the hills." He rises enough to scan where he'd spotted movement earlier but sees nothing. Risking the exposure, he stands, gazing down into the valley.

The vaporized concrete hangs in a solid cloud above the river, obscuring the face of the dam and the southern edge of the facility's walls. The larger guns that were mounted facing the town are silent or gone from the first missile strike. In their place is an erratic pop of gunfire that's coming not only from the remaining men on the wall but also from his own soldiers, their forms emerging from the town's cover to fire back.

"Full assault," Hiraku says over the ringing in his ears.

"Sir?"

"I said full assault. Get the boats in the water and lay down cover fire. Penetrate the outer wall."

"But the dam, sir! Look at the dam!"

A fountain of water sprays from a crater in the center of the sprawling structure. It curves down and splashes into the river below, forced by the titanic pressure behind the barrier. As he watches a chunk that must be at least the size of a tractor-trailer dislodges from the damage and plummets, bouncing once off the face of the dam, before plunging into the water.

He catches himself walking forward, transfixed at the spectacle, then he remembers Cree and how his skull looked glinting in the light. Hiraku backs himself behind the stone barricade, scanning the hill above him again before glancing down to the dam.

"Sir?" Draiman says, and Hiraku can hear his fear as if the man is speaking through a mouthful of it.

"Full assault."

"But sir, I—"

"Damn you, listen to me! Full assault! Now!"

His voice echoes loudly, his hearing slowly returning. There is a terrible pause in the other man's response. They will abandon him now, at the height of his fury, his crusade. If Shirou were here, there would be no question of his command; orders would simply be followed. It only amplifies his rage at the woman who took his friend from him, at everyone under his command, at himself.

The anger begins its pressure-cooker build, rising slowly before rocketing upward in a haze of red that mists his vision, and he grabs the radio to give the order again, but Draiman's voice issues from it before he can.

"Yes sir. Full assault."

He unclenches his hand from where it was gripping the sharp corners of the rock he hides behind, noting absently the blood running from multiple cuts on his palm. He wipes it on his pant leg before reaching into his chest pocket to draw out the folded paper.

He's taken to holding it when no one is around, never unfolding it; he hasn't been able to do that in some time. Even in the company of his men he's found himself reaching to touch the pocket where it's concealed.

Now he grips it tightly, the paper creasing in his fist, yet it is like a weapon, bolstering his resolve.

He inches forward enough to see his men moving toward the river on the bank far below. A barrage of gunfire pulses up and down their ranks as several squadrons move the tactical boats to the water's edge, even as the dam emits a low, almost primordial groan and another fountain of water springs from its center.

It will hold, or it won't, he thinks, unsnapping the holster at his hip and drawing out his pistol. Either way he'll get what he wants.

And for now, I can be more useful elsewhere.

Hiraku sidles from the boulder's cover into the nearest draw and begins to climb.

55

"What is that?" Zoey says, as the alarm blares again.

But Vivian isn't listening to her. Her mother's attention is focused on one of the several speakers set in the ceiling, a look of calm perplexity on her face. The baby wriggles in her blankets, and when Zoey looks down, she finds herself eye to eye with her daughter.

The blue vividness of her gaze drowns out everything else.

The alarm is still sounding, but from somewhere distant. For the second time in a matter of moments, Zoey opens her mouth without knowing what she will say. How do you greet a part of you you've never met before? For a heartbeat it is only the two of them, looking at one another.

The spell breaks as a static ripping sound invades the room overpowering the alarm. She has time to wonder why the noise would remind her of Riverbend, but then it crescendos to something beyond parsing.

Her eardrums fill with a reverberating blast as the floor shivers beneath them, tipping hard enough that she has to place an arm out on the couch to brace them.

Books rain from the shelves like injured birds.

The bottle of liquor falls from the desk.

Vivian stumbles to the floor as the lights flicker and plunge into full darkness before coming back on at half their power.

The baby squirms and begins to cry, eyes shutting with the effort. Her shrieks are muted, faraway beneath the buzzing in Zoey's ears, though now the girl has nothing to compete with, the alarm silent. She climbs to her feet, holding her daughter close as Vivian sits up, pushing herself to her knees.

"What the hell was that?" Vivian asks. Her hand comes up a dark red and it takes Zoey a second to realize the other woman fell in the Director's blood.

The door to the office bangs open, a middle-aged man in a lab coat who Zoey's never seen before, at the threshold.

"We're under attack! What do we do?"

Vivian gains her feet, wiping a bloody smear across her slacks. "Under attack? By who?"

"How the hell should I know? They bombed us or something. Where should I tell the staff to go?"

Vivian glances around the room, her eyes hovering on Zoey before moving back to the man. "Start emergency backup procedures. I want all data saved onto portable drives. Secure the incubation room. And tell every security personnel you see to report to level-five rooftop."

"Yes ma'am." He is gone in a swirl of his coat and they're alone again.

Vivian raises the pistol slowly, aiming it in Zoey's general direction. "You brought them here?"

"What? No, I—"

"You just told me we were going to be under attack and minutes later we are? That's too much of a coincidence, Zoey."

"I told you he knew the location. I didn't know how close he was."

Vivian seems to weigh something before motioning to the open door. "Move."

Zoey rocks the crying infant but doesn't move toward the hall. "What are you going to do?"

"I'm going to put both of you in a holding room until I can get control of the situation."

"You're not going to get control of the situation. Don't you see? He's here. His men will get inside." Through the thick walls comes a faint popping sound, like the cracking of a stiff joint. Gunshots. She stares at her mother. "Do you hear that? They're already fighting. Help me. Help me get her out of here. Please, if you ever really loved me, please help us." She sways in place, trying to calm the baby who continues to cry, her face splotchy and red.

Vivian blinks, looking down at the pistol in her hand, then to the Director's body. The room shudders around them and someone yells a curse out in the hallway as glass shatters.

"I won't let it all be for nothing," Vivian murmurs. She brings her head up and the gun follows. "Move. Now."

Zoey's heart drops as her mind careens through a dozen different options, all of them useless. "You're not going to kill me. You need me."

"That's where you're wrong. I need your eggs, Zoey, not you. So you can either do what I say or risk wounding your daughter."

"You wouldn't."

"Would you like to find out?"

She feels as if she's going to faint. The baby has begun to quiet with her constant movement and is looking at the nearby wall with curiosity. Zoey searches for another way out but Vivian pulls the pistol slightly to the side and yanks the trigger.

Zoey jerks at the report, instinctively hugging the baby closer as stuffing flies from the couch to her left.

"Don't test me, Zoey. You don't know what I'm capable of."

Zoey looks from the dark circle of the gun's barrel to her mother. "Yes I do."

She turns toward the door and starts to take a step but stops and bends down, retrieving a book that's fallen to the floor. Its cover is familiar, like seeing a friend's face after being away from each other too long.

The Count of Monte Cristo.

She scans the cover, flipping it open with one hand. Needing to be sure.

There are several ragged edges where the pages have been torn out. She recalls the night she watched Dellert strip them free and drop them to the ground, destroying the one escape from the prison of her life. Her one salvation.

Salvation.

"I won't tell you again, Zoey," Vivian says. She nods, moving toward the hall. "And leave the book."

Zoey pauses at the doorway and hefts the hardcover, feeling its weight, before facing her mother once again. "I always loved this story."

"Quite symbolic that Cleric Asher gave it to you."

"It kept me going most days. He knew me better than I knew myself."

"Yes. Well, I hope it was worth the cost of his life."

The baby wails and a muscle in Zoey's arm twitches but she turns away, taking one step toward the door.

"Zoey, I said to leave th—"

Zoey spins, whipping the heavy book around as hard as she can.

Vivian's gun hand is just where she knew it would be.

The tome connects with the back of her mother's wrist.

The gun goes off before it flies free of her grip, the report loud enough to reignite the ringing in Zoey's ears.

Vivian yells something incoherent and tries to launch herself forward, but Zoey's already driving the hard spine of the book at her face.

It smashes into Vivian's nose with an audible snap.

The older woman rocks back on her heels as if she's hit a wall. Blood gushes from both nostrils and she brings a hand up as if to touch the injury, but doesn't.

Zoey takes a single step and flings a hard kick into her mother's solar plexus.

Vivian staggers backward and slips in the congealing pool of the Director's blood. Her feet kick out from beneath her and she falls, the back of her head connecting with the low table between the chairs.

There is a sickening, fleshy thud, and Vivian drops to her side and lies still.

Zoey takes in a shaky breath. Her daughter squalls again, one of her small feet digging into Zoey's ribs.

"Shhh, shhh, it's okay, it's okay." She leans in, kissing the girl lightly on the forehead before retrieving the pistol. A subtle burning begins to enter her shoulder and she glances at it, surprised to see a slick of bright blood there. The bullet must have grazed her but she hadn't felt it. She works her arm and, besides the pain, it moves without issue.

Moving to the couch she gently lays her daughter down, tucking her in the valley of two cushions before crossing the gap to Vivian. She kneels over her mother, noting the dribble of blood leaking from the back of her head. Grasping her shoulder, she rolls her over and checks for a pulse at her neck. It is there, fast but steady. On her wrist Zoey sees a bracelet much like the one she used to wear except for a small clasp on the bottom. She presses it and the bracelet opens, slipping off the other woman's arm easily.

She begins to rise, knowing she needs to run, to get her daughter and herself out of the ARC, but she pauses for a moment, held there in limbo by a pang of remorse.

There is something deeply tragic about this woman, and despite the blood coating the lower half of her face, Zoey recognizes a hint of herself now. Perhaps it's her imagination, or maybe it was always there and she chose not to see it.

Her daughter cries, and beyond the walls comes an erratic string of gunfire.

They have to go. Now.

She starts to turn away but one of Vivian's hands shoots out, grasping her wrist with shocking strength. Her eyes, crazed and bloodshot, spring open and find Zoey's. "You had a chance to save the species." Bloody spittle sprays from her lips. "And you missed it."

Zoey grits her teeth, resisting the pull of Vivian's arm before leaning closer. "You had a chance to be my mother."

She yanks her wrist away and walks to the couch, gathering her daughter in her arms before moving to the hall.

"Zoey! Zoey! Zoey!"

She slams the door on Vivian's screams, silencing them to mutters.

The hallway is devoid of life, the stairs leading up and to the left toward the roof dark except for a single emergency light. Down the corridor is the set of doors she recalls from her first escape. In the center of the hall a light fixture has fallen from its mount, glass littering the floor in a semicircle.

She hurries to the doors and scans the bracelet that's sticky with blood. The door clicks open and she steps through, hugging her daughter close while sweeping the area ahead with the pistol.

She comes to the *T* in the hall. Straight ahead a dead end. To the right the glass-fronted laboratory, quiet and still. To the left the elevator.

Zoey presses the button on the wall, glancing back the way she came, all the while continuing to shift back and forth with the baby. "It's all right. Everything's going to be okay." She says the words even as the voice in her head tells her she has no idea if this is true while also reminding her she doesn't know what she's doing. "Then we'll figure it out, right? You and me, we'll figure it out together." The girl hiccups several times but slowly focuses on her, a shaky sigh coming from her chest that is part cry and part gurgle. "It's going to be okay. I promise." The baby's mouth quirks slightly, almost a smile.

Zoey starts to return it when something round and cold presses against the back of her neck.

"Drop the gun."

She hesitates, wondering how fast she can move without hurting the baby.

The metallic click of the hammer being drawn back echoes in the corridor. "Do it."

She lets the pistol drop to the floor. It's kicked away at once, spinning to a stop a dozen feet down the hall. The gun's barrel leaves her neck and she takes a step, turning to look at her captor.

Doctor Calvin holds the pistol in both hands, a cruel mockery of a grin on his face. "Got the better of her, huh? Doesn't surprise me. You're something, Zoey. I always knew you were special."

The elevator pings, drawing their attention as its doors glide open. Four men step out into the open. The first two are Redeyes, the next a guard wearing a thick tactical vest loaded with ammunition.

And the last is Reaper.

He wears a dark uniform and polished black boots. Only his colorless eyes are visible above the mask she knows covers his ruined features.

Everyone stops in place, the situation taking on the quality of a painting.

"I caught her trying to escape," Calvin says. "She probably killed or injured Vivian."

Reaper shoots a look at her and her insides shrivel as she clutches the baby tighter.

Here he is, the monster of her nightmares. She cannot recall ever fearing or loathing another human being more in her life.

"Get to the roof and provide covering fire over the gap in the wall," Reaper says, still looking at her. "Repel the boats and tell McGarry to start evacuation procedures."

The Redeyes and single guard hurry away down the corridor, scanning through the doorway, and are gone. The floor vibrates and a resounding blast comes from the south before the quick patter of gunshots continues like rain against a window.

"Where do you want me to put her?" Calvin says, glancing from Reaper to Zoey. Reaper moves toward the doctor, stopping by his side to face her once more. "Holding room or should I bring her to the roof for evacuation?"

"You performed her ovum extraction prior to her escape, correct?" Reaper asks.

A look of pride forms on Calvin's face. "Yes I did, sir."

"I thought so."

With a movement so fast Zoey can barely follow it, Reaper swings his right forearm toward the doctor's neck and slams his palm into the top of his head on the opposite side.

Calvin's skull snaps to a hideous angle, the vertebrae in his neck breaking with the sound of a dry branch.

Zoey lets out a startled cry, her eyes widening as the doctor's gun clatters to the floor and his body follows a second later.

Reaper stands over him and glances up at her, his gray gaze unblinking. "Follow me."

He strides away from the elevator toward the lab. Zoey watches him go, looking back to the elevator doors and down to Calvin's motionless body, rooted in place.

"Zoey, please. There's not much time," he says, motioning toward the right doorway at the end of the hall.

Indecision holds her in place for another moment before the baby coos, breaking her free.

She hurries toward Reaper, trying to ready herself for a trap as her mind replays what just happened. He disappears into the room as she nears, and now she remembers what's inside the area.

Rows of opaque tanks, the artificial wombs where both of her daughters were grown. In the center the tower with oscillating lights shimmers, its shape and aura almost like a sentient presence. To the left

Reaper is working at a panel full of electronics, its face lined with dials and monitors. There is an abrupt clacking sound and the panel swings forward and now she sees it is only a false representation. Behind it is a narrow doorway that opens as Reaper touches a button set into its frame.

Another elevator.

"Get in," he says, stepping out of the way.

She barely hesitates. None of this makes sense.

As she huddles into one corner Reaper steps inside the small space and punches another button on a panel. The door slips shut without a sound.

They descend.

"Where are you taking us?" she asks, her voice loud in the steel enclosure.

"We're almost there."

Their motion slows. Stops.

The door opens to a narrow concrete tunnel without windows, a sparse line of industrial lights running along its ceiling. A guard stands with his back to them, rifle unslung and ready. As they step into the tunnel he turns, his entire body going rigid before recognition enters his eyes.

"Sir, it's you. What—" The guard looks at her. Down to the baby. Back to Reaper. "Sir, what the hell are you doing?"

Reaper takes a step forward and the guard raises his weapon.

Again, the blur of motion as he moves, stepping into and past the younger man's weapon before he can fire. His fist sinks into the guard's throat, knocking him into the wall. The guard rebounds, legs going slack as Reaper catches his weight and tosses him to the cement where he lands in a heap.

The guard's weapon clatters away and its owner lies still.

Reaper straightens, his breathing making his back heave slightly. Zoey finds herself pressed against the opposite wall, the baby beginning to fuss again in her arms. He faces her and there is something in his gaze that catches her off guard. A softness. Almost like . . .

He points down the tunnel. "Follow it to the end and you'll find a staircase leading up. The code on the door is 3172021."

She pushes away from the wall and takes a tentative step, half sure he will suddenly grab her and force her back into the elevator, the last three minutes some kind of cruel joke. So when she tries to move by him and he raises a hand toward her, she flinches, holding the baby out of his reach.

But instead of grasping her, his hand opens, fingers only inches away from the side of her face. He moves as if to touch her and she shrinks back. His hand hovers there, trembling faintly before he drops it to his side.

"I'm so sorry, Zoey." His voice is raw and defeated. The mask he wears shifts as if he is trying to say something more before he looks away and strides to the elevator. She watches him go, a strange sensation stealing over her almost like the feeling of the current while standing knee-deep in a stream.

The door slides closed, gradually hiding him from her sight until he is gone.

The elevator hums before fading away.

Zoey wavers on the spot, feeling the edge of an epiphany in her mind, its shape concealed beneath gauzy layers of confusion and denial. But as she tries to pull away the cover, it breaks apart and recedes into a vague sense of sadness she doesn't understand.

The baby squalls, hiccupping herself into a full-blown cry.

The guard on the floor moans, one hand sliding across the concrete.

Zoey runs.

The tunnel travels gradually downward before leveling out. She tries to listen for sounds of the battle somewhere above her but there is nothing but the sound of the child, the pounding of her slippered feet, and the harried rush of blood in her ears.

A staircase materializes a hundred yards ahead. It is steel and concrete, perhaps a dozen steps. A reinforced door rests at its top and on the wall beside it a digital panel glows green.

She takes the steps two at a time, sliding to a stop on the top landing. Her finger pauses over the buttons. The code. What was the code? She had been so stunned by Reaper's actions she hadn't truly been listening. But there had been something deeply familiar about them for some reason.

3172021.

The code comes rushing back with a ferocity that nearly staggers her.

Because those numbers are one of the first things she was ever required to remember.

Her birthdate.

She spins, looking back down the silent tunnel but the elevator is gone. Gone like the man who led her out. Gone like Vivian had said he was.

A pulsating thrum comes from somewhere above her and a stream of dust drops from the ceiling. She faces the panel once again, fingers shaking so badly it takes three tries to enter in the code correctly.

The door unlocks, easing away from her on oiled hinges, and she steps through it into the raging sounds of battle.

56

Merrill, Tia, and Newton leapfrog between the buildings, timing their movements within the staccato beat of gunfire.

They are almost to the water, its surface a disturbed plain of waves and foam in the morning light. The sun hinted at an appearance after clearing the horizon but now is lost behind the crumpled curtain of clouds that coats the sky.

A bullet whizzes by Merrill's face, close enough to feel the air displaced by its passage. He leans back behind the tree they crouch next to. Hiraku's army has solidified from shadows into the men they are, all of them pushing forward after the initial attack on the ARC and the subsequent destruction of the dam. They are all around them now, squads scurrying from house to house, coming nearer to the river's edge where the heaviest fighting is going on.

Merrill peers around the tree again.

The soaring hole in the side of the ARC is lined with men, the muzzles of their rifles flashing continuously. On the shore the invading force has taken cover behind several rock walls and benches that overlook the water. Tracers zoom back and forth, their color almost lost in the daylight. But it's the dam that captures his attention.

Two waterfalls gush from the upper portion of the hole the drone left in its wake. He has no idea how many feet thick the structure is, but the blasts from the missiles must've been beyond powerful. The crater is at least sixty feet deep and over three hundred feet long. As he watches, several pieces of jagged concrete crumble beneath the water's pressure and fall, bouncing and tumbling into the river.

The pressure behind the dam is like a colossal blade poised at its pinnacle, ready to fall any second.

They have less than no time.

A clamor of men's voices overrides the shooting before even more gunfire erupts. A soldier two hundred yards to their left rises from a crouch, lifting a rocket launcher to his shoulder. He takes aim and fires.

The RPG sizzles across the river and through the gap in the wall, slamming into the building behind it.

Debris rains down, and a row of small boats launch into the water from their side.

"Merrill," Tia says from beside him. Her hand grips his shoulder.

"Let's move to the observatory. There's only two men there. We can take them out and hold until it's clear enough to cross."

"In what? We don't have a boat and the water's rising."

"We have to get across. We'll find something on the shore."

"It's suicide. We'll be blown away by one side or the other. We can't stay here, much less press forward, and you know it."

"No." He focuses on the boats as they cruise toward the gap in the wall. A barrage of fire comes from the guards in the ARC and the men in the two front boats jitter in time to the beat of the bullets. The boats careen to the side, missing the structure completely.

A tectonic rumble vibrates the ground beneath them and another massive chunk of concrete dislodges from the dam, breaking in two as it descends. The pieces send a splash up forty feet in the air, the waves nearly capsizing the closest boats.

"Damn it, Merrill, look at me!" Tia hisses, yanking him around. Her eyes are alight with intensity. "She's gone. It's over. We step out into this we're dead. And if we make it through to the ARC, that water's coming. If we go out there we're going to die." Her expression softens slightly and she drops her hand away from his shoulder. "She's gone."

Merrill sinks back against the house, unsure if his legs will hold him or not. A rending sensation fills him. He's being torn asunder from within, half of him already running toward the river, the other half being pulled up the valley wall to where he knows Chelsea and his unborn child wait.

He leans forward, giving the fighting another look. The leading boat has met the break in the wall and for some reason it seems completely wrong to him. In the next instant he knows why. Hiraku's men shouldn't be able to climb from the river onto the promenade surrounding the building—the gap is normally too much—but the water has risen significantly in the last ten minutes.

The sight galvanizes his decision.

He turns away, vision blurring the landscape of their retreat.

"Okay," he says hoarsely. "Okay."

They mark their next move, Newton going first. Almost all of Hiraku's men are past their position, and the few they see in the distance don't seem to notice them. Tia and Merrill follow, moving in halting spans between cover until they are outside the border of battle.

As they climb into and out of a shallow ditch near a crumbling roadway, Merrill realizes he is whispering to himself, the words a mantra of pain he hasn't let himself acknowledge until now. With a final look back at the ARC through the skeletal trees and decrepit houses, he says it again.

"I'm sorry."

57

Reaper strides through the security doors on the fifth level, the lights overhead flickering with another explosion.

He walks down the hall quickly, passing each doorway without a look before hearing a new sound that overshadows the fighting outside.

It's a voice coming from behind the Director's door, a soft pounding accompanying it. He reaches out his arm, bringing the bracelet he wears almost to the scanner above the number pad, but stops.

His wife's voice sounds shattered from yelling, but there is something else there, an unhinged quality that mirrors what's been growing inside her for the better part of two decades. Maybe it's been there much longer.

Reaper slowly moves his hand to the middle of the door as Vivian falls quiet, pressing his palm there for a moment before pulling it away. He had once stepped in front of a grenade for her and wears the scars to show it, but now he can no longer protect her because there is no protecting someone from themselves.

He walks away, leaving the renewed pounding and the cries to be freed behind him.

Up the stairs and through the door to the roof.

Into chaos.

There are at least sixty people there, scattered across the helipad and between the HVAC units. Many are members of Vivian's research and medical staff, those who have resided behind the walls in comfort for years without a true worry. Now their faces are different: drawn by terror, tear streaked, and broken. The extinction of fear isn't a good thing, not for people, he decides, moving past the closest to him. He's always been afraid, and the right amount of fear has served him well, kept him sharp and attentive to the risks around him. But it's also blinded him. And now the moment he's dreaded the most is at hand.

One of the helicopters is priming for takeoff, its interior packed with people. Two of his men stand guard outside the door as the rotor begins to turn.

"Sir, we've saved you a seat," the closest guard yells over the gathering whir of blades, but he doesn't stop. "Sir! Sir!"

He feels eyes land on him, the weight palpable. He moves past them toward the catwalk stretching to the closest sniper's nest. The metal bangs under his feet and he glances down, searching out the huge hole in the curving wall.

A line of his men stands firing out at the invading force, their stances strong, none showing any sign of retreat. But even as he watches, three of them fall, a hail of lead cutting through their bodies in mists of red.

He reaches the sniper's nest. The guard who had been manning it lies dead, slumped against the surround, a gaping hole where his left eye should be. Reaper retrieves the man's rifle from his death grip and settles it on the rampart. Below he catches sight of five boats streaming toward the gap in the wall. Two land and almost immediately pull away, their occupants fighting past the last of the guards.

So the defenses have fallen.

He always knew it would happen. From within or without was the only question. He had felt his own fortifications slipping over the years;

his belief and duty to the cause, always bolstered by Vivian's vision as well as his love for her, beginning to rust with time and the empty hole within he couldn't bring himself to name.

But now there is no reason not to. There is nothing holding him back at this final juncture, nothing keeping him from speaking of his failure and the love he wouldn't allow himself to free.

"Zoey," he says, settling his eye into the scope and finding the house the security tunnel leads to. He only has to wait a few seconds before he sees her. She emerges from the side of the structure holding her daughter—his granddaughter. He had been allowed to hold the two girls shortly after their artificial births and it had been this more than anything that destroyed the last of his defenses. The guilt of what he had done over the years for the cause he'd served rushed in, drowning and crushing, leaving him with only a single course of action, the only thing honorable left for a soldier like him.

And now the time has come to do it.

"Run," he says as the sound of the helicopter heightens behind him. "Run away, Zoey."

She does.

She flees up a small rise onto a narrow roadway hugging the river. A quarter mile ahead the sheer drop of the cliffs surrenders to a long, diagonal cut ascending between their ranks. They need to reach it before the dam crumbles and the billions of gallons of water come rushing forward.

Bringing his face away from the riflescope, he squints ahead of Zoey's path before adjusting the weapon's aim. Through the magnification he finds a pairing of men crouched behind an abandoned car. As he watches they turn their heads in her direction, no doubt alerted by the baby's cries.

His finger only grazes the trigger before the recoil nudges his shoulder.

The first soldier topples to the ground and he fires again before the man's compatriot can take cover. The second soldier spins in a half circle with the impact and falls as Zoey jogs into their vicinity.

Reaper repositions himself, scanning downstream once more. Another man runs in her direction, head down, seemingly oblivious to her presence, but he will not take a chance. After a lifetime of holding up his duty as a soldier while never living up to the title of father, he will not fail her now.

His shot takes the man in the head midstride, and he skids to a stop on his stomach, dead before he hits the ground. As Reaper gazes onward, tracing a line along the hills she'll have to follow, the helicopter's tone changes and without looking back he knows it has become airborne.

Wind buffets him from its rotors, but he doesn't turn to watch it depart. Those on board are thinking only of themselves, as they always have. Everything they pledged to and worked toward, gone the moment a threat presented itself.

Now the future lies with the young woman running for her life along the riverbank. And his greatest regret among many is that he never got to truly know her.

The helicopter rises and he's about to turn to watch it flee when there is a puff of smoke from one of the boats in the river. A high whistling fills his ears and he ducks instinctively as the RPG soars over his head and connects with the tail of the aircraft.

There is a bone-shaking boom and the tail section disconnects from the main body like a limb cut from a tree.

The main rotor spins the cockpit and cabin out of control, dumping several of the people within onto the roof while others fall out of sight over the northern wall with clipped screams.

Then the helicopter itself connects with the wall and rotates away and down, a trail of black smoke marking its descent. The tail section crunches into the roof, its smaller rotor detaching as it crashes.

Reaper sees what's about to happen and knows from years spent in conflict that there is no point in trying to move. Sometimes running is a waste of time.

Instead he closes his eyes as the rotor pinwheels toward him across the roof.

He's slammed into the wall behind him and slides down it, all feeling gone from below his breastbone. But there is no pain. Not yet.

He opens his eyes, blinking through a redness that coats his vision, then looks down at his chest.

The rotor struck him at an angle, entering between the joint of his shoulder and neck before continuing on its way over the side of the wall. He notes enough exposed muscle and bone to confirm it won't take long.

His breathing isn't painful, yet he can't inhale fully. It's as if something is sitting on his chest. An elephant maybe, like the one the doctor had told him would be there for a while after a terrible bout of pneumonia when he was ten. He had nearly died then, and now, so many years later, it is strange to recall the single memory of his mother's worried eyes watching him while he lay in bed, struggling to breathe.

As the red in his eyes begins to curdle and darken, he feels more than hears something vast give way. The entire structure trembles with its force and he wonders if his daughter and granddaughter will survive. In that moment he would like to see them safe more than anything, to watch them make it free of all this like his mother had watched him return to health.

But then the darkness thickens, dragging his eyelids closed, and the last thing he sees is a wave of vertical gray sky shooting up to an immeasurable height and washing away the clouds.

58

Vivian pounds harder on the door, her voice like slivers of glass in her throat.

Outside, between the rattle of gunfire and the muted explosions that send small shivers through the floor, there is the sound of booted footsteps. Thank God, someone heard her and is finally coming to let her out. She yells again, hammering the door for good measure even though she knows whoever it is has stopped. In a few seconds she'll be out and will assess the situation. It can't be nearly as bad as Zoey said.

Zoey.

She will have to be punished. Like any disobedient child she'll have to learn her limitations and how far she can push her mother. Especially if she is to be trusted going forward. There will be no room for discord among them if she is to be at her side in the new world.

Vivian's about to start beating on the door again with her bruised hand when a confusing sound reaches her ears.

The footsteps are leaving.

Whoever is out there is walking away.

For a second she's speechless. Why wouldn't they let her out? "Hey! I'm stuck in here! Hey!" Her voice finally breaks, turning into a dry rasp.

She lowers her aching hand and stands gazing at the door as if she can see through it.

She turns and wipes at her broken nose, sending a jolt of pain through her entire head. "That's fine." She steps over the Director's body and circles his desk, lowering herself into the arrogant bastard's chair. How many hours did he waste sitting here, pretending he was something he wasn't?

But he wasn't the only one pretending, was he?

She shakes her head. There's no room for any more distractions now. Now is the time for focus. She concentrates on the Director's ruined skull, wishing she would have killed him years ago. She tries to imagine how different things would have been if she had, but stops.

Regret is a waste of time, and time is the most precious thing she has.

No, the most precious thing you had broke your nose and left you trapped here.

Vivian discards the thoughts, gathering a handful of papers up from the desk. They are the latest reports from the blood and DNA tests that were run on Zoey's offspring. Everything about them is promising, especially the Beta-catenin levels.

"Just need to gather more data. Then she'll have to see reason," she says under her breath, shuffling papers.

Can't you see she was telling the truth? She's not like you. Her nature is completely different, and you can't fight nature.

Vivian shuts her eyes and takes a deep, cleansing breath that's ruined by the whistling in her smashed nose. Focus and control. That's all it will take to make things right again.

There is a reference number on one of the reports associated with a notation in a recent research paper. Does she have it here? No. There had been no reason to include it for the Director since nearly all of the data went completely over his head. She's not even sure now why she provided him with the reports. To keep up the illusion of his leadership she supposes. And how sad it is looking back and knowing he was needed as a figurehead, a fixture of purpose for those that lived beneath them simply because he was a man.

Disgusted, she rises from the desk, carrying the reports with her as the floor does a strange shimmy under her feet. How long will it take them to sort this incursion out? There is work to be done and almost no time to do it.

She catches herself reaching toward the scanner beside the door to let herself out. That's right, her bracelet is gone. She'll have to wait—

Her head jerks around, eyes landing on the Director's pallid out-stretched wrist and the bracelet around it.

She nearly laughs. Of course, why hadn't she thought of that before? Vivian moves to the body, setting down the paperwork while trying to keep her feet out of the blood. All of this was just a minor hiccup in the plans. She'll get the bracelet, then find Zoey and make her see reason. They will move forward together in the right direction and everything will fall into place.

Vivian turns the bracelet over, looking for the clasp that holds it on like her own but sees none. The realization is like another blow to her head. In his infinite wisdom the Director had insisted on having the same bracelet design as all the rest of the staff. He'd said it would build a sense of trust and commonality among them. She curses his logic under her breath and grasps the bracelet, trying to wiggle it free. It comes to the wide part of the Director's hand and stops, refusing to move any farther. She tries crushing the corpse's palm into a different shape but it's not enough to free the bracelet.

A tremor of rage runs through her. She yanks with both hands. The body jerks with her efforts and she grunts, bracing her feet harder against the floor. Even in death he is still hindering her, holding her back. A wordless cry leaves her as she pulls again with all her strength and feels something give.

The bracelet comes free and she stumbles back, elation blooming inside her. She raises it to her face unable to keep from smiling.

The bracelet's broken band meets her gaze, the tiny wires shining and exposed inside the rubber.

"No." She hurries to the door, nearly tripping over the low table. With a rising panic she scans the bracelet and punches in the code.

Nothing.

"No!" She tries again and again, but the result is the same each time. "No, no, no, no!" She slams her fist into the door and pain explodes down her arm. This wasn't supposed to happen. Everything is a mockery of what she'd planned. Of her hopes, her dreams.

The gunfire.

Explosions.

Zoey.

"This isn't right," she whispers, unable to stand anymore. She slumps to the couch, staring down at the useless bracelet. "None of this is right."

And as a rumble begins building around her, shaking books from the shelves and sending the furniture scattering about the room, Vivian wonders at what moment she lost control, or if she ever had it at all.

"None of this was right," she says as everything falls down around her and the world begins to spin.

59

The image of the dam hemorrhaging water hounds Zoey as she runs along the riverbank.

She hasn't looked back yet and knows if she were to, she might be transfixed by the sight—unable to do anything but absorb the promise of death.

A ditch appears before her and she clutches the wailing baby tight before plunging into it and up the other side.

Her feet hit cracked pavement, one of them bare, the thin slipper lost sometime since leaving the house where the tunnel ended. The sound of battle is still near enough for her to flinch each time a gun goes off, the reports coming slower now, in small bursts with punctuations of silence between them.

She catches sight of movement ahead as the shape of a man moves toward her. Even as she changes course to avoid him he's falling to the ground, his head partially disintegrating.

Ian.

No, the shot came from the wrong direction. It came from the ARC.

She has no time to reckon it as another explosion rips through the morning air, followed by the screeching of metal.

Everything is chaos. Everything fury and horror.

Except for the weight she carries in her arms.

With a burst of speed, she rounds a corner in the small street and sees her path ends near a dilapidated house, the bank of the river narrow below the sheer cliffs to the left. Without pause she plunges onward, feet leaving the roadway and sliding through dirt and detritus. Several large rocks present themselves, and she scrambles onto and over them, leaping to a sloping grade that runs parallel beneath the bluffs.

As she sprints across a patch of loose sediment, the ground does a strange jerk, the sheer face of rock beside her seeming to lunge out to nudge her shoulder.

Zoey's feet slip, mind crying out that she's going to fall.

The river looms, wide and strong, waiting to swallow her and the baby whole if she topples that way.

Her shin and knees connect with the ground, skin peeling away as she tries to shield her daughter.

They land in a skid of dust, small rocks burying themselves in her left arm. A roaring fills her ears and for a moment she thinks she's fallen so hard her hearing has been disrupted. There is only static around her, the baby's cries forlorn and distant.

A dozen areas on her body throbbing in time with her heart, Zoey sits up and looks back the way she came, and for a split second she doesn't understand what she's seeing.

The center of the dam is gone.

In its place is a raging torrent of water the color of the clouds above.

The water pours past the concrete, ripping gigantic chunks of the dam with it, discarding them like a child throwing toys, into the river hundreds of feet below.

There is an immense cracking that she can feel in her teeth, and the entire left section of the structure folds over, disappearing with a rending blast of liquid that rushes into the riverbed and slams into the side of the ARC.

A wall of water shoots straight up into the sky. It rises higher and higher until she's sure it's going to brush some of the clouds, expanding outward all the time. For a brief moment its shape becomes that of a massive hand, fingers extending, palm flat against the ARC, then it blasts over the walls, covering the facility completely.

Zoey shoves herself up, a cold terror filling her like the water will do if it catches them. She spins away but not before seeing the ARC—her home, her prison—crumble inward and begin to roll beneath the pressure of the deluge.

Higher ground. It's their only chance.

How many seconds until it reaches them? How much time does she have left with the tiny bundle of warmth against her chest? Five seconds? Ten?

Her legs burn along with her lungs, fear an acidic fuel in her veins.

The static rush of water builds behind them until it is something alive, a frenzied scream of all the voices she's ever silenced. They are in the wall of water blazing toward her, frantic to clutch her and the baby and wash them away as if they never were.

An outcropping of rock extends into their path, nearly blocking the way completely, and she can't see what's beyond it. There might be nothing but empty air and the chilling shock of falling, but she doesn't hesitate.

Zoey slows enough to grasp a handhold in the stone and swing their combined weight out and over a drop she doesn't look at, before leaping forward.

The ground is there.

The solidity of it is like a lover's embrace. And what's beyond makes her heart surge.

A cut in the land extends up through the towering hills in a wide swath.

She runs upward, several steps giving way in soft runoff from the last rain before she gains traction. A blast of air rips past her and she knows the water is there. If she were to look back it would be reaching for her, perhaps with another hand like the one that destroyed the ARC.

Up.

Up.

Up.

Step after step she gains altitude, climbing until her legs give out and she crawls, one arm holding her daughter, the other grasping for purchase and pulling.

Something cold and wet touches her feet.

Zoey cries out. She can't help it. The sudden caress of the water electrifies her nerves, snapping her muscles tight. A wave cascades to her right, up the steeper wall of the cut, and rolls back on itself, coming toward them.

Zoey lunges left, shoving off a larger rock. She's gaining ground, but the wave is ahead of her. There's no outrunning it.

She has half a breath to grab the boulder ahead of her before the water slams into them.

It hits them like a cold punch, rocking her back and away from the stone.

Her fingers hold, allowing the briefest hope to fill her before they give way.

She and the baby tumble sideways, tossed toward the opposite wall of the cut.

The ground takes hungry bites from her and she can feel her clothes tearing along with her skin. Her daughter's screams are cut off as the cold liquid closes over them.

Zoey's ears fill with the water's language. It is a hollow clunking that sounds like hideous low laughter. It is in her nose, her mouth, embracing her completely.

Something solid strikes her in the lower back, sending a lightning bolt of pain through her spine and legs, but her arm automatically lashes out, hand searching, scrabbling.

Her fingers close on an object too large to grasp and they slip. A sharp edge tears her fingers, and now her lungs are bellowing for air. She will have to breathe soon, and then it will all be over. Forever darkness for both of them.

Her torn fingers latch onto a handhold.

The water tries to jerk her away but she grips harder, opening her mouth and drawing in a breath because the urge is overwhelming. Her mind screams to stop but her body plows forward, the need for oxygen too great.

Water courses into her open mouth, down into her lungs.

Immediately she gags, vomiting while trying to inhale again.

She sucks in air.

It is polluted with water and her own bile, but she breathes it in. Glorious oxygen. Black motes swim around her and it takes another five seconds for everything to come into focus.

They lie against the angle of a long, flat stone, the tip of it still clutched tightly in her hand. Blood flows outward from where she holds it and it takes a long second of concentration to get herself to let go. She coughs, heaving up another watery mouthful. Spluttering she rolls to her back, looking down the way they came.

The river is there.

A dozen feet away it swirls and rolls against the cut's boundaries but rises no higher. The entire river valley is full up to the point at which they lie. Her mind struggles with the sight, the amount of water mind-numbing and mesmerizing at the same time. Many things float in the current as it washes by: trees, pieces of house, and bodies. Many bodies. Some people are still alive; they bob and thrash as they coast past, unable to fight the pull of water, their screams nightmarishly distorted against the rock and water. She looks away, a creeping sensation flowing outward from her middle.

They are safe, but something is wrong. And that's when the realization hits her.

Her daughter isn't crying anymore.

Zoey pulls the baby away from her chest.

The girl's eyes are closed, her lips a soft blue. Water leaks from the corner of her mouth and she is pale as starlight.

"No!" Zoey yells, her voice jagged, not her own. She cradles the baby, giving her a gentle shake. Nothing. An animalistic sound comes from inside her, driven upward by panic the likes of which she's never felt before.

Pivoting on the rock, she lays her daughter down, peeling away the sodden blankets to expose her small body. She is dressed in a tiny one-piece, her legs and arms bare and limp. Zoey picks her back up, unable to concentrate on what to do.

Get the water out.

It is like someone has spoken directly into her mind. She shifts the little girl facedown on the inside of her arm and pats her back.

Nothing.

She pats harder, the tiny body shivering slightly each time.

A stream of water runs out over her arm.

"There, there, there," Zoey says, the words a mantra. "Please, please, breathe. You have to breathe." She's crying now, eyes clouded with tears even as she goes into another coughing fit. She turns the baby over again.

The girl's mouth is open, water draining from both nostrils, but still no movement. Still no breath.

"Oh please, please, please, please." Zoey reverses her daughter again, resuming the patting on her back.

Time elongates, bloating around them.

It is seconds or minutes or hours before she finally turns her over again. The girl's skin is colorless, almost translucent. She can see the delicate veins beneath her skin, their blue lines like minuscule script, but it tells a story of only sorrow.

Her daughter is gone.

Zoey leans back, holding her to her chest, sobbing silently.

She thought she had known grief and anguish, but she was wrong. There is nothing like the void left by a life unlived, all the vacant years compounding at once into an unbearable weight.

Zoey sags beneath it. She must break; there can't be anything after this. She shudders, holding her daughter tighter. The rock digs into her back, unyielding, unkind. But that is the world now; it's what it's always been. If the smallest, most innocent life isn't allowed to live then the truth of the world is only the hardness of stone, the cold clutch of indifferent water, and gunmetal sky presiding over it all.

She feels her heart struggling free of her chest. There is no surprise, only acceptance. If this is the place and the time, so be it.

Fresh wetness soaks into her shirt, coating her skin.

Her heart struggles harder.

She freezes.

The movement she's feeling isn't on the inside of her chest. It's on the outside.

With a strangled cry her daughter coughs, spewing even more water as Zoey sits straight up, rigid with hope and disbelief. A long wheezing breath in then another explosive shriek, her arms and legs jerking about.

Zoey lets out a choking noise that is half sob, half laugh as she cradles the crying girl in her arms. "You're okay! You're okay. I've got you, I've got you." She rocks back and forth, distilled joy coursing through her. "You're all right." She laughs again, gazing down at her daughter's reddening features, the color coming back like the sun after a long storm.

Below, the water continues to gurgle and eddy, flotsam rising and colliding with the valley's walls before slipping beneath the surface again. What could've been part of a boat floats past and is gone as something white and glistening is whirled closer up into the cut, refracting the gray morning light.

Zoey watches the white induction gown float by like a ghost, its sequins shining wetly. The dress swirls once in a circle, as if the water is dancing within it, before it is towed away around the corner of rock.

She's so entranced by the dress's appearance she doesn't notice the clack of rock above her daughter's cries until a hand falls on her shoulder.

Zoey lets out a short scream, twisting in place.

Merrill gazes down at her, eyes shining, open wonder on his face. "Zoey," is all he manages before she is on her feet and in his arms. He holds her, the baby squirming between them. She leans into his warmth, more tears leaking from her eyes before he lets her go.

"How did you find us?" she says, noticing Tia and Newton approaching down the cut behind him.

"We were in the town beside the dam and circled up into the lowest hill before it broke. We heard the baby right before the water came through, and we spotted you as you went around the bend. We ran in the same direction and lost track of you until I heard the baby crying again."

Tia steps up to her, dragging her into a rough embrace. The older woman kisses the side of her head. "Damn you, girl. This is the very last time I let you out of my sight. I mean it."

Zoey laughs as Newton approaches, putting a hand on her shoulder. "O-o-okay?" he asks.

"We're okay."

And all at once it is like they realize what she's holding. "Whose? I mean, where?" Merrill says, gazing at the baby.

"I'll explain," Zoey says, exhaustion a physical force trying to drag her down. "But can we please get away from the water first?"

60

The baby is asleep by the time they climb to the plateau where the house sits.

They fashioned a sling from Merrill's shirt to hang around Zoey's neck and shoulder, and after only a few minutes of hiking, the girl was nestled in and quiet. At first her silence frightened Zoey, and she continued to check her breathing every few steps, but after a time she relaxed, content with the child's weight and warmth against her as she and the others climbed free of the cut and began to traverse the road leading toward the outcropping of hills and the lone structure atop the closest one.

Zoey moves past the ASV and slows as the front door opens revealing Lee, who looks like a statue for a split second before he's rushing down the steps and racing to her.

Then his arms are wrapped around her, his breath warm on her face and ear.

"How? How did you—?"

The baby shifts between them and Lee takes a small step back, eyes wide as he peers into the sling. When he raises his gaze to hers, she can't help the smile that forms on her face.

"This is your daughter. Your other daughter." And there is no question now, no doubt as before. She knows in her heart that it's the truth.

"I don't understand."

"They fertilized two eggs, not one." Now the others are gathering around her, their embraces continuous. Tears, joy, laughter—it all coalesces until her throat closes with happiness. The questions are a barrage, their voices mingling until she can't separate a single word, but she doesn't need to. There will be time to answer all of them, time to come to terms with what happened in the ARC, with what she learned.

"How about a proper introduction," Chelsea says, holding out a bundle of blankets. Zoey grins and removes the sling from her shoulder, gently handing the sleeping girl to Lee while she accepts her other daughter. "I think you both lucked out, she's a really good baby."

Unlike her sister, the girl is awake, eyes shining and searching as if they are sponges and she's soaking up the world through them. "Hello," Zoey whispers, bringing her face down closer to the child's. "Hello there." The baby focuses on her, blinking quickly before making a soft gurgle in her throat that almost sounds like a laugh. When she glances up at Lee, he is crying. He shrugs as if to say, *well, here we are,* and it is like a vise has been unclamped from inside her.

"What could you see from up here?" Merrill asks Ian, who cradles his rifle on one arm.

"Everything. It was catastrophic. The ARC is gone along with the town. Most of the army was washed away and those higher up on shore scattered."

Zoey watches as Chelsea holds out her arms, waving emphatically for Lee to let her hold the other baby. He pretends to deny her before transferring the girl over as Sherell and Nell huddle around her with Rita taking furtive peeks over their shoulders. A cool wind coasts through the flooded valley, raking the dead bramble and grass with its touch. Zoey shivers, hugging the baby tighter to her. Who would have thought it would end in the same place it began? But the symmetry feels right somehow, as if she's been not on a straight path, but a circle. And now with one of her children in her arms, watching the man she loves beside the family she's found, the circle has finally closed.

She's about to suggest that they move inside the house out of the weather when movement catches her attention over Lee's shoulder.

Hiraku stalks toward them with unhurried steps, gun outstretched in one hand, his other clutching what looks like a tattered piece of paper.

Zoey opens her mouth to cry out a warning, but Tia has spotted him as well and is trying to raise her rifle.

"Don't," Hiraku says, and the entire group spins to face him. He stops several yards away, the drop of the gorge at his back. His dark hair flutters in the wind and his eyes are dead calm. "I would suggest none of you make any sudden movements."

Behind her Zoey hears the distinct click of Ian's rifle's safety.

Hiraku studies each of them. They've formed a half circle with Zoey at the back. Lee stands before her, arms away from his sides as if preparing to lunge forward.

"Do you understand what you've done?" he asks, his voice low, and it is his composure that scares Zoey the most. "Years and years of planning. Lives lost, traded for the promise of something better. And now it's all gone." He aims the pistol toward Merrill who has edged around to the far end of the group. "Would you like to be the first to die?"

Merrill stares at him, hand resting lightly on his slung rifle. "It's over. Your men are gone. There's no need to do this. We just want to leave."

Hiraku blinks. "Leave? My life has been full of leaving. She left me. So did Shirou, and there was nothing I could do about it."

Zoey notices Ian moving closer to her right, his sniper rifle pointed low.

Merrill takes a step forward, hands held out before Hiraku. "I'm sorry for what you lost. We've all lost someone. Please. Put the gun down."

A ripple of emotion crosses Hiraku's features. His hand clenches the paper, working it within his fist.

Ian sidles around Lee who has also inched forward.

Hiraku's jaw tightens and his eyes glisten. "All I wanted was to be a father. And she took it from me." His gaze shifts from Merrill, skims over Lee, and finds Zoey as the baby kicks within the blankets and makes a loud cooing.

It is like a transparent veil falls over him as he looks from her face to the infant she holds. His expression softens as if he's seen something familiar.

"Jiaying?" Hiraku tilts his head and brings the handgun to bear on her.

Shouts erupt and movement is everywhere.

Ian steps forward and fires his rifle from the hip.

A hole appears in Hiraku's jacket above his navel and there is a spray of crimson behind him.

The handgun's muzzle travels away from her toward Ian as Hiraku stumbles backward.

He fires.

Ian jerks and loses his balance, rifle twisting from his hands.

Zoey hears screaming as she shields the baby and realizes it's coming from her.

Hiraku totters, somehow still on his feet. A ribbon of blood leaks from his bottom lip and paints a crimson goatee on his chin.

His eyes find hers, and there is true recognition there.

And hatred.

He raises the pistol toward her again.

But Lee is already in motion, running forward, head down, his feet coming free of the ground as he dives.

Lee's shoulder connects with Hiraku's stomach, forcing a hollow woof of air from his lungs.

The handgun flies free, landing in the dirt as both men crash to the ground.

They roll twice, arms and limbs entwined, bared teeth and flapping coats.

And before it happens, Zoey sees what's coming and tries to cry out but all her air is gone and she's lost in a vacuum of horror.

Lee and Hiraku tumble over the edge of the cliff, a bark of surprise coming from one of them.

Then they're gone, swallowed by the drop.

"No!" Zoey screams, rushing forward. It is a million miles and only a few harried steps before she's there, forcing herself to look down even though she knows what she'll see.

The river is seventy feet below, the current a swirling mass of debris and cloudy water. Neither man is anywhere to be seen.

The baby squalls, but she barely hears her.

Gone.

Lee is gone.

An arm encircles her shoulders, holding her upright as she sways.

The foul water chuffs and laps against the valley walls, and it is a sound of hunger, or perhaps satisfaction. Distantly she thinks that she's going to be sick. Zoey begins to turn away to do so when something moves below her.

An arm.

A wordless sound comes from her as she leans out as far as she dares, someone's hands grasping at her clothing.

Twenty feet down, a serrated shelf of rock juts out like a broken jaw. Lee lies upon it, his right arm, the one she saw move, twisted at a stomach-churning angle. A pool of red expands at an alarming rate around his head and his broken arm twitches once more and is still.

"Down there!" Zoey yells, pointing. Merrill and Tia follow the direction of her gestures and race to the ASV. A moment later the big vehicle is parked a dozen feet from the drop and Merrill steps from the interior with a stout length of rope he ties quickly around his waist. At the front of the ASV he pauses and with Tia's help attaches the rope to a cabled winch. Tia runs the controls, spooling out slack until Merrill has enough to lower himself over the edge.

The seconds tick by in complete silence with only the wind and the burbling river to break it. After what seems like an interminable amount of time, Merrill calls out and Tia begins winding the cable in, slow and sure.

Lee slowly appears. Merrill has trussed the rope around Lee's mid-back and hips, forming a type of cradle while Merrill himself clings to an extra loop in its bottom.

"Is he . . . ?" Zoey says as Tia and Merrill unhook the harness from around Lee's back.

"He's alive, but he hit his head and his arm is shattered. Where's Chelsea?"

"Here," she says, dropping to her knees beside Lee. "Tia, get my bag, it's over by Ian. Zoey, step back and give me some room."

She does as Chelsea says, a sense of unreality descending upon her. How long since she was thinking that they had time?

Enough time? What a foolish thought. There is never enough.

Zoey swallows the bile that's trying to surge up her throat and steps out of the way as Tia hurries past, clutching Chelsea's medical bag. Something occurs to her then that slipped free of her mind after seeing Lee fall.

Ian. He was hit.

She glances to where he fell, sure that if Chelsea is focusing on Lee, Ian must be only wounded.

The old man lies on his back, Rita, Sherell, and Lyle to one side, Seamus sitting motionless on his other. Lyle glances up at her as she approaches and quickly looks away.

"How is—?" But the rest of the question dies in her throat.

Blood covers Ian's chest. So much so that if she didn't know he'd been wearing a white shirt beneath his long coat, she would've guessed it was originally red. A dark hole to the left of his breastbone pumps a feeble stream of blood again and again.

"Oh no," she breathes, kneeling down beside him. His head is propped on someone's jacket, and his gray beard is soaked red. His eyes are open and they stare at the clouded sky between lazy blinks.

"Chelsea said it nicked his heart," Lyle murmurs as Sherell turns away, pressing her face into Rita's shoulder. Rita stares dumbly down at Ian's chest, her gaze wooden and unseeing. Seamus makes a deep whining sound and his tongue appears, licking once at Ian's temple.

Zoey finds one of Ian's hands, holding the baby with the other arm. He squeezes her fingers, his gaze coming to rest on her.

"Zoey." His voice is quiet but clear.

"I'm right here."

He nods. "I'm getting tired."

She stifles a sob. "It's okay."

"I'm so glad you found us."

"Me too."

He swallows thickly, trying to focus on her face. "Lynn?"

She hesitates but then squeezes his hand. "I'm here."

"Do you remember the animals at the zoo? Do you remember when I took you to the zoo?"

"I remember."

"You always loved animals." He smiles and his eyes drift partially closed. "And I loved you." His wound no longer pumps blood, and his chest falls, a final sigh coming from him, and he is still.

"I love you too," Zoey says.

Through her tears she places his limp hand on his chest and softly brushes his eyelids shut with her palm. Seamus whines again, nuzzling Ian's hair before Lyle rises to guide the big dog away.

"I'll take care of him," Nell says from behind her, lightly touching her quaking shoulder. When she doesn't move, Nell helps her to her feet. "You go be with Lee."

Zoey nods, brushing away tears to look one last time at Ian. If it weren't for the blood, he might be taking a nap. His face is serene and relaxed, many of the wrinkles smoothed out.

Her daughter begins to fuss. Amid everything, she has been mostly quiet, simply observing. Now her features crinkle with annoyance, and she twists as if she wants to crawl away.

Newton stands several yards to her right, awkwardly holding the other baby. He gives her a pained look but tries to smile even as Merrill, Chelsea, and Tia suddenly count to three loudly.

They've placed Lee on a blanket and are carrying him toward the ASV's open door.

"We have to get him somewhere that I can operate," Chelsea says as they slide him onto the floor of the vehicle.

"What's the matter?"

"I won't know for sure until I can get him on a table."

"Let's go, everyone!" Merrill shouts, climbing into the driver's seat. "We gotta move!"

Lyle and Nell carry Ian's body past, his form now wrapped in a dark sheet of some kind. *Shroud,* she thinks to herself. *It stopped being a sheet when they placed him in it.* Then it's her turn to get in the ASV.

As she prepares to climb the steps she spots something on the ground and picks it up. It is the paper Hiraku was holding before he was shot. She carries it with her without thinking as she takes a place on one of the benches beside Lee. His face is remarkably unblemished, only a shallow cut across the bridge of his nose. But then she notices the dark red blotch seeping through a white wrap of gauze around the side of his head.

Tia begins closing the door and Zoey catches a last glimpse of the house and the river valley beyond where the ARC once stood. Past it is the ruins of the dam, a broken mouth of concrete still gushing water.

Then the door slams shut and they're moving away from the plateau, away from the river, and on into the cold glare of the early day.

61

The long hallway echoes with her steps as she paces down its length, each insignificant feature becoming a landmark.

Here is the cracked tile in the floor, shattered like a mirror.

Here the long strip of paint drooping away from the wall where moisture invaded through a leak in the ceiling.

Here the wide door with light glowing from its rectangular window. The one she's not allowed past.

Zoey turns and begins her circuit all over again, moving slowly back down the corridor, past dark rooms and the smell of old chemicals to where some of the group waits. Her daughter, the first girl she's taken to thinking of her as since she was the infant Zoey traded herself for, lies asleep in her arms. The other baby rests with Nell who is feeding her from the makeshift bottle Chelsea created. The rest of the group either stands near the long bank of windows at the start of the hall or sits on a bench attached to the wall. Merrill is the only one absent besides Chelsea, and she wishes desperately he were either here waiting with her or she were behind the door with him. With Lee.

The nearest town with a hospital had been twenty miles away. It took them less than fifteen minutes to get there, the ASV seeming to become airborne over small bumps at times. After finding the medical center they had located the operating room on the second floor and hauled Lee inside, Chelsea's warning to stay out in the hall with the others still ringing in her ears.

How long has it been? Two hours? Three? She can't say. All she knows is the tension is eating her like acid from the inside out, the need to know, so much worse than anything else she's ever experienced. She is back in the hospital waiting for Eli to recover, but at least then she was able to speak to him, even if it was for the last time.

Zoey shoves away the notion of never talking to Lee again and gets herself to sit. She tries to focus on the child she's holding—her small, perfect face, the warm weight of her soft body. But almost at once she recalls Lee yelling to her before she was forced into the vehicle with Vivian. He was asking her what he should name the baby.

And now she wants to know the same thing. She needs to hear his confident voice, feel the strength of his arms around her, because she's not sure she'll be able to continue without him. Not now, not after everything that's happened. She imagines the door opening at the end of the hallway, Merrill's and Chelsea's stricken faces, the deadened hole expanding inside her, but most of all she sees the long days stretching out ahead without Lee. They are a wasteland, barren and cold with only the heavy weight of his absence to fill them up.

She adjusts herself into a more comfortable position, and something brushes the back of her fingers on her right hand. She grasps it and draws it from her jacket pocket.

Hiraku's folded paper.

She didn't open it on the ride here. She doesn't recall tucking it away, but she must have, and now an irresistible compulsion overcomes her.

Zoey unfolds the tattered page and stares.

Some of the brush-stroked ink is marred by streaks of blood, but the image is clear, the talent that created it undeniable. The woman in the painting is young and pretty, her dark hair cut near her shoulders, almond eyes full of life that gaze down to her arms where a swaddled infant lies looking back up at her, the baby's features subtly mirroring her mother's. How she knows the baby is a girl, Zoey doesn't understand, she simply does. The mother and child sit on a blanket upon a sandy beach, several gentle waves washing up behind them in the background. There is a slightly surreal quality to the picture; whether it is the angles of the subjects or the overall energy the scene gives off, she's not sure, but somehow she's certain that this is not a memory, it is a dream. A day imagined but never realized. Near the bottom is a small scrawl of illegible text in what appears to be a different type of ink than the painting, possibly a ballpoint pen, followed by a string of numbers.

49.6506° N, 125.4494° W

She frowns, struggling to determine a meaning from them. She's about to ask Nell, who's sitting across from her, to take a look when the door to the operating room opens.

Before she can read their expressions, Zoey is moving down the corridor toward Merrill and Chelsea. As she nears, she can see they both look exhausted. There is a spattering of blood on Chelsea's left shoulder and her shirtsleeves, which she's rolled up, are tinted crimson as well.

Zoey stops before them, glancing from one to the other and back again, but she can't get herself to utter any words.

"He's alive," Chelsea says, the calm assuredness of her voice unable to hide the ugly thing waiting beyond what she's saying. "But he's had major trauma to his skull and his brain has swollen badly."

Zoey swallows, feeling her lower lip trembling. "What does that mean?"

"It means I don't know what's going to happen to him. His breathing and heart rate are both stable now so that tells me his brain stem isn't overly damaged and we've been able to relieve some of the swelling by inserting a port into his skull, but I'm worried there might be some hypoxia."

"What's that?"

"It's a lack of oxygen to the brain possibly caused by the swelling."

"But you said you helped the swelling now?"

"I relieved some of it, but that's not the problem. If he does have hypoxia the damage may already be done."

Zoey glances from Chelsea to Merrill. "What are you saying?"

"Lee might never wake up again," Merrill says. "And if he does he may not ever be the same."

Sherell places a steadying hand on her shoulder as a frown creases her face. "But he's alive. He'll come back, right? If he's alive he'll wake up and come back."

"We don't know," Chelsea says, coming closer to place an arm around her. "I wish I could say something different, but right now all we can do is wait. There's no power here to perform any significant testing, and even if there was I don't know if I'd be able to interpret the results correctly or do anything past what I've already done. My experience with cerebral trauma was limited while I was learning medicine. I'm sorry, Zoey."

She feels the tears start to burn at the back of her eyes and blinks them away. She's so sick of crying. She's done with it. Lee isn't gone, he's alive.

"He's strong," she says, trying to smile and nearly managing it.

Chelsea nods. "We'll keep close watch over him. There's nothing saying he won't wake up."

"Can I see him?"

"Of course."

Zoey transfers her daughter into Sherell's waiting arms without waking her and follows Chelsea through the operating room door. There is a dank area with several sinks and cabinets then a set of double doors that squeak loudly as they push through them.

Three solar lanterns light the large space on the other side of the doors. It is circular, lined with rolling tables and alien apparatus while its center is taken up by a wide bed on casters. Lee lies in its middle covered in a heap of blankets, his chest rising and falling in slow rhythm.

"I'll leave you alone," Chelsea says, retreating.

Zoey moves forward to the bedside, a tingle of horror flowing through her as she spots a metal tube protruding from the side of Lee's skull close to where it rests on a pillow. Blood drips in slow drops from the tube into a shallow pan.

She reaches hesitantly beneath the blankets, finding his hand, and the fear that it will be cold dissolves.

It is as warm as the first time she held it.

"Hi," she says, studying the pallor of his face. She watches his closed eyelids, hoping to see the pupils move under them, but they remain still. "I know you can hear me. You're going to be all right. Chelsea did a good job, and now all you have to do is wake up, okay? The hard part's over. You saved us. You saved me." She pauses, the sensation of water closing over her almost as strong as it was after the dam broke. She concentrates on his hand as if it is the only thing tethering her to reality. And in that moment a memory surfaces so poignant it sends an ache through her chest.

"Before I found you in Seattle, I imagined us together. We were somewhere in the mountains at a little house we'd built. I saw you and our daughter, and we were happy. I never guessed we'd have two instead of one." She laughs but it is stilted and short. "What I'm saying is there's more to do. You left me once, and you promised you'd never do it again." She squeezes his hand with both of hers. "I believe you. So you come back to me and keep your promise."

A tear rolls down her cheek and she wipes it away, sniffling a little. She leans over and kisses Lee lightly on the corner of his mouth before tucking his hand back away and smoothing his blankets out. With each step she takes away from him it feels like the last, but she casts the thought aside. She cannot break now. Her strength is all she has left.

Merrill and Chelsea wait outside in the hallway. Chelsea gives her a quick hug before moving back into the operating room.

"Where is everyone?" she asks, giving the empty corridor a glance.

"Downstairs in a lounge Tia found. It's got some beds, so we're going to take turns sleeping. You need to go lie down."

"I'm fine."

"No, you're not. You're exhausted and grieving and in shock."

"What else is new?" She gives him a wan smile that he returns.

"He's going to make it."

"I know he will." Absently her hand goes to the corner of the painting that's sticking out of her pocket and her thumb begins flicking it back and forth.

"What is that?" Merrill asks.

She pulls the paper free and unfolds it, showing it to him. "Hiraku was carrying it. I think it might've been his family."

Merrill examines the page, eyes narrowing as the door opens at the far end of the hall and Lyle strides toward them, Seamus at his side. "Newton and I found some fuel in the building across the street. Not sure if the ASV will run on it or not, but it's worth a shot," he says, stopping before them.

"Good," Merrill replies faintly, still looking at the painting.

"I can't read what's written on the bottom," Zoey says, pointing to the obscure text. "And I have no idea what the numbers mean."

"They're coordinates," Merrill says looking up. "Longitude and latitude."

"They must be for the ARC. The defector gave the location to Hiraku before he died. It makes sense that he kept them with the picture; they were both precious to him," Zoey says.

Lyle wrinkles his nose and reaches for the paper. "May I?" Merrill hands it to him. The older man's eyes flick across the painting and down to the numerals at the bottom. He frowns.

"What is it?" Zoey asks.

"The coordinates," Lyle says.

"What about them?"

He finally looks up from the page, eyes wide and magnified behind his glasses. "When you asked me to destroy the ARC at Riverbend, I had to enter the longitude and latitude for the ARC into the guidance system for the missile. It was one of the requirements to arm it."

"And?"

Lyle turns the paper around, pointing at the numbers. "These aren't the coordinates for the ARC. They're for somewhere else."

62

They leave the hospital the day after Lyle and Tia locate the United States Geological Survey building at the center of the town.

The US maps Lyle found contained in a water-stained book are complete with topography, ancient earthquake activity, and most importantly, coordinates. The time before they departed had also been spent fixing a midsize car they located in the basement of a nearby parking structure. With the space required for Lee's transport there wouldn't be enough room for everyone to ride together.

When they depart, Merrill drives the ASV with Chelsea, Zoey, Sherell, Rita, and Nell riding on the bench seats behind him, Lee strapped securely to a makeshift stretcher at the very rear. They had found two child seats in the hospital for the babies, and both are nestled on the floor below Lee's seat, their eyes wide as the ASV rumbles out of the hospital's parking lot and heads due west.

They travel slowly, their progress hindered by washed-out roads as well as the need to keep Lee as still as possible as to not further irritate his injury. He hasn't woken up or so much as made a sound since their arrival at the hospital even though Zoey has continued to speak to him when they're alone, always holding one of his hands while she does so. The side of his head that took the brunt of the trauma is swollen and bruised so badly that half of his face is a mottled purple and black. The drain Chelsea inserted into his skull has quit dripping blood and she's told Zoey that it will have to be removed soon so as not to invite infection, but the chance that his brain might swell again is always there, an unsaid communication in the way Chelsea looks at her each time they discuss his condition.

It is the middle of the night when they reach the turnoff for Ian's home. Both the babies are sleeping after having eaten nearly a full bottle apiece of warm water and powdered formula Sherell discovered in the maternity ward. Zoey had tried the mixture first even though the expiration date was marked as over a decade before. The milk had tasted fine and after a lack of sickness or ill effects she began feeding it to the girls, who took to it almost at once. The breastfeeding Chelsea had instructed and assisted her with prior to that had been a challenge mostly due to the fact that her milk had been extremely slow to come in no matter how enthusiastically her daughters tried to coax it from her, which had left them increasingly frustrated and Zoey unbelievably sore. For now, the formula would have to be a supplement until her body became adjusted to the demands she was forcing on it, or until they found another acceptable food source.

They park on the road, brilliant moonlight etching the surrounding mountains in stark detail as black teeth rising up into the night sky. Merrill had tried to talk her out of what she'd suggested, but only halfheartedly; she can tell he wants it as much as she does.

It takes them nearly an hour to hike to the clearing near the house, carrying Ian's tightly wrapped body between them. The home's quiet solitude breaks something loose inside Zoey, which draws renewed tears from her, and she cries them without shame in the dark as Merrill begins to dig.

They all say something around the grave once it's completed: some fond memory or favorite quote that they remember Ian saying, but Zoey can't put into words what he means to her. She can only recall how his face looked as he bent over her the first time they met, her brain fogged with fever. She had thought he was God, and in nursing her to health along with his kindness, he had been in a way. He had saved her more times than she could count, and anything she said would've been a pale representation of how she felt.

When they move to leave, Lyle stops them and calls out to Seamus who has lain down beside the cairn. The big dog doesn't move from the spot, and when Lyle begins to walk toward him, Zoey grabs his arm.

"I think he wants to stay."

"But—"

"He was wild when Ian found him. He can take care of himself."

"Doesn't seem right," Lyle finally says, allowing her to guide him away.

"It wouldn't be right to make him leave."

Zoey gives the clearing a last look as they move down the mountain. It is bathed in the moon's glow, serene and peaceful as the first time she saw it. "Good-bye," she says, speaking to Seamus, to the meadow and house, to the only real home she's ever known.

63

The boat leaves the dock and Zoey feels the sea beneath her feet, unsteady and wild as they pull away from the mainland.

Behind her the enormous lodge on the shores of Fidalgo Island recedes into the morning mist. It had taken them a full day to travel from Ian's home to the northwestern coastline, and this is their second and last morning here. The interior of the huge building had been damp and musty, but overall solid, its grounds littered with the suggested remnants of a settlement long since abandoned. The thirty-foot charter boat had been inside a decaying boathouse, the roof partially fallen on top of the vessel, but when they'd launched it into the curling waves beside the dock, it had floated, merrily bobbing up and down as if pleased to be in its element again.

It had taken Tia and Lyle two long days of work getting the engines running, some of the wiring having been eaten away by rodents, but in the end the diesel motor chugged roughly away, drinking the fuel they'd siphoned from the ASV, which they left beside the lodge like a sentry. Zoey looks at its shape one last time, a pang of nostalgia surprising her as it disappears from sight, as if she is saying good-bye to an old friend.

Ahead dark slopes of land rise up out of the sea like immense aquatic beasts, the isles to the right partially obscuring their destination.

Vancouver Island.

Something about the way the name rolled off her tongue gave her a sense of security. The title had a solidity to it, the way riding in the ASV had felt—as if you were surrounded by armor and as long as you stayed inside you were invulnerable. Not everyone had shared her feelings. The group had been almost perfectly divided: Tia at one pole argued over and over that they knew nothing about the place or what they were walking into, while Zoey had been at the other end, continuing to point out the fact that if Hiraku and his men had set their sights on the island, it must have some significance. Besides, they knew of no other settlements, excluding Seattle, that have the kind of medical care Lee needs.

Because beneath it all, the real truth fueling her reasoning is the seconds ticking away, the feel of Lee's pulse under her fingers and how each time she reaches for his hand the fear that it will be cold and stiff as stone nearly overwhelms her.

If there is a chance for him and the rest of them, it is on the island.

The waves increase in height the farther out to sea they travel, though Tia stays as close as she dares to the nearing islands, the threat of hidden rocks or wreckage they can impale the craft upon always present. Zoey watches Tia pilot the boat from where she rests beside Lee, their daughters buckled into their seats inside a small inflatable raft she insisted they blow up and place on the vessel's deck before leaving shore. She knows Tia's father used to be a dockhand, but now she wonders, after seeing the other woman's proficiency in all things related to the ocean, if he also had some type of craft they spent time on when Tia was younger. It's something Zoey intends to ask her when they're on land again. And at the moment, that point in time can't come soon enough.

A fist of nausea forms in her stomach, and she fights down the urge to vomit, gripping harder onto her daughters' seats. Beside her feet is her rifle. She stares at it, imagining having to use it if she's wrong about the island, if it isn't what she's hoping for. And what of her children? If all seems lost and their situation goes from hopeful to hopeless, what will she do then? What terrible choice will she make if forced to?

The large swath of Vancouver Island expands before them, its rocky coastline giving way to serrated tops of coniferous trees, beyond which the suggestion of mountain peaks forming into reality. The map's representation of the island doesn't do it justice, and as the land continues to widen, its inlets and bays taking shape in the moist air, she forgets the discomfort in her stomach, a sense of awe settling over her like a heavy blanket.

She's about to ask Lyle, who's holding the map, where they're going to land when she hears Merrill swear. His gaze is focused on the southernmost point of the island and the two boats that have just rounded it toward them.

"Get ready," he says, tightening his hold on his weapon.

The two boats grow in size quickly, their speed apparent, and soon she sees the designation "boats" should be replaced with "ships." They are long and elegant in design, steel prows jutting high above the waves, conning towers lined with dark windows and guns. It is only minutes before the vessels are directly before them, the small shapes of men darting back and forth behind looming gunwales.

"Oh, God," Lyle says, letting the map drop to the deck. "We don't have a chance."

Zoey watches the ships. They've stopped several hundred yards away, and Tia has stilled their own boat's movement, though she keeps one hand on the throttle and the other on the steering wheel.

The moment stretches out. Gulls duck and dive overhead, their calls shrill in the midmorning air, the briny smell of the ocean pungent.

The mist has lifted and the clarity of the scene is like the edge of broken glass.

Zoey's heart thuds as she holds tightly to the handles on her daughters' seats. Both of them have begun to cry, from hunger or the need to be held, she doesn't know. Now that the time has come, she can't get herself to decide what she will do if this is the end. Does she have the courage?

"UNIDENTIFIED VESSEL. YOU ARE IN PROTECTED WATERS. DISCARD YOUR WEAPONS OVER THE SIDE OF THE BOAT." The male voice, amplified many times over, carries across the water and reverberates in her eardrums.

"Fuck that," Tia says, glancing at Merrill. "Should we run?"

"No. They'd blow us out of the water before we could turn around."

"Then what do we do?"

Merrill looks at Zoey and she swallows, her throat tightened to less than a needlepoint. After a beat she nods, only in that second truly deciding what has to be done.

"Throw the guns over," Merrill says, motioning to everyone as he casts his rifle into the churning ocean.

"Are you crazy?" Tia asks, gaping at him. "They're going to kill us!"

"They can do that now if they want," he says. Zoey is next to discard her weapon. It splashes into the water, slipping away in an instant as the others who are armed follow suit. Tia curses and shakes her head, but unholsters the pistol on her hip and throws it overboard.

"BRING YOUR SPEED UP TO TEN KNOTS. IF YOU HAVE NOT FULLY COMPLIED WITH DISARMING YOU WILL BE FIRED UPON."

Merrill taps Tia on the shoulder as she pushes the throttle forward. She stares back at him defiantly for a long time before rolling her eyes and reaching behind her to pull out the small handgun concealed in the waistband of her pants. She tosses it over the side and says something about Merrill's mother that he ignores.

The two ships turn with their passing, flanking them to either side. The large-caliber machine guns mounted to the decks follow them closely, the men manning them mostly hidden behind their bulk.

After rounding the point, the ships guide them into a large inlet that gradually takes shape. The land transitions from rocky and tree encrusted to the first impressions of human habitation. A long concrete seawall branches out from the island, a tall lighthouse at its end. As the lighthouse gets closer, Zoey sees that its top has been removed, leaving it open to the weather, and what at first she thinks are some type of communication antennas branching from its sides and top are in fact gun barrels that follow their progress past. Men move along the seawall behind low concrete barricades, several of them stopping to watch them cruise by.

Farther into the port are massive piers extending into the water, each of them complete with reinforced battlements, the outline of what appears to be a tank situated where the docks meet the shore.

"MAKE PORT AT THE LAST DOCKING AREA AND PREPARE TO BE BOARDED. ANY AND ALL RESISTANCE WILL BE MET WITH DEADLY FORCE."

"Well that's comforting," Tia says, guiding their boat to the last pier. A dozen men wait for them as they pull even with it, all of them armed and wearing vests and helmets. Beyond them Zoey spots a sniper's nest higher on the shore above a tall concrete barricade, the flash of the riflescope bright and fleeting.

A rope is thrown down to them from above and the closest man sweeps his rifle across their number. "Tie off and climb up. Slowly." Merrill secures the boat and glances at them all before moving to the steel ladder attached to the pier's side. Tia is next, followed by Newton. Zoey picks up the older of her two daughters from her seat. She's come to think of her only as older because she's the first of the two she saw as well as being larger. Zoey holds the crying child to her chest as Chelsea picks up her other daughter. When the man covering them with his weapon sees the two babies, his expression changes and he blinks, his rifle lowering slightly.

"Get a ramp," he yells over one shoulder, and a minute later a wide steel ramp is lowered and secured over the side of the pier, extending to the deck of their boat. Zoey walks up it on unsteady feet, the unmoving quality of the ramp throwing her off after the jostling of the boat. Two soldiers pass her and move toward Lee where he lies on his stretcher.

"Be careful, his head is injured," she says to them as they check Lee for weapons before picking up the stretcher. Zoey steps onto the pier and sees everyone is being patted down, their clothing searched by two men and . . .

She does a double take.

Two of the people searching the rest of the group are men, but the other two are women: one of them dark haired with hazel eyes, the other with short lengths of blond hair extending from beneath her flak helmet.

"Ma'am, please step over here," the soldier who called for the ramp says. And it's then that she realizes she's given him the correct title. He is a soldier along with the rest of them. They move with a militaristic fluidity and positioning that is both familiar and strangely different than any other organized force she's witnessed. They are stoic and calmly authoritative but the threat she felt when first seeing the ships approaching them is gone.

She moves to the place the man indicates, and the blonde female soldier approaches her, the woman openly startled as she takes in the youth of Zoey's face as well as the crying child in her arms. She is perhaps forty years of age, maybe younger, with clear blue eyes. She hesitates only another instant before patting Zoey down, guiding her hands over any place a weapon could be concealed.

"They're all clean," the female soldier says to the man who seems to be in charge. He steps forward, running his gaze across them all, hovering longest on Rita, Sherell, and Zoey.

"Where did you come from?" he asks, directing the question at all of them. None of them.

Merrill clears his throat. "Washington. The Cascades."

"What are you doing here?"

"We came for safety and medical attention. Our friend needs help." He motions to Lee. "We heard this is a safe haven."

"Heard from whom?" The soldier's voice hardens.

"It's complicated. But we're alone. It's just us."

The soldier says nothing, and Zoey sees him calculating what Merrill's said. She imagines him nodding to the rest of the men and women and watching their weapons come up. Imagines the feeling of bullets ripping through her, the weightless fall back toward the boat. Instead he simply nods.

"Follow me."

They form a line behind him as he walks up the pier and passes through several concrete barriers. Soldiers silently watch them move by their posts, the only sound beyond the sea wind the constant shriek of gulls.

At the top of a long set of stairs they exit onto a street lining the harbor. There are buildings everywhere that have been stripped and repurposed from their original construction.

Here is what appears to be a seaside restaurant that now is a fortification with a dozen men inside.

There a home with its front torn away to reveal stacks of sandbags protected by a rusting tin roof.

Stretching away down the shore from the last building is a ten-foot-high chain-link fence, its top looped with razor wire that's gone dark with age and weather. Waiting for them on the street are two low vehicles and a van, all of them green and black camouflage. The soldiers carrying Lee bring him to the rear of the van and load him inside as the lead man gestures toward the other two military vehicles.

"Get in, please."

"Where are you taking us?" Zoey asks.

"To processing."

"But he's hurt. He needs medical attention," she says, motioning in the direction of the van.

"He'll be brought to the treatment facility and cared for."

"I want to go with him."

"I'm sorry but that's not an option." When she doesn't move the soldier's expression softens. "He'll be looked after, I promise."

Reluctantly Zoey heads toward the waiting vehicle, giving the van a last look before climbing inside. Chelsea sits next to her, and Sherell, Rita, Newton, and Merrill all get in as well. The rest of the group rides in the transport behind them.

Motors rumble to life and then they're moving swiftly down the street, taking two left turns before driving straight for several blocks. The city they're in is much larger than Zoey's first impressions of it. It sprawls away in rows of buildings several stories high with lower structures lining many of its street fronts. The skeletal shapes of trees line the roads on both sides, their branches overhanging the lanes as well as several open expanses of what would be green lawns in the summertime.

Then they're pulling out from behind a dark-shingled apartment or hotel complex ten stories high and into an open expanse and her attention is caught by the structure situated across the clearing.

It is an immense stone behemoth with wings expanding out in regal stature to either side of its central towers, all of them capped with greenish domes, a golden statue atop the tallest of them. They turn toward the massive building and pull to a stop before its front entrance. Zoey notes Lee's van continuing past them deeper into the city. It is there and gone behind another storefront. *Please be okay,* she has time to think before the doors are opened and they pile out.

They are herded up a wide bank of stairs, the building towering above them in rows of windows and balustraded balconies. A set of huge double doors are opened by two soldiers standing beside them, and they are ushered inside, down a hallway with rounded ceilings and arched doorways that empties them out into a sprawling rotunda. The floor is a beautiful mosaic of small tiles, the outside of the design floral while the center suggests a starburst or compass points. Zoey hears a small intake of breath from Chelsea and follows the other woman's gaze up as they pass through the chamber, and for a moment she is dumbstruck by the sight.

The tallest dome she saw from the outside is directly above them, at least a hundred feet overhead, its center shining with light.

"This way," the soldier escorting them says, motioning to another hall across the space. They follow him to an inconspicuous wooden door that opens onto a square room with globe lights hanging from its tall ceiling. Two doors at the end of the room beside a large desk are both closed. The soldier gestures toward a bank of seats and sofas before the desk while he takes up a position beside the entrance.

It is deathly quiet in the room except for the occasional squall of one of the babies. Zoey catches Merrill's eye and he gives her a slight nod.

The left door beside the desk opens and a woman appears. She is compactly built, standing a little over five feet tall with a tight bun of silver hair tied back from a squarish face. She wears a plain gray suit with a white blouse beneath, flat dark shoes on her feet. She rounds the desk and slows, her initial confident stroll diminished, then gone as she stops before them. Her eyes are deep brown and unblinking as she takes them in.

"Hello," she says after a moment. They rumble a group greeting, their voices mixing. The woman slowly smiles. "My God, I almost don't believe it. When Major Adams there informed me of the reports of a fishing boat carrying at least six women heading toward the island I thought he was hallucinating." She beams at them. "Ah, where are my manners, my name is Eleanor Scott. I'm the mayor of Victoria. Welcome to the first city."

64

They are fed and handed bottles of water, encouraged to sit and rest, all the while Eleanor speaks to them, leaning against her desk casually.

"Victoria started out as a research center for British Columbia a year after the Dearth began. Prime Minister Evans had the foresight to begin fortifications of the city almost immediately. Thousands of troops were based here, and the perimeter fencing you probably noticed on the way in was erected."

"How far does it run?" Merrill asks.

"Good question. I haven't the foggiest. Adams?" She directs her gaze at the soldier still waiting by the entrance.

"Approximately sixty kilometers, ma'am."

"There you are, sixty kilometers. It basically surrounds the city, though the strongest defenses are concentrated in the major ports. We have twenty-four-hour patrols around our borders as well as a functioning surveillance system and early warning marine detection apparatus, which alerted us to your presence this morning." She smiles at them again, and there is something so genuine about the woman, Zoey feels herself already liking the mayor.

"You said research center," Rita says through half a mouthful of food. "Can you explain that a little, because honestly, we're not too keen on research centers."

Eleanor laughs. "I can only imagine. Our centers were nothing like the National Obstetric Alliance. Prime Minister Evans and his advisors were deeply concerned about the direction the United States was headed early on. Our programs were volunteer only. We had nearly six thousand women and their families arrive here in a matter of months only to have them slowly leave again as things worsened across the world."

"Why did they leave?" Sherell asks.

"Because this wasn't their home. I've found in a time of crisis or worry, there is no place people would rather be than home. So even though we offered protection and hope, many still chose to leave. Some did find their way here over the next years as the situation deteriorated; I can't claim my country didn't have its fair share of senseless violence and bloodshed." Her face darkens. "That's why four years after the Dearth began we shut our borders. There was a lot of fighting in those days and twice we were raided, once betrayed from the inside." Eleanor looks off into space above their heads and Zoey knows she's reliving some terrible memory. She takes a deep breath. "So after that we instituted the first law that's kept us safe since that point."

"What's the first law?" Zoey asks.

"Once you arrive at the island, you can never leave."

There is a span of silence before Tia says, "What's this horseshit?"

Merrill sighs. "Tia."

"No, I mean it. You're saying we can't leave?"

Eleanor nods. "I'm afraid not. We can't take the chance of word reaching the wrong people."

"Uh, it's a little too late for that, sister." Tia holds her thumb and forefinger a quarter inch apart. "You came about this close to having your asses handed to you."

Eleanor tips her head to one side. "Enlighten me."

The group collectively looks to Zoey. She clears her throat and begins talking.

It takes her nearly thirty minutes to briefly explain Hiraku's arrival in Seattle as well as her and the others' history at the ARC and beyond. Eleanor listens intently, asking only the odd question from time to time. When Zoey's finished, she falls silent and takes a sip of water to quench her dried throat.

"That's an incredible story," Eleanor says. "The people of Victoria are in your debt. I'm sure you saved countless lives by your actions, though we do have contingency plans for such an occurrence."

"Like what?" Tia asks.

"We have fallback positions located in the mountains to the north. If our defenses are overwhelmed our entire population can fit inside and wait out the incursion."

"For how long."

"Six years," Eleanor says evenly.

Tia squints at her. "That's a long fucking time," she says finally.

"It is a long fucking time," Eleanor replies deadpan, and Zoey's initial like of the woman instantly doubles. Tia bursts out laughing, and any lasting tension in the room seems to dissipate.

"It was him, wasn't it?" Zoey asks after nearly a minute has passed.

"Was who, dear?" Eleanor asks.

"The man who gave Hiraku your location; it was him who betrayed you from the inside."

"Yes," Eleanor says in almost a whisper. "Yes, I believe it was." She seems to recede into herself before focusing her attention on Zoey again. "One question to clarify, Zoey. You said 'daughter' earlier. I'm not exactly sure what you meant by that."

"My daughters," Zoey replies, nodding to the sleeping child in her arms as well as the girl Chelsea cradles.

Eleanor frowns before leaning back farther on her desk. "You're saying these two infants are . . . female?"

"Yes."

The older woman is struck silent. She blinks, truly taking in the two babies for the first time. "I assumed they were your sons. I'm having trouble wrapping my head around this."

"You can change their diapers if you need proof," Zoey says. The room erupts in laughter and Eleanor slowly joins in herself. When the mirth dies down, the mayor straightens, appraising them all more closely, as if she is trying to see through any possible false facade.

"I have a feeling we will be spending quite a lot of time together, Zoey," Eleanor says. She stares at Zoey before clapping her hands together. "I think we've all been well met, right, Adams?"

"Absolutely, ma'am."

"So next—"

"Eleanor?" Zoey says.

"Yes?"

"One of our group, Lee, he's badly hurt. Some of your people brought him to a medical facility—I'd like to go there now."

The mayor looks to Adams before nodding. "That can be arranged. First we need to process you, get you settled into your quarters—you'll be staying here in the parliament building for the first month as a precaution, then situated in your own homes throughout the city. And don't worry, dear, our doctors will take good care of him."

Zoey feels such a swelling of gratitude it blocks off her windpipe. "Thank you," she manages before having to look away.

"Of course. Now, to get you situated . . ." Eleanor moves around her desk and picks up a phone.

"You have electricity *and* you've got working phones too?" Chelsea asks.

"Oh yes. We run a fairly tight ship around here, you'll see. It's imperative to keep up with all our residents and their needs."

Zoey feels her brow furrow. "Residents. You mean women?"

"Yes."

"How many live on the island?"

"Our last count was six hundred sixty-seven." Eleanor smiles at their expressions. "Glad I could offer one surprise to balance out the many you brought me today. Their presence is mostly due to President Benson Andrews. From what I learned through the prime minister's administration, Andrews contacted him personally only days before the rebels detonated the atomic weapon. The president told Evans that he was deeply leery of NOA and their practices and feared he had given them too much power. The day before he was killed, he had a special forces team smuggle over five hundred women and young girls out of the safe haven near Washington, DC. Our own Adams over there was the youngest man on the SEAL team."

Adams inclines his head slightly as they all turn to look at him. "The president was a good man," he says quietly. "He made mistakes, listened to the wrong people, just like a lot of us did. In the end he was going to shut NOA down but he wanted to get as many women and children safe first. Only he didn't get much of a chance."

"That is why we call the island the first city," Eleanor says. "For all the chances missed and ill choices made, this place is a new beginning for many." She looks at Zoey. "I hope it can be for you as well." Eleanor punches in a number and waits before saying, "We have some new residents. Send Tenner in please."

Every head in the group snaps up, attention first on Eleanor before traveling to Chelsea at the mention of her last name.

"What . . . what did you say?" Chelsea asks, her voice airy.

But before the mayor can respond the other door behind her desk opens and a female soldier enters. She is petite with chopped red hair that frames her face, and the moment she glances around at them Zoey has the same jarring impression she experienced the first time seeing Nell.

She recognizes this person because she is nearly a mirror image of Chelsea, only slightly younger.

The soldier steps up to the mayor's desk saying, "You called, ma'am?" But that is all she is able to get out before Chelsea stands and the two women's eyes meet.

"Janie?" Chelsea breathes.

Janie's eyelids flutter like moth's wings and she leans heavily on the desk before launching herself forward into her sister's arms.

Quiet sobs of joy come from them both as they cling to one another. They rock in place for a time before Chelsea steps back, grasping Janie with one hand while still cradling Zoey's daughter. "How? Where did you go? Oh my God." The words run together as she hugs her sister again.

"I looked for you, I did. I'm sorry. I'm so sorry," Janie says.

Zoey smiles, gazing around at the rest of the group. There are tears and grins everywhere.

"It's okay, it's okay. I thought you were gone. I thought you were gone forever."

"I've been here. I looked so long and then I found this place." Janie parts from her sister but doesn't let her go completely. "I can't believe I'm looking at you."

"I can't believe it either."

"Janie came to us over a dozen years ago," Eleanor says, whose eyes are lit with emotion. "She's been an incredible asset to the island, I don't know what we'd do without her."

Janie is introduced all around the group, shaking hands and hugging everyone, though she continues to keep a hold on Chelsea's sleeve as if she's afraid the other woman will vanish if she lets her go. And all at once Zoey feels such a longing for Lee it is nearly a physical ache. She realizes watching Chelsea reunite with Janie has brought her back to the moment she saw Lee for the first time in Seattle, the tempest of warring emotions still vivid. What she wouldn't give to have him here now.

She smiles again as Chelsea kisses Janie's forehead and puts a palm to her face, soaking in the sight of her sister.

"Well I can't think of a better way to start off your stay here in Victoria," Eleanor says. "May every day be as wonderful. Now let's see to your rooms."

◆　◆　◆

The hospital is half a dozen blocks from the parliament building, closer to the center of the city. Victoria rises and falls with the land, at times allowing sweeping views of the sea while at others giving the impression of a labyrinth made of buildings that partially block out the sky. The city is well kept, the streets as clean and maintained as any Zoey's seen. Every so often she spots a woman moving along the sidewalk or climbing into a vehicle, sometimes holding the hand of a small boy or walking arm in arm with a man.

They park beneath the front awning of the hospital, the structure itself a low, sprawling concrete facility that looks as much like a military stronghold as it does a medical center.

Major Adams leads them into an unremarkable atrium lined with counters behind which several men sit, typing away at computers. Rita, Sherell, and Merrill follow her through the space, the others having stayed behind to settle into their rooms at the parliament building.

At the far end of the atrium is a bank of elevators. Adams presses the button marked "3" once they're inside, and they ride quietly and smoothly upward. The third floor opens to them in a cross-section of halls, a corner counter extending out to their left as soon as they exit the elevator. Adams speaks with a matronly woman with short curly black hair manning the station who points down the right hall without giving any of them more than a cursory glance. They pass four doors, Adams finally stopping at the fifth.

"This is it," he says. "I'll have a man posted on ground level to bring you all back to the parliament building when you're done, and I'll start working on getting you a set of wheels of your own." He smiles warmly at Zoey. "Hope he gets better."

She thanks him and steps through the doorway, heart beginning to slam in her chest. Inside is a large hospital bed beneath a wide window looking out over a forest to the north. Lee lies propped slightly up in the middle of the bed, his head wrapped in fresh gauze, a clear tube running into one nostril. At least six wires extend to various places on his body and a steady electronic beep comes from a machine on a stand beside him.

Zoey crosses to the bed and grasps his hand. It is dry and loose, like a glove filled with water. But it is warm.

"Hey, we're here," she says, rubbing his arm. "We made it." The others cluster around the foot of the bed, each of them saying hello in turn. Lee doesn't move. Zoey watches his closed eyelids.

Nothing. Not a twitch.

"Hello," a voice says from the doorway, accompanied by a soft knock. A middle-aged man stands there in a white long-sleeved coat. He is tall and balding, his scalp shining through wisps of light brown hair. He wears glasses and has a long face that seems to match his height. "I'm Doctor Fost," he says, shaking hands with everyone. "You're the family of this young man?"

"Yes," Zoey says.

"Okay, could I get his name for reference?"

"It's Lee Asher."

"All right," Fost says, scribbling on a chart he holds in one hand. "Well, to be honest, I don't have a lot of good news for you. His head trauma was apparent when he came in as well as the broken arm. Whoever worked on him prior to this did a good job. The arm is set well and should heal fine, and the cranial vent was inserted correctly. We did an MRI, or magnetic resonance imaging, and noted that there is still some swelling of the brain, but that's not the worst of our worries." Fost pauses, glancing around at them. "I'm afraid there are some signs of hypoxia, which is a lack of oxygen to a certain area of the body. In this case it's Lee's brain. All of his autonomic functions are fine but obviously cognitive areas have been affected. At this point we don't know how severe the lack of oxygen was; only time will tell. If the person who treated him is available, they might be able to answer some further questions for me."

"She is. I'm sure she'll be able to come in today," Merrill says.

"So you're saying that there isn't anything you can do for him?" Zoey asks.

"I'm afraid not. We've sterilized the vent and are monitoring his condition closely, but for now it's a waiting game."

The pressure that's been building in her chest becomes painful. "Will he wake up?"

"I'm sorry, I can't say one way or another. In cases like this, patients sometimes remain in a coma for an extended period. Others wake up but never regain speech or mobility. Some have made remarkable recoveries; it all depends on the person. I wish I could tell you more or give you a definitive prognosis, but I can't."

Zoey gazes at Lee. He looks so small, so insignificant lying in the bed, like an afterthought of the person he once was. How can he be here but not be here all at the same time? The fact that there is nothing she can do to help him is like a thorn jabbing her skin somewhere she can't reach, its needling point digging deeper and deeper with each minute.

Fost shifts in place, transferring the chart he holds under one arm. "I'll be his physician for the length of his stay here, so any questions or concerns you have can be left for me at the desk down the hall. I'm almost always on call, so I'm not too hard to find." He gives them a half smile. "One thing that's immeasurable in the world of medicine is the resilience of the human spirit. Keep talking to him, let him know you're here. I've seen it do wonders."

"Thank you, Doctor," Zoey says.

"You're welcome." Fost takes several steps toward the door before Zoey stops him again, forcing herself to look away from Lee.

"One last thing, Doctor."

"Of course."

"Do you have any testing and treatment procedures for cancer?"

Fost frowns. "We do. Why do you ask?"

Zoey swallows, trying to gather the remaining amount of her courage, willing herself to press forward even as the words try to submerge within her. She turns to Rita and Sherell. "You both might want to sit down."

65

Zoey settles onto the bed beside Lee's, an exhausted sigh escaping her.

The babies are finally both asleep after nearly an hour of struggling to get them down in their cribs across the hospital room. She nestles herself into the blankets and reaches across the space between them to grasp Lee's hand.

Their first month on the island flew by in a blurry haze of days that melted into one another. There was always somewhere to go, someone to see. The processing Eleanor had mentioned upon their arrival was a series of interviews by psychologists, doctors, social counselors, and a dozen other officials from various departments of the city. Their questions ranged from the standard (*How are you feeling today?*) to the bewildering (*When was your last bowel movement?*). But most of Zoey's time had been spent in Eleanor's office. The mayor had been extremely interested in the ARC as well as Vivian's research, which wasn't surprising given that the island's initial purpose was the same as the National Obstetric Alliance's had been. Slowly over time the research and experiments had been dialed down, much more of the resources and efforts channeled toward protection of the citizens and continuation of life on the island.

But now things have changed.

Zoey had been processed much faster than the others and allowed to move into a shared room with Lee at the hospital. This wasn't only due to her wishes but also to the fact that it was so much more convenient for the testing she lent herself to each day. The scientists, those who were originally tasked with finding a solution to the Dearth decades ago as well as the trainees and apprentices dutifully trained for succession, had made significant progress in the process of isolating her Beta-catenin. Their theory was that introducing the refined protein from her body into an embryo would create the same reaction that had produced her daughters. They continued to be tested as well, their results always normal and healthy.

Healthy.

Zoey shifts uncomfortably on the bed, partially due to the soreness in her shoulders from rocking the girls to sleep and partially because of the guilt. Because she is healthy and so are her children.

But Rita is not.

She recalls telling them that first day, standing beside Lee's bed, the warmth of his hand the only thing that got her through it. She remembers the look on Sherell's and Rita's faces as she told them about the enzymes that had been added to their food since their arrival at the ARC as well as the terrible effects the overexpression of Beta-catenin could cause.

Sherell's tests had come back normal. Rita's had not.

Malignant tumors had been found on both of Rita's ovaries and had begun to spread outward, reaching hungry tendrils toward the rest of her body. The doctors had operated immediately, removing both ovaries nearly two weeks ago, and she had held Rita afterwards, the younger woman crying not only out of fear, but also of loss. Loss of the possibility for children she had never truly voiced out loud as a hope, not until it was gone. Radiation therapy was planned to begin the following week, and only that day Doctor Fost had explained the side effects that would begin almost immediately after the first dosage. Nell had held her daughter's hand the entire time, rubbing her back and murmuring encouraging words. She'd slept in a bed beside Rita even before the initial surgeries and hadn't left her alone for more than a few minutes since. If the older woman's mettle was any indication, Rita had inherited more than enough strength to make it through the treatment.

But despite those assurances Zoey's stomach churns with nausea at the thought of what her friend will have to go through in the coming months. She rubs Lee's hand with her thumb, veering her thoughts away from what Rita will endure, and focuses on Lee.

He is much the same as he was the day they arrived. Only less. He has lost weight and a certain amount of his color. But it is more than the physical that has diminished. He seems farther away sometimes to her, a thinning of some indefinable trait she can't see but feel.

It is as if he is in a boat without oars, drifting more out to sea with each day spent locked in himself while she waits on shore.

The thorn of frustration at her inability to help him has become a lance through her center. And it is killing them both.

Her pillow is wet and she realizes then that she's crying. She wipes at her face and readjusts her hold on his hand. "Eleanor offered me a job today," she says. She's taken to talking to him at night, sometimes whispering for hours while their children sleep across the room. "She doesn't have a title for it yet, and she won't tell me exactly what I'll be doing. Only that I'll be working closely with her and the administration for 'the betterment of the island,' as she puts it. I think she knows what I'm going to propose even though I haven't written anything down yet. She's very insightful when it comes to people. Probably why she's in charge." Zoey traces a vein in Lee's hand with her fingertip. "The problem is I don't know if it's the right thing to do or not. No one can fight the world and win, I know that now, but if I'm wrong . . ."

She lets the thought trail off as one of their daughters makes a soft noise in her sleep. "I named the girls today," she says quietly. "I wanted to wait until you woke up, but . . ." She swallows. "The one we traded me for is Ellie. I asked Tia if I should spell it just like Eli spelled his name and she said I better not because then I'd be condemning her to spelling out her name for everyone her entire life." She laughs before saying, "And the other one is Lynn for Ian's daughter. When she gets older we can tell her about him and where she got her name."

Zoey looks away, afraid that the tears will come again, but her eyes are dry. Maybe she's exhausted her stores; it wouldn't surprise her. She shifts closer to Lee, enfolding his arm against her, wrapping both of hers around it. She's impaled again by helplessness, the feeling having robbed her of so many nights of sleep, but she anchors herself to the warmth of his body, the quiet breathing and night sounds of their daughters.

And for now it is enough. For now, it has to be.

66

Three months later Zoey wakes in the middle of the night, not sure of what brought her free of sleep.

She begins to push herself up, guessing it was one of the girls stirring and hungry for a feeding, but stops.

Lee's hand rests in its customary place within hers but his head is turned toward her instead of facing the ceiling.

He is looking at her and he smiles before his eyes close again.

EPILOGUE

NINE MONTHS LATER

Zoey holds the flowers as she walks through the bar's rear doorway into the wide courtyard.

The area is more crowded than she expected. Merrill and Chelsea sit on one side of a long table near the fence surrounding the space, Merrill holding their son Ian who sits in the crook of his father's arm watching the world with the intensity that only babies and poets seem to possess. On the opposite side is Janie, her military uniform gone in exchange for a business suit, her customary dress since gaining the title of senior military advisor nearly six months ago. To Janie's right is Tia, her face reddened in mid-laugh and, Zoey guesses, by the contents of her mostly empty glass. There are three more tables nearly full with an assortment of soldiers, business owners, and several families all enjoying the cool fall air that's finally broken the strange heat spell of the past weeks.

Tia sees her first and she grins, eyes going from Zoey's face to the flowers she holds. "You do that just to piss me off, don't you? You know how much I hate flowers."

"And you know how much I love them," Janie says, standing to take them from her while giving her a hug. "They're beautiful. Thank you."

"I guess they're passable as far as flowers go," Tia says, standing to give Zoey a hug as well.

Zoey laughs. "I would've brought you some of your favorite white whiskey, but I thought flowers were more appropriate. Congratulations, both of you."

"She had to make an honest woman out of me eventually," Janie says and grins, brushing away some loose hair on Tia's head before running her fingers down to rest on her shoulder. It is such a comfortable, loving gesture it nearly overwhelms Zoey with emotion. Tia and Janie's relationship had grown slowly and steadily since their arrival, the spark between the two of them obvious to anyone who spent more than a few minutes in their company. So it was really no surprise when they announced their engagement two days ago.

"So glad you could join us, Minister," Tia says as they all settle down at the table.

"Oh, don't call me that. Not here," Zoey says. "I'm officially clocked out."

"But having drinks with the minister of domestic affairs is such an honor."

Zoey rolls her eyes. "You just get a thrill out of being one of the few people able to insult me and get away with it."

Tia smiles evilly. "Maybe."

A waiter comes and takes her drink order and they begin chatting about plans for the wedding that will be held in the spring.

"We tried to get Eleanor to agree to shut down immigration for a day so we could have the ceremony in the middle of the bay on one of the bigger ships, but she told us no," Janie says.

"If it weren't for me, that might've been an option," Zoey says, sipping her wine.

"If it weren't for you, the island wouldn't be running like it is," Merrill says. "You've done a lot in the last six months."

A part of her knows he's right. The referendum she drafted, after the very first election in Victoria's history, was agreed upon almost unanimously. She hadn't expected it to pass through the two divisions of parliament on its first vote, and when Prime Minister Scott, who had been elevated from the position of mayor during the election, signed it into law, Zoey had nearly broken down with worry that they had made a fatal mistake, her self-doubt a constant whispering in the back of her mind.

The Open Borders Act, or what the general populace called Bridger Law, had been the first step of many in the legislative movement to send an emissary mission to Seattle, notifying the city of their presence on Vancouver Island along with the recent breakthroughs in their scientific sector.

When the new leadership of Seattle had learned female infants were being born once again on the island, there was an almost overnight draft of allegiance drawn up between the two cities and the influx of men to Victoria's port had begun a month later. Zoey had been filled with terror during the interim, half expecting each morning that she would wake to see a fleet of warships approaching across the water, their decks lined with men coming to plunder, steal, and violate. Coming to do what had always been done: to take. She had voiced her concerns over and over to Eleanor, who continued to support Bridger Law despite Zoey's reluctance.

You're not giving yourself or the movement enough credit, Eleanor had told her not long after the emissary mission had left Vancouver Island. *I always knew one day we would have to reach out into the world and take our chances to continue to support the growing population here, and now you've given us the opportunity to do it. It's not just that you're carrying the key to end the Dearth, Zoey, it's your belief as well. There's a reason the law went through as quickly as it did; it was nothing short of inspired. The hope and faith for the future was just what this place needed. You're what this place needed.*

Despite Eleanor's confidence that they had taken the right path, Zoey had still worried the entire movement would be a disaster simply because people were unpredictable even when the correct choices were clear.

But the outcome couldn't have been more opposite.

The influx of men and several women, who had learned of Victoria through rumor, was organized, calm, and peaceful. In the last months, Victoria's army had almost doubled in size, its flood of volunteers fueled by the new residents, and a steady trade had begun between the island and Seattle's port, bringing in vital resources the people of Victoria had done without over the past decades.

To put it simply, the idea had started to form within her after arriving on the island, and once it had bloomed and flourished into life, it couldn't have gone more according to plan. Their government became stronger along with the military, which ensured safety, new industry had taken off in dozens of exciting new directions, and by utilizing a stabilized form of her own Beta-catenin within embryos, women had begun giving birth to female infants again. There had already been five children born and another twenty women were expecting. All in all, the results had eclipsed her wildest hopes and dreams.

The conversation between her friends has moved on, leaving her floating in her own memories and emotions. She brings herself back to the present.

"I haven't seen Rita very much in the last few weeks," Chelsea says, taking Ian from Merrill's arms. "Guess her new occupation is taking up a lot of her time."

"Do you mean being in the military or the tall blond-haired guy who follows her around like a lost puppy?" Zoey asks. Everyone laughs, but she knows they couldn't be happier for Rita. Her recovery had been an arduous one, but only a month ago her doctor had declared her in remission.

"They've only been dating for a couple months, but I've never seen her happier," Merrill says. "Nell told me the other day if he doesn't do it soon, Rita's going to propose." They laugh again.

"How is Sherell and Newton's little one doing?" Tia asks.

"She's great," Zoey says. "I stopped by to see them yesterday. I don't think Newton's quit smiling since she was born."

It hadn't been a shock to any of them when Sherell and Newton announced their pregnancy. What had been a surprise was that the fetus was a girl. Apparently the protein and enzyme therapy Vivian had employed at the ARC had not only worked on Zoey but on Sherell as well. Both of them were still cancer free, and Sherell's baby had been born healthy and without complication nearly two months ago. Already Sherell was donating portions of her day to the scientific community in an effort to harvest some of her Beta-catenin for the eventual distribution among women who wanted to give birth to girls.

"They're going to be great parents," Janie says. They all murmur their agreement and fall silent. Zoey can feel what's coming and wants nothing more than to leave the table before it does. She doesn't want or need the pity she sees in their eyes whenever her own family comes up. She quickly finishes her wine and opens her mouth to say her good-byes, but Chelsea touches her hand before she can.

"And how are you doing, Zoey?"

"I'm fine. Just . . . fine." She smiles tightly before looking anywhere but at the people who know her best. Chelsea starts to ask something else, possibly about the girls, but she cuts her off. "I really should get going," she says, rising from the table.

"You just got here," Merrill says.

"I know, but it was a long day." She makes her way around the table, hugging each of them in turn. Merrill holds her for an extra second after she releases him, kissing her on the brow before letting her go. He says everything he needs to in the last look before turning away, and she smiles as she waves her good-byes and makes her way out through the bar.

The smell of ripe apples drifts across the highway to the parking lot from the massive orchard and she breathes it in, taking a moment of solace for herself. As she walks to her vehicle she brushes back a strand of loose hair from her forehead. It's grown nearly to her shoulders in the fourteen months since she cut it, but she's not sure it fits her anymore. Each time she looks into a mirror it is like gazing into the past, one she still doesn't truly understand. Maybe she'll end up cutting it again soon. Perhaps that's better since some things can never go back to the way they were.

Zoey climbs into the four-wheel drive SUV and pulls away from the bar, giving the enclosed courtyard where her family is celebrating a last look.

She drives north through the outskirts of the city, the elevation gradually bringing her up and away from the sprawling neighborhoods that are beginning to come to life again. She winds her way past several stores that have popped up in what seems to be only the last few weeks and turns right onto a dirt drive threaded between thick stands of red cedar.

At the top of a rise she turns into a driveway that curves twice up the side of a foothill, emptying out in a clearing, at the back of which is her house. It is a tall timber frame with a front porch and deck overlooking the sweeping view down through the Douglas firs and spruce trees that line the mountainside. A swelling of happiness fills her just as it does every time she returns here. Home. The place she's always wanted is finally hers. She pulls to a stop beside Nell's car and climbs out, hauling in the few supplies she picked up in town prior to stopping at the bar.

Inside, the air is warmed by the fireplace she can hear crackling in the great room. Sunlight slants across the wide kitchen and the smell of cooking onions wafts from a pot on the stove. Zoey moves to the cabinets and begins unloading the groceries, listening for, and after a second hearing, the sound of tinkling laughter in the next room. Her smile fades only briefly as she closes the cabinet and her eyes fall on the pictures taped there: each type of food normally stored within, along with its name.

She walks to the sink and washes her hands, not really seeing the other labels around the room: the phone by the door with the word "phone" above it, along with numbers to her office at the parliament building and the emergency services in Victoria. She begins to move toward the great room but her eyes catch on the photographs beside the door, these of her own face as well as the girls', their names below each one.

Zoey pushes through the door.

The great room is much warmer than the kitchen, the afternoon light pouring through the rows of windows lining the front of the house. Nell sits on the closest chair holding Lynn in her lap, the girl's chubby arms raised above her head in a triumphant pose. Ellie sits near Nell's feet, one hand on the edge of the low coffee table.

"Hey, you're home early," Nell says, standing.

"Yeah, meetings were quick today so I got out of there and stopped for a celebratory drink with everyone on the way." Zoey grins as she takes Lynn from Nell, kissing the little girl on the cheek. "How are you, beautiful?" Lynn laughs as Zoey nuzzles her neck, tickling her under the arm at the same time.

"They were really good. Both took an hour nap this afternoon, so they shouldn't be cranky like yesterday. How is the happy couple doing?"

Joe Hart

"Great. They've already got a lot of the planning done. It's going to be a beautiful ceremony."

"That's wonderful. Say, I hate to run, but Rita and Daniel are coming over for supper, and I promised I'd whip up my fish stew. I've got soup going on the stove, should be done in an hour." Nell gathers her bag from the floor beside the couch before kneeling to kiss Ellie on the top of the head. "You be good for mama. And you too," she says, sliding her finger off the button of Lynn's nose.

"Nell?"

"Yeah," the older woman says, pausing by the doorway.

"How was he today?"

Nell's expression darkens slightly. "Pretty good. He got a little upset this morning after you left when he couldn't remember my name, and he tried to fix the bathroom doorknob that's loose upstairs."

"Oh no. Did he break anything?"

"No. He threw his toolkit when he couldn't figure out what to use on the screws."

Zoey nods, disentangling Lynn's fingers from a length of her hair as the girl starts to pull on it. "Okay. Thanks for everything."

Nell smiles, but there is a hint of sadness in it. "No problem. Same time tomorrow?"

"Yeah."

"Okay. Have a good night."

"You too."

Nell pushes through the door and is gone.

The fire crackles in the hearth. Ellie picks up a plastic rattle and inspects it before shaking it hard enough to nearly knock her over. Zoey gazes at her daughter for a moment before looking past her to the couch in front of the picture windows.

Lee sits to one end of the sofa, hands folded in his lap. He stares out at the sunlit drop below the house, eyes tracing the movement of the treetops in the wind.

Zoey walks to the couch and lowers herself onto it, holding Lynn in her lap. "Hi honey," she says.

Lee doesn't look at her at first, then his head turns and she sees the dim fugue state slowly recede from his gaze.

"Hi," he says, a crooked smile pulling at the corner of his mouth. His forehead wrinkles in concentration and his jaw works. "Zoey," he says at last, as if the word was stuck behind a dam inside him.

"How was your day?"

He struggles, wringing his hands together. "I think I got angry once."

"It's okay." She reaches out and takes his hands apart, holding one of them in her own. "It's okay."

The small hope she harbors throughout each day from the time she leaves the house to when she walks through the doors in the evening falls away. The doctors all concurred that it was a miracle Lee recovered at all, and they had explained that he might need constant supervision and special care for the rest of his life, even after the rigorous therapy he'd undergone. Deep down Zoey understands this, but she can't help the ember that begins glowing inside her every day; the thought that when she comes home Lee will be there, her Lee. Not the man who has to check the photographs hanging by the door several times a day to remember their names.

She recalls two nights before, waking sometime in the early morning hours to find Lee's side of the bed empty, the door to their room wide open, Lee gone. She'd rushed through their home, terrified he'd fallen and hurt himself or simply walked away from the house into the night and forgotten how to return.

She'd found him on the front porch, crying softly into his hands, a spoon beside him on the bench. She'd hugged him close, whispering that it was okay until he'd calmed enough to tell her he'd woken hungry and come downstairs for something to eat, but after taking out a bowl and spoon for some leftover stew, he'd forgotten what the spoon was called. It bothered him so much he couldn't get himself to eat.

So each day she hopes that somewhere in the tangled neurological pathways of his mind a connection will be made that will in turn create another link forging a chain to draw him back to the man he once was, the man who could engineer anything he could imagine. And yet despite the challenges, he is here beside her. The life with him that she dreamed about is a reality. And that is enough for her, because the love he feels for her is there, strong as ever when their eyes meet or their hands touch.

"What smells so good?" Lee asks, looking past her toward the kitchen.

"Soup. It should be ready pretty soon. Do you remember what we use to eat soup with?"

The look of concentration returns to his face. "No," he says after a time, defeat thick in his voice.

"A spoon. We eat soup with a spoon." When he doesn't look up she says, "It's okay, honey, you're doing great."

He is quiet for a long time, the sound of the fire and the occasional rattle of Ellie's toy the only things breaking the silence. She is about to rise and begin preparing their meal when Lee squeezes her hand.

"I remember this," he says, glancing up at her. "I remember holding your hand in the hospital and before in another place."

"At the ARC," she says. "That's right, we held hands at the ARC."

"The wall. I remember the wall. I can see it, and it's like it's here in my head," he says, bringing his fingers up to brush his temple. "I know if I can get to the other side, things will be there; everything I've forgotten. You'll be there."

Her vision blurs. "We're going to get through the wall together because I'm not on the other side, I'm right here, I'll always be right here."

He smiles, a choked laugh coming from him. He leans forward and kisses her gently before gazing down at Lynn. "I almost forgot," he says, rising. He stops, frowning in a way that makes her think the wall inside him isn't so thick after all, because for a brief moment he is her Lee from before. He grins and shakes his head. "That's really funny; me saying I almost forgot." He moves to where Ellie sits beside the table and picks her up, setting her on her feet. "Okay . . . El . . ." He looks at Zoey for a second before nodding. "Okay Ellie, let's show Mom what you can do."

For a beat, Zoey's worried, sure that Lee is misremembering something or confused, but then he lets go of Ellie and the girl doesn't slump to her bottom as she usually does after pulling herself up to a standing position.

Instead she takes a hesitant step forward.

Then another.

And another.

"Oh my God," Zoey says. "She's walking!"

Lee smiles, following a pace behind his daughter, hands held out to either side of her in case she falls. "She did it twice earlier today. I'm sorry you didn't get to see the first time."

"That's okay," she hears herself saying. Lynn burbles and flaps her arms in Zoey's lap, and she hugs her close, watching Ellie walk and Lee follow her; their child and the man who would die for her, even if he cannot always recall her name.

"Everything is going to be okay," Zoey says, and in her heart she truly believes it will be.

ACKNOWLEDGMENTS

Thanks so much to my family, who supported me through the process of writing the trilogy; you mean more to me than you know. Huge thanks to my editor, Jacque Ben-Zekry, for believing in Zoey, in the story, and in me. Many thanks to Kjersti Egerdahl, Sarah Shaw, Dennelle Catlett, Jeff Belle, Mikyla Bruder, and everyone else on the team at Thomas & Mercer; you are the best of the best, and the books wouldn't be what they are without you! Big thanks to Caitlin Alexander for the dynamite edits! Thanks to all my author friends who I bounced ideas off throughout the trilogy; you know who you are.

And thanks last, but definitely not least, to the readers; without you I wouldn't be doing what I am today. Thank you for following Zoey and Lee and all the others to the very end, thank you, thank you a million times over!

ABOUT THE AUTHOR

Photo © 2015 Jade Hart

Joe Hart is the *Wall Street Journal* bestselling author of eleven novels that include *The River Is Dark*, *Lineage*, and *EverFall*. *The First City* is the final book in the highly acclaimed Dominion Trilogy.

When not writing, he enjoys reading, exercising, exploring the great outdoors, and watching movies with his family. For more information on his upcoming novels and access to his blog, visit www.joehartbooks.com.